TRAITORS
in the
GESTAPO

A JENZ RAMSGRUND NOVEL

J.H. AHLIN

ISBN   Softcover   978-1-956998-07-8

To order additional copies of this book, contact:
Bookwhip
1-855-339-3589
https://www.bookwhip.com

CONTENTS

Prologue vii

Chapter 1   Hitler Youth Camp - 1936 1

Chapter 2   Growing up in Düsseldorf, Germany – 1926 9

Chapter 3   The Early Years 12

Chapter 4   Meeting Zeke... 16

Chapter 5   Arbeitslosigheit (Unemployment) comes to
             Germany...19

Chapter 6   Rising Anti-Semitism.. 23

Chapter 7   Defending Zeke 27

Chapter 8   My Fifteenth Birthday 34

Chapter 9   The Coming Olympic Games 1936 37

Chapter 10   Leaving for Hitler Youth Camp......................... 40

Chapter 11   Gestapo Visit, Summer - 1936 52

Chapter 12   Kristallnacht Comes to Düsseldorf.................... 64

Chapter 13   The Gestapo Visits the Leven's Home 75

Chapter 14   A Letter from Ilsa... 84

Chapter 15   A Visit to Hannover 89

Chapter 16   Ilsa Meets her Tormentor 102

Chapter 17   Trapped by a Monster 108

Chapter 18   Ezekiel Leven has a Name Change.....................114

Chapter 19   Protecting a University Student from the
              Gestapo 123

Chapter 20   Taking out the Trash..................................... 128

Chapter 21   Evaluation by the SS 131

Chapter 22   Reporting to Dachau and Auschwitz for
              "Training" 141

Chapter 23   Ensnared by the Gestapo 151

Chapter 24   Apprehended by Gestapo Agents on the
              Train to Hannover 160

Chapter 25   Parental Concern and Acceptance.................. 168

Chapter 26   The Gestapo Comes Calling For My Parents 172

Chapter 27   Peenemünde...................................... 180

Chapter 28   Pulling Zeke Out of a Gestapo Trap 187

Chapter 29   Modifying the V-1 204

Chapter 30   Encounter with Wehrmacht Deserters...............213

Chapter 31   Joseph Göebbels Comes to Peenemünde 219

Chapter 32   The Gestapo Interrupts Dinner......................... 225

Chapter 33   Planning for The Failure of the V-1 and V-2 233

Chapter 34   The First Vengeance Weapons Arrive 237

Chapter 35   Delaying the V-2.. 243

Chapter 36   Labor Camp Prisoners Building Rockets...........251

Chapter 37   Downtown Nordhausen.....................................255

Chapter 38 A Chance Meeting with Gestapo Agents...........261

Chapter 39 An Exit Plan to Get Out of the Reich 268

Chapter 40 The Gestapo Provides Our Transportation 277

Chapter 41 Our Hasty Retreat to the Land of the Danes ... 284

Chapter 42 On the run to Northern Germany 298

Chapter 43 Fleeing the Reich 311

Chapter 44 The Danish Border 318

Chapter 45 The Wehrmacht Air Base at Aalborg................ 322

Chapter 46 The Gestapo Comes Calling at Aalborg........... 326

Chapter 47 A Very Hard Goodbye 340

Chapter 48 Into the Lion's Den 345

Chapter 49 My Appointment with the Gestapo...................352

Chapter 50 A Return Visit to the V-2 Factory.....................359

Chapter 51 V-2 Missiles to Aalborg Air Base 365

Chapter 52 Facing the Gestapo without Ezekiel 371

Chapter 53 Sweden Bound 376

Chapter 54 America Bound 381

Chapter 55 Freedom.. 383

The Author's Family History 385

Author's Note 387

PROLOGUE

I have delayed telling our story out of fear and loathing for the regime in which I was an unwilling participant. However, at my advanced age, now in my late nineties, I want other people to know what my friend Ezekiel and I went through growing up in *Nazi* Germany during the 1920s, 1930s and early 1940s.

The term "traitors" was the kindest term the *Gestapo* ever called us. They considered us terrorists and worse: we were Germans considered disloyal to the *Third Reich. The Reich* included all the *Nazi Party's* political thugs who became by far the worst war criminals of all history.

The term *Gestapo* is an abbreviation of the words *Geheime Staats Polizei* or Secret State Police of Nazi Germany and German-occupied Europe. It was created by Hermann Göring on the 26th of April, 1933, and contained only a few dozen agents. Near the end of World War II, there were 32,000 members of the *Gestapo.*

Ezekiel and I worked together tirelessly to thwart the overwhelmingly popular *Nazi* regime and its ambitions. Our efforts are detailed here. I have delayed documenting the details of our story. I know the long tentacles of the *Third Reich* or perhaps the *Fourth Reich* are a dark and sinister, yet still active force.

Lastly, some of the abject cruelty and other information on the *Gestapo* methods of torture have never been released and might be surprising and difficult for some readers. In addition to witnessing many of these atrocities first hand, letters, research, and personal accounts verify the cruelty of these war criminals.

I have been in America for over six decades now so my German might be a little dated. It is sometimes hard for me to understand many of the new words and phrases the younger German teenagers use in their every-day language.

CHAPTER 1

Hitler Youth Camp - 1936

"**D**ieter, try and hurt me!"

"I will if you would just stand still for a minute."

Dieter was my friend at Hitler Camp. We had been paired up as boxing partners because we were both pretty good size boys for sixteen-year-olds. He was almost six feet, and I was six feet four and a half inches tall. We would wrestle and compete in all sorts of strength tests and sports.

I had an excuse for my size. Mom was five feet eleven inches and had a very athletic figure; Dad was six feet five inches and very strong. The combination of genetics left me with an oversized and quite healthy body, which no one at the Hitler Youth Camp could beat in almost any sport or activity.

Dad encouraged me to let other boys win some of the wrestling or strength contests because he didn't want me to stand out. We had a family secret and it was important to keep the secret to ourselves in *Nazi* Germany in 1936: My mom was Jewish, and Dad was Swedish Christian.

Dad thought Hitler Camp might help disguise our family's Jewish heritage. It allowed me to learn how to love and to hate. The hate came easily. All the campers, including me, had to wear black swastikas on red armbands in addition to the other atrocious

Hitler garb. We were taught to hate the sinful Jew and everything Jewish.

All of the activities had an anti-Semitic bent to them. We were always pretending to attack, blow things up with hand grenades, or mow down Jews with machine gun fire. The dreaded Jew was always stealing from us, hurting us financially, or taking our place in line for food.

The love came to me entirely unexpectedly one late afternoon when Dieter and I had finished a long ten-kilometer hike for Hitler Camp. We decided to sneak down to the lake for a swim before dinner and cool off. Since we didn't have swimsuits, we were going to swim in our shorts. It was so warm we figured we would dry off quickly before dinner.

Dinner was the only formal part of Hitler Camp. We were served by younger campers who were supervised by young enlisted men in the *Wehrmacht*. We had to sit ram-rod straight, with no horsing around, no joking or teasing. It was very formal and polite. Manners were stressed. Hatred toward Jews and all different approaches to anti-Semitism were always the underlying themes: "Oh, we were always so much better bred or informed than the masses of Jewish heathens." The whole attitude made me sick. If I didn't get so hungry, I would have skipped the evening "formal" meal.

The food wasn't too bad but was served institutional style by the younger campers. The dessert was usually one cookie. I can never remember having enough to eat to feel full. I always thought I could have eaten another meal or at least a plate of several cookies after our meals.

One warm spring day our Hitler Youth group had returned from a long march in the forest, it must have been at least 10 kilometers. We were all hot, sweaty, tired from carrying a heavy pack, and hungry. One of my fellow campers, Dieter, had the bright idea we could go down to the lake and swim to cool off. We tried to get Horst, another fellow camper, to join us, but he said he was too worried about getting "written up" and receiving a bad report from the *Wehrmacht* camp leader.

We tore off our shirts and shoes and ran across the meadow down to the lake. We were both pretty worn out from the hike. Dieter was very athletic and ran ahead of me and was first into the calm cool waters of the lake.

We had been swimming a few minutes when from out of the bushes we heard giggling and laughter.

The women's equivalent to the Hitler Camp was called the *Bund Deutscher Mädel.* Their camp for teenage women was nearby. The giggling came from a camp counselor who had come down to the lake. She thought two large boys frolicking in the serene lake was somewhat humorous.

The bushes partially hid her; all we could see was the outline of her body and her hair. She looked tall and curvy; the sun was low on the horizon and shown through her hair, turning it into spun gold.

By the time I went to Hitler Youth Camp, I was tall, but still painfully shy with girls. I did have enough courage to call out to whoever was hiding up in the bushes.

"Who, who's there?" I called. All I could see was an image of a tall girl with golden hair. As she came out from behind the bushes, Dieter and I got a better look at her. Her beauty was mesmerizing.

Dieter was terrified. He shouted, "We better get back, Jenz, we'll be missed, and we will be late for our dinner!"

"You go on up, Dieter, I'll be right behind you shortly."

He ran like a scared rabbit out of the water and up the hill toward our camp.

"Wha. Wha, what is your name...Miss?"

It was not quite evening, and the day was slowly dying; it was almost twilight, but the sun was still up. I got enough courage to ask, "W,would, you like to swim?" I didn't want her to think Dieter and I were hogging the entire small beach area by the lake.

As she came down to the water's edge, her beauty was undeniable. I was enthralled.

"My name is Ilsa," she mouthed. "Are you enjoying Hitler Camp? What is your name?"

Truthfully, I couldn't even respond; I just kept staring at her like a goof-ball. My face was getting red, and my breathing came in short breaths; my shorts were clinging to me, and my privates were starting to embarrass me. She probably thought I was brain-dead.

I backed into deeper water to hide my embarrassment.

I finally mumbled, "J. J, Jenz. My name is Jenz."

I couldn't stop staring at her beautiful mouth. When she talked, her lips kept smiling at me.

I was delighted she was talking because no sound would come out of my mouth. I was standing in waist-deep water and felt anchored in cement. If I could have moved, I probably would have fled with Dieter up to the dining hall.

She kicked off her shoes and came into the water fully clothed and splashed me-- probably trying to get me to say something. I could barely think, let alone utter a coherent sentence. As she came near me into the water, her head only came up to my neck.

As she approached me, she reached out and put her hand on my chest; I was on fire with embarrassment. My chest was tingling underneath her hand. I thought for a moment she might have had something in her hand, my chest felt so odd.

She was laughing and smiling and asking about the Hitler Camp. Then she started gently stroking and massaging my chest muscles; my whole body started tingling. I felt frozen in stone, except my privates kept swelling.

She then pushed hard on my chest. I toppled like a fallen tree, over backward into the fresh cool water. I considered staying under until she left, but she grabbed my arm and pulled me up to a kneeling position in shallower water.

"Come on up here, you good-looking man."

She knelt close to me and stared into my eyes. Her eyes were a light blue and had a very intense look of longing and desire in them. My eyes were steel-blue-gray and broadcast I was scared to death.

She smiled and led me by the hand to a mossy glen in the woods just at the edge of the lake. I felt like a slave with no power to resist. I was completely captivated by her beauty. Her hair was the color of a golden sheath of wheat.

I couldn't talk and only mumbled.

Ilsa gently pushed me into the moss and stripped off my shorts.

I was too embarrassed even to open my eyes. I do remember my body was on fire and the moss felt cool and comforting on my backside.

She held me and kissed me on the lips. Her kiss was the first time I had ever experienced anything so delicious. Her lips were soft and full. Even now, in my advanced years, I can still taste and feel their elegance. She ordered me to relax; I could only mumble or murmur. Nothing sounded very intelligible.

She put her arms around my neck and kissed me hard on the mouth. I tried to resist what was happening inside of me; my whole body betrayed me and went stiff but with no resistance to her gentle touch. She put her hand on my privates and squeezed. My entire body exploded with pleasure. I just moaned like an idiot while she kept stroking my privates and legs. I couldn't catch my breath even though I was breathing quite hard.

She just held me close to her and told me I was very good looking. My breathing started to calm down. She slipped out of her wet dress and underclothing and continued to rub my chest and the upper part of my legs. I was utterly helpless in her arms.

I certainly had no idea as to what to do, but what I lacked in knowledge and experience, she made up for whispering encouragement in my ear.

She breathlessly told me her name, Ilsa meant "Devoted to God." I was instead hoping God wasn't witnessing my embarrassment right now. She also said her Hitler Youth Bund encouraged them to have children and motherhood.

I told her I was only 16 years old, and her retort was a question: "Are you upset or have regrets?"

"N, No." I squeaked. My voice just would not come out from my mouth.

She held me and kissed me deeply. I tried to explain to her I would miss dinner, and I should get back to the camp; anything coming out of my mouth was pure gibberish.

She held me tightly and gently stroked and pinched my backside while she kissed me on the chest. When she placed my hand on her breast, my privates started to swell uncontrollably again.

Although I was doing everything in my mind I could to leave and get back to the camp, my strength had wholly left me. I was powerless to move.

She rolled on top of me and gently guided me into her special place. The warmth and excitement flowing through my body were uncontrollable. She moved smoothly and rhythmically on top of me until I could no longer even see, hear, or care about anything she was whispering in my ear.

The passion, kindness, devotion, and thanks I felt for this young German girl was overwhelming. I wanted to be with her forever.

An electric flow of energy traversed my body from the tips of my toes and fingers into my privates. I could not prevent the overwhelming excitement exploding into Ilsa.

She started moaning uncontrollably; I thought I might have hurt her. I opened my eyes, and she was staring intently into mine.

She assured me she was feeling the same pleasure I was feeling and talked about wanting to have my child.

Although I tried to tell her I was only 16, she reminded me I was a man. I guess my six foot four inch plus height had her thinking I was older. I did, however, have the feeling she knew exactly what she was doing.

I was just very thankful for her affection toward me and wanted to see her again soon. We promised each other to meet in the glade the next week if we could get away from the Hitler Youth activities. Ilsa told me her Bund encouraged lovemaking with Aryan men. She seemed very straight forward about wanting me again.

By 1936 membership in the Hitler Youth had become compulsory. All German boys ages fourteen to eighteen of Aryan extraction had to join. I kept wondering how the Hitler Youth folks would feel about me being half Jewish and enjoying going to synagogue with my Jewish classmates.

There was some strange dichotomy of feelings running through my mind as I walked back up the hill to the Hitler Camp. I was exceedingly proud of my Jewish heritage, yet I was surrounded by anti-Semitism wherever I looked. I was always pleased and honored by the inventiveness, scholarship, and culture, of my Jewish background and teachings in the synagogue. However, to celebrate my Jewish Faith could mean discrimination, banishment, and even imprisonment in my own country.

The anti-Semitism raging throughout my country made it almost impossible to be a normal sixteen-year-old German Jew.

CHAPTER 2

Growing up in Düsseldorf, Germany – 1926

Ezekiel was my best friend growing up. Although he was a half-year older than me, we grew up together during the 1920s and 1930s. I was born on September 16, 1920; Zeke was born six months earlier. The Great War was finally over, and Germany was suffering widespread poverty no one thought we would ever have to face.

There were always long lines of people trying to get even basic necessities like bread, meat, and coal for heating and cooking. The only vegetables I can remember in my early years were root based: onions, potatoes, and occasionally carrots and beets. I never tasted fruit until I was six years old.

Although I was only a child and knew nothing about economics, our families lived through the rapid devaluation of the German currency. The German government was trying desperately to pay off reparations imposed by the Allies after The Great War. The German *Reichsmark* was printed by the millions and billions. So many *Marks* had been printed our currency became almost worthless. I can remember my parents saying, "We will be lucky if our life savings will even buy a loaf of bread."

When my dad got paid at work, Mom would have to run with the money to the meat market and bakery to purchase our necessities before the price would rise out of sight. I would play with bundles of worthless German bank notes, and use them as building blocks as I was growing up.

My dad complained: "This is an example of what can happen when a country tries to inflate their currency to avoid indebtedness. In 1914 the exchange rate of the German Mark to the American Dollar was 4.2 to 1. Nine short years later it was 4.2 Trillion to 1." Although our family never went out to eat, Dad heard in the restaurants in Germany in 1922, waiters would have to stand on a chair or table and announce the price changes every half-hour.

Often the market and shops wouldn't sell the food at the stated price. They would complain they couldn't get more meat or bread for several days. In reality, they were waiting for an hour or two for the price to go up so they could make a small profit. It seemed continually tricky for my parents and our neighbors to get adequate food, clothing, coal for heating and cooking, or other supplies in the early years after The Great War.

By 1923, America had loaned the German government enough money to slowly rebuild our economy. My preschool years were filled with the happiness of a little boy who could not possibly recognize the poverty all around our small town and nation.

Quirks in the German school system put Ezekiel and me together in the first grade of our school. We had known each other since we were six years old. Although Zeke has gone to be with the Lord, I will never forget my friend who helped me survive the Nazi occupation of our government as it overran most of Europe in the late 1930s and early 1940s.

Occasionally, I am startled awake in the middle of the night by the horrors Zeke and I lived through. His parents were practicing Jews, and despite our best efforts, were lost in the Holocaust.

I have lived in America since the late 1940s. I have tried very hard to push our experiences with Hermann Göering, who initially established and ran the *Gestapo*, and the *SS* run by Heinrich Himmler, to a distant edge of my mind. I'm very grateful to America for allowing me the freedom to express my views.

CHAPTER 3

The Early Years

"Jenz, come on, it's time for school." My mom was a victim of German punctuality.

"Okay, I'm coming."

Mom was going to walk me to school since it was my first day of grade one; Dad had already taken the bus to work at his plant.

I have always admired my dad. He was a hardworking Swede who was always committed to his work and his family. All my life, I tried to emulate his work ethic.

My school was only a few blocks, a pleasant walk, from our house. The heat of summer was fading to the coolness of fall. The days were getting shorter, and there was a damp chill in the air. Mom wanted to make sure we weren't late. I had a little trouble keeping up with her, she always walked with long strides. She did almost everything with purposeful energy.

The school building was near the center of our small town outside of Düsseldorf. The school building was just a short walk from our home. It was a bit cloudy, with a touch of dampness. The dampness seemed to penetrate to my bones. Even though the sky was just a little hazy, my thoughts contained lots of darkness and nervousness.

I met Ezekiel on the first day of grade school. Our last names placed us opposite each other, so we sat on either side of our row of desks. The school building was the largest building I had ever seen. I was jittery and excited. There were so many kids of varying ages; their parents were all milling about, trying to find their children's classrooms.

Some of the younger children were upset and crying. Although their parents were trying to be consoling, the general hubbub and confusion led me to believe this was not going to be a very good day. It wasn't raining, but there was an early morning fall mist in the air. The mist gave dampness to my clothing and was unsettling. I remember leaving footprints of dew on the school's front cement walk.

The school building was a large intimidating brick building with at least four floors. There were cut stone arches over the outside doors and windows. If someone had told me it was a prison, I would have believed them. Most of the children milling about with their parents didn't seem at all sure they wanted to be there.

My mother talked with me on our way to school and tried to settle me down with reassurances of all the fun and new things I was going to learn. I knew it was irrational, but I felt like I was on my way to an execution.

"Jenz, once you get the 'learning bug' and enjoy learning new things, you will enjoy school and look forward to being here."

I told Mom, "Me happy here. I don't need school to make me happy."

Mom pulled me along to the central administrative office on the first floor and got directions to my classroom from a bulletin board outside the school office. To my mind, we had gone about as far as I wanted to go. I was thinking about making a "final stand" right there outside the principal's office.

"Come on, Jenz," was my mother's encouragement. "We are going to make this day enjoyable and memorable for you. And I will have a special treat for you when you come home. I will be here when school is out at the end of the school day and walk home with you."

Food was my Mom's favorite bribe. I was rapidly growing, was continuously hungry, and she knew it would always work. Unfortunately, I have always been a slave to my stomach, especially during my teenage years. I cannot ever remember passing up a favorite pastry. Even now, in my late 90's, a couple of bites of dark chocolate always puts me in a great mood.

We trudged up to the second floor and started searching for the correct room. There was a distinct smell of wax and cleaning solution throughout the building. The odor of cleaning solution was not helping my nervousness as we climbed the stairs. The floors all seemed shiny and reflected the overhead lights. Although I was a little oversized for my age, Mom seemed to have no trouble "guiding" me through the school building in spite of my reluctance.

Mom was a rather large woman. Not obese, but athletic and very strong, and tall. She was almost five feet eleven inches tall with an active and gracious body type. My dad was even taller, nearly six feet, five inches. Dad was slender but exceptionally strong. He could lift Mom and me at the same time. It was strange when I think back, I never saw either of them ever do any strength training or regular exercise of any sort all their lives.

They loved each other very much but had a secret I didn't hear much about until early in my pre-teen years: Dad was a Swedish Christian, and Mom was a German Jew. Their different religions never made any difference to me. I attended church and synagogue throughout my youth. At an early age, I had no idea of the complications this relationship was going to have on my later life.

After locating my classroom, Mom told me in very gentle, loving terms, "Jenz, you go find a seat and meet your teacher and classmates."

Our teacher, Frau Ohlendorf, chimed in, "Children, find your seat with your name on the desk. *Bitte*, no talking." She clapped her hands for emphasis. The moms were not allowed into the classrooms; they waited out in the hall for a few minutes before they fled for a saner part of their day.

My first impression of my teacher was of a harsh old lady who was out to enforce strict discipline with an emphasis on precision and order. Although she was only about half the size of my mom, I had the impression she might be someone to be feared. She had dark hair tied back in a severe bun. Her skin was very light and almost pasty looking. Her body language shouted, "Do exactly as I suggest, and no one will get hurt."

Interestingly enough, as I got to know her, she became quite likable; her features softened, and the harshness left her voice. By the end of my first year of school, her mannerisms seemed to grow more friendly, almost as if she might actually like small children. Thinking back, she was quite pretty; probably in her mid-twenties, just not too experienced with handling a room full of very busy first graders.

CHAPTER 4

Meeting Zeke

"**H**i, I'm Jenz," I said to the young boy who sat next to me. There were three rows of desks, two desks together in each row. There were five desks deep in each row. There were four or five empty desks in the back of the classroom, so there must have been about twenty-five students total in the class.

The chairs were attached to the desks, and since I was undeniably the largest boy in the class, I had a little difficulty getting into my chair. I probably should have been embarrassed. I remember the desk came right into my stomach.

"I'm Ezekiel," shot back my classmate, "My friends call me Zeke." Zeke and I chatted quietly until Frau Ohlendorf cast a stern look in our direction.

After lunch, all the first-grade students were let out into the schoolyard for playtime. Zeke and I mostly ran around and kicked a soccer ball about the yard. Over our first school year, we became friends.

Zeke was a little smaller than most of the boys in our class, and I was a good bit larger. He had dark wavy hair and a smooth dark complexion. My complexion was light, but not pasty. My mom would always say in private, "Thank God you have some German Jewish blood in you. Otherwise, you would look completely pale."

I did have a girlfriend in the first grade. By girlfriend, I mean a delightful playmate who always seemed a little frail and sickly to me. Of course, I was a bit oversized, so if Marlene seemed smaller, it was probably more a feeling of comparison. This six-year-old playmate was a big help for me with all kinds of paperwork after the war, when I immigrated to America.

I had sandy hair but was somewhat self-conscious about my size. Compared to my classmates, I looked slightly oversized; in some folks mind probably freakish. But, what did I know, I was only six years old and starting to enjoy the social aspects of joining my classmates in the first grade.

The classroom was pretty stark. I remember in the front of the room, Ms. Ohlendorph sat at a large desk on a six inch raised platform. Perhaps her raised height let her better oversee all the students. I was almost as tall as she was. There was a large blackboard behind her on the wall with chalk in a tray underneath.

I remember one embarrassing incident during the first week of school. I had tried to cram too much food into my mouth at lunch, so I wouldn't get too hungry before school was out in the afternoon. I'm sure I ate too fast in addition to too much.

My stomach was sore and cramped. I raised my hand and asked Ms. Ohlendorph if I could use the bathroom. The teacher ignored me, since we had just started the lesson. When I raised my hand again, the teacher told me to wait. I couldn't wait and vomited my lunch right on the floor. Everyone in the class laughed at me except Ezekiel. He helped me get to the boys' room and wash up. I was so embarrassed I felt like crying or at least quitting school. I have never forgotten Ezekiel's kindness to me.

In the future, whenever I did raise my hand, Ms. Ohlendorph was quick to respond and call on me.

All my life, Ezekiel was encouraging and helpful to me, even with our most difficult encounters with the German State Police in later years.

Our classroom had political posters on the walls extolling the virtues of the new German industry and its' political leaders. The year was 1926, and although I was oblivious to economic circumstances, Germany was still having a difficult time trying to pay for the sins of The Great War. Reparations were stunting economic growth, and the German people were suffering and frustrated with the dismal economic conditions.

I can never remember being poor. I was always hungry, but more because I was growing pretty fast, not because my family didn't have enough to eat. I remember our diet didn't contain much in the way of fresh fruits and vegetables, although Mom always tried to get vegetables in the summer.

In the winter, we had some very cold nights. Although we were often cold in our home, coal was hard to come by because of the expense. I can remember on the coldest nights sleeping under several blankets near the coal stove in the kitchen. Mom would place a pan of water on the stove to help keep the air from being too dry. Dad would block of the doorway to the kitchen with a blanket so the kitchen was quite comfortable even on the coldest nights in the winter.

CHAPTER 5

Arbeitslosigheit (Unemployment) comes to Germany

By the time I entered the fifth grade at the same school in 1931, there seemed to be some encouraging news from the economic front. The German industry had shown some signs of improvement. The problem, according to my dad, was the large number of unemployed Germans. The entire world was experiencing economic depression. In May of 1930, there were approximately 4 million unemployed Germans; by the end of the year, *arbeitslosigheit* (unemployment) reached 5.6 million people in Germany.

With so many unemployed and millions of Germans suffering from lack of necessities, it was somewhat understandable many would look toward political leaders who would promise to improve economic conditions. Many devils emerged from the rise of politicians in the *Nazi Party*.

The *Nazi* Party was solidifying their power base. Heinrich Himmler was recognized as a rising star in the Party. In 1929, Himmler was named *Reichführer* of the *SS*. He was developing the power of the *SS (Schutzstaffel)* or protective echelon around Hitler. Later in the year, Himmler recruited Reinhard Heydrich to form the intelligence service within the *SS*.

Heydrich was said to have a heart of iron. Hitler considered him the ideal *Nazi*. Later in Czechoslovakia, he was known as the "Butcher of Prague." This individual was the chairman of the *Wannsee Conference,* which was responsible for formalizing the plans for the *Final Solution* for the Jewish Question. This conference on 20 January 1942 decided on the deportation and genocide of all Jews in Germany and *Nazi*-occupied Europe.

By the time Hitler gained absolute power in Germany in January 1933, the *SS* was the most powerful organization in Germany except for the German Army *(Wehrmacht).* Germany was getting to be a dangerous country for anyone of the Jewish Religion, Communists, Gypsies, homosexuals, and anyone with handicapping deformities. Germany was not a safe place for anyone who disagreed with the basic ideas of the *Nazi* Party.

Later, the concentration camps became the prisons and death camps for Jewish Citizens, Catholic Priests, Protestant Clergy, and almost anyone who didn't go along with the "Pure German Blood" theory the *Nazi* Party envisioned.

Because Germany had suffered such upheaval after The Great War, our nation had enormous debts to pay. The political leaders at the time thought devaluation of the currency would make it easier to pay off the war reparations. The cheaper *RMs (Reichsmarks)* was a disaster for our country. The late 1920s and early 1930s were a time of gradually renewed industrialization in our country. The nation was slowly undergoing economic recovery.

The worldwide Great Depression brought further misery to Germany. We were already suffering from high unemployment after a decade of rampant inflation. Our country was ripe for a leader who promised to unite a country, remake it into a mighty nation, and rid the causes of our misfortune.

By 1932 the frustration of the German people gave rise to politicians who would promise economic prosperity and dramatic increases in industrialization.

Adolf Hitler was the most charismatic orator of the 1930s. His vociferous denunciation of communists, gypsies, Jews, and homosexuals ignited the people most affected by the harsh peace terms of the Versailles Treaty thrust on the German people ending The Great War. Hitler hinted these denounced people were taking the jobs, money, and the spirit of hardworking and unemployed German workers.

The tone of Hitler's speeches resonated well with the middle classes in Germany. Many of my countrymen looked the other way when industrial progress went toward munitions and weapons for the *Wehrmacht*. However, the treatment of Jews was abhorrent.

Many Germans only saw the beautiful buildings, parks and new railroad stations springing up throughout the country. The railway station in Berlin was a monument to modern Germany. The latest and efficient railroads connected most major German cities.

Our port cities contained many industries, and shipbuilding was in high gear. Many men and women worked in the design and implementation of one of the most significant industrial revivals in history.

New highways, including the *Reichsautobahn*, seemed to appear out of nowhere. This first significant highway was completed and opened on August 6, 1932, by Konrad Adenauer, the then mayor of Cologne. The superhighway went from Cologne to Bonn with no speed limit. I was twelve years old. Unemployment, which was rampant in the 1920s and early 1930s dried up and anyone who wanted to work was able to find a job.

President Hindenburg appointed Adolf Hitler Chancellor of the *Nazi Party* on the 30th of January, 1933. Many Germans felt the new *Führer* of the *National Socialist German Workers Party* or *Nazi Party* was responsible for a brighter future for Germany. But there was an evil face of this industrialization lurking just under the surface.

CHAPTER 6

Rising Anti-Semitism

In April of 1933, a piece of legislation passed by the *Reichstag* was a harbinger of the evil lurking in the hearts of the *Reich* political elite. The law was titled: "Law for the Restoration of the Professional Civil Service." It sounded innocent enough. On the surface, it looked like an excellent idea.

The reality of the law was very different. The sinister and disastrous part of this proclamation was it effectively barred Jews and other non-Aryans from being employed in various organizations and professions in the civil service. I was thirteen years old. Dad said, "It spells a dark day for Germany and the German people."

The real problem was the politicians who seemed to be blaming a religious group, Jewish people, for many of the issues everyday Germans might face: shortages in the markets, lines for the bakery, or banking problems. The politicians in the *Nazi* party seemed to overlook the fact the vast majority of people, including Jews, were all suffering the same issues.

My parents were concerned about the new anti-Jewish Laws enacted and passed between 1933-1935. Ezekiel and all Jews were banned from attending public schools. Jews who owned medical or legal practices and prosperous shopkeepers were discriminated against and targeted.

My parents and many Germans were concerned about the political climate in Germany after the currency lost value in the early 1920s from hyperinflation. This concern only deepened when in April of 1925 the *Schutzstaffel* or *SS* was formed ostensibly as a "Protective Echelon" for the leader of the *Nazi* Party, Adolf Hitler.

My dad asked this question with his colleagues at work and with our family: "Why would a popular politician like Adolf Hitler need a special protection guard when the country was struggling with so much economic chaos? Wouldn't our resources be more prudently spent on stimulating economic growth?"

This was a time of generalized rapid industrial growth and constricting anti-Semitic and restrictive laws in Germany. Zeke and I were maturing and enjoying grade school.

In the early grades, Zeke and I were in the same classroom most of the time. As we grew up, we saw each other at our respective family's homes as they also became friends. Our family even spent many of our weekends together with Zeke's family. We were always trying to take the most fun traditions of each family's holidays and claim them for ourselves.

Our families often went hiking together in the nearby forests. As our parents became friends, we would often go on short weekend vacations together. Although we had other friends, Zeke and I depended on each other for homework assignments and sat together during most school lunches.

Zeke's parents, Dr. and Mrs. Leven lived in a lovely section of town and had a large yard. They had several apple trees and a hedge of fir trees demarcating the large back yard. Mrs. Leven had an excellent cook named Hilda. This lovely cook always had something for us boys to munch on after school. The Leven's were so kind to my family and me during my early grade school years.

Their home was large enough to get lost in, the upstairs bedrooms were huge. Zeke and I would often play in the attic or yard. His birthday parties were always an excellent time for me to eat Hilda's delicious baked delicacies and enjoy the spectacular fountains, gardens and apple orchid in the Leven's backyard.

Their attic was always dark and mysterious to me. There were trunks, boxes, and other treasures scattered about in no particular order. Zeke and I could entertain ourselves for hours up there. Mrs. Leven only had one rule: come when called for meals. Nobody ever had to call me twice when it came to food. Mrs. Leven was a wonderful mom to Zeke. She was always a little nervous around me, perhaps because of my size. The anti-Semitism engulfing Germany didn't help anyone's state of mind.

An incident in the third grade stuck in my mind and helped to cement my friendship with Zeke. We often played kickball out in the playground. I found out much later in life the rules were similar to American baseball, except we kicked the ball instead of using a bat. It was a fun game, and I was pretty good at it because of my size.

I had started to grow even more significantly and stronger between ages six and nine and was then by far the largest boy in the class. I was as tall as most of my teachers. I never realized I was much stronger than the other boys in our class, and I was always a little timid to even participate in soccer, rugby, or in any team sport dependent on strength or endurance. Competitive sports just never interested me.

If I connected with the ball in kickball, sometimes we would never find the ball because it would fly way over the fence into an adjacent property. Once I kicked the ball so hard it exploded and deflated. In addition to being tall, I started to put on weight and muscle mass. I had no idea I was robust, strong, and powerful.

On more than one occasion my friendship with Ezekiel was instrumental in saving my life. I had no idea true hatred toward the German State Police would gain control of our lives. I was dumfounded when this hatred turned me into an individual who could kill or severely injure another human being without even thinking too much about the consequences. I was always quite timid and not at all aggressive when it came to sporting events or confrontation with my classmates. All our teachings in the Synagogue taught us to respect the individual and to avoid conflict.

CHAPTER 7

Defending Zeke

One warm spring day our class was let out a to the playground after lunch. Zeke had left me in the lunchroom because I hadn't finished eating. In reality, it took me longer to eat most meals, because I could usually eat twice as much as any of my classmates. By the third grade, my mother was continually trying to get me to eat a little less. She might have had concerns about my size. I remember during those early school years, I was continuously hungry. No matter how much I ate, I would rarely feel full.

As I went out of the school after lunch and into the playground, I found it warm enough to be without my sweater. The blossoms and leaves were coming out on all the trees. It was a glorious day with hardly a cloud in a bright blue sky. I looked around for my friend Zeke but didn't see him in the schoolyard. I remember being very happy to be in school. I enjoyed having a good friend like Zeke.

I did see a small crowd of boys and girls at the edge of the yard playing a game of some sort. I remember thinking, *Maybe Zeke is over there with those children playing a game.*

As I got closer, it looked like two of my class-mates had ganged up on Zeke. They were both good sized boys and could pick on him and make fun of him. My thinking at the time was they probably were making fun of him because he wore a small hat on his head during the Jewish Holidays.

I yelled at the tormentors:

"Leave Zeke alone!" I shrieked at the top of my lungs. "Pick on someone your size!" I had hoped a teacher would hear me and notice these bullies beating up my friend.

Zeke was on the ground, covering his head from being kicked by the larger of the two bullies.

One of the bullies shouted back at me, "Hey, he's just a dirty Jew! He needs a beating."

"Why are you hitting him?" I yelled. "Stop it right now! Cut it out! I'll have to call the teacher!"

One of the boys had grabbed Zeke, pulled him up, and had his arm around Zeke's neck. "Go ahead, call anyone you want. He's just a Jew and needs to be beaten up." It looked like he was choking him. I grabbed his arm. "Hold it, stop," I yelled, and pulled his arm off Zeke's neck. Unfortunately, I pulled his arm with such force I dislocated the tormentor's shoulder. He went down, screaming in pain.

The other boy tried to punch me in the face, but I had developed quick reflexes like my dad. I caught his fist with my left hand and just slapped him in his face with the flat edge of an opened right hand. I didn't mean to, but I hit him hard enough to fracture his upper jaw and break his two front teeth.

Also, I accidentally squeezed his fist headed for my face. I squeezed so hard I could hear his fingers breaking and feel them crunching in my fist.

I tried explaining everything to the headmaster: "Sir, it was not my intention to hurt those boys, I just wanted them to stop hurting Zeke. I certainly didn't want them both to wind up in the hospital."

I also mentioned,

"Zeke was on the ground, and the larger boy was kicking him."

"Why didn't you call one of the teachers over?"

"There was no time, sir. I didn't want them to hurt Zeke."

My mom came to school, and we walked home. It was early afternoon. The leaves had started to come out, and the blossoms were falling; the air smelled wonderfully sweet. I remember catching my breath as I tried to explain to my Mom why I had hurt those boys.

"Mom, those boys were trying to kick Zeke because he sometimes wears his funny hat to school, mostly during the Jewish Holidays.

"Zeke is my friend. I will never let anyone hurt my friend. Two bullies in our class had ganged up on Zeke and were kicking and choking him. They called him a 'dirty Jew.' I didn't mean to hurt them and send them to the hospital. I just wanted them to stop bothering Zeke."

"What caused them to start hitting Zeke? Was he provoking them in some way?"

"No, Mom. He was waiting for me in the schoolyard to come out after lunch."

In general, I would have to say my parents were understanding but furious. My explanation of the whole incident seemed to make them even more upset. When he got home from work, Dad explained to me to be very careful of my strength. Also, he cautioned me about never expressing my views about religion or politics or the *National Socialist Party* in public.

"Son, unfortunately, we are living in times where it could be perilous to express a political or religious opinion. Any opinions different from those of our political leaders, or the *National Socialist Workers Party,* are not to be discussed or talked about in public. These thugs are steering our country in a direction limiting our freedoms of expression. You must understand how careful you have to be with Zeke and his family. No one should know of our friendship or connections with them."

He emphasized, "Jenz, always avoid fighting with other classmates. They could someday gang up on you, or you could hurt someone else quite seriously." Even at the age of nine or ten, my strength was a wonder to my parents. I had no trouble lifting an eighty-pound bag of cement or even lifting either parent.

"However, and listen to me son, if you ever find a fight with another person is unavoidable, hit him first, and wallop him. Make sure you hit him hard enough, so he stays down and doesn't want to get back up on his feet."

All through my grade school years, I was never much interested in sports or even exercising. As I matured, I found muscles I didn't realize I had. My back and chest muscles far exceeded any of my classmates in middle school years.

Once when I was twelve or thirteen, our family car went off the road during an ice storm and got stuck in the snow. I got out of the car and lifted the back end of the automobile, with my parents in it, back onto the pavement so Dad could gain traction and back it out of the icy ruts. My parents were amazed.

My hand strength developed to the point where I could break a brick with one hand. My father warned me, "Be very careful when shaking hands with anyone, men or women. You do not want to hurt them. Always avoid any fights with women; and as you mature, you will find it is best not to argue with them either."

My body was maturing and getting exceptionally strong. I would always wear loose fitting clothing to cover up the muscles on my body. I would apologize and make excuses whenever I had to lift machinery or anything substantial for any reason.

Even though participating in sports didn't particularly interest me, I was fascinated by the spectacle and excitement of the upcoming Olympic Games. One of my teachers in my high school class, Herr Lautenziner, strongly "encouraged" me to join the Hitler Youth and attend the Hitler Camp next summer. He said I should probably train for the Olympic Games.

I talked with Dad, "My teacher has suggested I go to the Hitler Youth Camp this summer. Many of my classmates are going, and they talk about it all the time."

Dad commented, "Yes, son, I hate to say it, but it probably would be good for you to attend, perhaps it is even mandatory."

"But Dad, what about all the anti-Jewish signs? They are everywhere saying 'Jews Out,' or 'Jews Not Wanted.' Won't Hitler Camp be more of the same? I can't go without Zeke. He's my best friend."

"Jenz, you must keep our family secret. You cannot let anyone know you are part Jewish and have a best friend who is Jewish. Zeke must understand this, and he will know why you are going to the Hitler Camp. The Camp will further hide the way our family feels about the Chancellor and his regime of cutthroat thugs. You must never speak of the *Reich* in anything but glowing and positive terms.

"Besides, with the upcoming Olympic Games, much of this disgusting anti-Semitism might get toned down or disappear. Herr

Hitler will not want the world to know about what is happening to the Jews in our country."

Another issue for my family, which included me, my mom Hannah, and my dad Rolf, was we were quiet, almost "secret" members of the *CC* or *Confessing Church*. The head of the church and pastor, Dietrich Bonhoeffer, was a very popular and charismatic preacher. However, he was not at all popular with the German political elite.

My father warned, "Pastor Bonheoffer's sermons regularly criticize the ideology of anti-Semitism and the proliferation of the concentration and work camps. The *Gestapo* thugs are watching him. Jenz, listen to me. You must never involve yourself or Zeke or Zeke's family in any conversations about politics or religion with other people."

Occasionally, we would travel into Berlin to listen to Pastor Bonheoffer's sermons at the large and very impressive *Zionskirchplatz*. He would often preach about "The Church and the Jewish Question."

Many citizens and pastors in Germany during those years had no idea what the real meaning of *Gleischaltung* or in English, synchronization, really meant. Our country was undergoing a total reorganization along with the racist ideology of the *National Socialist Party*. Only a few of the politically connected knew how fast this horrific change was taking place in our nation.

Dad warned, "Be especially careful with your language at the Hitler Camp. Anyone could overhear you and might pass on your words to the *Gestapo* or a politician. I have heard stories from colleagues at work who talk in confidence about some of their Jewish co-workers being dragged out of the office, arrested, and sent to work camps."

Dad was a chemist for *Interessen-Gemeinschaft Farbenindustrie AG*, also known as *IG Farben.* He joined the company when founded in 1925 from the joining of six smaller German chemical companies. His division developed edible dyes, food colorings, and chemicals for food enhancements.

Little did I know as a young boy growing up in *Nazi* Germany with a Jewish best friend how invaluable some of my father's work could be to Zeke and me as teenagers and young adults.

After April 1933, many more laws with a distinctly anti-Semitic flavor to them were passed and put into place at the national and local levels. Even our little village, just outside of Düsseldorf, had printed signs warning Jews to stay away from individual businesses and for the non-Jews to have nothing to do with Jewish businesses. The effect for our family and many of our neighbors was to concentrate our shopping in Jewish only companies. We did not want them to suffer economic hardship.

The total effect of the myriad of anti-Semitic legislation in those years was very depressing for the Jews and many others in my country, but it seemed to draw Zeke's family and our family even closer together. The only negative aspect of the new laws I can remember was my parents discouraged me from going to Synagogue with Zeke's family. However, Zeke would often come to our church during our grade school years.

CHAPTER 8

My Fifteenth Birthday

On my birthday in September 1935, I turned fifteen-years-old, Zeke was already fifteen. Of course, I was excited to celebrate my birthday with Zeke. His parents came over to our home, and we celebrated with baked goods and candy. Even though I have lived in America for many years, I still cannot get the smell, texture, or deliciousness of German baked goods out of my memory.

My mom, bless her heart, whom I loved deeply, was not the best cook in the world. Often my dad would help with the cooking duties around the kitchen. On this birthday celebration day, the Leven's cook, Hilda, had prepared some special German delicacies, which I can still taste in the back of my mind.

We celebrated with caramelized almond and vanilla custard small cakes called *Bienenstich*. We ate these along with little *Berliners* -- something like small jelly doughnuts. The Leven's also brought a type of spice cake called *Baumkuchen*. My dad liked this type of baked dessert. However, Frau Hilda knew my favorite, which I can still taste to this day.

Prinzegententorte is a Bavarian cake with at least six thin layers of chocolate buttercream. The entire cake is drenched with a dark chocolate glaze. Eating a slice of this delicacy made me want Frau Hilda to join our family. I even asked Dr. Leven if he could loan her to us. This Bavarian tort cake was also Zeke's favorite. Occasionally I still dream about those chocolate glazed cakes.

What most stuck in my mind on this particular birthday, however, was the reaction of Zeke's parents and my parents to the news broadcast over the radio. The radio announcement placed a dark cloud over the celebration.

The day before my birthday the Nationalist Socialist German Workers Party, the *Nazi* Political Party, held a rally in the southern German city of Nuremberg. At the rally, the *Nazi* Party announced the creation of what became known as the *Nuremberg Laws*. These laws were to go into effect immediately on the date, 15 September 1935.

The German people understood these laws would codify the racial theories embedded in the *Nazi* Party's ideology. It was explained why these new *Nuremberg Laws* were made up of two fully enforceable laws: the *"Reich Citizenship Law"* and the *"Law for the Protection of German Blood and Honor."*

The announcement didn't mean too much to Zeke and me, but our parents spoke in hushed tones, and their facial expressions indicated they were distraught. My dad and Dr. Leven talked about how this could be the end of Germany as they knew it.

"If the Jews cannot make a living in Germany," Dr. Leven asked, "how are we to stay in a country which will not even acknowledge our citizenship?"

My dad voiced his theory: "Von Papen, the Vice-Chancellor or other non-Nazis in the government might be able to hold the *Führer* in check and contain his temper and often brutal tendencies."

Mom said, "Look, Hitler was named Chancellor in January 1933. Has Von Papen done anything to make anti-Semitism less brutal?"

Mrs. Leven started crying softly, "Hitler is out to destroy our religion and our people. The *SA* has already been to my husband's office in the hospital. These *Brownshirts* have bullied the hospital staff and intimidated my husband. They have accused him of malpractice, poor surgical technique, and treating Aryans and non-Jews without permission."

SA stood for Storm Detachment or *Sturmabteilung.* "These stormtroopers seem to be everywhere," said Mom. "They look and act like a bunch of bullies and ruffians."

Dad's comment, "I thought Hitler put an end to this group of thugs last year in June of 1934, with the killing of their leader, Ernst Rohm."

Dr. Leven added, "The *SA* thugs have overrun many organizations and companies in our country. The *Gestapo* and the *SS* have also infiltrated all aspects of German life."

None of us had any idea of the power of the *Gestapo,* which was the German State Police, and the *SS* to intimidate and terrorize the German population. Our neighbors and friends were fearful of being reported to the *Gestapo* for being critical of the *Reich* and thuggish politicians. The *Waffen SS* was the elite armed wing of the *Nazi Party's SS (Schutzstaffel).* This organization struck terror into the hearts of all law-abiding Germans, as well as the entire Jewish population.

CHAPTER 9

The Coming Olympic Games 1936

The years between 1933 and 1935 were a time of great upheaval and change for Germany. One day there were thousands of anti-Semitic placards and signs in every city and town, and almost overnight after the beginning of 1936, virtually all of them had disappeared. I asked Dad, "What happened to the outrage of anti-Semitic activity? It almost seemed the politicians in Germany had regained their sanity."

"No, son. Hitler is cautious of world opinion with the upcoming Olympic Games.

"Also," claimed Dad, "Perhaps the general population has realized what damage could be done to our economy and our nation if one of the most productive population groups in Germany is not allowed citizenship."

"I will feel much better about going to Hitler Youth Camp this summer as long as there is no anti-Semitic political movement. Maybe the camp won't be so bad."

In the summer of 1936, I was sixteen-years-old and full of hope for the German athletes at the summer games and full of hope for Germany. We had so much potential. I was growing stronger and taller. At six feet four and one-half inches, I think I was at my full height. My mom said she would be pleased if I didn't grow too much more significantly.

Dad's admonishment for summer camp, "Be sure you blend in, Jenz. You shouldn't stand out in any way; never voice your opinion of the *Third Reich* unless it is in positive tones. Always stay in the middle of any group of athletes, work projects, pistol shooting, or marches. Try not to excel or get noticed. Please do not let anyone goad you into a fight or want to test your strength. You could wind up seriously hurting one of your fellow campers.

"But remember what I told you when you were in grade school. If an unavoidable fight is looming, first, try walking away. If it is impossible to walk away first distract the tormentor...and then, unfortunately, put them down with a rapid blow to the head. Strike them, and don't hesitate! You do not want them to get up.

"If you hit them hard enough, they will never get up. A direct blow to the face could kill your opponent with facial bones lodged into the brain. A hard enough blow to the side of the head could crush their skull like an eggshell. Be very careful of your strength! The forehead and top of the skull are very hard, avoid those areas. Also, if you are going to hit someone, think about putting on a leather glove for protection of your hands.

"Remember, it is best never to make an opponent angry with you."

"Dad, does the camp offer military training in fighting tactics?"

"Probably son. Be very aware and do not hurt any of your fellow campers."

"Will the use of firearms be included at our camp?"

"Learn well, my son. Unfortunately, someday you might have to use those tactics and firearms against the *Gestapo*."

"Dad, I couldn't turn against my countrymen!"

"Son, these men are monsters. Whatever they were in civilian life, the political atmosphere has changed them irreparably. They are no longer our countrymen. They have sworn allegiance to Hitler or the *SS,* and son, believe me, they are dangerous. I have seen how evil and destructive they can be in our plant at Farben."

CHAPTER 10

Leaving for Hitler Youth Camp

The next week I left for camp. It was a warm, beautiful late spring day with the scent of fruit tree blossoms and early spring flowers in the air. There were still some small patches of snow in the forests and the evenings were still cool, but you could tell the warmth of summer was almost upon us.

There was an excitement I couldn't quite describe, almost like meeting a pretty girl at school. I was anxious and shy at the same time. Whenever I became concerned about a new situation, Zeke would usually come to my rescue by talking over the positives and negatives of the case. He was always the voice of reason ever since I had known him. His perspective in difficult situations was always calming to me.

The camp was a short two-hour train ride away. I was a little shaky, similar to what I was like on my first day of school at age six. The only problem was I didn't have Zeke or my parents to lean on. I read the material given to all the boys on the train about how vital summer camp was for the Hitler Youth. I read Hitler's quote of what he expected of Germany's youth when the Hitler Youth Movement was formed early in my life in 1922:

"The weak must be chiseled away. I want men and women who can suffer pain. A young German must

*be as swift as a greyhound, as tough as leather, and as
hard as Krupp's steel."*

A bus picked up the campers at the train from Düsseldorf and brought us into the country. The forest and the meadows were beautiful. It looked like such a tranquil and peaceful place. The camp itself was set on a hillside with a large dining hall at the top. All the campers could eat together in the building. There were some smaller outbuildings and tents for about two hundred campers. The camp was nestled in the rolling hills and countryside dotted with lakes, streams and pastures.

My first day at camp included getting uniforms and participating in close order marching drills. The younger boys had to have their heads shaved. Since I was sixteen, I just received a tight haircut. It was like an induction into the *Wehrmacht*. There were lots of anti-Semitic posters and literature around with huge *Nazi* flags with the *swastika*. They were all hanging and decorating the inside the dining hall. We all had to wear armbands on our left arms with the *swastika* on them. Most of the campers seemed proud of their uniforms and were quite excited to wear them.

To me, the uniform made me feel dirty. Wearing it just seemed to betray my family, my religion, and Germany. It made my skin crawl. I never would say anything, however.

Our Hitler Youth leaders were mostly from the enlisted ranks of the *Wehrmacht*. They kept drilling us in close order marching, calisthenics, and rifle practice. Also, we learned the best way to throw hand grenades. We would try to pitch the fake weapons into a circle with a stake in the middle. The ring was 25-30 meters away. The closer to the stake you landed your grenade, the higher was your score. I always had the thought the stake might not be far enough away if the weapons were live.

There was plenty of fun exercising also. We played soccer, rugby, and variations of kickball.

I remember writing my dad from the camp, "It seems like Hitler is trying to build some super, racially pure society." The idea of racial purity was encouraged and beaten into us from the first day of camp.

"You may be on to something son," He wrote back, "The *Gestapo* has already been to our plant and harassed many of my colleagues who work with me. The German political structure is insisting our company develop munitions, explosives, timing fuses, and dyes for military applications. It makes no sense unless the *Wehrmacht* is planning for another war. I don't think the German people would stand for such nonsense."

I wrote to my mom, telling her I missed not socializing with Zeke.

She wrote back a very understanding letter with the warning not to mention any of our friends in my messages, "Because, the wrong people might be reading them."

She also advised me never to send correspondence to Ezekiel or his family or to talk about his family. My question was, "How could this be happening in our country?"

While at the camp, my body was developing in ways I didn't understand. Girls seemed to be attracted to me, and there was a whole Hitler Youth segment for young girls.

The youngest girls, ages ten to thirteen, could belong to the *"Jungmadelbund,"* or the "League for Young Girls." Once the girls turned fourteen years old, they were "encouraged" to join the

"Bund Deutscher Madel," or "The League of German Girls." There was a *Bund* for the older girls somewhere near our camp.

I have to admit, whenever I got near a beautiful girl in the senior *Bund,* my whole body seemed to react weirdly. My speech all of a sudden became slurred and almost incomprehensible. I would get shy, and my face seemed to turn red with a flush. I would often get embarrassed about my privates, and I had to leave the room. Usually, I could barely remember my name.

Hitler Camp was a cross between the Boy Scouts and military training. The Boy Scouts and most religious youth organizations had been blended into the Hitler Youth by the mid-1920s. The Lutheran youth group before 1930 was over six hundred thousand members strong in Germany. After 1933 it was outlawed and wholly absorbed into the Hitler Youth movement.

By December first, 1933, the Hitler Youth movement became a state organization, and all other non-*Nazi* youth movements were banned. Many families throughout Germany were becoming so concerned they were making plans to immigrate from the *Nazi* State, even though their homes, businesses, and very lives were linked to Germany.[*]

The part of the Hitler Youth camp I enjoyed and found most interesting was the marksmanship and strength training, and of course my chance meeting with Ilsa. My time with Ilsa was cherished. I think I knew then there was something extraordinary about her.

---

[*] *Before the war broke out, over eighty percent of our Jews under age twenty-one had immigrated from Germany. None could leave once the war broke out. All the Europeans of Jewish ancestry who were trapped in Germany or any of the conquered territories were subsequently rounded up and sent to concentration camps for extermination.*

Our hand to hand combat training was extensive. We learned to kill an enemy with bare hands, a club from a stick, with knives, or a pistol. I learned a quick punch to the throat could easily crush a persons' ability to breathe and could cause death in a few minutes. The throat blow could ultimately kill an enemy. I had to be careful when sparing with other campers. I followed my father's advise and pretended to be somewhat awkward and usually let my partner win the exercise.

We went to the firing range in groups of twenty boys. The field was more of an elongated clearing of about 100 meters deep in the woods. The backdrop was the forest. There were targets of cardboard cutouts of soldiers at twenty-five, fifty, and one hundred meters distant.

My friend Dieter and I were in a group of ten boys. As we marched up to the firing line, we had issued one *Pistole Parabellum* or *Lugar Pistol* and ten rounds of ammunition. Before we were able to load our firearm, we had to take the gun apart, clean, lubricate, and reassemble it.

Dieter asked me, "How do you load these pistols?"

"Quiet on the firing range!" ordered the instructor. "No talking!"

The Lugar felt very small in my hand. Although the first site needed a slight adjustment depending on the range distance, I was able to hit all the targets, even at the one hundred meter mark.

Our instructors were very racist and derogatory toward Jews. "Pretend it's a swarm of Jews heading to harm your family, and you have to eradicate them all," was the cry from one of our instructors. This type of discourse was unsettling to me. All I could do was to bite my tongue. I felt like aiming for the instructors' head.

What was most detestable was the *Nazi* policy of a deep hatred of Jews in our country. My family's Jewish heritage was concerning. Zeke's family heritage was even more concerning. Dr. Leven had talked about some of the anti-Semitism he had experienced at work. Most of the campers were extremely anti-Semitic. I remembered my father's warnings and kept my mouth shut.

What was rather thrilling for me was about a week after seeing Ilsa, my friend Dieter spoke to me at our noon meal and handed me a note from her. She wrote she would like to meet me at the same spot near the lake after the evening meal.

"Dieter, was she serious?"

"I think so. Ilsa sure smiles a lot."

I suggested, "She is a very kind girl, but I don't want you or me to get into trouble with our councilors here at the Hitler Camp."

"Meeting her would probably be okay," Dieter returned, "I think she is one of the leaders in the girls Bund."

"If you say so, Dieter, I'm out of here right after dinner."

I ate only a little, and quickly, which was not my usual style. I can't for the life of me, even remember what I had for dinner. Besides, I hadn't the faintest idea what she wanted. I guessed she wanted to talk about the "swim" and "after swim" time we had in the mossy glade.

I hoped I wasn't just naive or worse, just plain stupid. I was looking forward to seeing Ilsa again.

I rushed through dinner and slipped out of the dining hall through the kitchen exit. I tried to walk casually across the meadow and down toward the lake. The sun was about a half-hour from setting; small birds were darting around the field. It was a beautifully warm early summer evening.

I remembered small common German flowers covering the field. They made a beautiful white carpet of flowers, but for the life of me, I couldn't remember their name. I had difficulty thinking of anything other than Ilsa.

The air smelled sweet from the spring grasses and trees. There was freshness and purity about being alone on the meadow. The contrast between the racism and hatred spewed by the Hitler Camp leaders and the virtue of the empty field was positively delightful. I was lost in thought and looking forward to seeing Ilsa.

Something about the open field and the flowers and thoughts of Ilsa made me think of something from Song of Songs in the Bible about going out to the countryside with my lover. The interesting thing was, I couldn't remember if I learned the phrase from my church or at my synagogue.

I picked my way down to the lake and looked for the little beach where Dieter and I had been swimming. To my surprise, there were two people in the water. At first, I thought I might be in trouble, it looked like Ilsa, and another person was splashing about. My second thought was there go my chances of being alone with Ilsa again.

"Hello, Jenz, this is my friend Gretchen."

"Ha. Hi. G, Gretchen. It is ah,n, nice to see you."

Gretchen had light brown hair, a very pretty perfect roundish face, and a stunning figure in her bathing suit. She had a quick wide smile with brilliant white teeth. Her eyes were a dazzling deep bright blue.

I could see my plans for being alone with Ilsa were just not going to materialize.

"Come on in the water, Jenz, it's very refreshing." chided Ilsa.

I hesitated at the edge of the water deep in thought. *Me, swimming with two beautiful women, this just can't be happening.*

"Come on in Jenz." Gretchen admonished, "You can't be afraid of us."

"No. N, No," I stammered as I stepped out of my shoes and removed my shirt.

Thinking about it later, they probably wanted me in the water as a way to get me partially undressed.

The water seemed a little chilly when I stuck my foot in, but I didn't want to seem hesitant. So I ran and dove under the water to get wet quickly. Both girls started splashing me and teasing me about my size. I told them I wasn't overweight, just overgrown.

Both Ilsa and Gretchen talked about how their Bund leaders encouraged them to have relations with Aryan men to serve our *Führer*. It flashed through my mind, could it be possible, maybe they both wanted me? I swam away from them and started to back slowly out of the water.

Ilsa called out to me, "Where are you going, silly." She caught up to me and held my hand and pulled me close to her. "Didn't you enjoy the other night in the glade?"

"Y, Yes." I stammered. "But, I, d, don't want to be unkind or embarrass your friend."

"Better yet, I don't want to embarrass myself."

Gretchen came up to me and reassured me, "I am tough to embarrass, Jenz, "and besides," she articulated in a low husky voice, "you are attractive to me. I promise you we would not ever embarrass you."

She placed her hand on my chest and made a remark about my muscles.

I know my face was turning red, and my chest was burning where her hand lingered.

"Thank you," was what I tried to say, but it came out "tank ooo." I felt pretty stupid. Each girl had hold of one of my hands and was leading me out of the water. I know I should have made a run across the meadow for the camp, but my legs felt wooden; they would only move where they were taking me.

Ilsa sat me down in the mossy glade and ordered me to relax and enjoy myself.

She said, "Look, it isn't every day a handsome man gets the company of two beautiful women."

I just groaned and said something unintelligible. Gretchen gently pushed me onto my side to face Ilsa.

She then slipped out of her bathing suit and pressed her body against my back. Perhaps they were trying to see if I would get frightened and run away. The truth is, I couldn't move. All I could think of saying, "Is this what our Chancellor wants of us?"

Both Ilsa and Gretchen answered, "Yes!" at the same time.

I had no idea what to do. All I remember is I couldn't move.

Ilsa had removed her bathing suit and had slipped off my wet shorts.

My privates had swollen beyond my comprehension. Gretchen rolled me toward her and gently climbed on top of me.

She kissed me on the mouth and whispered, "You sweet man, it's my turn."

She was holding my manhood and was slowly gliding it into her. "Relax," she whispered, "I'm not going to hurt you, I just want you to feel pleasure." She started a gentle, but slow, rhythmic motion setting my body on fire.

I couldn't kiss her back because her head only came up to my chest.

Ilsa started kissing me on the cheek, then my mouth while whispering in my ear to go slowly and relax.

Slowly! I was frozen in place, even though my body was on fire.

Gretchen stopped moving on top of me and ordered me to go slowly. Well, I wasn't going anywhere. I couldn't move if I wanted to. Then, since Gretchen couldn't reach my mouth to kiss me, she started kissing Ilsa on her stomach and lower.

My body became an electric circuit; it began thrusting and squirming, I exploded into Gretchen, I just could not stop myself. Both girls just moaned and giggled with pleasure.

I almost passed out from lack of air. Even though I was breathing hard, I had a difficult time staying conscious. My heart was racing. Gretchen had her head on my chest.

"Your heart is racing and telling me you are enjoying this. Am I right?"

I couldn't talk coherently, "Y, Yes! Definitely yes!"

I remember thinking somewhere in the depths of my mind, I should hurry back to camp before I was missed. And I would have hurried up the hill, if I could have moved. My body would not respond to my brain. I wasn't even sure if my brain cells were still functioning.

Ilsa whispered to me, "Stay right where you are and just relax. It's my turn to make sure you are relaxed."

My speech was slurred in my response to her. " Ilsa, it's not possible for me to be any more relaxed. I'm barely conscious. I hope I didn't hurt Gretchen."

"I'm fine," she replied as she rolled me on my side and started rubbing my back and buttocks.

Although the back rub felt soothing, it exposed me to Ilsa who started kissing and rubbing my chest. "Oh Ilsa," I protested, "They will miss me at the camp, I must get going!"

"I'm a camp leader at the Woman's Bund," she giggled. "I will tell you when you can go."

After Ilsa's comment, she started kissing me on the lips. I tried to protest and tell her I couldn't possibly stay longer. But she clutched my genitals and started squeezing gently, then a little harder.

"Oohhh, you feel divine," Was all I could say.

She kept messaging me and squeezing me gently. She climbed on top of me, but held her hand under my genitals and wouldn't let go. She kept on gently messaging me while gliding me into her.

Gretchen kept kissing my cheek and whispering in my ear. In a low tone, she said, "Jenz, you will not forget us, will you?"

"No. Never, I murmured. I will always remember your ki, kindness to me."

Then Gretchen started kissing Ilsa and Ilsa squeezed harder on my genitals. I tried everything I could to hold back, but then Ilsa began a low groaning moan and a rhythmic thrusting of her body. There was no controlling my body. I started thrusting profoundly and rapidly and suddenly could hold back no longer and just exploded into my dear Ilsa.

"Mein Gott in Himmel," Ilsa moaned as she kept messaging under my genitals.

I couldn't have moved even if I had wanted or had to. I was completely paralyzed. The girls moaned and giggled as they rolled me on my side and rubbed my back and chest.

My heart was beating so hard, I couldn't move or think. My heart was pounding in my ears. They both continued chatting and laughing, but I couldn't understand anything they were saying. My ears were ringing, and I couldn't make out their words.

They said something about getting together again soon, but my hearing was shot. Ilsa and Gretchen dressed and left me naked in the glade.

After a time, I regained some alertness, dressed as quickly as I could and hurried back to the camp on wobbly legs. It was completely dark. After the pleasant and unexpected evening, I was pretty sure the 10-kilometer hikes were not going to be my only challenge all summer.

It was a strange summer filled with the hate and racial venom of the Hitler Youth Camp and the love I shared with Ilsa and Gretchen. I really discovered myself at Hitler Camp in the summer of 1936. I learned to love the two women who were so kind to me, and really hate the racism and anti-Semitism dished out daily at the Hitler Youth Camp.

At the end of the summer, my parents asked about the camp. I tried to answer in generalities, but Mom asked, "Jenz, was there anything, in particular, you liked about the Hitler Youth Camp?"

I longed to share my experiences with Ilsa and Gretchen but thought better of it. I answered, "There were some parts I enjoyed, but most of it seemed like military training."

"Dad," I asked, "Will I have to join the *Wehrmacht?*"

"You will have no choice, Jenz. It now is a law in Germany. All Aryan men over age 18 must join the Wehrmacht in some capacity. There are severe consequences for shirkers or resisters.

"More importantly, I need to talk with you about the visit this summer from the *Gestapo* to our home in Düsseldorf."

CHAPTER 11

Gestapo Visit, Summer - 1936

"**W**ha, what happened, Dad?

"Why would they come to our home?"

"There were two of them, Jenz. They asked about my work and if I worked with or knew any Jews who might be troublemakers. They never introduced themselves and only flashed a government identification card and a badge.

"They were both cruel looking men with dark clothing and grim faces. They looked like the type of people who would kick a helpless little puppy and not think twice about it. They wreaked of cigarette smoke.

"One of them had a pinched nose on a narrow face. This agent had piercing penetrating eyes set too close together. His forehead was lined with deep furrows bordering a receding hairline. He wore black clothing and a black fedora. I don't think I'll ever forget him.

"The other man was heavyset with thin sneering lips; he never smiled. His pockmarked face expressed a deep hatred for anything if it didn't go exactly his way. When he spoke, he spit out his words between crooked, tobacco-stained, yellowing teeth.

"Of course," I told them, "Possibly some of my co-workers might be Jewish, but I could only guess.

"They were very intimidating and used harsh words, right in front of your mother. They both had facial expressions which radiated pure evil."

"Mr. Ramsgrund," they continued, "if you are not completely truthful with us, things could go very harshly for you and your family."

I decided not to respond.

"Where is your son?" the pock-faced agent asked.

Fortunately, I was able to say, "He is at Hitler Youth Camp near Münster."

"Excellent." They both replied in unison.

Then pock-face held his jacket aside and displayed a large handgun in a leather holster while giving Hannah and me a sneering smirk. It was my understanding all firearms had been confiscated by the *Nazi* party. Their display of the large handgun left no doubt in my mind: these were dangerous men.

"I understand you officers completely, could we offer you something... tea perhaps?"

"They left without actually brandishing the pistol, but your mother and I got the message."

"Jenz, you and Zeke have to be very careful when together. I am anxious to talk with Dr. and Mrs. Leven about what they intend to do if he is let go from the hospital. Since the Olympics are over, there seems to be much more anti-Semitism in our country."

"I will talk to Zeke and see when his parents could come over. The director at Hitler Youth Camp strongly hinted all of our communications with fellow Nazi's should be direct and personal, not by telephone or written down.

"The implication was, You can never be sure who might be listening.

"I'll go over to the Leven's home this afternoon and see how they are doing."

"Be careful, Jenz, you never know who will be watching them or their home."

Later in the afternoon, I walked the three miles to Zeke's home. I took a bit of a circuitous route. I don't think anyone was following me, but I saw other men on the streets. I hadn't yet learned how to spot the *Gestapo*.

The wind seemed to go right through my light jacket and sweater and chilled me, even as I walked briskly toward the Leven's home. The grassy areas appeared to retain some white hoar frost, and there was a skim of ice on the puddles of water in the street. It was late afternoon, and the sun looked like it might set within the hour through a partly overcast sky.

I took another detour to wind up on the Leven's street and still have a good view both up and down the road. No one seemed to be following me; there were only a few folks out and about in the neighborhood. I had the feeling it wasn't just the coolness of the weather keeping people indoors. It was almost as if a plague had descended on our small part of Düsseldorf. A plague of fear.

As I knocked on the Leven's front door, I noticed two men out of the corner of my eye about a block away on the other side of the road. Mrs. Leven came to the door; I entered quickly before the two men could spot me.

"Mrs. Leven," I spoke rapidly and a little breathlessly, "I may have been followed. Is Zeke home? I was hoping we could talk. Besides, my dad was hoping he could have you over to discuss the political situation with you and Dr. Leven."

We were standing in the foyer of their grand home. There was a thick round oriental carpet on the black and white marble tiled floor and some magnificent art on the walls. Mrs. Leven seemed pretty calm. She offered to take my jacket and asked me to wait in the library just off the foyer.

Their library also had a beautiful oriental carpet with muted colors of red and gold surrounded by shelves full of interesting medical books and world-class literature. The furniture included a large desk with a leather insert on top and a comfortable dark red leather couch and matching armchairs.

Everything smelled elegant and quiet. The bay window looked out on a manicured side lawn with fruit trees decorating the landscape. Many of the books were about surgical technique and surgical procedures. Dr. Leven was a highly skilled thoracic surgeon.

Mrs. Leven came in and commented,

"Jenz, you seem so out of breath, are you okay?"

"I just walked quickly on the way over here. I didn't want to be followed."

"Who would follow you here?"

"Mrs. Leven, the *Gestapo* is everywhere and thoroughly evil."

"Jenz, these political fops shouldn't scare you. Our country should have some protection from these evil brutes," added Mrs. Leven.

"I'll get Ezekiel. Would you two like some tea out on the front porch?"

The Leven's home had a large front porch supporting two matching columns either side of the front entry. The porch wrapped around one side of the house. There were two painted wooden chairs each side of a table on the side porch, perfect for an outside meal or afternoon tea.

"No. No, Mrs. Leven, my father has said we are to be very careful about being seen or heard together. He thought you and your family would understand because of the particular political circumstances. Also, it's a bit cool for sitting outside."

Zeke came down an impressive winding staircase from the second floor and came directly into the library.

"Hey, Jenz. It's nice to see you. How was Hitler Camp this summer?"

"Zeke, you wouldn't believe me even if I told you. Most of it was boring military stuff, but I did learn how to kill an enemy with my bare hands."

"We also learned how to march ten kilometers with a thirty-pound backpack, shoot the Lugar pistol and a rifle at stationary targets."

"Fantastic," said Zeke. "Thanks for filling me in on Hitler Camp. Our *Fuhrer's* camp scares the hell out of most of the Jews in our country."

"I don't blame you for being wary of the Hitler Youth, they are a frightening bunch. How do you think I felt being half Jewish and getting a daily dose of hateful bigotry toward my Mom's side of our family every day. It was disgusting. It took a lot of discipline just to remain calm and not express my outrage.

"My family sent me over so you, your parents, and my parents could get together to try to ease the burden of increasing anti-Semitism since the Olympic Games. It seems for folks who are Jewish or part Jewish, life is getting more and more difficult this year."

My additional comment was, "I wonder how our *Führer* felt about a Negro man, Jesse Owens winning four gold medals including the 100-meter dash during the Olympic games?"

"It makes you wonder about his theories of racial superiority," said Zeke.

"Even the art museums are displaying anti-Semitic art," I added. "In the library of the German Museum, there is a display of what the museum calls degenerative art. My dad went to Munich to see with his own eyes the display titled *'Der Ewige Juden,'* The Eternal Jew. The exhibit opened in November 1937."

Dad's comment was, "Not only was it disgusting, but it wove the stereotypes of the 'Eastern Jew' with common anti-Semitic feelings of many Germans." He mentioned, "Up to five thousand people each day went to see all the disgusting nonsense."

Mrs. Leven joined the conversation. "What do your parents suggest, Jenz? Life here in Düsseldorf is getting increasingly difficult for us and many of our Jewish friends and families in the synagogue. The authorities have even sent out an order for all Jewish businesses to write the word Jew on the front of their doors or store windows."

"Dad feels it would be best to be organized in some sort of unobtrusive resistance to the political climate. He warned me it could be nothing overt. The *Gestapo* is everywhere. He has even heard if you are arrested on suspicion of disloyalty to the *Reich*, consequences can be disastrous.

"He mentioned one of his colleagues at his chemical plant was hauled out from his work station for just making comments on the local politicians. He was never seen again."

"How is it possible?" Mrs. Leven asked. "Are we no longer a country of laws?"

"Unfortunately, No. Since the *Nuremberg Laws* of 1935, we can no longer be thought of citizens of the *Reich* or expect legal protection under the law."

I convinced Mrs. Leven to let me wait until Dr. Leven returned from the hospital, and then after dark take all of us in the car on a circuitous route to my home.

"Why to wait until it's dark?" queried Mrs. Leven.

I reassured her, "The *Gestapo* is everywhere. I would not be surprised if they were watching your home and noted my visit today."

Dr. Leven came home shortly after 6 pm. It was already dark outside. Mrs. Leven's cook had prepared some food and packed it in a basket to take with us. Dr. Leven drove the long way to our house. We drove into the back driveway of our yard, and we all entered through the back door. There were very few cars on the roads, but no one seemed to be following us. No one was lurking around our home when we drove down the driveway to the back of the house.

I think Dr. Leven understood the gravity of the situation, but I wasn't sure Zeke or I did. I was able to attend secondary school, but Zeke and all Jews had to attend private schools or were homeschooled. Jews were not allowed to participate in public schools or universities by this time in Germany.

Mom welcomed the Leven's into our home. All of us understood why we met in the back of the house around the kitchen table by candlelight.

The adults talked about how bad the political climate was becoming; Zeke and I just listened. It didn't seem possible our country would re-arm again and get involved in another war, but the adults seemed to think it was what was happening.

Dad said, "The restrictions are becoming more and more stringent for all Germans of the Jewish faith."

Dr. Leven commented, "The outright hostility of the hospital staff, patients, and even the cleaning personnel toward me and the other Jewish doctors and nurses is becoming intolerable.

"No one seems to want any Jews on the hospital staff or even in the hospital. I go to work every day and fear for my safety."

"Our chemical plant has the same atmosphere," remarked my dad. "Some workers, even crucial personnel, have been fired, let go, or just disappeared and haven't returned to work.

"Also, our whole focus has changed at *Farben*. We are now developing high explosives for artillery rounds, rockets, and bombs. It seems our *Führer* is guiding Germany into preparations for war. We have even developed a highly secret liquid rocket fuel to be mixed with liquid oxygen."

"What are these madmen dreaming up?" asked Dr. Leven.

"Stan, I would never say this anywhere, but here with you people," Dad continued. "Hitler is acting like a crazy man. Who in his right mind would denigrate one of the most productive groups of people in Germany and then ban them from citizenship in the *Reich*?"

"These are challenging times," Dr. Leven mumbled in a low voice, almost a whisper. The politicians need to do something before Hitler ruins our economy or forces or blunders us into a war. What would you think, Rolf?"

"We need to be very careful and cautious in planning. The *Gestapo* seems to be into every company in Germany. It would be imperative not to trust or confide in anyone. Jenz and Ezekiel, you must not speak about politics to anyone, even friends you trust."

"If it comes to actual war, I will try to get some materials out of the plant. Some of the explosives might be useful for resisting political thugs."

"If war does come, I might be able to alter the formula for the explosives slightly. But it is just conjecture. We have to be extremely cautious."

"Does your family have anywhere you can go if the authorities come to your hospital or home with too many questions, Stan?"

"I don't think the *Gestapo* will bother the doctors in the Reich, Rolf. Especially so soon after the Olympics. Won't the eyes of the world still be looking at Germany?"

"Hitler has no concern what the rest of the nations think about his treatment of the Jews in Germany. His only concern is solidifying his power. My associates at *Farben,* feel Hitler and the *Gestapo* are trying to rid the country of all Jews."

I blurted out, "Dad it just doesn't make any sense!"

"Quiet down Jenz; nothing is making any sense to educated Germans. A madman is leading our country - and the majority of the population is listening to him."

Ezekiel cried out, "Isn't there anything we can do? We just can't let them confiscate our property and send us to work camps."

"Zeke," Dad declared, "Since the enactment of the Nuremberg Laws in September 1935, the Jews in our country have received appalling treatment from the local police, the *Gestapo,* and all Germans who have hatred in their heart. The cruelty of these laws and these people is unprecedented in all of human history.

"Homes and businesses are confiscated, schools and universities are restricting Jews; the marking of stores with the Star of David makes an easy target for anyone in the country with hatred for Jews."

"Dr. Leven, Stan, any suggestions?"

"Rolf, I think we should prepare for the worse. The Jewish head of surgery at our hospital had his automobile confiscated last week. He was told to "ride the bus like everyone else." Dr. Leven continued, "The 'gentlemen' from the *Gestapo* then told him to sell his home to an Aryan broker for a pittance."

"Otherwise," he was told, "You could have an accident, or your house could be set afire by an angry mob."

"Rolf," Dr. Leven continued, "This well-regarded surgeon is now in fear for his life and the welfare of his whole family. He is considering moving out of the country. This doctor is afraid to go to work and has quietly asked his friends if they would like to purchase, at any price, the family artwork, jewels, silverware, or China. He has quietly put his family home up for sale.

"His main problem is all of his friends and acquaintances are under similar threat of confiscation of property, loss of businesses, and possible arrest. It has become impossible for him to sell anything to anyone. He is contemplating leaving everything behind and just trying to get his family out of the country.

"His two children can no longer attend the university, and their careers as an engineer and professor for the *Reich* are no longer possible.

"What is this leading up to, Rolf?"

"God only knows, Stan."

"Although the risk is great, I will start, very slowly, to bring home small quantities of explosive material. Unfortunately, all the firearms and ammunition have been confiscated under threat of arrest and imprisonment by the *Nazis*."

"Be very careful, Rolf. Knowledge of your activity at *Farben* could easily lead to your arrest and the arrest of your family for treason."

"I am aware of what the *Gestapo* is capable of Stan, I have heard rumors of their torture techniques.

"Colleagues at work informed me the *Gestapo* is known to show up in the middle of the night with a loud knock on the door. The arrest is sudden, and the targeted individual has little time even to get dressed or pack up any essentials.

"I suggest you return home. Our family will keep close contact with you through our sons and any other means possible. Jenz can stay at your home whenever you would like, but I would suggest you make plans to leave the country as soon as you possibly are able. Let's not let the *Gestapo,* or the growing *SS* menace threaten our families any further. We must resist somehow. Let's meet again within a week."

"I don't feel comfortable even showing up at the hospital." None of the staff or the patients seem at all friendly; most are unequivocally hostile."

"Are you fearful of your safety?" asked Dad.

"Not... quite... yet. But it is getting close. Sometimes yes."

"As soon as anyone says something threatening to you, please stay at home and notify us at once. My family will do everything we can do to protect each other and others from the synagogue from the insulting thugs who are running our country."

"Let's have a word of prayer before partaking of the food Hilda has so graciously prepared for us." Mrs. Leven suggested.

"Dear God," Dr. Leven intoned with firmness, "Please watch over and protect our family and the Ramsgrund family from the deadly and hateful intent of the *Nazi Party.* Please guide us to the best path to take to ensure our children can live with religious freedom with a loving God. Amen."

The Leven's cook had prepared ham and cheese sandwiches and slices of apples wrapped in waxed paper for us, which we attacked with enthusiasm.

Dr. Leven remarked, "Our country has gone insane. Many Jewish businesses are ruined. New laws prevent Jews from living normal lives."

After those comments, the Leven's crept out the back door into the night and drove a circuitous route back to their neighborhood and entered their driveway with the lights off.

CHAPTER 12

Kristallnacht Comes to Düsseldorf

There was no moon with an overcast sky and drizzle dampening the windshield and coating the streets. It turned the light covering of snow into slush. The gloom intensified the Leven family's depression about their future. By this time Hitler had installed Herman Göering as Speaker of the *Reichstag* and Paul Joseph Göebbels as head of the *Nazi Party* in Berlin. It would turn out both of these men were very dangerous for Jews and anyone else who would speak against the *Reich.*

Since the 19th of August, 1934, Hitler had become *(Führer und Reichskanzler)* Leader and Reich Chancellor. The entire internal policy of Germany was to be controlled by members of the *Nazi Party.* The *Nazis* were firm believers in violence against the Jews and the eradication of Jews from the *Reich,* including, eventually, the occupied territories.

By 1938 the future of the Jews and the Jewish Faith in Germany had become very dark. The *Waffen SS,* the armed wing of the *Nazi Party's SS (Schutzstaffel)* organization had grown to 50,000 strong. The hatred and violence against Jews were becoming commonplace.

Germany marched into Austria in March of 1938 and annexed the country in what was called the *Anschluss.* Many of the German-speaking Austrians welcomed this joining of the two countries.

In August and September of 1938, the Wehrmacht marched into a part of Czechoslovakia known as the Sudetenland. Their presence was not nearly as welcomed as in Austria. Many Jews and political dissenters from both countries were arrested and deported to labor (concentration) camps. These labor camps were increasing throughout the *Reich*.

The next day a misty sun drove away the last vestiges of the overcast and rain. It was cold for November with frost on the grass and walkways. Only an inch or so of snow had fallen in Düsseldorf, but the chill in the wind let you know winter wasn't too far off.

I telephoned the Leven residence. "Mrs. Leven, I would like to see Ezekiel today about some homework assignments I need for school. Could Zeke help me with the calculus for my mid-terms next week?"

"I will get him Jenz, just a minute."

"Hey Jenz, How are you. Thanks for calling. Dad came right back from the hospital this morning. The President of the hospital informed him his surgeries had been canceled and his appointment at the hospital was no longer valid. Dad is pretty upset. He had procedures scheduled all morning, and all his patients are his friends. He doesn't know what to do."

"Would you mind if I came over," I asked? "I need a little math help for the midterms. I know you can't be in school, but you understand this stuff much better than me. Also, my father has some suggestions possibly helpful for your family."

The Leven's home was in an expensive section of town with more substantial homes with well-tended yards. Their back and side yard had fruit trees, and the back yard had many medium-sized emerald green Arborvitae forming a boarder around their yard. The evergreen trees gave the large back yard plenty of privacy.

It took me over two hours to get my books together and walk a circular route to the Leven's home. It was the 8th of November 1938. The decent day still had some sun, but there was a cold breeze with a hint of snow in the air. I got there just in time for Hilda to make me lunch. I thought Mrs. Leven might make a bit of a joke about my arrival in time for lunch because I always seemed to be eating whenever I went over to their home. However, the household mood was very somber when I arrived.

There was almost a feeling of dread in the air. All the curtains and blinds were down, and no one was around. I knocked on the door and then rang the bell.

I had never seen Dr. and Mrs. Leven so sad and melancholy. I tried to lighten the mood a little by remarking, "I hope I didn't disturb your lunch, Mrs. Leven."

"Not at all, Jenz." Hilda has been waiting for you so you and Ezekiel can eat in the sunroom."

Hilda was one of my favorite people. She would always make me two cheese sandwiches, and she never joked about my size. Also, she knew I had a particular fondness for anything she baked.

While Zeke and I were munching cheese sandwiches on the sun porch, Dr. Leven came in. He wanted to show us a newspaper article.

"I'm so sorry about the situation at the hospital, doctor. Is there anything the medical association can do?"

"I don't think so, Jenz. There is so much anti-Semitism in our country now, no Jew feels very safe no matter what they do."

"Take a look at this article in the Düsseldorf Newspaper. It describes how a well-respected Rabbi, Abraham Joshua Heschel, was expelled from Germany last week. The *Gestapo* came to his door, and the Rabbi was given five minutes to pack only one suitcase before he was trundled off to the train station for a one way trip out of the country to Poland!"

"As Jews were taken from his neighborhood, their remaining possessions were seized as loot by the *Nazi* authorities and neighbors!"

"Jenz, I am distraught for my family. I'm not so concerned about the hospital appointment, I can work in almost any hospital in the world, but I'm worried about Jews being taken out of their homes and deprived of all their possessions and possibly sent out of the country or to work camps. I don't know how Phyllis and Zeke would survive in a labor camp."

"Do you have any weapons in your home, doctor?"

"No! They have all been confiscated by the *National Socialist Workers Party* under the penalties of lengthy imprisonment."*

---

* *Heinrich Himmler, the German commander of the Nazi Police, issued an order forbidding Jews from owning any firearm weapons and imposed a penalty of twenty years in a concentration camp for any Jew in possession of a firearm after the summer of 1938. In Berlin, Himmler effectively disarmed the entire Jewish population by confiscation of all hand weapons and rifles and thousands of rounds of ammunition.*

Everyone knew a twenty-year sentence in a concentration or labor camp was indeed a death sentence.

Then, the ban on firearms was imposed on every German citizen unless they belonged to a law enforcement organization or the Wehrmacht.

Jews in Germany at this time could not attend secondary schools, gymnasium, or the public universities per order of the Nazi Party.

"Doctor Leven, would you mind if I stayed with your family for a few days? I could go to school from here and bring Ezekiel back our assignments, so he could keep up without going to school."

"We have plenty of room, Jenz, and you would be welcome. But you should check with your parents. These are challenging times in Germany, and they may want you home."

"Don't take this the wrong way, doctor, but my dad suggested this plan to me about a week ago. He and Mom are very concerned about the anti-Semitism and what is happening to Jews in our country.

I said, "Let's see what we can make or improvise over the next few days. At *Hitler Youth Camp*, we were taught to be ready for any situation."

The doctor looked distraught. "Are you suggesting we take up arms against the dreaded *Gestapo?*"

"Only if they come for us or any member of our family," was my reply. "Let's hope it never happens, but we should be ready."

Doctor Leven replied, "Perhaps you're right, Jenz. I have heard some real horror stories from patients at the hospital. It's hard to believe people could be dragged from their homes and beaten for no apparent reason other than their religion. If these stories and newspaper articles are correct, Jews no longer have civil protections in Germany."

I left for school from the Leven's home early the next morning. I remember it was Wednesday, the 9th of November, 1938. There was a light dusting of snow on the ground, and the sidewalks were a little slippery. An icy wind was forecasting the coming of winter. Most of the leaves were off the trees, but a few apples were remaining on the Leven's fruit trees; those remaining were hanging on for dear life in the cold breeze.

I only had a thin jacket on, but I walked as briskly as possible on the slushy walks and didn't feel the cold. The sadness of missing Zeke and the anti-Semitism in Germany was getting me down.

On the way back to the Leven's home, I purchased a newspaper because of the headline *Juden Raus! Auf Nach Palastina!*, (Jews Out! Out to Palestine!) caught my eye. Although I started to read the article on the walk back to the Leven's, the walking was too slippery. I had to pay attention to where I was going. Even the headline was too disgusting to read. I folded the paper and put it under my arm.

Hilda greeted me at the door. "How was your day at school, Jenz? I have a snack for you and Ezekiel."

"Thanks, Hilda. I could use a discussion with some sane people right at the moment."

I left the folded newspaper on the kitchen counter and met Zeke in the library. Hilda had milk and a plate of cookies for us.

"How is it going with school, Jenz?"

"Not well, Zeke."

"Most of my classmates and even the teachers seem to have gone nuts with all the anti-Semitism baloney. Students and most teachers seem accepting of what is happening in our country, and some even seem smug and encouraging about perpetuating anti-Semitism."

Just then, Dr. Leven came rushing into the library.

"Jenz, did you bring in the newspaper? Did you read the headline article?"

"No, I purchased the paper on the way home from school at the newsstand by the bus terminal. But, since I was walking, it was too slippery to read without slipping."

Dr. Leven finished the article and then explained: "A Polish Jewish teenager named Hershel Grynszpan shot and killed a German Embassy official named Ernst vom Rath in Paris yesterday."

"I hope the *Gestapo* doesn't use this as an excuse to bring retribution to all Jews in Germany."

"Wouldn't it be very unlikely, Dad?" Zeke exclaimed.

"With the thug politicians we have in our country, son, nothing is unreasonable or surprising. It is now crystal clear. The political goal is to rid our country of all Jews. They appear to stop at nothing. If they can't deport us and steal our possessions, they will put us in labor camps or beat or kill us. We will have to make a plan to leave the country or go underground and hide somewhere."*

Dr. Leven mentioned Chaim Weizmann had written earlier in 1936: "The world seemed to be divided into two parts: those

---

By the spring of 1938, Germany had annexed the country of Austria. Almost 250,000 Jews had already fled Germany and Austria by the time of the Évian Conference July 6th to the 15th in Évian, France. This conference, initiated by then U.S. President, Franklin Delano Roosevelt, addressed the issue of Jewish immigration to other countries. Those in the Nazi Party looked at the Évian Conference as Hitler's green light for genocide.

Roosevelt, although he was reluctant to discuss it, seemed to want to preserve "quotas" for the number of Jewish refugees admitted to the United States.

Meanwhile, the country of China took in over fourteen thousand refugees fleeing religious and racial persecution from Germany and Austria.

Hitler's comments after the Évian Conference:

"I can only hope and expect the other world, which has such deep sympathy for these criminals [Jews], will at least be generous enough to convert this sympathy into practical aid. We, on our part, are ready to put all these criminals at the disposal of these countries, for all I care, even on luxury ships."

places where Jews could not live, and those places where Jews could not enter."

It was late afternoon; Hilda was preparing dinner for the family and me. The kitchen smelled delicious with the cooking food.

Mrs. Leven came into the library and exclaimed, **"There must be a huge fire in the town, the whole skyline is lighted up like daytime!"**

"Turn on the radio, Phyllis. Perhaps there is some news," exclaimed Dr. Leven.

In addition to *Nazi* propaganda and military music, the radio had almost no news from outside of the country. Late this afternoon was no different. There was a lot of ranting about the recent shooting in Paris and the "retaliation of honest Germans out to cleanse the country of the scourge of the Jew Criminal."

The news broadcaster led with "the destruction and elimination of all signs of the Jew in our precious country."

His lead news was the "Eradication of the Jew Dwellings of Worship."

"OH NO!" cried Mrs. Leven, **"The *Nazis* are burning our synagogue!"**

"Jenz… Zeke" cried Dr. Leven, **"let's go see what is going on at the shul. Quickly now, let's see what is happening."**

There was a knock at the door. It was a neighbor crying hysterically, **"They are burning and looting our synagogue!"**

Dr. Leven, Zeke, the next door neighbor and I ran through the cold night air. The atmosphere was thick with smoke and sparks. We ran to the only Jewish synagogue in our part of Düsseldorf four blocks away. I had grabbed my jacket, and it was some protection from the flying sparks and cinders. The temple was an inferno of fire and destruction.

"This is not believable!" shouted Dr. Leven. **"Why would they do this?"**

I said in a rushed voice, **"Hatred and ignorance by the Brownshirts** (*Sturmabteilung*). **Let me run into the vestry and see what I can save."**

"NO," shouted Dr. Leven. He held up his hands to stop me from even thinking of entering the inferno.

But, I ran in anyway. I knew, from being in the house of worship many times, the chancellery held many books and vestments sacred to the congregation. I soaked my jacket with some slush from a nearby lawn and covered my head with it and ran into the synagogue.

I heard one of the bystanders cheer, **"There goes another crazy Jew into the furnace!"**

Smoke filled the synagogue; I could barely see. I kept my soaked jacket tight around my head with just a peephole for my eyes. I took very shallow breaths into my slush-filled jacket.

As I neared the front of the chancellery, sparks and cinders were raining down from the high ceiling. I was running on pure adrenaline. I was looking for ceremonial items and books, but it looked like someone, probably the *Nazi SA or Stormtroopers,* had already been there. The ritual items were gone or scattered around the front of the synagogue. My breathing was rapid, shallow, and labored. I knew I wouldn't last long if the ceiling fell on me. I grabbed a ceremonial cloth and a book from the floor and ran out the side door.

I found Dr. Leven and Zeke across the street from the burning inferno and gave the doctor the items I had retrieved from the front of the synagogue. I told him most of the ceremonial items were missing. "I hope they were saved and not looted."

Besides, I added, "It wouldn't surprise me if the thuggish *Brownshirts* had looted the synagogue before they torched it!"

As I came around the side of the building, I noticed the fire brigade all standing around and not attempting to put out the fire. I mentioned my surprise to the doctor, and he said, "Let's go and talk to the fire marshal."

We found him in a group of other firefighters. He was tall and very slim with a retruded lower jaw. He was wearing a Fire Marshal's Badge. **"Sir, why aren't your men placing the fire under control?"** shouted Dr. Leven

"Orders from our *Führer,"* cautioned the fire marshal, **"And strict enforcement by the police!"** We watched the fire until the roof collapsed into the ruined sanctuary. Tears were in the eyes of many of the onlookers, both Jewish and Christian neighbors.

On the 9th of November, 1938, the German embassy spokesman in Paris, Ernst vom Rath, died of his wounds inflicted by the Polish Jew, Herschel Grynszpan.

In the afternoon, learning of Rath's death, the *Führer* issued the following statement through his Propaganda Minister, Joseph Göebbels:

> *"Demonstrations should not be prepared or organized*
> *by the party, but insofar as they erupt spontaneously,*
> *they are not to be hampered."*

With these words, Göebbels unleashed a pogrom against the Jews in Germany and Austria.

On the 10th of November, 1938, Hitler's head of the *Nazi Security Police, SS Obergruppenführer,* Reinhard Heydrich instructed the *Sturmabteilung (SA)* not to interfere with the riots unless foreigners or non-Jewish businesses were at risk. The police were notified to seize Jewish archives from the synagogues and to arrest and detain "healthy male Jews who are not too old" for eventual transfer to labor (concentration) camps.

Many in the crowd of onlookers were crying. Some were shouting epithets at the firefighters. A few were almost jubilant. Some well-dressed observers were holding up their children "for a better look at the new Germany."

Dr. Leven, Zeke and I were aghast and saddened, almost inconsolable.

"What are we going to do, father," wailed Zeke.

"We are going to get home and make a plan, son."

"At least now we know the Nazi's will stop at nothing to rid all Jews from Germany!"

On the nights of November 9th and 10th, 267 Synagogues were burned or destroyed in Germany and Austria. Desecration occurred in over 1400 Jewish temples or reading rooms.

Göebbels ascribed the events of *Kristallnacht* to the "healthy instincts" of the German people.

In addition, over 30,000 Jewish men, were arrested by the police and *Gestapo* and taken to concentration camps; primarily *Dachau, Buchenwald, and Sachsenhausen.*

In the aftermath of *Kristallnacht,* the *Nazi* regime ordered the Jewish community to pay a one billion *Reichsmark* "atonement tax" and rapidly enacted many more anti-Jewish laws and edicts.

CHAPTER 13

The Gestapo Visits the Leven's Home

Dr. Leven, Zeke, and I watched from their darkened living room as the *Gestapo* entered their neighbor's home across the street and dragged off the husband. The family looked like they had no notice; the husband was dragged out without a suitcase.

Zeke and I were still looking out the window from back in the darkened front hall when a large black car pulled up in front of the house. It looked like there were two men in the automobile.

"Dad!" yelled Zeke. **"They're here!"**

I told Dr. Leven, "Sir if you let them into your home, because we will have to, we cannot let them leave. You cannot let them take you to a labor camp or worse. It would be the end of your family."

"I understand Jenz, but what can we do, there are two of them, and they are undoubtedly armed."

"Dad," cried Zeke, **"It's either eliminate them, or they will eliminate us."**

Mrs. Leven cried hysterically, **"Are they here to beat us or kill us?"**

"Either way Mrs. Leven, we cannot let these evil men harm us. Zeke, sneak around the side of the house and see if anyone else is in their car."

"Dr. and Mrs. Leven, please wait upstairs and don't come down until I call you twice. Please do not come down the first time I call up to you, only the second time.

"Do you understand?"

"Yes, Jenz. On your second call."

Bang - Bang, Bang!

A loud knocking sound on the front door signaled the *Gestapo's* presence at the front door of the house. The Leven's ran upstairs.

I was very polite while answering the door. "May I help you, gentlemen?"

They were carbon copies of the thugs Dad had described on the *Gestapo* visit to our home last summer. The leader was a little taller and was the spokesman for the two-person hit squad. He had a pockmarked face and a squirrely look in his eyes. His eyes radiated pure evil. He had thin lips and refused to smile. I knew I would have to take him out first.

The second thug was shorter, overweight, and lacked a lower jaw. His face seemed to drop off right after his nose. His receded lower jaw looked almost malformed. I would take him out second, but I was a little unsure where to hit him.

Both of the *Gestapo* "gentlemen" made a point of opening their black trench coats so I would get a clear view of their Lugar Pistols.

"We are here to bring in Dr. Leven for questioning at *Gestapo Headquarters.* The taller thug called out in a loud voice.

The Lugar pistols I had fired at Hitler Camp carried a clip of seven 9.mm. Parabellum bullets and one in the chamber. So between the two of them, they brought two semi-automatic pistols capable of firing sixteen rounds in rapid succession.

It wouldn't be prudent for me to let their hands get anywhere near their firearms.

It wasn't a question of strength, I was a head taller and probably 60 pounds heavier than the leader, but I had to distract him somewhat.

"Wait just a moment while I call for the doctor, he is in his upstairs study."

"O, Dr. Leven," I yelled upstairs, **"You have some visitors, come on down."**

Both *Gestapo* thugs looked upstairs. As the leader raised his head to look up to the second floor, my closed fist flew sidearm into his exposed throat, crushing his windpipe. The look of surprise and shock registered in his face as his eyes bulged out and his face turned beet red. He went down, clutching his throat. Blood trickled out of the corner of his mouth, probably from his crushed trachea.

It looked like he was trying to say something, but he went down without saying a word. Some guttural noises were emanating from him; I knew it would take him 4-5 minutes to suffocate to death. Thank you, Hitler Youth Camp training! His thrashing and kicking in the hall almost tipped over a small table.

The other thug just looked at his partner in crime in abject shock and surprise. The *Gestapo* was not used to being challenged. Their use of intimidation was so formidable and complete.

While "pock-face" was writhing on the floor, slack-jaw opened his coat and started to go for his weapon. His concentration, however, was on his very distressed partner on the floor and he never saw the side of my closed right fist as it flew at his head. I hit him on the left temple with the side-edge of my fist as hard as I could. I felt bones crunching as my fist fractured the temporalis portion of his skull. Blood splashed out from the impact.

As he was reeling and heading for the floor, I gave him a knuckle blow directly over the carotid body and carotid artery on the side of his neck in an attempt to crush the artery and close off any hope for half of his cranial blood support. The immediate rush of blood and reddening in the area led me to believe I had damaged his carotid artery. He went down on top of his partner like a sack of sand. I was pretty sure it was lights out for him also. To make sure, I put my weight on my knee and buried it in his stomach to collapse his diaphragm and force any air from his lungs. I left my knee on his collapsed diaphragm for two or three minutes.

I checked both of them for a pulse and confirmed they were no longer a threat to the Leven family or any family in the Reich. I opened the front door to look outside, I couldn't find Zeke.

He came around the corner of the house. It was hard to see him with no lights on around their home.

"Zeke, is anyone else in the car?"

"Nobody," Zeke called out quietly.

"Come on in here Zeke; I need you."

As Zeke came in the front door, his jaw almost hit the floor. **"What the hell happened to the two *Gestapo Agents*?"**

"They ran into an accident," I suggested. "Neither agent will be getting up."

Zeke went white. **"What are we suppose to do with them now?"** he queried in panic.

"Easy, Zeke, we have to think. Perhaps your dad will have a suggestion.

"My God, Jenz. You can't kill two *Gestapo Agents* and get away with no repercussions. They will torture you and kill your family, and us."

"Easy Zeke! Let's take this one step at a time."

I called upstairs, **"Dr. and Mrs. Leven, could you come down now?.... Please?"**

As the Leven's hesitatingly came down the circular staircase, the look of surprise and alarm registered on both their faces. There was a good bit of blood around the head of the second agent.

"Jenz, what the hell happened?"

"Sir, they came here to take you to their headquarters for questioning. I have heard they question Jews under extreme torture. I wasn't about to let these evil men take us anywhere."

Mrs. Leven cried, **"Oh Jenz, they will catch up to us. We have nowhere to go and only a little money or resources, and no papers to flee the country. These people will track us down and put us in a camp. We will be cut off from our friends and family."**

Mrs. Leven was getting hysterical and getting the rest of the family agitated. Two dead agents of doom in their foyer might be almost a little too much for anyone to handle.

"Look on the bright side, Mrs. Leven. Your husband and son are not down at *Gestapo Headquarters* right now being questioned, tortured or even worse."

"Also, we now have two very nice Lugar firearms for self-defense."

"I suggest we keep one, put both thugs in their car and drive it into a ravine deep in the woods down by the river. Dr. Leven and I can make it look like an accident with blunt force trauma from the automobile accident."

"If you have any alcohol, Dr. Leven, we can make it look like they had been drinking a little."

"I'll see what we have, Jenz."

I suggested we keep just one of the Lugar firearms.

"If we kept both pistols, the authorities might get suspicious. However, with just one missing, it might have gone into the river or gotten lost in the woods, or a passerby could have retrieved it."

"Let's bring their car around back and load these nice folks into it. They are about to go for their last ride."

I said a silent prayer for myself, asking for God's forgiveness. Although I knew the mechanics of how to end someone's life, I had never put my knowledge to the test. I was a little surprised how easy it was with these two members of the *Gestapo*. What was even more disconcerting for me was I never did feel much regret or anxiety over their deaths. The take-down happened so quickly, my racing heart didn't have a chance to catch up to my actions.

The night was ink-dark. I dragged pock-face down the back steps by his feet and into their back seat. I heard his head bang against each step on the way down. I figured additional head trauma wasn't going to be a problem after we crashed their car.

Dr. Leven and Zeke trundled slack-jaw into the back on the other side. I'm not sure why they were so careful not to bruise the dead *Gestapo* agent further, but I was just glad they were getting on with the task.

I told Zeke, "Watch over your mother. Two dead agents in her front hall have undoubtedly been a bit of a shock for her. We will be back in a few hours after we have taken out this trash. You might consider cleaning up the front hall. It's a little messy from the first agent's blood while he was thrashing around. Also, the smell was from him emptying his bowels and bladder."

Dr. Leven was nervous, he asked if I wouldn't mind driving. Of course, neither one of us wanted to be stopped with a couple of dead *Gestapo Agents* in our back seat.

We headed out away from the synagogue and the crowd surrounding the area. Dr. Leven knew the back roads pretty well. We drove through the country to a secluded spot near the Rhine River. We estimated it would take one to two hours to walk back without being seen. We were near a small copse of woods off Rotterdamer Street.

We parked on a hill overlooking the river. First, we placed pock-face in the driver's position; the keys to the automobile had been in his pocket. We put slack-jaw next to him.

I suggested we splash some alcohol on their clothing and the front seat of the car. We were on a hill with no lights on because we had removed the inside car light bulb. It was very dark with no traffic and no lights anywhere except for some dull half moonlight filtering through the clouds.

I remember thinking, I should have dressed warmer. The wind off the river sent a chill right through me. Also, I was a little concerned about being caught.

We splashed some alcohol around the front seat, wedged a shoe from pock-face over the gas pedal, pointed the car toward the trees at the bottom of the hill.

"Stand clear, doctor, while I put the car in gear."

I held the clutch down with my right foot; the car engine was racing. I pulled it into gear.

My foot snapped off the clutch as I slammed the door and rolled free.

The sleek black *Gestapo* car rocketed toward the tees, crashed, and rolled over into the river. It took a few minutes for it to sink entirely because we had forgotten to roll down the windows. It floated out into the river but eventually dropped out of sight.

The good doctor and I started our long hike back to his home. It must have been over five-kilometers, but we were able to take a few short cuts. Dr. Leven knew the area well.

We returned to the Leven's home late; Zeke and his mom were still up wandering about the house and worrying.

"How are we going to sleep," fretted Mrs. Leven.

I had to smile a little, and a hmmph came out of my mouth. I certainly didn't intend to make fun of the Leven's concern about the authorities, but I answered as straight-faced as I could.

"Probably much better than at *Gestapo* headquarters!"

The Leven's let me sleep late the next morning. I showed up in their kitchen around 7:30. Hilda was bustling about and fixed me a breakfast of three eggs over easy with ham and a thick slice of bread with jam. I joined Zeke in the sunroom. I guess the walk the night before helped me sleep pretty well.

The Leven's joined us in the sunroom and closed the door. No one wanted Hilda to hear or know anything about the events from last evening. They both seemed pretty well rested.

Mrs. Leven asked me what I thought would happen once the authorities realized they had two missing agents.

"I assume they will go looking for them," was my short answer.

"What if they come here?" she asked.

"Just remember, Mrs. Leven, you have not seen or heard of any *Gestapo* authorities coming to your home or town.

"We will face the problem if it comes up," I answered. "If agents come, it will probably be at night. I will talk to my parents about what has happened so far. They will probably encourage me to spend a few more days with you, if you folks wouldn't mind?"

"Thank you, Jenz, for what you have done for my family and me," said Dr. Leven. "I don't know how you disarmed and overcame those two agents."

"Sir, they were very evil men. Please try to get Mrs. Leven to understand. I'm not sure she realizes how dangerous they could be at night, in a Jewish family's home."

"I'm just glad they didn't discharge their firearms. Please keep in mind you and your family will need to leave the country as soon as possible. Please do not underestimate these thugs. They have the force of a corrupt government behind them."

"Try to get the two agents who showed up last evening out of your mind. Our country will not have to worry about those two monsters again."

"I'm going home and skipping school today. I want to confide in my parents about last night's confrontation with those agents. If it is all right with you folks, I will be back by early evening after supper."

"I do not recommend opening the door to anyone, even if you think you might know them. And remember, if anyone questions you or your family about a visit from *Gestapo* agents, you know nothing about any visit, and you do not know any agents."

CHAPTER 14

A Letter from Ilsa

I tried to sugar coat my explanation of last evenings proceedings as much as you can sugar coat two dead *Gestapo Agents* tossed into the Rhine. My mom was beside herself with confusion and worry. I had to repeat the whole story when Dad got home from work. He was more understanding and said,

"I'm grateful you were over at their home. The news on the radio said almost 30,000 Jews were arrested last night and early today and sent to concentration camps at Dachau near Munich, Sachsenhausen near Berlin, and Buchenwald near Weimar. I am sure the Leven's were thrilled not to be among them."

"I will be going over to their home this evening if it is okay with you both?" I asked.

"Jenz, this is a deadly business with these *Gestapo* or *SS* agents," remarked Dad. "I hope your summer at Hitler Camp prepared you for the unforeseen."

"Dad, your suggestions on when not to fight were the most helpful. I did not want to allow those two thugs to get up off the Leven's floor."

"Since I turned eighteen, I now have to go to the Central Registration Office and sign up for the *Wehrmacht*."

"I would like to see if I can also procure a school deferment."

"Oh, thanks for reminding me of something, Jenz. Your mother has a postal letter for you from someone named I. Huber. Does the name sound familiar?"

"It's on your desk."

"Thanks, Mom."

I immediately went to my room to read the letter. I. Huber didn't sound familiar, but I opened and began reading. It was from the girl I had met at summer camp, Ilsa Huber. I just never really knew her last name.

> *Dear Jenz,*
>
> *I hoped you remember me from Hitler Camp last summer. I want you to know Gretchen and I think about you and hope you are doing well in school.*
>
> *I hope you don't mind me contacting you, but I have a problem with someone who is giving me and my family trouble because of a political issue. I didn't know who to turn to because I cannot go to the local police.*
>
> *If you think you could help in any way, please send me information at my family's home near Hannover. Perhaps we could meet to talk.*
>
> *Love and remembrances,*
>
> *Ilsa*

How could I not remember Ilsa? She had been on my mind ever since summer camp ended in August. Although I would love to meet her, I would need to take the train to Hannover on the weekend and find a place to meet.

The only place I had ever met her was in the glen at Hitler Camp. The glen by the lake was a little too cold for an idyllic spot this time of year.

I wrote her a brief note. Her plea was a bit of a mystery to me, but I hoped it had nothing to do with me being part Jewish.

> *Dearest Ilsa,*
>
> *Thank you so much for contacting me. I think of you very often. I'm not sure I would be the best person to help with a political issue; however, I would be happy to travel to Hannover and meet with you to discuss anything troubling you.*
>
> *Let me know if you can meet me at the railroad station a week from Saturday.*
>
> *I will never forget your kindness to me,*
>
> *Jenz*

I spent the next week in and out of the Leven's home. Zeke helped me catch up on my math skills in calculus, and I discussed in specific terms what was going on in our last year of secondary school. Both of us were concerned about not being able to attend the *Technische Hochschule* in Berlin. I was probably going to spend time in the army, and Zeke was barred by the Nuremberg Laws, from attending the university.

Fortunately, there were no new late-night "knocks on the door" over the next week at the Leven's home.

The newspapers and radio had a continuous message of anti-Semitism permeating our country. Killing the *Nazi* official in Paris by a Polish Jew was the excuse offered by Göebbels for ridding Germany and Austria of all Jews and their houses of worship. In reality, the pogrom against the Jews looked like it had been planned long before the 9th of November 1938.

I did a little research on the Polish man accused of killing the German official in Paris. It appears there was substantial evidence the killing might have been a homosexual dispute before the shooting. The homosexual incident was never mentioned by the German officials or in the press.

Most of the pogrom of *Kristallnacht* against the Jews was halted on the night of the 10th of November 1938. By this time over 1400 Jewish Synagogues had been damaged or destroyed. Priceless artifacts in synagogues were looted and sold to or appropriated by national museums in Germany.

Göebbels, who initiated the destruction of the Jewish synagogues, businesses, and families, halted the carnage with the following statement:

> *"The justified and understandable resentment of the German nation of the cowardly Jew murder of a German diplomat in Paris extensively manifested itself last night. Reprisals have been taken in numerous towns and cities of the Reich against Jewish buildings and shops.*

"At present, however, the entire population is earnestly warned immediately to abstain from any further demonstrations against Jewry, no matter what kind.

"The final and correct answer to the Jewish outrage in Paris will be given Jewry through laws and decrees."

Göebbels issued his desist order at 4 pm on the 10th of November, 1938. By this time, over 7,000 Jewish businesses in Germany and Austria had been destroyed and looted. German citizens looted clothing stores, jewelry shops had their windows and display cases smashed and looted. Some Jewish restaurants had their windows, tables, and chairs destroyed and burned.

It was as if the entire population of Germany had suddenly forgotten these Jewish businesses and houses of worship belonged to their neighbors and fellow Germans. It was sheer madness. "The Night of Broken Glass" left many of the remaining Jews, including the Leven's, afraid to leave their homes for fear of beatings or worse.

CHAPTER 15

A Visit to Hannover

I spent the rest of the week hanging out at the Leven's, after eating dinner at home. My parents were very understanding.

Wednesday I received another letter from I. Huber. Now my parent's interests were piqued. I told them I was eighteen, and this was a girlfriend whom I had met at the Hitler Youth Camp. "Ilsa is a wonderful girl, Mom. I don't know her too well yet."

"Next Saturday, I am taking the train to Hannover to meet her at noon at the railroad station. I need to get to know her a little better."

"Be careful, Jenz. These are difficult times. Occasionally, difficult times can lead to desperate situations. It would be your father's and my pleasure to meet Ilsa anytime."

"Thanks, Mom, I'll be cautious. I'm taking the 8:30 train and should be back by Sunday evening."

The rest of the week after *Kristallnacht* I spent getting the requisite papers for the *Wehrmacht* and a one-year delay so I would be able to attend the *Technische Hochschule* in Berlin.

I packed an overnight bag and was on the 8:30 train to Hannover on Saturday morning. The German trains were punctual, comfortable, and fast. I was in Hannover courtesy of the *Deutsche Reichsbahn* or German National Rail with only six stops from Düsseldorf. The train got in by 11:45 in the morning.

Looking around the railroad station, I spotted Ilsa right where she said she would be: near the ticketing booth in the center of the station.

"Hello Ilsa," I called from about six meters away.

She turned and ran to me. "Oh Jenz, thank you so much for coming!" She planted a big kiss on my cheek and mentioned, "I want to talk to you, but could we go someplace quiet where we could be alone?"

My first thought was someplace, where we could be close and hold each other in private. But then I wasn't sure how much talking we could accomplish. My next thought was of my stomach.

"Have you had lunch?" I asked. "We could find a quiet restaurant for a bite to eat." For some reason, at my particular stage of life, it seemed I could never really get enough to eat.

"I know the perfect place!" Exclaimed Ilsa. "Their lunches are reasonable, and they give you plenty to eat. It isn't too far from here on *Welfengarten Strasse* near the *Leibniz University*."

By the time we walked there, almost 45 minutes, my insides were screaming "feed me please."

The restaurant seemed a little like a student hang-out, so I hoped they were used to feeding hungry men. Ilsa chatted about her schooling and her family, but I could tell she had something serious on her mind. I remember saying yes quite often to her inquiries, but my mind seemed to be hovering over a plate of food.

We settled in a booth in the back of the eatery and ordered. Ilsa immediately launched into her predicament. She began by telling me she thought it was horrible what the *Nazis* were doing to Jewish business and synagogues. Ilsa thought it might be the work of the *Gestapo* or the *Brownshirts.* Then she told me her story.

"Jenz, about a month ago I was shopping for some clothing in a shop on *Schulenburger Landstrasse,* which is our main street for shopping in Hannover. I was approached by a mean looking middle-aged man who said he was from the *Gestapo* and showed me a badge. He had a pinched face with eyes set too close together. He radiated an evil aura of doom; he was all dressed in black, including a black fedora. He stank of stale cigarette smoke.

"He said he had some serious questions for me and suggested we talk privately in a quiet section of the shop. He then proceeded to sit on a bench much too close to me and told me the Gestapo was watch*ing me* because I had a Jewish aunt on my father's side of the family.

"I confronted him and said the woman he was referring to was like an adopted aunt my father's parents had taken in when the woman's husband had died. She and my grandmother were friends from north of Hannover in the town of *Langenhagen.*"

I asked, "What was your grandmother's last name?"

"My grandmother's name was Möller, and her friend's name was Fischer."

"The agent said in this case, the blood relative was close enough, and then he discussed in detail all the problems I might encounter if the *Gestapo* had to arrest me. He threatened my family and me with the interrogation, which he said would be most unpleasant at their headquarters in Berlin.

"He then said he could make sure the notes and information the *Gestapo* had accumulated on my family and me could be quietly set aside if I would offer him sex once each week for the summer in Berlin near his office."

As she was relating her difficulty to me, our food came, and she quieted down for a couple of minutes. I could tell she was quite upset; she didn't touch her food. Her facial expression was one of pleading and helplessness.

Although I was sympathetic, I couldn't think too well without digging into my food. I made a plate of meatballs disappear within a few minutes. I used the wonderful Italian bread to finish up the delicious sauce.

"Ilsa, have you seen this man before, or have you noticed anyone following you at college or shopping?"

"No, not ever! But then again, I have not been looking for anyone following me."

"This agent, I'll call him 'beady eyes' wants me to meet him in Berlin next weekend for sex. I don't dare go to the police. I'm afraid the police would make even more trouble for me or my family."

"You are correct, Ilsa. It would be best if you and I could settle this matter personally without involving the authorities. Let me get just a few more meatballs while I think of a plan to fix this problem. You haven't eaten much of your lunch."

"Oh, Jenz, you finish it. I'm so upset; I'm not at all hungry."

After polishing off Ilsa's lunch, I said, "Let's walk a bit, I can think better out in the fresh air."

There was a chill in the air. Pedestrians had their chins burrowed under their collars as they bustled around town. Most of the shops seemed intact without damage from the thuggery of Kristallnacht.

Ilsa confided in me she wanted to think of me as her boyfriend as we wandered toward the outskirts of Hannover.

I told her, "Nothing would make me happier."

She told me, "Jenz, you are the only man for me. **Forever!**"

As we were walking through Hannover, it occurred to me I was changing. Although I was quite strong physically, I realize my heart was not at all secure. More to the point, I was losing my heart to Ilsa. It made me feel weak and vulnerable. If I ever lost my Ilsa, my heart would surely break.

Ilsa interrupted my thoughts and mentioned we were within 5 kilometers of her home and she would like me to meet her parents. I thought meeting her parents would be okay, although my mother's warning about being cautious came to mind. I still had my overnight bag with no place to sleep at night, or it would be a nighttime train back to Düsseldorf.

As we approached her home, Ilsa made the admission she wasn't sure her parents would be home yet. They were visiting relatives in Augsburg, which, as I remembered, was near Munich, in the southern part of Germany.

"What do your parents think you should do with the beady-eyed *Gestapo* agent?"

"Oh, Jenz, I haven't even mentioned this monster to them."

"Have you mention this agent to anyone else?"

"No, I'm too embarrassed and frightened."

"Are you positive you haven't talked to anyone about this situation."

"Yes, Jenz, I'm positive; I haven't discussed this horror with anyone but you!"

"Then I think I can help you. Let's go into your home, and I will discuss a plan for us to convince agent 'beady-eyes' of the error of his ways."

Her home felt somewhat warm because we were out of the wind. Ilsa put a bit of coal in the stove, and her kitchen was soon quite warm and comfortable. It was getting dark early, and the sun had already set. You could see a few flakes of snow swirling and dancing in the occasional car headlights passing on the road.

There was a note on the kitchen table from her parents:

Hi dear, home tomorrow afternoon, plenty of food in the icebox. Love, Mom.

It went through my mind being away might have been arranged by Ilsa, or possibly Ilsa and her folks. Either way, I was in heaven.

She held me and kissed me a little more than a peck on the cheek, and asked with all seriousness, "How would you suggest we deal the beady-eyed *Gestapo* blackmailer?"

"There is only one sure way to make sure he never bothers you or your family again."

"Do we have to bribe him? My family isn't wealthy. And besides, I don't want them to know about this monster. How can we deal with him, we aren't powerful politicians?"

"There is only one answer," I said quietly. "We have to eliminate this agent and make it look like an accident, or he disappears forever."

Ilsa went very quiet.

The fact she had a near-Jewish relative or close association with a Jewish person, and did not want her family involved or hurt, gave me some courage to continue.

"Ilsa, this *Gestapo* Agent threatened you and your family. He even detailed some of the procedures and tortures you and your family might have to suffer."

"This man has forfeited his right to walk on this planet among civilized people. He is a direct threat to you and your family, and so he is also a direct threat to me and other law-abiding Germans."

"In the morning, before I head back to the train for Düsseldorf, I will explain what we have to do."

"This evening we can think about other things." I said. "For example, I need to find accommodations for proper sleeping arrangements this evening."

"Oh Jenz, have you forgotten?"

"I am one of the leaders in the woman's *Bund*. I will tell you when you can leave!"

I started to smile and stifled a laugh.

With her comment, she put her loving arms around my neck and pulled me down to her level and gave me a very tender kiss on my mouth.

I started tingling all over. My voice seemed to have resorted to squeaks and groans as I mumbled, "Darling, I was hoping you might suggest as much." At least I tried to express a thought. It came out something like: "Daring, I hops as such."

Her room upstairs seemed a little cold to me. Ilsa lit a small stove vented into the same chimney as the stove in the kitchen. She had a bucket of coal beside the stove, and in no time at all, the room was comfortable. She also opened a vent in the floor, and the heat from the kitchen flooded into the room.

She led me to her bed and very slowly undressed me. Her slowness was driving me crazy because my entire body and privates were tingling with desire. Ilsa probably knew what was happening to me and was deliberately torturing me by going so slowly.

She ordered me to lie down on the sheets and pulled up my shirt and kissed me on my stomach. Ilsa's kisses on my stomach almost did it for me, but she backed off and continued to take my sweater and shirt off slowly.

She loosened the lacings on my shoes and dropped them on the floor one at a time before she stripped off my pants, one leg slowly, then the other.

I could barely control myself, but Ilsa was still fully dressed.

She slid off my underwear and then slowly began to undress. As she slowly began folding her clothing and putting her garments away, I began losing control of my senses. My body started aching and moving uncontrollably.

She put her hand on my chest and told me to relax. She was teasing me unmercifully, so I thought I would get her back a little bit.

I said, " So where is your friend Gretchen?"

She gave me a cross look and emphatically stated with firmness, **"I am never sharing you with anyone ever again."**

I told her, "It's okay with me, but please come to bed."

She slid in next to me and put her hand on my stomach.

I thought I might explode, but she just whispered in my ear to relax and enjoy her company. She tried to calm me down by saying, "my parents will not be home until late tomorrow afternoon, and this evening, I insist you enjoy yourself."

I felt a momentary twang of guilt. We might be deceiving her parents, but any guilt I might have felt quickly evaporated when she started rubbing my shins with her feet.

She talked about how many people everywhere in Germany had so many worries and fears with Hitler in control of the government. She said in a low voice with all the anti-Semitism and other problems she had with the Gestapo, I should relax and let her control my pleasure for the evening.

She started rubbing the inside of my thighs, not hard, but just barely brushing them with the back of her hand. She must have known I was right on the edge of my wits; she kept whispering to me to relax and enjoy myself.

Ilsa seemed to know exactly what she was doing. At one point she told me she was going to get on top of me, but for me to stay very still.

She then ordered me not to move while she guided me into her. She urgently kept repeating by whispering in my ear, "do not move darling."

I was in a state of suspended ecstasy.

Every time I started to move or thrust, she would firmly tell me to **"stop...wait, stop!"**

She was in complete control. Although my body was on fire, I felt utterly helpless in her arms. She had me firmly in her grasp.

I was like a mad-man. Every time I started to move or squirm, Ilsa would stop me.

She started kissing and biting me softly on my chest. Then she would rub my chest whispering, "I hope I didn't hurt you."

I loved everything about her. Her voice electrified me; the smell of her hair and skin sent shock waves through my body; the touch of her body against mine caused me to shudder with delight and ecstasy.

She told me, "Jenz, think about other things." But my brain was blank except for an unrelenting longing for her touch.

She started moving slowly and rhythmically on top of me while commanding me by whispering in my ear, "**do not move, let me control your pleasure.**"

Suddenly my body became utterly ridged, electricity shot through my body, and I exploded into my dear Ilsa.

All I could do was moan, "I hope I didn't hurt you, darling."

She just moaned with pleasure, "Yesssss.

As we fell asleep in each other's arms, I started thinking of ways of dealing with agent "beady-eyes."

The next morning was cold in the room; Ilsa was up making us some breakfast. She had put some coal in the stove, but it hadn't caught up enough to warm the bedroom very much. I hopped in the shower, dressed, and got myself ready to explain what we had to do for her tormentor.

Over breakfast, I discussed with Ilsa what she had to say and do to finalize a meeting with agent "beady-eyes."

"When he contacts you, be sure and very reluctantly agree to meet him. Make him promise to bring any notes or reports about your grandmother's Jewish friend with him so you may see them. Ask if there is anything else you can do to avoid having weekly sex with him. It is essential he thinks you will very reluctantly do anything to protect your parents and grandmother and her friend."

"Agree to meet him only in a public place of your choosing, and then tell him he can take you to someplace private."

"Why do you want me to meet him in public?" she asked.

"So I can follow you to his apartment without any hindrances. I need him alone and distracted. If he is with you, he will be distracted."

"What will you do to him?"

"Ilsa, you have to trust me."

"You write to me as soon as he contacts you. Give him the time on Saturday you will be able to meet him in Berlin. I would suggest around the middle of the afternoon near his apartment so it will be a short walk to his place. It would be good if you can get his last name or his apartment address, but he probably won't give you his information. I will have to follow you to his apartment.

"Carry some chalk so you can mark his apartment number without him noticing. Place a small inconspicuous line under his mailbox slot. If it is a large building, I need to know where he is taking you."

"How well do you know Berlin?"

"Pretty well," she replied. "I have relatives in Lichtenberg, just outside of Berlin."

"Good. First, find out where the agent wants to meet. Then name the most known landmark you can think of near there and tell him you are very nervous about meeting him, but he needs to bring any evidence he has against your family so you can read it."

"Make it very clear to him you will agree to his demands, but you must have protection for your family. Emphasize the idea of protection, and only after he assures you of complete protection, you will be willing to meet his sexual demands."

"You need to act intimidated and frightened, for yourself and your family."

"Don't imply he is a perverted devil; both of us already know what he is all about."

"Always act a little frightened, timid, and shy, even reluctant unless he brings his notes of proof of Jewish collusion and can reassure you no harm will come to your family."

"You also have to dress a bit provocatively, yet keep your smile fearful. But let the agent know you intend to carry out your end of the deal."

"Oh Jenz, I couldn't even think about having anything to do with the monster!"

"Don't worry, Ilsa. I won't let him even get close to you."

We spent the rest of the day talking, having lunch, and discussing the next weekend. Toward late afternoon, I caught the 4:40 train to Düsseldorf.

The next week was relatively uneventful, I processed my application for the *Technische Hochschule* in Berlin and made sure my deferment was in place. The radio was full of anti-Semitism and bombastic nonsense: loyal Germans all need to fulfill their duty to the *Reich*.

Meanwhile on Thursday, 260 miles to the east of Düsseldorf at his office in Berlin, *Gestapo* agent Klaus Friedrich, also known as agent "beady-eyes," was preparing a dossier on Ilsa Huber's family. His cubical was in an open room with eight other office cubicles. All the agents were following up on families who might have a Jewish relative in the *Reich*.

Agent Friedrich's office was in a granite-grey marble block and stucco building on Prinz Albrecht Street number 8 situated near the Reichstag. This nondescript building was also known as *Gestapo Headquarters*. There were rumors there were soundproof rooms in the basement where the agents could elicit just about any information from anyone given the proper time sequence, torture tactics, and family kidnappings. In other words, if you wouldn't break and provide them with the information the *Gestapo* wanted, you might change your mind if your children's, wife's or close friends fingers were amputated one by one. It was a torture chamber where the *Gestapo* could systematically and ruthlessly brutalize their prisoners.

Passersby could hear the faint screams of torture victims through the ventilation system out in the street.

I received a note from Ilsa on Thursday. She was meeting agent "beady-eyes" at the main entrance to the Tiergarten in central Berlin on Saturday at 2:30 pm, on the steps of the Reichstag.

In the afternoon I took a bus to the Düsseldorf railway station and purchased an 8:05 am ticket to Berlin on Saturday morning. I explained to my parents I was meeting Ilsa in Berlin to take care of some minor problems for her and would be home late Sunday for school on Monday. They were kind enough, or intuitive enough, not to ask any particulars about my sleeping arrangements.

I should also mention after dispatching the two *Gestapo agents* in the Leven's home, my parents never questioned me too closely about any of my decisions.

CHAPTER 16

Ilsa Meets her Tormentor

The Tiergarten was originally a private hunting reserve for the nobility in Germany in the 1600s. Friedrich Wilhelm was the first noble to have the reserve enclosed into *The Grosse Tiergarten*, large game park. In 1938 it contained approximately 500 acres and was a beautiful place for Germans to picnic and stroll on weekends. There are many small lakes, private paths, and beautiful gardens in the park. All the wild animals had long ago been hunted to extinction, although there are still small animals like fox and deer with hundreds of species of birds. The Berlin Zoo boarders the southwest corner of the *Tiergarten*.

The *Reichstag* or German Parliament building was, in 1938, only serving as a rubber stamp for Adolf Hitler and the *Third Reich*. Since the suspicious fire on the 27th of February, 1933, the *National Socialist Workers Party, Nazi Party,* was in firm control of the German government. The communists were blamed for the fire and forced out of government offices, even though, it was probably the *SA* or *Brownshirts* who started the fire.

Early Saturday morning I was at the train station in Düsseldorf long before the 8:05 to Berlin. The journey to Berlin was approximately four to five hours, and I planned to be near the

Reichstag well before the meeting between my beloved Ilsa and agent "beady-eyes."

The train pulled into the center of Berlin at 12:40 pm. During the journey, I formulated a way to eliminate the troublesome *Gestapo* agent. Unfortunately, I would not have time to communicate the plan to Ilsa; she was taking my word on faith.

Even after almost two weeks, there was still a great deal of evidence of *Kristallnacht*. Almost everywhere there were boarded up businesses, shops, and restaurants. Many of these shut businesses were visible from the train. It was, unfortunately, evident each business owner had lost a lifetime of savings and future earnings. Money and time lost forever. A life's work destroyed in an instant of rage and insanity.

I asked one of the conductors on the train, "What did people think when they destroyed all these shops and stores?"

He got extremely agitated and defensive and replied in a hushed voice, "Oh...it's best not to talk about such things."

The conductor seemed almost dazed by my question. He got a far-away look in his eyes, and his expression went blank. It was a question he was not prepared to answer or even express a comment. As he hustled on down the train car toward the exit, he kept shaking his head to justify his ignorance.

He was obviously frightened to talk about the events of the evening on the ninth of November 1938.

As I got off the bus to the *Tiergarten*, I noticed a lot of people wouldn't make eye contact with me, not even a glance.

Ilsa positioned herself inside the *Tiergarten* where she could watch the steps of the *Reichstag* from a respectful distance without being seen. She was sitting down in the window of a small cafe drinking a cup of hot tea. From her position, she could watch the people who were coming and going on the front steps of the German Parliament building.

There was only one man who seemed to linger around the front of the steps. From her vantage point, she was too far away to be sure it was the beady-eyed agent. He was the only figure who stayed on the steps. He dressed like an office worker with a tie and overcoat. It was 1:20, and she wondered if Jenz had seen him.

At the same moment, a group of college students walked across the front of the building. The tall one in the bright blue sweater had to be Jenz. He kept going with the group of students and disappeared from her view down a side street parallel to the *Tiergarten*.

She slowly finished her tea and started walking toward the *Reichstag*. The man who looked like an office worker was staring in her direction. It was a sunny but cold day. The sun was low over the building, and Ilsa couldn't be positive, but it looked like the tall student out of the group had stopped and walked up to the other side of the steps. He had on a brown jacket over his sweater, and a hat pulled low over his forehead. He then slid behind one of the columns in front of the building. She thought it has to be Jenz.

Ilsa knew the history of the Reichstag. It was constructed between 1892 and 1894. Since the fire in January 1933 much of it had been damaged and boarded and off limits to the public.

Ilsa walked across the grass toward the building. She tried not to look at the beady-eyed man in the trench coat who was following her with his eyes. Even his gaze at this distance seemed evil and disconcerting. As she approached him, he gave her a thin smile without any warmth in it and said, "Good afternoon, Miss, you have shown excellent judgment in meeting me."

Ilsa looked disarmingly beautiful as she tried to humor her tormentor, "Thank you, Mr., I guess I don't know your name." *Or, Ilsa thought, should I call you the "beady-eyed" one?*

"You may call me Klaus."

"D...Do you have the information concerning my grandmother and m, my family?" Ilsa kept a slight stuttering motion going as her lower lip faked a noticeable tremor.

"Of course, dear girl. It is in my apartment not far from here."

"Is the only way I can read it by going to your home?"

"But of course, dearie, remember our agreement? My apartment is only a kilometer or so from here."

They walked almost in total silence. Ilsa was desperate to know if Jenz was following them but didn't dare to look back. At one point, Klaus tried to hold her hand, and Ilsa's retort was, **"Klaus, I remember our agreement!"**

As they approached Klaus's apartment, it looked like an extensive home converted into several apartments. Grey wooden steps were leading up to a wood-shingled home. It was an older home, and some of the shingles looked like they had slipped or were misaligned. But there were curtains in the windows, and it looked tidy enough from the outside. The neighborhood was middle class with homes grouped closely together. Many of the larger houses had been converted into apartments. The community emanated a feeling of safety, yet a coldness crept into Ilsa's stomach.

The sun was setting, and there was a wind whistling down the street. The chill of the wind was nothing compared to the overpowering feeling of helplessness and hopelessness creeping into and chilling Ilsa's soul.

As they reached the top step, Ilsa stole a backward glance to see where Jenz might be in the area. Her heart sank. There were other people in the street, but she could not spot anyone as tall as Jenz.

"Right this way *Liebchen*, let me check the post."

His comment made her skin crawl. *Where was Jenz?*

"I am on the second floor. Right this way."

"Lead the way, Klaus."

As Klaus started up the stairs, Ilsa sat on the first step and took off her shoe.

"I'll be right along, Klaus, I have a stone in my shoe."

As she feigned emptying her shoe, she wrote 2 on the stair riser in chalk.

"I'm coming Klaus; I hope you have all the information about my family so I can read it first."

As he was unlocking his apartment, he said with a sarcastic tone over his shoulder, "Of course I have it, it's all laid out on my desk. You have to trust me."

Ilsa thought, *"I could never trust you with anything you beady-eyed monster!"*

As soon as Ilsa cleared the threshold, Klaus slammed the door and locked it with the inside lock and chain and secured the bolt.

Slap! Klaus hit Ilsa with a sharp blow to her face. She was temporarily stunned.

"You deserve a slap for not trusting me!"

By then, I was already in the house, saw the chalk mark for the 2nd floor, and heard the bolt as it was thrown to lock the door to "beady-eyes" apartment securely.

As I crept up the stairs, I could hear some muffled talk from his apartment. I put my ear to his door and listened to Ilsa, crying, **"Why are you doing this?"**

Klaus had handcuffed Ilsa to his metal bedpost with *Gestapo* issued handcuffs.

Klaus's retort, "You didn't think I was just going to let you read the dossier and then run out on me, did you?"

"No, No, of course not!" she cried.

Klaus grabbed her other hand and secured it to the other side of the bed with an additional set of agency issued cuffs.

"I would advise you to be very quiet, or we can go to *Gestapo* headquarters where no one will ever see you again."

Klaus busied himself securing her feet to the bottom of the bed frame with short ropes he had positioned at the foot of his bed.

"Now, my beautiful concubine, you will be my adoring slave for as long as I say. It might be an hour, or it might be a month. I will let you walk around the apartment under supervision, but you must never leave this apartment until I say."

CHAPTER 17

Trapped by a Monster

As Ilsa started to protest in a loud voice, Klaus's face became very dark, and he seethed in a very firm tone, **"You are now completely under the control of the *Gestapo*. I will let you live if you do what I say. I will not subject you to torture, but I am going to cut your clothing from your body."**

He left the room in a huff only to return from the kitchen with a huge knife. He delighted in bringing the blade close to Ilsa's face and with a guttural voice, sounding like a completely different person, "Stay very still and I won't have to cut you as I slit off your pants. I will leave you in your underwear unless you fight me."

She fought and tried to kick.

"You leave me no choice *Liebchen* but also to cut off every bit of your clothing! And, if you continue to fight me, you have no idea of the drugs and pain I could inflict upon you. I will turn you into a drug addicted whore and share you with my fellow agents if you are not careful. I can assure you it would be most unpleasant for you."

"You will pay for this mister *Gestapo* man!"

"If you are not quiet, I will put a washcloth in your mouth and tie it to your head. It would be a shame to have to cut or bruise such a pretty face."

Klaus's entire appearance transformed into something evil. His eyes became narrow slits, his eyebrows furrowed into the middle of his forehead, and his lips seemed to curl into a ghastly mean sneer.

Klaus cut off Ilsa's underwear with a flick of the knife under the front of her bra strap. He smiled like a sadistic animal as he explained what more he could do to her if she were still uncooperative.

"If you prove uncooperative, I have drugs. These drugs will destroy your power to think and make you an addict. would you prefer addiction to drugs?"

Ilsa gasped, "Please don't hurt me."

Just then, there was a soft knock at the door.

"I'm sorry my dear, but I have to put this cloth in your mouth; I wouldn't want you crying or spoiling our fun now would I,"

Klaus seethed his words out of the corner of his mouth. He then gave her an evil grin as he thrust a washcloth in her mouth and tied a rope around her head to firmly hold it in place. His facial features seemed to grow hideous. His eyes bulged out, and his pupils radiated evil. His whole body transformed into an evil and depraved beast.

The knock persisted. From the other side of the door, a voice called, "Agent, it is Bruno from the agency. I have important papers for you to sign."

"Slip them under the door to my apartment you fool. Why are you bothering me at home?"

"The papers in this packet will not fit under your door. These are important dossier papers and have to be signed and returned today. Just crack the door, and I will pass them to you."

"Leave them outside, and I will pick them up later."

"Okay, Sir, the dossier papers are leaning up against the door. Please return them directly to headquarters after you have read them and they are signed."

Jenz stepped back approximately three to four feet.

There was some shuffling and mumbling from within the apartment, and then Jenz could hear the bolt slide open.

As Klaus kept the chain lock engaged, he cracked the door and firmly stated, **"Give me the papers you idiot!"**

I hit the door with a short run from four feet away. There were 235 pounds behind my shoulder, traveling for an instant at about 30 miles per hour. The door and chain lock and Klaus never had a chance.

The door flung open badly bruising Klaus and blooding his nose. "You fool, you have broken my nose!"

I sincerely hoped the racket hadn't traveled to the neighbor's apartments. I grabbed Klaus by the collar, spun him around with blood from his broken nose flying everywhere. With a lightning-like flick of my wrist, I hit Klaus on his temple with the side of my clenched fist. There was a splash of blood where my fist cracked his temple. The floor rushed up to meet the felled *Gestapo* agent.

I knew he wouldn't be getting up for a while. I could feel bones crunching as my fist flew into the agent's head in the temporal region. I just hope I hadn't killed him.

Muffled sounds were emanating from the bedroom. I carefully closed the door and engaged the bolt; the chain was hanging by the door plate. I rushed into the bedroom and saw Ilsa sprawled spread eagle tied to the bed completely naked with a large knife on the bedside table.

"*Mein Gott*, Ilsa, are you all right?" as I pulled the cloth from her mouth. She looked terrified.

"I think he was about to cut or drug me! Thank you so much for coming in when you did. Where is he? Is he dead?"

"No, for the moment he is sleeping in the hall. We have to get him undressed and into the tub."

"Why do we care if he is in the tub?" asked Ilsa.

I held up one finger for the "wait" sign.

I then went to the front door to make sure it was secured and checked the bolt and relocked it. I then rushed back into the bedroom to free Ilsa from her handcuffs and ropes. I cut the leg ropes off with the large knife by the bed and found the key to the *Gestapo's* handcuffs in Klaus's pocket.

Ilsa dressed as best she could in her torn clothing.

We carefully undressed Klaus, folded his clothing, including his underwear, and placed them carefully on a chair. I then dragged his naked body into the bathroom.

"Why are you folding his clothing so neatly?" asked Ilsa.

"Because our poor Klaus has had an accident in the bathtub. He has fallen, hit his head, and drowned. I want everything to look like an accidental fall. He probably would have gotten dressed again right after his bath."

"I will fill the tub and place him in it, but he might wake up when his head goes beneath the surface of the water. I need you to be ready to help hold him under."

"Why don't we just hit him again to make sure he never wakes up?" queried Ilsa.

"We need this to look accidental, sweetheart. We need to have the water in his lungs. Klaus is an important *Gestapo* agent. The authorities may investigate his death, but only if they don't believe this was an accidental drowning."

"Let's get him in the tub. It is half-filled with water, which should be plenty."

"Easy, you take his legs. We don't want to cause any additional bruising. I am going to wipe the blood from his nose, face, side of his head and lips and smear it on the faucet and spigot for the tub."

As I eased his head underwater, old Klaus started coming around with some thrashing and kicking. I probably shouldn't have used just the cold water. I held his head under water, and Ilsa kept his feet from kicking and splashing out too much of the bath water. We helped him stay underwater for about five minutes. We waited for a couple of minutes after the bubbles stopped coming up from his nose and mouth. He was looking pretty pale when we released him.

We placed his towel where he could have reached it as he got out of the tub.

We next went through his apartment and cleaned all traces of his blood off the door and floor. I repaired the chain lock I had broken when I busted into his apartment. I found some larger screws in a kitchen drawer. Ilsa put the handcuffs in a drawer and replaced the knife in the kitchen. We collected every bit of information we could find on Ilsa's family and tied it into a bundle for easy carrying.

It was getting dark. We turned one light on in the apartment and one in the bathroom. We left separately and agreed to meet at the end of the street in 10 minutes.

I checked on Klaus. He was still under the water with no pulse. The bathroom scene looked natural enough for an accident. I left the bathroom light on, locked the apartment door, and crept down the stairs and out of the building. I silently prayed God would forgive me for ending this evil agent's life.

Ilsa and I walked back to the train station in Central Berlin. There were lots of people out, but there were also several shops owned by Jews boarded up or looted and completely cleaned out. Ilsa commented, "In Hannover, we also lost our main synagogue and two other smaller synagogues and several Jewish reading rooms."

Neither of us wanted to talk about the *Gestapo* agent we had just drowned. We were both relieved Klaus couldn't hurt us or anyone else anymore. But we both dreaded what he had planned for Ilsa. We consoled ourselves by saying Germany was safer without him.

"Please come home with me. My parents are home and would love to meet you. We are both adults. I will make this point clear when I arrange for our sleeping accommodations."

"Are you sure it will be okay with your parents, Ilsa?"

"They said they would look forward to meeting you."

The train to Hannover arrived at 9:30 in the evening. The walk from the station to Ilsa's home took us almost an hour. The night was cold, and we could see our breath; walking briskly kept us warm enough. We promised each other not ever to discuss the evil *Gestapo* agent who had been cruel to Ilsa.

Ilsa's parents were delightful people and seemed to have no problem with both of us sharing Ilsa's room.

Ilsa was kind, warm, and very loving toward me when we got into bed. She awakened me early in the morning by kissing my stomach. I couldn't have been in a happier place.

The next day I caught the noon train to Düsseldorf. I had been somewhat concerned over the weekend about the Leven's. I hoped they hadn't been bothered by any further incidents from the *Gestapo.*

CHAPTER 18

....

Ezekiel Leven has a Name Change

It was almost midnight by the time I returned home to Düsseldorf. Dad was still up, but when I started to tell him about the *Gestapo* agent in Berlin, he got Mom up to hear the story. Since Mom was a worrier, I wasn't sure getting her up was such a fantastic idea. We sat in the kitchen where it was a little warmer. Mom fixed me a cheese sandwich and some tea while I told them the details of my trip to Berlin.

Mom almost lost it when I talked about drowning the *Gestapo* agent. "Jenz, I have never seen you violent before, but now you have murdered three men."

"I am so sorry mother, I hope God will forgive me, but these men were evil and going to hurt my friends. I couldn't let anything happen to the Leven's or Ilsa."

"What have you heard from Zeke this weekend?" I asked.

Dad commented, "It's been tranquil in their neighborhood since the 10th of November."

"Good, I will try to spend more time at their home this week, if they are OK with my being there."

It seemed excellent to be able to sit at the kitchen table and discuss adult topics with my parents. I told them I was in love with Ilsa and would like to be with her forever. I told them as soon as it was practical, I would love for them to meet her.

The next week I spent most evenings at Ezekiel's home. My parents didn't seem to mind, and I have to tell you, Hilda was a terrific cook. Her baked German delicacies were of professional quality.

The nights were getting colder with intermittent snow squalls. Although the Leven's always kept their home nice and warm, the feeling of joylessness permeating their home was palpable.

I encouraged the Leven's to make arrangements to leave the country without delay, but they were pretty set on staying in their neighborhood and seeing what could happen politically in Germany. They had the feeling the political atmosphere toward Jews had to get better.

I remember Dr. Leven saying, "After all the synagogues and businesses have been burned or destroyed, what else could the government do to the Jews?"

I decided to retell the story about my previous weekend in Berlin with Ilsa. I described what the *Gestapo* agent was like and what he had planned to do to Ilsa.

"These men are animals, doctor. You cannot reason with them. Their views are evil and dangerous. My recommendation is for you and your family to apply for passports and seek asylum in Switzerland, Hungry or France, or Spain. Even Austria, Denmark, or Sweden would be an improvement."

Then I gave the Leven's a hint of what I would do over the next year.

"I am planning on moving to Berlin this next year. I want to get an apartment, study at the university, and have Zeke join me."

"Oh No," sighed Mrs. Leven. "Zeke would not be allowed to attend the *Technische Hochschule* in Berlin; Jews are not permitted."

"I'd love to go," said Zeke, "but Mom is probably right. I would bring you nothing but trouble."

"No more trouble than having the *Gestapo* revisit your home."

"I'm afraid their next visit might not work out so well for you or your family."

"Look, Ezekiel, we are going to have to make you Aryan whether you like it or not. Once I get settled, I will find someone who will get an Italian drivers license and passport for you. Give me an idea of what kind of Italian name you would like."

"From what I hear on the news," I continued, "Jews are being rounded up all over the country and sent to labor camps. If they resist, they are beaten or worse. We cannot let anything remotely similar happen to our families or us."*

Melancholy and depression settled over the Jews in Europe like a dense blanket of fog. Fewer and fewer options were open to folks of the Jewish faith in Germany. Jews in the Conquered Territories were fair game for the *Gestapo, Wehrmacht,* and the *SS*. The Einsatzgruppen were particularly dangerous for any Jews left in the concord territories, if the Jews had not been killed by the Wehrmacht. Jews, leaders in other religions, political opposition, and anyone not in full agreement with the *Nazi* idea of "pure German blood," were systematically hunted down, killed, or imprisoned in concentration camps.

From Hitler's rise to power in January of 1933, the official *Nazi* policy was the persecution of Jews. This slow strangulation of the Jewish religion became much worse in late 1938 and 1939.

---

* *It was just eight weeks later on January 30, 1939, when Hitler warned the Jewish bankers: "If Jewish financers start a war against Germany, the result will be the annihilation of the Jewish Race in Europe."*

"Zeke, I will travel to Berlin next weekend and secure an apartment for myself and my roommate, with an Italian last name. I hope it is okay with your parents. Let me know what you would like for the last name, but I would like us both to enroll in the university and receive deferments from the Wehrmacht. You will most likely not need a deferment since you will be a foreign student."

"Could I be Vitali Carapezza? My dad has a friend with the same last name. He was a dentist just outside of Rome in Ladispoli, Italy."

"Of course, I will get the apartment in both our names."

Later in the week I wrote to Ilsa to tell her of my plans with Zeke.

Early Saturday morning, I took the express train from Düsseldorf. My parents gave me their blessing and enough money for my first month's rent in Berlin and a little food. It was clear to me both Zeke and I would have to have some gainful employment to live in Berlin.

We found a moderately priced apartment in a home in the Kreuzberg section of Berlin, just south of the center of the city on a side street just off Leibnizstrasse. With all the trees and bushes, it was hard to believe we were in the middle of a city. It was within walking distance of the university and the train station. Zeke was now Vitali and enrolled in the *Technische Hochschule* in Berlin after completing the entrance examinations.

Now we could go to work.

My roommate and I both got decent low-level jobs through the *Technische Hochschule*. He worked in the library, and I worked as a waiter in one of the restaurants on the campus. Together we earned enough to cover our rent and most of our food. I was almost continuously hungry.

If the books were too expensive, Vitali would get them out of the library on "loan." His boss, a very understanding librarian, said, "Use them as long as you needed them for each course." Each course usually lasted 2-3 months. We were very grateful for her understanding.

We joined the mechanical engineering class in the winter term. In addition to studying at the *Technische Hochschule* and working as a waiter and assistant librarian, Vitali and I masked our real intentions for being in Berlin.

Yes. We both wanted to study engineering and physics. But, more important to us was protecting innocent people from the dreaded *Gestapo*. This collection of low-life thuggish anti-intellectual scum was not only terrorizing Jews, and Jewish sympathizers, but also political dissidents, students, disabled students, gypsies, and anyone who might dare to marry a Jew or in any way dilute "German blood."

An additional danger was brought to our attention. Lurking in the university and in Berlin were Jews who collaborated with the *Gestapo* for money to turn over to the authorities fellow Jews or anyone who disagreed with the Nazi philosophy of "pure Germanic blood."

Ezekiel and I were warned about Stella Kübler, perhaps one of the more notorious *"greiferin"* or catcher of Jews for the *Gestapo.*[*] Zeke and I had to be very careful of the *Greiferin* in Berlin.

---

[*] *When Stella and her family couldn't obtain visas to flee the country, the Gestapo subjected Stella to torture. She agreed to save herself and her family by going underground as an Aryan because of her blond hair and blue eyes. She received 300*

By attending lectures and classes during the day and working evenings Vitali and I stayed away from the political spotlight and under the fascist radar. It turned out many students at the university were Jewish sympathizers but deathly afraid to say anything to anyone.

Zeke (Vitali) and I decided to take no one else into our confidence for what we were planning. There were too many chances for leaks, or any information getting to the *Gestapo* through spies and just loose talk. We trusted each other but were very reluctant to fully trust someone else who might undergo torture for information about our mission.

Our goal was to protect Jews who might be on the receiving end of the *SS* or the *Gestapo's* long arm of terror. Our mission was pretty clear to us. We wanted to save Jews from the *Gestapo,* but we told no one about our partnership or what we were doing. Nothing was written down on paper. We never spoke of our mission to anyone.

If the SS or Gestapo arrested *anyone,* anything could happen to you. Many arrested Jews were subjected to unspeakable pain and atrocities. Under torture, most reasonable people would give up information on their friends, parents, or siblings to be free of the degradation and suffering.

Reichsmarks for each Jew she betrayed. These Jews hiding as non-Jews were referred to as submerged or in German untergetauchter.

She eventually betrayed between six hundred to three thousand fellow Jews. But in spite of her collaboration, the Gestapo eventually imprisoned and killed her parents in the Theresienstadt concentration camp. Stella was arrested by the Russians after the war and served ten years in prison for her crimes. She eventually committed suicide by throwing herself out of her apartment window in Freiburg, Germany in 1994.

One of our mutual friends, a student at the university, was picked up by the *Gestapo* because he had a Jewish grandmother. He underwent 36 straight hours of "interrogation" at *Gestapo* headquarters in Berlin. The authorities were looking for resisters, Jewish sympathizers, and anyone who knew anything about Jews in hiding.

This unfortunate student had three fingers removed, electroshock treatment to his genitals, and a severe beating. He confessed everything he knew about his Jewish friends, relatives, and student resistant movements. Zeke and I were so glad we hadn't confided in this individual. We learned a lot about the workings of the *Gestapo* when we visited the student in the hospital. We were surprised the *Gestapo* had let him live. They probably let him live to spread terror to any Jews or Jewish sympathizers in the student community. He was never able to resume his studies. He had a thousand-yard blank stare in his eyes.

When I asked, "Did the agent from the *Gestapo* mistreat you in any way?" He just held up his hand with three fingers missing and mumbled about his beatings. It was hard for him to talk with so many missing and broken teeth.

It was the beginning of 1939. Our engineering classes were going pretty well. Ilsa and I were able to see each other on some weekends. On the 30th of January, Hitler addressed the *Reichstag* (German Parliament). His message was basically if the forces of Jewry plunge our country into another world war, then the result would be "the annihilation of the Jewish race in Europe." He received a standing ovation.

My dad could see the changes happening at Farben. He pleaded with the Leven's to try to emigrate to another country. Both Zeke and I strongly recommended his parents leave at their earliest convenience. They kept trying to get visas at different embassies, but without success.

It was evident to my dad, because of the changes at Farben, the politicians in Germany were re-arming the country and placing it on a war footing. Late in January of the new year, 27 January 1939, Hitler announced Plan-Z. Dad said, "This is a code name for the build-up of the *Kriegsmarine* (German Navy). Hitler wants a navy a strong navy able to defeat the British if war comes again to Germany."

"Dad, would the German people put up with military expansion for another war like The Great War?"

"Son, it's already happening! In March, on the 22nd., 1939, Germany took the Memelland, part of Lithuania, by declaring it part of the German State.

"Also three days later, German troops marched into Bohemia and Moravia, essentially taking over the entire country of Czechoslovakia.

"Jenz, listen to me. The Jews in the Eastern Territories are as frightened as in Germany. If the Wehrmacht takes over Poland, East Prussia, Czechoslovakia, and France and the low countries, there will be millions of Jews and their families affected. Where will they go?"*

In the United States the Wagner/Rogers bill was introduced in Congress to allow the admission of up to 20,000 Jewish children under the age of 14. The bill sponsors were Senator Robert Wagner, a Democrat from New York and Representative Edith Rogers a Republican from Massachusetts. The bill proposed the immigration of 10,000 Jews under the age of 14 from Nazi Germany into the United States in 1939 and another 10,000 in 1940. The law never came to a vote because of Democratic Senator Robert Rice Reynolds of North Carolina, an avowed anti-Semite. Most of the children this bill was aimed to save wound up in the gas chambers and ovens in the Nazi concentration camps.

"Jenz, be very careful with your work at disrupting *Gestapo* activity. It is rumored the *Wehrmacht* has been tasked to march into Poland this summer. If the Wehrmacht marches, it could be the start of a second world-wide war."

"We are cautious, Dad. No one knows about our plans or actions. Our next target will be the agents who are harassing and interrogating students at the *Technische Hochschule* in Berlin."

"How do you hope to discourage this particular *Gestapo* agent or agents and get these cruel men to change their barbarous methods?"

"They are probably interested in picking up another student who has been quite vocal about his opposition to the *Nazi Party*. When the agents swoop in to arrest him, we will be waiting."

"You and Zeke be careful, Jenz. Your mother and I are distraught something will go very wrong and you will both be swept up in the search for student dissidents."

CHAPTER 19

Protecting a University Student from the Gestapo

Zeke and I took my parents concerns seriously. Ilsa was also anxious about us and our dealings with the *Gestapo* and the *SS*. I promised we would make every effort to stay under the *Gestapo* radar and keep a low profile in the academic setting.

Both Vitali and I had warned this particular student the *Gestapo* might be observing or following him. Günther, however, claimed it was impossible. "I'm from an ancient family with a history of parents, uncles, and grandparents in the *Wehrmacht*."

"Günter, calm down," I whispered in a low voice, "You never know who might overhear you and decide to cause some trouble. You do not want to be questioned by the authorities in this political climate, especially if they're going to take you to *Gestapo* Headquarters.

He answered in a rather loud and brash voice, **"These political thugs wouldn't dare touch me!"**

I just looked at Vitali, and we walked away. There was just no dealing with someone who had a death wish. He had no idea of the political climate, or who might overhear and report such talk.

Vitali and I decided to keep a close watch on Günter and see if the authorities might come for him with some questioning, interrogation, or an arrest warrant.

Vitali and I would switch off. One of us would go to Günter's classes, and one of us would watch his apartment until midnight. From the Leven's experience, we figured the authorities would probably come to his residence in the late evening.

They came the second night just after 11:00 pm. I was a half block down the street studying in a small cafe closing at midnight. I saw the car drive up with two men dressed mostly in black with fedoras and bulky long coats.

I used the cafe pay phone to call our apartment. Vitali said he would hurry right over.

The authorities entered the rooming house where Günter was renting a room. I figured I would let them get inside of Günter's apartment before I walked in.

By this time in 1939, the anti-Jewish policies put in place by the *Third Reich* were complete. Zeke and I knew first-hand how the Jews in Germany had been slowly terrorized since Hitler came to power in January of 1933. Jews were initially deprived of citizenship, the ability to work, and fundamental civil rights. Now they were being hunted down by the *Gestapo* and the *SS* in the most despicable and ruthless way possible. Hitler's goal was to make Germany and the conquered territories free of all Jews, dissidents, communists, people with handicapping disorders, or anyone else who might disagree with the "pure German blood" philosophy of the *Third Reich*.

There was a slight chill in the fragrant spring air, and I could almost see my breath. I was wearing a school sweater and leather gloves and carrying a couple of books.

I knocked on Günter's door and walked in yelling, "Hi Günther, sorry to bother you this late, but I need the reading assignment of tomorrows mechanical engineering class."

"Oh, sorry! I didn't realize you had company."

I remember thinking, yikes, these guys are pretty big. How would be the best way to put them down. I am going to have to distract one while I lean on the other one. I better take out the larger one first if he is the leader. It didn't look like Günther was going to be much of a help. He was whimpering in the hall halfway out of his bedroom.

I came in with two rather large engineering books under my left arm. Günter looked white as a ghost.

Günter moaned, "These agents want me to go to their headquarters, I'm under arrest!"

I dropped my books in supposed surprise. My books clattered at the feet of the largest and most significant agent. He looked down at the floor where the books had landed at his feet.

He never saw my leather gloved left fist as it caught him squarely under the chin.

As his chin bounced up, he never saw my gloved right fist crush into his larynx and windpipe. He hit the floor as good as dead although he was making awful grunting noises. His legs and arms were flailing while he writhed on the floor. The takedown of this brute took less than five seconds.

The other agent, although stunned at his partner's impending demise, had his pistol out in his right hand and was bringing it to bear on me. I grabbed his right arm and spun him around so hard I broke or dislocated his arm at the elbow, and he dropped his weapon.

The agent let out a howl before I hit him in the back of his neck so hard I was sure his neck was broken; I might have severed his spine.

Günter whined, "Jenz, what the hell are you doing?"

"Saving you from being arrested and tortured at *Gestapo* headquarters, you idiot. You would probably wind up in *Dachau* or worse, if you survived their torture session. Their very effective method of torture is removing fingers, one at a time."

"I, I don't know what to say," Günter replied in a low whimper.

"How about 'thank you'! My friend Vitali will be here soon. You can help us dispose of this trash. They will be missed. I recommend you keep going to class as if nothing has happened."

"And for the record, you never saw or met any agents from any government authority. Also, let me remind you, **never, ever,** brag about how you come from a prominent family and the *Nazis* would never dare to lay a hand on you. My advice is to always speak of the *Third Reich* in positive, even glowing terms."

"When Vitali gets here we are going to need access to a car. Do you know where you can get one or borrow one for about one hour?"

"I can borrow my father's car. They live about thirty minutes away. I'll get a taxi."

"Hold on Günter, let's see which one of these gentlemen drove."

I searched the pockets of the smaller agent and found the keys and his wallet. Although both agents had cash in their wallets, we left the money because I had decided to stage an accident with their automobile. I didn't want this to look like a robbery. I replaced the firearm in the second agent's holster.

"Günter, please get me an old blanket to wrap the first agent in before we transport him to the trunk of their car. We can use the same blanket for the second agent and then return the blanket to you."

When Vitali arrived, he asked, "Was the big guy hard to put down?"

Günter responded, "Jenz was amazingly fast for an ordinary student. I had no idea he possessed such astonishing and incredible fighting skills."

"Pretty routine stuff at Hitler Youth Camp," I added.

"Günter, remember, **never - ever** talk about this evening to anyone. You know **nothing** about these agents visiting you; and be careful, because more agents may question you, especially if these agents kept a schedule with your name on it at *Gestapo* headquarters."

"If asked or questioned extensively, you do not know Vitali or me. **Never**, under any circumstances, let on to anyone else or even hint to anyone you know us. Remember, one ill-placed word from you could mean the amputation of your fingers or much worse."

"The next time the Gestapo has your name on a list, you may not be so fortunate. We can hope your name is only on these agents agenda, and not on a master list at headquarters."

CHAPTER 20

Taking out the Trash

"**V**itali let's place these agents in the trunk. I'll back the car into the driveway, close to the walk to minimize the chances of anyone seeing us load these blanket wrapped packages into the car."

"Günter, we need a glass bottle with a screw top and a length of garden hose approximately four feet long. Do not ask what they are for; get them as soon as you can. **Now!**"

Günter returned from the cellar with a clear glass pickle jar and a length of garden hose he had just cut. He poured out the preserved cucumber pickles into the sink and rinsed out the container.

Vitali and I put the two agents, the glass pickle jar, and the length of hose in the trunk of the car. I left my books with Günter, with instructions for him to return them to me at our next class.

We left with one final admonishment for Günter, "**Remember, Günter, No one came to visit you here this evening, and you never heard of us!**"

Vitali and I stopped on a secluded street, I suctioned a pickle jar full of petrol from the automobile and drove off looking for a suitable crash site spitting traces of gasoline out the window.

We found a deserted street in Wedding, in the northeast section of Berlin. It was a leafy tree-lined street with no houses in the immediate vicinity. We looked for a tight curve in the road at the bottom of a hill for a plausible crash site. We couldn't see any lights from any houses in the vicinity, which wasn't unusual because most of Germany, especially near the major cities, was in blackout mode by this time.

We braced ourselves and ran the car off the road into a tree on a dangerous curve in the street. We hauled the agents out of the trunk and placed them in the front seat with the smaller agent in the driver's seat. I used the tire iron to smash the windshield from the inside in two spots to simulate where the heads of the two agents would have struck during the crash. Zeke poured petrol over the dead agents and onto the front seat. He then lit the automobile on fire, and we walked briskly back to the main road leading to the railway station. We thought it only fair that we empty the agent's wallets for future use.

I looked back once, as the roaring fire had consumed the agents and their automobile. It made quite a beacon of light in an otherwise gloomy night. Looking back, I decided in the future to always keep any cash from our Gestapo victims. They certainly were not going to need the money.

There was a spring mist in the air hanging around us like guilt. I had to make sure Vitali was going to be okay.

"Thanks, Zeke, for your help. You have been a help for me all through school. Are you doing okay with this dastardly business this evening?"

"I'm okay, Jenz. This is the third and fourth time we have removed Gestapo trash. So far, we have been pretty lucky. I hope our luck holds out. It looks like Hitler wants a large army with a vast network of the secret police."

We were back to our apartment by 1:30. A note on our door said an agent from the *SS* had been asking about me. He wanted to talk with me before noon the next day at their headquarters on Prinz Albrecht Street; a *Schutzstaffel* officer had signed it.

CHAPTER 21

Evaluation by the SS

The next morning the sun seemed to be in a tug of war with a thin cloud cover; by 10 O'clock, it was evident the sun was going to be victorious. It was a pleasant late spring day with a fragrance from new blossoms no one would find objectionable.

I showed up at *Schutzstaffel, (SS)* headquarters at number eight Prinz Albrecht Street relatively near the *Reichstag,* at 11 am. dressed in a suit and tie. Vitali was much more nervous than I. He had visions we were all going to be arrested and interrogated because of last night's activities.

Since it was unlikely the *SS* had learned about our accomplishments from last evening, I thought it unlikely their interview could be too disastrous.

The building was a large stately building. It occupied most of the block of buildings. It was built around the turn of the century. It had large curved windows, between enormous granite blocks. A solid looking building; it didn't look too intimidating from the outside. I didn't know at the time, but this building was also the headquarters for the feared *Gestapo,* the *Sicherheitspolizei (SiPo)* Security Police, *Einsatzgruppen* deployment groups, and the *SD* an abbreviation for *Sicherheitsdienst* which was the intelligence agency for the *SS.*

I hadn't heard too much about the *Einsatzgruppen*, or deployment groups, but learned later these unpleasant thugs made up roving death squads responsible for the murder of priests, Jews, anyone in the political sphere who demonstrated disagreement with the *Nazi* philosophy of racial purity. Their dastardly tasks were mainly carried out in the conquered territories of Hungry, Poland, and Czechoslovakia.

These deployment groups killed thousands of people in the occupied territories, including innocent women and children. Their favorite killing mechanism was the rifle or pistol shot at close range after the males had dug their graves for their families. This vile contemptible behavior helped Ezekiel and me not feel too guilty when it came to eliminating *Gestapo* agents. After the war, most of these despicable groups were never prosecuted for their heinous and hellish crimes against civilians. The proof of their nefarious crimes was buried in the earth.

The young woman at the front desk was charming. She had beautiful smooth skin, reasonably straight and dazzling white teeth, and a lithe, athletic figure declaring there were not too many miles of frustration on it. I introduced myself as Jenz Ramsgrund from Düsseldorf, and this delightful and rather beautiful creature led me down a corridor to a quiet interview room with a desk and two comfortable chairs on either side of it.

As I sat in the room, I noticed there was no doorknob on the inside of the door, but I didn't give it too much thought. I wanted to keep positive thoughts going through my mind. The room was painted all off-white with framed prints of German accomplishments: buildings, bridges, armaments, and highways on the walls in addition to the large black and white photograph of our *Führer.*

After about 15 minutes, an *SS* officer in full uniform came in and offered me coffee or tea. I stood up, and we shook hands. I declined a beverage but thanked him. I wasn't sure if he was being friendly or trying to catch me off guard.

"Jenz Ramsgrund," he began, "I have reviewed your file and recommendations from your time at the Hitler Youth Camp and your professors and employer at the *Technische Hochschule* in Berlin."

I breathed a silent sigh of relief. Where the hell was all this going?

He continued, "You possess the facial features, athletic appearance, and the strength of a potential member of the *Schutzstaffel.*"

I thought to myself, how would he feel if I told him I was half Jewish and enjoyed going to Synagogue with my Jewish classmates.

"In two weeks, you will be allowed to attend a briefing and training session for new *SS* officers. You should understand this is a direct commission and a high honor. You will report for duty no later than 0800 on July 1st. Our country needs loyal men like you to counter the threat of rising Judaism in Germany. This nefarious element is propelling our strong country into a war, and we must be ready for any eventuality."

He was waiting for a response from me. I just waited to see if he was going to add any further baloney.

"Do you have any questions?" he finally asked.

I was too dumbfounded to reply immediately, so I said nothing. I wasn't sure if the officer was going to keep on espousing the virtues of the *SS* or what this "valuable" organization was doing for the German people.

I eventually mouthed, "Sir. It would be a great honor to serve the *Reich* in any capacity."

The *SS* officer stood shook my hand and offered the Hitler salute. After shaking his hand, I took a step back and saluted with a stiff arm I hopped look authentic. He said I would be getting orders within a week, and the *SS* training would last one month. He then offered his congratulations.

"You have made the right choice; you make our *Führer* proud."

I didn't see I had a lot of choice in the decision, but at the time it seemed best not to initiate a debate.

He took a unique key out of his pocket and let me exit the interview room. I wondered at the time what he would have done if I had just declined his offer with a polite "no thank you."

I nodded a greeting and a toothy smile to the young lady at the front counter, and briefly wondered what she would look like without her clothes. I immediately felt a pang of guilt and wondered when I was going to see Ilsa again. I also was curious about what Ilsa might think of my new station in life.

The atmosphere was close and musty in the *Schutzstaffel* headquarters. Once I got out on the sidewalk, the air never smelled so sweet. I took several full breaths to clear the hate and disgust I felt toward the *SS* in general and *Herr* Himmler in particular. Then I tried to picture how I'd look in an *SS* uniform. I wasn't too impressed.

I looked down at the basement windows by the sidewalk and wondered why they had bars and blackout cloth over them. It wouldn't be too long until I found out.

My parents had mixed feelings about having a new *SS* member in the family. Dad thought it proved we had done an excellent job at masking our Jewish background. Besides, he stated, "It might save you from the *Wehrmacht*. Mom was wary of the appointment and thought it might be some *Nazi* trap to ensnare the family and discover our true heritage.

Zeke was pretty calm about it and quipped, "It is always good to have a friend on the inside."

He did wonder and then mentioned, "What would the *Schutzstaffel* think of hiring and indoctrinating a half-Jewish patriot into their fold who was committed with his friend, who happened to be 100% Jewish, to put an end to their corrupt and fiendish methods."

Ilsa wasn't sure what to make of it. She was happy it might keep me from going into the army, but she worried about the rumors of the leader and founder of the *Schutzstaffel*, Heinrich Himmler. Those rumors included the beatings and murder of Jews in Austria and from some cities in Germany. He was also instrumental in setting up *Dachau,*[*] a concentration camp(*Konzentrationslager)* in Bavaria in southern Germany. I had never met the man and hoped I never would, but understood he was ruthless. Cruel didn't even begin to describe him.

---

[*] *Dachau was the first of many concentration camps in Germany and Poland. Dachau was set up in what was originally a munitions factory in 1933 by Himmler. It was designed to handle political prisoners at first. It was later expanded to be a prison for Jews, Communists, Catholic Priests, gypsies, homosexuals, and anyone else the Nazis felt they needed to eliminate from their pure blood Germanic society. Many religious leaders were imprisoned there, including over 2700 Catholic, Protestant, and Orthodox Clergy.*

One Catholic priest was imprisoned because he talked with a young woman who was thinking of giving up her religion and marrying an SS officer. Another priest was sent to Dachau for presiding over a funeral service for a member of the communist party.

It was, however, not set up as a death camp. The crematorium was for the disposal of inmates who had died while imprisoned at the camp. In practice, as history was to prove, prisoners were very likely to die while serving their sentences because of the deplorable food, horrific living conditions, forced labor, and rampant disease.

The next week went quickly. I spent time talking with my professors about a leave of absence. Vitali and I spent time discussing all the ramifications of my becoming an officer in the *Schutzstaffel*. Even I was getting a little anxious. What would become of me in such a feared and hated organization?

My letter orders came by post in one week. I was ordered to report to the *SS* training facility at *Dachau!* I was to report to the camp commandant, *Hauptsturmführer* Alexander Piorkowski, no later than 1 July 1939, for indoctrination and training.

My first thought was I could likely be a prisoner at *Dachau*. However, the letter continued about my being fitted for my uniform and training for conduct befitting an *SS* officer. My next thought was perhaps I might have a future in the acting industry. How was I going to pull off the greatest deception of my life? I was going to have to appear as a hardened *Schutzstaffel* officer while helping my fellow Jewish countrymen from the horrors of the camp at *Dachau*.

My parents, friends at the university, professors, and Hitler Camp instructors were interviewed and investigated by the *SS* about my suitability for the organization. I continued to take my engineering classes and study or work in the evenings.

"Jenz, could you come to my office after class at the end of the day?" It was a request from my mechanical engineering professor.

I had no idea what was on his mind; I hoped he wasn't angry I had asked for a leave of absence.

At 4:00 pm, I found my way to his office in the basement of the engineering building.

"Sit down Jenz. I wanted to talk to you about a recent visit I had from the *SS*."

"Yes, sir, my apology. The *Schutzstaffel* had me in for an interview last week and offered me a position with their organization."

"Do you know what this group does, Jenz?"

"I believe I do professor. They were formed in 1925 as a protective echelon for our *Führer*. Over the past few years, they have been expanded to provide guard duty at some of the political detention camps."

"Oh, Jenz, although what you have stated is true, this group of 'echelon guards' is much more dangerous and lethal to many of our citizens. They routinely round up Jews, Jewish sympathizers and anyone who disagrees with the *Nazi* philosophy of racial purity in our universities and cities and towns."

Here I had to be very careful. I didn't dare to confide in this professor. If I told him my goal was to protect our Jewish brothers and sisters and I was half Jewish and was working with a Jew from the engineering class, he could purposefully or inadvertently turn me over to the Gestapo.

"Sir, my goal is to serve the Fatherland with whatever means are at my disposal. I will try to be the best engineer for Germany and use my skills to advance learning, production, and value for our country."

If my response wasn't enough claptrap and bullshit for him, I had a bit more.

"Besides, sir, I want to be an excellent example of an officer in the service of our country."

"But Jenz," the professor continued, "You don't understand. The officer here indicated they were considering you for the *Waffen SS!*

"What the devil is the *Waffen SS?*" I asked in a surprised voice.

"Jenz, this is the elite armed wing of the *Schutzstaffel!* It is made up of the Aryan German elite who can trace their roots back several generations. It is mostly upper-middle and upper-class Germans with university degrees. However, if war ever came to Germany, these elite highly trained armed guards would be utilized to the fullest in positions of leadership and terror toward our fellow citizens."

"Thank you, professor. I appreciate your comments; I would love to have teaching as my profession, not the military."

"Go in peace, Jenz. Be careful of yourself. May God be with you."

The next few weeks were busy getting ready for my initiation into the *Schutzstaffel* and encouraging the Leven's to leave the country. I tried to emphasize if war did come to Germany, it would be much more challenging to obtain a visa or flee the country as a refugee.

The Leven's were understandably very stubborn about leaving everything they knew behind. They had many friends, patients, a home, and other possessions they hated to abandon to the will and plunder of the *Nazis*. Dr. Leven expressed his views repeatedly:

"Jenz, the *Reich* will continue to need physicians and surgeons. Why would the government want to put us in a labor camp? It just wouldn't make sense!"

"Because, doctor, our government is no longer rational or responsible to our Jewish citizens or anyone who disagrees with their philosophy of German racial purity. Anyone who voices disagreement with the *Reich's* leaders including Hitler, Himmler, and especially Hermann Göring from the *Gestapo* could be in serious trouble very quickly. It seems like these three thugs are in some contest: who can be the nastiest, most despicable, and the cruelest of them all."

"What is most worrisome, suggested Dr. Leven, is the *Gestapo* has now implemented *Schuzthaft* or 'protective custody' which is a method of detaining and imprisoning anyone without even a hint of judicial proceedings. The *Gestapo* is empowered by German law to execute, without judicial review, anyone deemed to be a traitor to the *Reich!*

"Equally concerning," Dr. Leven continued, "Is since 1936, an *SS Obergruppenführer* (General) named Reinhard Heydrich has taken over as head of the *Gestapo*. His moniker was well known in Jewish circles; some locals in Prague just nicknamed him *Der Henker* (The Hangman). His new position as of this year is head of the *Reichssicherheitshauptamt* (Reich Security Central Office). Essentially, he is in charge of all security and secret police in the *Third Reich*.

"Jenz, be extremely careful of this man. He is a danger to every student dissident in the universities, every Jewish family in Germany, and anyone they deem a danger to the Reich. He is not to be trusted or believed."

"Perhaps he should be eliminated, Dr. Leven."

"Jenz, **never** mention anything about eliminating anyone in a public place or even to close friends and relatives. I would only trust your family and our family. Who knows what someone may divulge under extreme torture? I would encourage you to keep those types of thoughts to yourself."

"Good point, doctor. Has Zeke filled you in on our latest 'trash' removal?"

"Yes, you boys are courageous, but bordering on the foolhardy. Please be careful. To say these men are extremely ruthless and depraved is not an exaggeration. May God be watching over you both!"

"Dr. Leven," I responded, "God has been very excellent in protecting your son and me, and we are extremely grateful. Our principal worry is you and your wife. Please do everything humanly possible to leave the country immediately. I promise you, even as a new member of the *SS,* the political and hate climate in Germany could get much worse than anyone could envision."[*]

---

[*] *Before the war started, over eighty percent of German Jews under 21 years of age had fled the country. However, after the start of hostilities in September 1939, no Jews were allowed to leave Germany or the conquered territories; they were trapped! The Jews of Europe were rounded up, hunted down, and systematically murdered.*

CHAPTER 22

Reporting to Dachau and Auschwitz for "Training"

I reported to the Commandant of the *Dachau* Labor Camp facility at eight O'clock in the morning on the first of July. Vitali drove me up to the gate in his dad's car, but the guards wouldn't let us enter with the automobile. The guards refusal was all it took for Zeke to say, "I've seen all I need to see, Jenz. Best of luck with your Hitler training. Call when you can or drop me a note."

A guard at the gate grabbed my bag and escorted me to the commandant's office. It was a warm summer day with a deep-blue sky. There were no hint of clouds nor any turmoil at the camp. If it were not for the double rows of barbed wire fence and the guard towers, I could have been entering a resort. We stopped walking in front of a large sign. It read: ***Hauptsturmführer* Alexander Piorkowski, Camp Commandant.**

It was a sturdy factory-like building with the commandant's office on the second floor straight ahead from the entrance. For some reason, climbing those stairs reminded me of my first day of school back in Düsseldorf. I had the same pangs of apprehension and fear of the unknown. However, it looked like this assignment would be much less pleasant.

I did recall grade school was my first meeting with Ezekiel. I certainly valued our friendship and wished he were here to join me now.

The inside of the factory-like building had a strange odor I couldn't quite place. It was somewhat moldy with the pungent smell of cleaning solution or bleach. I wasn't sure if I should ask the guard what the smell was coming from, but he stopped and knocked at the door with the commandant's name on the plaque — black lettering on a painted white sign.

The secretary bid us to enter, and the guard dropped my bag by her desk and immediately left after wishing me well with my training.

The older secretary looked emaciated with a full head of dead grey hair, pasty skin, and several missing teeth. Her back looked permanently hunched, and it appeared painful for her to raise her head to look up at my six foot four and a half inch frame.

I smiled and introduced myself, but didn't even think about how she would look without her clothes. She asked me to sit down and wait for the *Hauptsturmführer.* Her voice was kind enough, but it came out like a wheeze. I noticed an ashtray full of cigarette stubs and one half-smoked sitting in a tray on her desk. A small curl of smoke was coming from her last half-gone cigarette. I was now having severe second thoughts about my ability to maintain my sanity while hiding my real feelings in an *SS* uniform.

The General was a tough old bastard. He must have been somewhere in his fifties. The stiffness of age hadn't entirely caught up with him, but his girth made him struggle to get out of his chair when I entered his office. The general then gave up and slumped back down into his chair. He was pleasant enough while he explained the camp routine for the month of training. He advised my entering *SS* colleagues and me not to discuss anything with the prisoners or their guards. He explained most of the guards were also prisoners, but these individual prisoners or *Kapos* were somewhat more trustworthy than the general prisoner population. They also received better food and separate rooms. Sometimes they could also wear civilian clothing.

The commandant also advised me never to discuss any of the medical experiments ongoing at Dachau.

In my blatant stupidity and naiveté, I asked, "What medical experiments?"

The commandant advised me, "We have a famous doctor here a Dr. Rascher, who is conducting experiments geared to saving our downed flyers and Wehrmacht officers who are exposed to extreme freezing weather."

I decided to keep my mouth shut and say nothing. But the commandant's words were confusing to me, so I decided to ask one of the Kapos after lunch exactly what medical experiments were being conducted at Dachau.

I talked with a Kapo named Glender after grabbing a quick lunch at the officer's mess hall.

Glender's description of the freezing experiments almost left me paralyzed. It took me several minutes to regain my focus.

Glender stated Dr. Rascher's experiments were divided into two groups: The first group was to see how much cold a human being could endure before he died. The second group was designed to see what was the best means of rewarming a person who had been exposed to extreme cold.

I asked Glender, "How did they determine the results?"

"Oh, stated Glender, "Dr, Rascher just tied the prisoner to a stretcher, placed a thermometer in the prisoner's rectum, and left him or her outside in freezing weather. Every hour the doctor or his associate would throw a bucket of cold water on the prisoner. He had to conduct his experiments away from the camp buildings because of the terrible heart-rendering cries and pathetic howls of the prisoners."

He did mention it took much longer for the female victims to die. "The women would sometimes last all night."

"I'm sure the cries of the suffering would rent the night," I exclaimed. "Did anyone have any compassion for those poor souls?"

"Compassion for prisoners meant an immediate trip to the ovens," claimed Glender.

I had heard more than enough. Communicating these horrors to Zeke would strengthen our resolve to maximize our efforts to reduce the population of the *Gestapo*.

My next thought was to complain about the medical experimentation to the commandant, General Piorkowski. Glender's warning echoed in my brain. As I approached the commandant's building, he was out front speaking to a group of new *SS* trainees.

The General informed us the last group of new trainees would be transferred in one hour to a new labor camp for additional training at Auschwitz in the new territories. We left mid-afternoon. *I thought to myself, perhaps a new detention facility would have better facilities for the detainees and surely no medical experimentation on live patients.*

I was very wrong.

Our first evening I ate dinner at the central dining commons for the *SS* officers, guards, and all the trainees for the work camp officers at Auschwitz. After our meal, we had a series of short talks from the *SS* guards who were training the new officers for essential positions within the *SS*.

Interestingly enough, one of the guards was a woman! I'm not sure why I found it surprising. I had heard and seen many of the detainees (prisoners) in the camps were women and children.

What was surprising was the forcefulness of her presentation. She started in a kindly almost meek, grandmotherly voice stating concerns many of us expressed about watching over such a large population of prisoners. As her presentation progressed, her voice became more and more strident, almost jarring. It seemed like she might actually explode in a cloud of venom. When she started bellowing about prisoner treatment, I felt like running out of the room.

Then a strange thing happened, she got quiet, and a handler brought in two wolfhound dogs. They were both on short choker chain leashes and muzzled. Both dogs seemed very friendly to the woman speaker and controller, but they were about the scariest hounds I had ever seen. They looked like a combination of wolfhound and German Sheppard. I'm sure they each weighed over one hundred pounds.

I had been bitten once by a large dog as a child, so I had a natural disinclination to get too friendly with any of "man's best friends." But it was the speaker's next statement which left a mark on my psyche: "We find my two ravenous dogs are the best means of controlling our prison population. If a prisoner steps over the line of our rules here at Auschwitz, Hansel and Gretel will make short work of them. They particularly enjoy not only tearing a prisoner apart but also chewing on their genitals!"

This woman, I could never forget her name, Juana Bormann, was the first woman I had ever met who made me feel physically sick; I thought I might start crying. I was so distraught I had to continually concentrate on not let my emotions show, or she might turn the dogs loose on me!

Just when I started thinking the situation couldn't possibly get any worse, the guard who brought in the dogs spoke up. The new *SS* guard trainee next to me whispered, "This guard is an extraordinary case. Her name is Irma Grese. She often beats the prisoners into unconsciousness, throws women and children to her dogs, selects women and men who won't have sex with her for the gas chambers, and enjoys target practice with her pistol on live prisoners."

Although traumatized by my initial introduction to labor camp life, the rest of the training went more smoothly than I could have hoped. Most of the training was a lot like Hitler Camp with a somewhat fancier uniform. We only "dressed up" for our parades and graduation. The primary emphasis was on ruthlessness toward "Jews and other undesirables (*Untermensch*)," and courtesy toward fellow *Nazis* and their families.

The training made us hard, ruthless, and uncaring for a particular portion of the German population and people from the occupied territories and anyone from the East. The term "*Untermensch*" referred to non-Aryan or "inferior people."

On several occasions, I wanted to vomit.

After training at Dachau and Auschwitz, my next assignment was to a labor camp in East-Central Germany. *Buchenwald* was a forced labor camp near the town of Weimar. It was a beautiful August day when I arrived. It was a Tuesday when I was driven up to the detention camp from the railroad station by an enlisted *Wehrmacht* corporal. I wanted to ask him about train schedules because I wanted to make plans to get the train to Hannover and see Ilsa the next weekend.

I reported to the commandant of the prison camp at 11 am on August 1st, 1939. My heart sank as I entered the detention center and got a good look at what was taking place. Then my fears were confirmed when I met the commandant, *SS-Oberführer* Hans Loritz.

"Good Morning Herr Commandant," was my rather benign greeting. His face was disarmingly handsome with a kind look aged by a flurry of wrinkles, strain, and probably the ambition of rank. His demeanor, however, was the harshest, cruelest, and most sadistic for a camp commandant I had ever encountered. He had just been transferred from another labor camp, *Sachsenhausen*, and did not look happy to be at his current posting.

He initially ignored me then grunted, "Son, you will learn to work within our system here at *Buchenwald*. We have many hardened criminals in our camp, and we are rapidly expanding. We have many Jewish men, women, children, and all sorts of handicapped and retarded *untermensch* living in close quarters. Do not turn your back on them and do not show them any mercy, **ever!**"

The bile and anger were rising in my throat. I knew my face could not relay my true feelings, so I said, "Yes, Sir. I will find my quarters."

In the evening one of the older guards, Slater, had a word of warning for me. "Be very careful of all the guards, even the female guards. There is one named Koch the inmates call the 'Bitch of Buchenwald.' Avoid any contact with her or any of the people close to her."

"What is the problem with this particular guard?" was my foolish query.

Unfortunately, Slater told me. "This guard enjoys whipping and beating inmates. Those poor prisoners who have tattoos on their bodies are immediately killed, their skin is removed with the tattoo, and this Koch guard makes the prisoner's skin into lampshades, gloves, and coverings for her books!"

I heard all I needed to hear about guard Koch. I did eventually hear she married a new commandant at Buchenwald. Guard Koch married another *SS* officer, who was her equal in being ruthless brutal and cruel.

From the moment I arrived, I started planning a way out. This camp was one of forced labor, and the inmates were in horrible shape. I started thinking of some way to be transferred.

All the *SS* guards except Slater I had met the first day seemed to be a very disagreeable group with not a shred of a sense of humor. They were all from the *SS-Totenkopfverbände* (Death's Head) units. Maybe one had to be mean and ugly to even get into this unit. I certainly wanted no part in it.

I could have been wrong, but my best guess was between the commandant and the guards, most of these folks had found a dead-end for their military careers.

In the evening I wrote to the Commandant of the *SS* Headquarters in Berlin stating my engineering expertise would make me more valuable to the Reich if I were more effectively allocated. I did use a little poetic license in exaggerating my engineering experience.

By writing to the Head of the Berlin office of the *SS* before my paperwork got cleared for check-in at the labor camp, I was hopeful I wouldn't have to go up through the chain of command.

Sure enough, within the week I had orders to a "special weapons facility" in a secret location on the coast of northern Germany. The orders looked official enough. I was to take rail transportation to Hamburg and meet with the head of the *SS* in the *Neuengamme* Concentration Camp. The commandant of the camp would issue me "final orders."

The orders for the special weapons facility arrived on a Wednesday, the week after my getting to the Buchenwald Camp.

I was to transfer to another labor or concentration camp. I had one week to get there. It occurred to me Hamburg was on the way, sort of, to Hannover. Perhaps I could manage to see Ilsa in between postings.

After the evening meal, I talked with the secretary to the Commandant of the Camp. She seemed like a reasonably kind middle-aged woman with, I hoped, no particular ax to grind.

"Frau," I asked, how far from Hamburg is my new posting at *Neuengamme?*"

"Herr Lieutenant, you will need to take a taxi approximately 12 kilometers south-west of the center of Hamburg."

"Thank you so much; you are a dear person. By the way, just how many of these prison camps are there now in Germany?"

"The number is a state secret, lieutenant, but many more than you could imagine."

I didn't want to press the issue, but it got me thinking, what the devil were the politicians going to do with all these labor camps? Why do the *Nazis* have so many? Do the politicians intend to imprison everyone in the *Reich* who disagrees with them? Is unthinkable medical experimentation going on in all the labor camps?

The Wehrmacht had already gone into and annexed Austria and Czechoslovakia. The current rumor was Hitler was considering marching the *Wehrmacht* into Poland. My feeling was another war might be right around the corner.

My ride to the train in Hamburg was uneventful. As I walked through the station, I couldn't tell if people were staring at me out of respect or just hate and disgust.

CHAPTER 23

Ensnared by the Gestapo

It was in Hamburg where the very clever concealment of my true feelings toward the *Nazis* and the *Third Reich* seemed to unravel a bit.

A *Gestapo* agent met me on the train platform. Initially, I thought he was there to give me a ride to *Neuengamme* Concentration Camp. I told him I needed to make a call before we got in his car for the trip. I wanted to call Ilsa and let her know where I was to set up a time for our visit over the weekend. I asked the agent to get my bag I had carried out onto the platform.

"Lieutenant, get your own bag! I am here to arrest you and to escort you to *the Gestapo* headquarters in Hamburg. We have some questions for you."

The platform wasn't crowded, so I was pretty sure no travelers could over hear the agent. It was kind of a sleepy summer day with the bustle of passengers going in several different directions.

I tried to act very relaxed about his words. But his tone sounded like a death sentence. His face got all pinched and narrow looking, almost rat-like but with a high forehead going quickly to what was probably a balding dome under his black fedora.

I assessed one on one, he would be no problem for me to take out. I didn't know what he might have for back-up in his automobile or at *Gestapo* Headquarters. Also, I was somewhat interested in what the hell had sparked his curiosity.

"Agent, surely, you are mistaken, but let's go to headquarters, to iron this out."

I started to get in the front seat of his car, but he stopped me.

"Lieutenant, you get in the back seat. Do I need to handcuff you? Do not cause trouble."

I thought to myself, what the devil is going on. Germany has become an actual police state. I quietly wondered if any of our deceased Gestapo friends could have been linked to Zeke or me.

"As you wish agent. But for the record, you are making a serious mistake."

"It is you, Lieutenant, who has made a mistake. You have betrayed the Fatherland."

"On what basis are you making these absurd accusations, agent?"

I tried to settle into the back seat. I stretched my legs to the other side of the automobile, otherwise, my legs just wouldn't fit. I appeared comfortable and relaxed.

"I have done some research on my own and discovered you might have Jews in your family! I have done some looking into another *SS* officer named Otto Rahn and found he also had tainted Jewish blood through his mother."

"Have you had a chance to 'interview' my mother?"

"Not yet, Lieutenant, we will get to your family next week. Your interview this afternoon will depend on how extensively we will need to question your family. I'm planning on you being cooperative, so we will not have to send your parents to *Dachau.*"

"You couldn't be more ridiculous. Have you shared any of these crazy thoughts with any of our colleagues?"

"No. Not yet, Lieutenant. I will question you at *Gestapo* Headquarters first. I sincerely hope I do not have to use 'extreme' measures."

I remarked, "I will report my answers truthfully to my ability. However, I want my answers recorded and given to your superiors at headquarters; in case there are any adverse repercussions for you."

I was trying to plant a little insecurity in the agent's mind. I remained silent for the rest of the ride to headquarters. I did notice there were no door handles on the inside of the rear doors of the automobile. What is wrong with these people!

Gestapo Headquarters was a massive turn of the century building housing the *Gestapo* and several other *Nazi* government organizations. It seemed the favorite *Nazi* architecture was made from large slabs of granite and cement. I was led directly to an interview room in the cellar where Agent Keller introduced himself and ordered me to sit in the lone chair in the middle of the room. The room had an odor of cleaning solution I couldn't quite place. It wasn't overpowering, but it was pervasive. I wondered at the time if the smell was part of the torture routine in this chamber.

There must have been some sort of sound deadening material in the walls and ceiling. There was no sound reverberations; our words were immediately swallowed by the soundproofing.

The agent then proceeded to handcuff me through the arm rails of the chair. He assured me it was for procedural reasons only. The agent chained me to a large wooden chair with secure looking wooden armrests. I didn't resist, because I knew I could pick up the chair and bash the agent's head with it if the interrogation got too intense.

Then the *Gestapo* agent Keller removed my hat, put on leather "work" gloves and smacked me sharply across my face with the warning, " **You will now tell me the truth. What are your origins?"**

I replied in as calm a voice as I could muster with my nose bleeding and my top teeth feeling loose when I ran my tongue behind them, **"Agent Keller, you have just made the most grievous mistake of your life. You might say a most serious, career-ending mistake."**

"I don't think so, Lieutenant. When I share my findings with my superiors, you will wish I had killed you quickly. With some more consistent and frankly horrific techniques we use here at *Gestapo* Headquarters, you will tell us everything we want to know and more!"

Agent Keller seemed pretty sure of himself. He had a rather cold smirk on his face. I could taste the saltiness of my bleeding mouth. His brazenness irked me even more because I was a little hungry.

I had to plan my next move rather carefully. Timing is everything in these situations. The door was locked from the inside with a key; I did not want to be interrupted after the agent took another swing at me with his padded leather gloves.

I could see him wind up for a sidearm swing at my face. As the blow was about to hit me, I jerked my head back and caused the chair to tip backward. I caught a glancing blow, but only with the brush of his knuckles.

I continued to push the chair back with my heels until it crashed back onto the floor. I dropped my chin to my chest so the back of my head wouldn't bang onto the cement. As I was going over backward, I forcibly squeezed my shoulders together and brought my elbows suddenly into my chest. My chest and forearms were amazingly muscular, even when I was a young teenager. As a result, both wooden chair arm rails snapped right off the chair. Sometimes I don't know my strength. But, I will have to admit, Agent Keller's slaps to my face got me a bit angry. I will also have to admit I hadn't had anything to eat since breakfast. Perhaps I should have warned Agent Keller I get a little testy when I'm hungry.

This little maneuver freed me from the chair. As I got to my feet, I clasped my hands together in a praying grasp and hit agent Keller as hard as I could on the side of his head. I was almost a head taller than him, and I had at least fifty pounds on him. He went down with a splash of blood, holding his head and staring at me in total surprise. I knew I had fractured his skull; he went down pretty hard.

He was down, but not quite out, so I straddled him and collapsed his windpipe with my thumbs until he stopped breathing. I kept my knee on his chest to keep him stable. Also, I pressed my knee into his diaphragm to quickly expel any air stored in his lungs. I then shouted into his ear: **"This is what I meant by a career-ending mistake!"**

He quickly turned crimson red then purple. He was angry but helpless. He tried a futile kick to my groin, but then his legs went into spasm. I was not about to let go of his throat. I held on until I couldn't feel any carotid pulse.

My next task was to position the agent so it looked like he slipped during the interrogation. I smashed the back of his head onto the cement floor and smeared a little blood around on the floor.

I then pieced back the wooden arm rails of the chair after placing my handcuffs around the arms of the chair. I then sat back and waited.

Patience is not my best attribute, especially when I'm hungry. It was getting on toward late afternoon. I waited for over an hour before there was a knock at the door. I yelled, "Come in, quickly!" and the Chief of Station, *Gestapo Headquarters*, Hamburg, burst into the interrogation room, leaving the door wide open.

"What has happened?" he shouted.

I explained, "I had been handcuffed to the chair, and Agent Keller had started to question me."

I then showed him by pointing my foot how he had slipped on the floor and hit his head, but, "I had called and tried to get help, but he must have lost consciousness and passed out. Perhaps no one could hear my call for help."

"No," the agent remarked, "These rooms are sound-proof for a reason."

"Okay," I replied. Please release these stupid handcuffs immediately. Are you people accustomed to questioning the loyalty of *Waffen Schutzstaffel* Lieutenants?

"I can't set you free! Agent Keller must have restrained you for a reason. You will have to wait until a shift change at six O'clock when I can consult with the station chief."

"Is there no one else here? Or anyone you can call?"

"Sorry no, Lieutenant. I cannot release you, and there is no one else in our department. There must be a warrant or charge for you to be held and restrained here at headquarters."

"Agent, what is your name and rank?"

"Why do you need my name and rank?"

"Because, dear friend, you are the second person today to make a career-ending mistake!"

"What the devil are you talking about?"

"This!" I shouted as I leaped out of the chair and caught the shocked agent with a sharp uppercut to his lower jaw. I hit him with the side of the chair arm. My fist was wrapped tightly around the arm.

His astonishment was complete. As his head snapped back, I landed a swift punch to his throat, crushing his trachea. He went down, clutching his throat, making horrible gasping sounds; I think he was swearing. Blood was gushing from his mouth where his broken teeth went through his lip.

He watched me walking over to pick up my hat. I gave him a look of disdain, and forcefully remarked, **"Now do you understand what I meant by a career-ending mistake?"**

It took three or four minutes for him to stop squirming around before his ungodly death rattle.

I solved the dilemma of what to do with the two dead agents while I was waiting for the second agent to die. I thought if these folks could torch and burn almost fourteen hundred synagogues on the ninth and tenth of November last year, I should be able to torch one *Gestapo Headquarters* with a clear conscience.

There were no flammable liquids I could readily find, but I came across a gas jet outlet and coils of tubing attached to a blow-torch-like mechanism. It passed through my mind this device might be used to burn people during "extreme" interrogation and torture. I began to think of a way to turn this gas outlet into an inferno for the headquarters building. I opened the valve on the gas jet for a moment, and the smell of gas was quite evident.

The awareness the *Gestapo* could burn people for torture solidified in my mind, these people were indeed animals. I asked myself, where is God during these horrific interrogation events? I hoped the good Lord would forgive me for my actions this day.

My goal was to burn down the building and destroy any evidence of my incarceration and at the same time, make it look accidental. The accident must look like it might have happened during an unsuccessful interrogation session.

There was a pack of cigarettes in the second agent's pocket. I withdrew and lit two cigarettes and placed them on the seat of the broken chair approximately two feet off the floor. I then opened the gas petcock to fully open, maximum flow, and quickly left the room and closed the door.

I was halfway down the street getting into a taxi when there was a tremendous clap of thunder and deep rumble in the block behind me in the direction of the office building I had just left. The noise was much louder than I anticipated. Parts of the building flew in all directions.

The taxi driver remarked, "I thought we were supposed to be bombing Poland, not the *Reich!*"

My comment, "Please take me to the Neuengamme Camp. The loud rumble was probably just a gas explosion."

I reported to the Commandant *SS* officer *Sturmbannführer* Walter Eisfeld at the *Neuengamme* Concentration Camp just after 7 pm. early in the evening. The sun was starting to get low in the sky, and there was a bit of a cool breeze. I was still a little shook up from my close encounter with the ruthlessness of *Gestapo* Agent Keller.

The commandant greeted me warmly and gave me orders. He gave me a quick tour of the open areas and showed me to the officer quarters. He remarked, "Lieutenant, this is a forced labor camp. Also, our food supplies are inefficient. Most of our inmates die in the first three months of their imprisonment from malnutrition and diarrhea. I will tell you, however, certain groups of prisoners are allowed food packages from their families or the Red Cross. These 'gifts from our *Führer*' are for those who are valued workers."

I couldn't help myself with the comment, "Wouldn't the *Reich* be better served if the all the inmates were better fed?"

The commandant's harsh retort, **"Do not let anyone hear you talk of such things!"** Then he continued quietly, "Most of the beef, grain, dairy, and vegetables are reserved and supplied to the *Wehrmacht*, *SS* and important *Nazi* politicians."

The commandant suggested I open and followed my new orders to the letter and leave as soon as possible. He then emphasized, "At Neuengamme the philosophy was the same as camps throughout the *Reich:* **extermination through labor!"**

His face became distorted, almost disfigured as he snarled the words through curled lips. His transformation into something vile and evil encouraged me to make a hasty retreat and plan my train ride to my next duty station: Peenemünde, Germany. The orders were explicit in dictating the time I was to arrive and my mode of travel, but I still unsure of the type of facility awaiting me.

Although he gave me a feeling of foreboding, Commandant Eisfeld arranged a ride for me to the railroad station to get the train to Peenemünde.

CHAPTER 24

Apprehended by Gestapo Agents on the Train to Hannover

I had to wait three hours for an overnight train going through Lubeck and Rostock and then probably painstakingly slowly on to Greifswald with a bus to Peenemünde. Instead of waiting for a train heading toward Peenemünde, I took a train heading for Hannover directly from Hamburg. It seemed very doable since I had about a week before I needed to show up at Peenemünde. I was not at all sure what awaited me at my next duty station, so I was in no rush to arrive early. I sincerely hoped it wasn't another labor camp.

I called Ilsa before boarding. She said she would meet me at the central railroad station in Hannover and meet the train from Hamburg. Out of caution, I never identified myself or used any names at all. On the train to Hannover, I tried to consider if I should confide completely in Ilsa and let her know of Zeke and my plans for somehow easing the terror engulfing the Jews and many others in our university and country. She was already well aware of my elimination of Klaus, the *Gestapo* agent who had terrorized her. I thought it important for her to know my plans since my heart was already dedicated to her. It would be critical; however, she would confide in no one else.

The train ride indeed wasn't luxurious, but if anything a little tiring. It felt good to relax and put the horrors of the recent "interrogation" behind me. The rhythmic clack of the train motion helped me relax.

As I was reading over the evening newspaper left on the seat by an earlier passenger, two men dressed in dark clothing approached my bench seat and said they would be joining me. They sat directly across and immediately began a conversation; it sounded a lot like an interrogation.

"What is your name, Lieutenant, and where are you going?"

"What business is it of yours; are you part of the military?"

"We are Gestapo, Lieutenant. Let me introduce Agent Schroder, and I am Agent Becker." The agent flipped open a wallet and showed a badge. "**Again, I will ask you for the last time, your name and destination.**" Becker was loud and obnoxious. Other passengers were looking at the three of us.

It passed through my mind as I was trying to frame a decent reply, these Gestapo Agents haven't been the brightest people I've ever run into. I wonder how the Reich recruits these cretins.

"I am *SS* Lieutenant Jenz Ramsgrund," I replied in a calm and measured tone of voice. "I have orders for the Army Weapons Research Center in Peenemünde, Germany* for no later than September 1ˢᵗ, 1939." I pulled out my orders and showed them to agent Becker, who seemed to be in charge.

---

* *Peenemünde was a small town in Northern Germany located on Usedom Island in the Baltic Sea. The Reich Air Ministry had purchased the entire northern peninsula of the island for 750,000 Reichsmarks in 1936 to use as a research center to develop and test military rockets. The Wehrmacht had found a loophole in the Treaty of Versailles ending The Great War: the treaty did not cover the development of rocket technology for military use.*

"Should I remind you, Lieutenant, this train is traveling away from the destination of your orders?"

"I am traveling in the direction I wish to go. I still have one week before I am required to be at the Army Weapons Research Center."

"Lieutenant, we have several other questions for you regarding your family and friends. Are you aware members of your family are Jewish and they are friendly with other Jews in Düsseldorf?"

"I'm not sure who or what you are referring to Agent Schroder. My family has many friends in Düsseldorf, and I am not of aware of all their religious backgrounds. However, if we could talk somewhere quietly, where we could not be overheard, it would be better for security purposes. My orders are highly confidential. I'm sure I can explain my orders and family background to your satisfaction."

"I hope you can, Lieutenant. Follow us to the rear of the train. Consider yourself under detention, and I should remind you we are both armed."

As we got up, several of our fellow passengers watched with quiet resignation. It was almost as if they knew I was in trouble and might be under arrest by the *Gestapo*. The middle-aged woman directly opposite me had a terrible frown on her face. Perhaps this woman had experienced recent terror in her life.

I put a casual smile and look of disdain on my face and gave her a wink of acknowledgment to try to alleviate her immediate concerns and perhaps the fears of the other travelers. I wanted to assure the agents I had nothing to hide. I straightened my uniform jacket, grabbed my hat from the overhead compartment, and walked between the agents to the rear of the train. I had to duck between the cars to clear the doorways. The openings were just not meant for individuals much over six feet tall.

I had to be very careful with these two. These agents were a little larger than previous rat-faced thugs portending to be *Gestapo* agents. Becker was quite muscular with a thick neck. Schroder while quite tall, but looked more like a school teacher with pasty skin and no lips. Becker was the one to eliminate as a threat first. He was following directly behind me. Schroder would have to wait his turn to be put down. I just had to figure out how to get to them.

The train was swaying gently back and forth and had some jerking motions as we hit curves and straight-aways. The larger more substantial agent was behind me, but he hadn't drawn his weapon. I was walking steadily and wasn't causing any delays or adverse movements. I tried to see the reflection of the agent behind me in the windows of the train as I moved toward the last car. He stayed about three steps behind me.

As we entered the last car on the train, it was empty. There was a small table bolted to the floor and seating on the sides of the compartment. There were windows in the car, but the shades were drawn even though it was almost dark outside. There was a lantern burning on the back wall, but there was only minimal light in the car. It reminded me of a dark tunnel with a light at the end of it. It passed through my mind, this car could be set up for interrogation purposes. The rest of the passengers would not hear the sound of their fellow riders being tortured.

Becker was the last one to get fully through the door, and he turned away from me to close and lock the sturdy wooden oak door to the caboose. Agent Schroder was facing away from me as he proceeded into the end of the railroad car straining to see in the dim light.

At the same moment the train jerked slightly, I pivoted on my right heal and brought all my weight with my elbow in a hammer-like blow to the left side of Agent Becker's head. The blow was directly over his temple just above his ear. I could feel bone-crunching under the weight of my elbow. His head snapped back and made a severe cracking sound onto the oak door he had just locked. Blood spattered from the angle blow of my elbow down onto his cheek.

Becker's head cracking against the door alerted the other agent. So I shouted at Agent Schroder, **"Please do not make a career-ending mistake!"** But he drew his weapon anyway. As he brought it up toward me, I took two quick steps forward and gave his hand and pistol a vicious kick sending the gun sprawling to the far end of the car. Schroder then made an additional mistake of turning and going after it.

It took only a quick two strides for me to pounce on him like a furious and enraged jackal. A hard blow to his back just below his neck snapped his head back and sent him flying onto the small table. I grabbed him off the table and gave him a rabbit chop to the trachea which seemed to put him entirely out of action. The second blow was probably unnecessary because I think I broke his neck with my first strike. He hit the floor and didn't move.

I immediately went to check on Agent Becker, who was bleeding profusely from his head where it had struck the locked door. Also, blood was flowing freely from his left ear and around the temple area. However, he was still alive and staggering around swearing loudly at me. I took off my uniform pants belt and wrapped it snugly around his neck, tightened it with all my strength and synched up and locked the belt for maximum tightness. He clawed at his throat and tried to reach for his pistol. I pulled his arm away from his holster and dislocated his elbow over my knee and broke it. It snapped like a wooden tree limb. He watched me with dying eyes as I went to check agent Schroder.

I couldn't resist shouting at Becker, "**Let this be a lesson to you. Never disrespect an SS officer, especially when he is hungry.**" I probably shouldn't have tormented the poor bastard, but I couldn't resist.

Both agents were dead within five minutes, but now I had the problem of disposal of their sorry carcasses. I removed all identification and their pistols and holsters. Since they had no use for it, I also took their available cash.

I removed Schroder's shirt and cleaned up Becker's blood on the door. I then proceeded to retrieve my uniform belt and put it back on. I dragged both agents to the front of the last car and dumped them on the tracks between the train coaches. Schroder went first because he was the lightest. There was a slight almost negligible bump as the train wheels sliced up the corpse. There was a slightly larger bump as Becker was sliced and diced by the steel train wheels.

I wanted the bodies so dismembered by this and future trains so they would not be able to be identified. I hoped additional trains, weather, animals, and time would minimize any of their remains.

Their pistols were taken apart and tossed out the window one piece at a time. The holsters followed. Their wallets were taken apart, and the identification ripped up and tossed. Their badges were flatted with my heal and scaled into the first body of water we came near.

God would have to deal with me later. It took me a while to get my heart beating normally again. It surprised me I wasn't overwhelmed by guilt. I went back and sat in the back of the car one car behind from where I was initially sitting and fell fast asleep while praying God would find me fair and just. I don't think I moved until the train pulled into Hannover. I did, however, have some pleasant thoughts about my dear Ilsa.

I met Ilsa at our usual spot near the ticket office. It was so good to see her again. Although my face had a broad smile, she could tell something was on my mind. She hugged me and asked, "What is going on in your complex brain, Jenz?"

The station was cavernous, but there were a few travelers about and I didn't want to be overheard. I was getting a little paranoid about the *Gestapo* being everywhere.

"I am anxious to tell you everything as soon as we are sure of being alone. It is late, but do you mind walking."

"No, not at all. My parents are expecting us."

"Dearest Ilsa, what I am going to tell you cannot be shared with anyone. You cannot confide in your parents, relatives, or even your closest friends."

We were walking out of the station on the city streets. Her home was north of the city center seven or eight kilometers from the railroad station. Although late evening, there were quite a few folks about near the station. It was a chilly but pleasant evening with a brilliant half moon high in the sky. As we got away from the city center, the stars came out and walking was quite enjoyable after the stress on the train. Walking seemed to energize me. It felt good to stretch out my legs.

I told Ilsa everything in pretty gritty detail. "My Jewish friend Zeke and I are doing everything we can to disrupt the *Gestapo* and the *SS* from hurting our Jewish friends, fellow students, neighbors, and countrymen. We have eliminated a half dozen of these creeps in addition to Klaus Friedrich, the agent who tried to terrorize you in Berlin."

"Believe me; he did more than try! Jenz, it sounds so dangerous! What will happen if they catch you?"

"They have already tried to trap me twice with armed agents. So far, we have been fortunate to outmaneuver them. I probably sound crazy, but the Good Lord might be on our side right at the moment."

We were coming to a more rural area with middle-class neighborhoods and parks. We were close to the banks of a river before we turned uphill to Ilsa's parents home. Their home was a modest home in a decent neighborhood with a small lot of land and a vacant lot next door.

I wanted to make sure her parents were okay with my staying with their daughter.

"Ilsa, are you sure your parents don't mind my being in your home?"

"Not only are they looking forward to your visit, but they would like an update on the military news. There is so much in the papers about the Polish question. Also, they want to hear a military view on the Anschluss in Austria and what is happening in Czechoslovakia."

"From what I can tell, my dearest Ilsa, our country is building many labor camps throughout the *Reich* and the protectorate countries. These labor camps imprison people who are Jewish or who disagree politically with the *Nazi Party* in general or our *Führer* in particular."

As we were entering her home, I remarked, "Remember, not a word to anyone!"

CHAPTER 25

Parental Concern and Acceptance

Ilsa's parents were very welcoming and offered me hot chocolate when we got to their home. After a bit of conversation about recent political and military events, they told us they were going to bed because they needed to get up early to get to work. Ilsa fixed me two chicken sandwiches because she knew I was always hungry. I didn't think it would have been appropriate to mention I could have eaten a third.

After her parents had retired, Ilsa began teasing me. "I know you have had a busy and stressful day. Would you like to use our guest bedroom, or would you prefer to sleep with a warm and caring woman."

I decided to give it back to her. I asked her with a sincere and inquiring look on my face, "how is your dear friend Gretchen?"

She put her arms around me and pushed me into a stuffed chair.

"I will show you how she is, and it will make you forget all about her forever."

She kissed me on the cheek, grabbed my hand, and pulled me upstairs into her bedroom.

Ilsa then proceeded to strip off all my clothing until I was completely naked on her bed. It was a little chilly, but when I tried to pull the sheet over me, she pulled it away, leaving me somewhat exposed. She was still fully clothed and was ignoring my swelling privates.

It was almost as if she was thinking about something else when she decided to notice my privates and issued a quick slap directly on them.

"Oh, she smiled with mock surprise, did I hurt them?"

Her eyes were shining and twinkling with desire as she whispered in my ear, "I will need to kiss them to make them better."

I had no idea of what she was talking about until she gently grasped my genitals and started kissing me on the stomach while massaging the underside of my genitals.

As she inched lower, my entire body started to vibrate inside. I don't think it was outwardly apparent, but I had tingling all over. The sensation seemed to emanate from my midsection.

I wasn't sure what to do. I couldn't move, even if I had wanted to.

She murmured, "I want to make sure it is **all** better," as she started kissing my member. She kept talking while kissing and licking me with her tongue. "I want to make sure I didn't hurt you, darling." All this time, she kept a steady stream of one-sided discussion while she gently massaged, squeezed, and licked my genitals.

If I had tried to join in the conversation, my speech would have been slurred and unintelligible.

I began to wonder if this was where the term "died and gone to heaven" had originated.

Then she stopped. I urged her to "please don't stop. I will do anything you would like, don't stop!"

"Oh, dear me Jenz, I'm getting warm and should take off some of my clothing."

Next, she started the slowest strip tease anyone could do. She shed her garments one at a time and folded them neatly on a chair. When she got to her underwear, I was very clearly out of my mind and crazy with desire for her.

She slowly got on the bed beside me but would not let me get on top of her. Her excuse, "We have to go slowly; it has been too long since you have been here."

I was not rational by this point, and she was very definitely in control. She seemed to know exactly what she was doing. She toyed with me by gently squeezing my genitals and then pinching and nibbling me on my chest.

She then got on top of me and held my member while gently gliding it into her.

I couldn't hold back any longer, but as I started to thrust, she put her hand on my chest and said: "**stop**, wait, enjoy me."

Enjoyment was probably the furthest thing from my mind. Enjoyment had turned into an urgent need.

She whispered in my ear, "I hope you will never forget me, Jenz." as she rhythmically started moving on top of me. "Don't you move!" she whispered. "I will do the moving for both of us."

Ohooo. was the only sound coming out of my mouth. I couldn't respond with anything intelligible, so I started kissing Ilsa on her head and telling her how much I loved her.

Then she whispered, you deserve to be treated better and started a more rapid rhythmic thrusting.

I could hold back no longer. My body went through some short circuit where my internal tingling vibrations changed to almost violent thrusting motions as I exploded into my dear friend Ilsa.

Afterward, she seemed to lie there and moan with pleasure. I hoped I hadn't hurt her. I told her she was absolutely correct, "I can't even remember your girlfriend's name. We both fell into a deep and welcomed sleep.

CHAPTER 26

The Gestapo Comes Calling For My Parents

The next morning Ilsa walked with me to the train station. It was cold, overcast, with a bit of snow in the air. I caught the early morning train to Düsseldorf. It was terrific to see my parents, but they were not happy with my *Gestapo* stories. I urged them and the Leven's to leave Germany as soon as humanly possible. Even though I was in the *SS,* I had no political clout and could be under an even further investigative cloud at any moment.

"Dad, it is important for you and Mom, and the Leven's to get out of Germany immediately. I have seen what goes on in the labor camps. They are working the inmates to death with inferior nutrition. If the work and poor food don't kill you, the diseases will. These poor folks have everything wrong with them from simple diarrhea to serious infections."

"Jenz, it would mean the Leven's and our family would have to leave everything, including our friends behind."

"It will be well worth it, Dad. You don't want to get near those concentration camps. The misery and suffering is overwhelming. The main problem will be if war does come, Germany's borders may be sealed. No one will be able to get out!"

It was getting late. I happened to glance out the front window and saw a dark sedan automobile pull up to our front walk.

"Mom, Dad!" I shouted with a loud whisper, "are you expecting visitors this late in the evening?"

"No son, why?"

"A dark, government-looking car just pulled up out front. Two very unsavory men are coming up the walk."

Mom asked, "Jenz, what could they possibly want at this time of night?"

"It can only be the *Gestapo*." was my quiet reply.

"I cannot let them take you to their headquarters for questioning. You will wind up in a concentration camp or worse."

"What can we do?" pleaded Mom.

"This will be tricky," I suggested. "The first agent has already drawn his weapon, and I will have to get rid of their automobile."

Bang, Bang, Bang. There were three loud knocks at the door; more like three hard bangs. It sounded like the first agent was using the butt of his pistol.

"Coming," I shouted. "Mom, Dad, quickly get into the cellar. Do not be alarmed if you hear a gunshot."

As soon as the cellar door had closed, I opened the door with a full sweeping motion and asked, "May I help you gentlemen this evening?"

They had a look of surprise on their faces when confronted with an *SS* officer in full uniform standing in front of them.

"We are here to interview Rolf and Hannah Ramsgrund and to learn the location of Dr. and Mrs. Leven. The Leven's are not in their home." The second agent opened a leather wallet with an ID card and badge of the *Gestapo*.

I replied as kindly as I could, "My parents are out for the evening, but I might be able to get you some information about the Leven's.

"If you will holster your weapon I will get you some coffee so we can discuss your request. Sir, I have to advise you, do not point the weapon in my direction."

I led them very carefully into the kitchen.

The first rat-faced agent replaced his pistol into his holster. They both followed me into the kitchen. They were both polite enough to remove their black fedoras.

I started to make coffee and asked how they liked it. Both wanted it black and the second agent, whom I felt some sympathy for because I knew what was ahead for him, asked for a small amount of sugar.

The larger, more substantial agent, who had entered our home first, had almost no neck. He was approximately five feet nine inches with a fair amount of muscle. He looked pretty muscular and had to be the first to go down. The second agent was thin, but wiry-looking with a beak-like nose and blotchy, uneven skin with stringy hair on its way to balding. I guessed they were both somewhere in their forties.

As I was preparing the hot coffee, I placed a heavy iron frying pan on the stove as I was getting out the coffee pot. I filled the pot with hot water from the tap and put it on the gas flame turned up high.

I had time while the water was heating to plan my next moves. With two armed men, one had to be a little careful during the take-down. I did not want any accidents.

As the water started to boil in the coffee pot, the take-down decision was made for me.

The larger of the two agents asked to use the restroom facilities.

I could hear him in there doing his business. The thinner agent with the beak-like nose turned and glanced toward the hall area leading to our bathroom.

I took the opportunity to pick up the heavy iron pan off the stove and quickly smash it over the stringy-haired agent's head. He never saw it coming and went down like a sack of sand. I literally brained him. Blood splashed on the wall, ceiling, and was all over the heavy cast iron pan. I put the pan in the sink; I'd wash the blood and hair fragments off later. I quickly dragged the agent into the living room and placed a throw cushion from the couch under his head so he wouldn't bleed out on the carpet.

I came back into the kitchen and turned the light off in the hall, so the splash of blood on the wall and ceiling wasn't too noticeable. The second agent was coming out of the bathroom.

He immediately asked, "Where is agent Shiller?"

"He went out to the car to get something he said he forgot," I answered while looking directly at the no-necked agent.

He started to go to the front hall of the house to see what the agent had forgotten.

I said, "Here, here's your coffee," I stammered, as I grabbed the cup and filled it with coffee. He took the cup, then turned to walk quickly to the front door.

I knew if he got to the end of the passageway, he would be able to look to his left and view the laid out dead agent. The agent was bleeding profusely with his head on the throw cushion.

As the agent arrived at the end of the hall, he glanced left and saw the dead or dying agent stretched out on the living room floor with his bloody head on the cushion.

As he realized what he was seeing, I brought the iron pan down on him as hard as I could. Unfortunately, the agent had turned his head enough so the glancing blow only stunned him temporarily. It did leave a sizable bloody gash on the side of his head behind his ear. He staggered and then went for his weapon. He was turning to look for me and bringing his gun to bare. I hit him again with the edge of the frying pan. I aimed for the base of his neck near the back of his head.

His legs shot straight out from under him, and he toppled like a tree. He smeared the wall with his blood which was gushing from the first glancing head blow. The neck blow must have pithed him like a frog, damaging his spinal cord.

His reflex action pulled the trigger on his weapon as I hit him at the base of his neck. The shot sounded like a cannon in our hall.

Both parents rushed upstairs. Dad yelled, "**My God, Jenz. What has happened! What have you done to these men?**"

I was on the floor, making sure the skinny agent had stopped breathing. I was pretty sure he had since I held my hand over his beak-like nose while pinching his nostrils together tightly. I couldn't feel a pulse in his carotid artery.

It was amazing how useful the Hitler Youth Camp had been for me.

"These *Gestapo* agents wanted to take you and Mom to their headquarters for questioning, and they wanted to know where the Leven's were located. You do know what happens to you once the *Gestapo* gets you to their headquarters, don't you?"

"Why would they bother us?"

"Mom, they would torture you until you confessed your faith; perhaps chopping off one finger at a time. After you confessed everything you knew about your family, the Leven's and your friends, they would send you both to a concentration camp. You would be lucky to last three months.

"The *Gestapo* has been rounding up Jews and anyone else who may disagree with the government policies.

"These two agents made a career-ending decision to get involved with my family; now we have to dispose of this garbage of human refuse carefully."

My mom could hardly speak. "Wha...What can we do with them, Jenz?" She was shaking pretty badly. I had turned the hall light back on. She nearly fainted to see all the blood on the walls and ceiling. I quickly rinsed the iron pan and cleaned it of hair and blood and placed it into the sink rack before she could see the tissue remains on it.

"Mom, get yourself under control, Dad and I will dispose of them and their automobile."

I dug the keys to the car out of the larger agent's pocket and put their car in our driveway behind the house. Dad and I put their blanket-wrapped bodies in the trunk one at a time.

The more substantial agent took both of us to carry, he was heavy with muscle. I was lucky to get him with the second blow from the iron pan; it was sloppy of me not to get him down on the first blow. Dad will have to refinish the floor where his bullet entered near the rug. I wasn't sure if the round had gone into the cellar.

We drove the agent's car and followed a route taking us south of the city on Volklinger Street and across the Rhine at Kolner Strasse. We turned off into a small park adjacent to the Rhine River. It was very dark in the park, but there was a slight slope going down to the river.

We needed the car and occupants to disappear into the river, so I opened the back windows to fill the vehicle with water quickly. The river was pretty deep and swift at this curve in the flow. We could see very few lights of the city across the river, and a few cars were following Hammer Deich Road on the other side. Much of Germany was following black-out requirements in the large cities.

I found a large flat rock for the gas pedal. Dad and I placed both agents in the front seat. The more substantial agent got to drive since the keys were in his pocket. After securing the rock on the accelerator and holding the steering wheel toward the water, I put the car in gear, released the clutch, and jumped free. I slammed the driver's door before I rolled away from the automobile.

The car rocketed into the swift-flowing Rhine and floated for a few seconds before filling with water. As it slowly sunk beneath the surface, I believed these two Gestapo Agents would not bother our fellow countrymen again. I uttered a prayer to God my father could hear: *please God forgive me for ridding these evil security police from our midst. Please watch over and protect my family, the Leven family, Ilsa's family, and our country. Amen.*

We walked back across the river until we came to the Hamm section of the city near the railway station and caught a taxi for home. Although it wasn't unusually cold in the city, I could feel a chill as we walked crossed the river.

Mom must have been emotionally exhausted. It was after midnight when we arrived back home. She was sprawled out on the couch, sound asleep with all the lights burning. Perhaps she didn't realize she was resting near the feet of where the dead agent had been lying. Fortunately, I had disposed of the pillow soaked with the agent's blood. Dad got her up to bed; she had a thousand questions. Dad just said, "we took care of the agents by giving them to God and the Rhine."

Dad and I scrubbed the blood from the wall and floor using dish soap and hot water.

CHAPTER 27

Peenemünde

I slept late the next morning and came down for breakfast at around 8 O'clock. I looked at the train schedule to start my trip to Peenemünde. The 11 am train to Bremen, and Hamburg seemed like the best bet. At 4 pm there was a train from Hamburg to Mecklenburg continuing to Greifswald. From Greifswald, I had to take about a 30-mile bus ride over some secondary roads to Peenemünde. It would have been hugely helpful if I had known what to expect at this duty station destination. I quickly learned it was not a concentration camp, although it was very well protected with high fencing and well guarded by the *SS* and a contingent from the *Wehrmacht*. Also, the workers at the Research Center, who were involved in the manufacturing of the weapons, were from the concentration camps.

I showed my orders to the guards at the main gate. They read: Report to the Peenemünde Army Weapons Research Center, no later than 1 September 1939. As I entered the base, there was some general excitement about the *SS* and the *Wehrmacht* marching into Poland. The Polish city of Danzig (renamed Gdansk after WW II) was not too far from the research center on the Baltic coast.

At this point in my life, it was hard to understand why the politicians in Germany were hell-bent on capturing more and more territory and expanding German influence into Eastern Europe.

I knew the German people felt unfairly treated by the results of the treaty ending The Great War. Invading another country was no reason to double down and further jeopardize the settlement and peace in Germany?

The guard at the main gate scrutinized my orders and had someone take me to the officer's quarters by motorcycle. My small overnight bag and I bounced around in the sidecar as we traveled up the bumpy road dodging the occasional pothole.

The quarters weren't luxurious by any stretch of the imagination, but they were a step up from the officer's quarters at the concentration camps. In the evening I learned where the officer's mess was located and learned about my one day of orientation for the Weapons Research Center.

The next day was spent touring and studying the different parts of the base. I also had to sign a non-disclosure agreement. The agreement specified I could not disclose anything I learned, observed, worked on, or invented with anyone outside the base, regardless of his rank or political position. The penalty was immediate imprisonment for not less than ten years!

It was on this first day of orientation I learned of Operation *Kirschkern* (Cherrystone) and Operation *Maikafer* (Maybug). These were popular German names for the development of an early cruise missile powered by a pulsejet engine. This weapon was a new flying bomb or *Vergeltungswaffe*. It eventually developed into the Vengeance Weapon 1, also known as the V-1.

This missile was called a reprisal weapon and was being developed to bomb cities indiscriminately in England and Europe. The guidance system in these weapons could only approximate where they were going to land within a 5-mile area. They were designed to bring terror to the population of targeted cities.

The use of the letter "V" was used initially to designate experimental *(Versuchsmuster)*. However, as the missiles were perfected, they became more compelling and useful in the *Reich's* terror bombing champagne and were termed "Vengeance Weapons."

I was one of a team of engineers who were enlisted to perfect and iron out the problems of the V-1 flying bomb. There were two main issues with this weapon: improving the guidance system and completing the fusing mechanism of the bomb.

The flying bomb was impressive as probably the first cruise missile. It was pretty evident to my fellow engineers and me at the *Heeresversuchsanstalt Peenemünde* (Peenemünde Army Research Center) Germany was headed for another war. This missile had a rudimentary guidance system with a warhead containing 1000 kg. of Amatol-39. The warhead had the explosive power of approximately 2000 pounds of TNT. The first problem my group of engineers was to solve was a way to fuse the warhead for maximum destruction.

The Amatol-39 was a mixture of TNT and ammonium nitrate. Although this mixture was highly explosive, the missile lacked accuracy. It flew for approximately one-half hour at almost 400mph, but when it ran out of fuel, it would plummet to earth and explode.

The cruel truth of this missile was whenever it happens to run out of fuel, the target was directly below. It was indeed a terror weapon and developed to instill terror into the cities and populations in its path.

My concern was this weapon could be used against my father's country, Sweden, or any of the cities or countries within its range. For me, it became a moral issue of the use of military weapons which were not defensible. Also, they might be used against our own country if the secret got out to Germany's victims or opponents in a war. I needed to talk about these issues with my father and my friend Ezekiel.

During my first week at Peenemünde, I consulted with the chief engineer leading the V-1 program, Herr Frits Gosslau. "Sir, would it be of any help to you to bring on another aeronautical engineer from the *Technische Hochschule Berlin* to aid with the guidance system of the V-1 missile?"

"Do you know such a person, Lieutenant Ramsgrund?"

"My suggestion is a trusted friend who is very skilled in physics and calculus, although he knows nothing of this particular system."

"Nor should he," shot back Gosslau. "Tell me more about this individual."

"His name is Vitali Carapezza, Sir. His home is in Italy, but he speaks fluent German. He is also an engineering student at the *Technische Hochschule* in Berlin. His field is Aeronautical Physics." *I had to stretch the truth a little to get Gosslau interested.*

"Thank you, Ramsgrund. He could be instrumental here. Of course, he will need to be checked by the usual channels and the *SS,* but I will let you know what they come up with in a few days. Please write down the spelling of his full name and the department for his course of studies."

Herr Gosslau called me into his office in 4 days. I feared the *SS* had discovered Vitali Carapezza was my boyhood and lifelong Jewish friend Ezekiel Leven.

"Ramsgrund, I have talked with Carapezza's Mechanical Engineering professor. He has assured me Mr. Carapezza is one of the brightest students he has had in decades."

"I thought you might appreciate his credentials, Herr Gosslau."

"Yes. Mr. Carapezza might do very well in the Flight, Guidance, and Telemetering Devices Laboratory. Dr. Ernst Steinhoff, a well-known rocket scientist, is in charge of the laboratory and has expressed a need for additional engineering staff.

"Both Dr. Steinhoff and Dr. Walter Thiel, our deputy director, would like help on improving the guidance system. These doctors, along with our engineering director, Wernher von Braun, are all trying to improve the guidance and fusing systems.

"The propulsion system has had some success," Gosslau continued, "because of the work of Dr. Hermann Steuding, our Aeroballistics Laboratory specialist. His testing of the pulsejet engine at the Luftwaffe testing facility at Peenemünde West and the development of a reliable propulsion mechanism for the V-1 program has added immeasurably to the German Luftwaffe missile program.

"I have been a strong proponent of the pulsejet engine as designed by the Argus Motoren Company and have been modifying and improving it for this particular project.

"Ramsgrund, I am authorizing you to travel to the university and bring this brilliant student mathematician to our facility. I could use additional help and human resources with the guidance system, the fusing issue, and the overall design of the fuel mixing system.

"Hitler seems to want a war with our neighbors. It is going to take more than tanks and machine guns to defeat the major powers in Europe. Our little flying bomb might come in handy for our *Führer*. However, right now the V-1 is more of an unguided missile. We have had many failures, and occasionally one of these monsters seems to want to circle back to bite us on the backside."

"Oh no," I uttered in mock surprise. "We cannot let such a malfunction happen!"

"Our *Führer* has many thousands of these missiles planned. It would be very unhealthy for us here at the Research Center to have a catastrophic failure with a warhead coming down in one of our cities or back here at Peenemünde," concluded Herr Gosslau.

"Our research here depends on funding from the *Reich*. We cannot afford to have a runaway cruise missile ruining our research."

"When would you like me to leave for Berlin, sir?"

"Go to the travel office over in the power plant building," Gosslau continued, "And draw a voucher for your trip. The travel orders will be ready by late this afternoon."

He continued reinforcing, "By tomorrow at 0800, there will be orders in the travel office for Vitali Carapezza to travel with you to our facility.

"Ramsgrund. Be careful not to disappoint the facility or your fellow engineers here at Peenemünde. Even more importantly, do not disappoint the *SS*."

With a not so subtle warning, I returned to my desk to look over the plans for the guidance and fusing systems. The missile was simple enough, but the guidance system was rather too rudimentary. The guidance system might get the rocket to a city but could not pinpoint a target.

Later in the afternoon, I found myself in the vacant *SS* office to do a little research on some of the major players in the V-1 hierarchy. It was in those files I found some interesting facts about one of the prime military officers at Peenemünde: *Generalfeldmarschall* Erhard Milch. His record had been sealed with a "**TOP SECRET**" stamp placed on the upper center part of the file.

This officer was primarily responsible for recommending the propulsion mechanism for the V-1 missile. Also, he was placed in the highest priority for the testing of the engine at the Luftwaffe's *Erprobungsstelle* coastal test center at Karlshagen, part of the Peenemünde West testing facility. The surprising news, buried in the files, was Milch's father was Jewish!

I had to smile. *How does the Reich even operate with so many foreigners in its ranks? It made me consider a few more additional opinions in the government might bring some needed sanity to the German body politic.*

Generalfeldmarschall Milch was either clever about hiding his Jewish origins, or he was important enough to have a superior officer cover it up for him. I thought it best to tuck this bit of information away for further use in case my background ever became a problem. I closed up all the files and left the building. In the morning, I picked up our orders.

CHAPTER 28

Pulling Zeke Out of a Gestapo Trap

Later in the day I took a bus to Greifswald and boarded a train for Vorpommern with continuing service on to Berlin.

I found Zeke in the evening studying at the front desk in the university library where he was working. There were several students in the library, and most of them looked up at me when I walked in.

"Vitali, how are you." I was in full *SS* uniform and was probably somewhat of a surprise to the students in the library, as well as Zeke. I towered over most of the students. Some of them looked surprised; some looked shocked. Most averted my gaze when I looked at them. A few even looked worried.

"Herr Lieutenant, it is a pleasure."

"Vitali, you look great." Then in a somewhat hushed voice, "Is there somewhere we could talk? I know you are working, but this won't take too long."

"Jenz," he articulated very quietly, "We can talk just over here in the private reading room."

I entered, and Zeke closed the door behind us.

"Where have you been, Jenz, I have tried to get in touch with you all week. The Gestapo has arrested my parents!"

"Oh, no!" I was not shocked. "Where have they taken them?"

"We cannot get any information. One of my neighbors told me when I was home last week and found no one at home."

"Zeke, we need a plan. I will try to get information through the *SS,* but we might get better information if we work together. If you can find out where they were taken, I will go there and personally demand their release in my custody."

"Won't going to a labor camp be most dangerous for you, Jenz?"

"It would be well worth it to get your parents out of one of those hell-holes."

"How can we work together, Jenz? Wouldn't it be dangerous for both of us?"

"Here, take a look at my orders. They state I am to come here to the *Technische Hochschule Berlin* and bring you to the Army Research Center at Peenemünde."

"Why me?"

"I recommended to the brass up there you were a whiz in calculus and physics. And you could probably be of enormous help to the scientists' with particular problems they were having with a specific weapons system."

"What weapons system? And how is traveling to Peenemünde going to be helpful for my parents."

"This particular facility," I stated, "uses forced labor to construct the many thousands of these weapons the *Führer* has planned for Germany. I will do everything I can to see if your parents could be transferred there. It's a long shot, but these are very confusing times in Germany. The food and living conditions at the research center are much improved over the average labor camp."

"This winter could be very tough for anyone in a labor camp. Perhaps we could make life a little easier for your parents if they were working at this weapons facility.

"I can't divulge what the work will involve until the head engineer of your department briefs you. It is important you return with me as soon as you can secure a leave of absence from your professor."

"You mean I leave the University right away?"

"Tomorrow would be best.

"And, let's face it, Zeke," I started to speak barely above a whisper," An idiot is running Germany. Last week Hitler invaded Poland. Who knows what could be next!"

I was very concerned to hear Zeke's parents had been arrested. They could be anywhere in the system. If tortured, it would not be surprising they would reveal Zeke and I are working together to help Jews arrested by the *Gestapo*. And, to date, we have eliminated many agents.

After discussing some of these possibilities with Ezekiel, he came to realize he might do well to get involved with the Army's Research Center and get out of Berlin without delay. He then mentioned he thought someone had been following him and watching him.

My immediate thought, I did not share with Ezekiel, was perhaps his parents had been tortured. Had they divulged where Zeke was working, and maybe what he and I were doing?

I suggested we go to his room, pack up his bags, and get the hell out of Berlin immediately.

He left his desk at the circulation center of the library and left his work on the counter. He mentioned to his colleague and co-worker he would be gone for about an hour.

We walked briskly because of light snow spitting in the air. On our way back to his apartment, it did appear someone might be following us. The same figure was on the same street with us even when we took a short detour to Zeke's apartment.

I told Zeke, "Pack only essentials in a small bag. Perhaps a change of clothing and your slide rule."

He asked if he should take the pistol we had received from a previous *Gestapo* Agent.

"Let's not complicate our journey back to Peenemünde. The SS guards could search us when we arrive."

Just then there was a loud knock on Zeke's door. Bang, Bang-Bang.

I immediately asked Zeke, "Do you have any leather gloves?"

"Yes," was his quick reply. "Right here in the kitchen drawer."

"Let me have them for a moment." I put the right glove on even though it was a little tight and held my hand behind my back. I opened the door to a lanky pinched faced official who looked like he hadn't been out in the sun for decades.

He looked surprised to see someone in a full *SS* uniform standing before him.

"Pardon me, lieutenant," he said as he introduced himself, "I am Agent Janke from the Berlin *Gestapo* office."

He pulled out a leather carrying case and showed me his badge.

"I am here to take Vitali Carapezza into headquarters for questioning about student activities."

"Of course, Agent Janke, could I look at your credentials?"

At this point, I called out, "Vitali, there is a gentleman here to see you." At the same time, I fumbled the agent's leather carrying case, and it dropped to the floor at the agent's feet.

"Oh, excuse me, Agent Janke."

As Janke bent down to pick up his case, my knee flew up to meet his chin with a sickening crack. I was pretty sure I had broken off the heads of the condyles of his lower jaw. As his head snapped back, my gloved fist found his larynx and trachea, which I crushed with a hard direct frontal blow with my gloved fist. I put much of my weight behind it.

He squirmed on the floor for a couple of minutes, making only gurgling noises through his nose before he turned purple and stopped breathing.

"Jeeze, Jenz, what are we suppose to do with this guy now?"

"I'm not sure Zeke, please check out front to see if he has a partner, these agents usually seem to like to travel in pairs."

As Zeke went to check out the front, I took the time to tie up the deceased agent in one of Zeke's blankets. With the rope around the quilt, it made for more comfortable carrying. He was quite tall, but I dragged him into the bedroom out of sight of the front hall.

"Jenz," exclaimed Zeke, "There is a black car idling out front; someone is behind the wheel waiting."

"Okay, Zeke, we will just wait here for him to come to the apartment."

Our apartment was pretty spare. It had one small bedroom and a day-couch arrangement I slept on whenever I was staying in Berlin or attending school. There was a small kitchen, but neither of us cooked too much. We both were severely spoiled by the Leven's cook and dear friend, Hilda.

Our school dreams were on hold for a while, but we did hope to continue with our engineering studies next term. It's a little strange, all my life I worked as an engineer but my only formal training was the semester at the Technical University in Berlin.

It took about ten minutes for the second agent to knock on the door. He had his weapon drawn and brandished it when I opened the door. He didn't expect to be greeted by a member of the *SS* in uniform.

I greeted the agent like a close colleague, "Come on in, Agent Janke is in the kitchen with Vitali having coffee." This second agent was even taller, probably about 6'2", with a skinny neck, and not too much common sense.

As he turned and lowered his pistol, he didn't see my gloved fist as it crashed into the side of his neck. I struck him hard, and I was pretty sure I had separated his spinal cord at the first cervical vertebrae. He went down hard, but his legs kept twitching for another couple of minutes. He started to foam at the mouth and suffocated on his saliva. My hand was sore even with Zeke's leather glove protecting my fingers. His neck was bright red where my fist had struck him, but the rest of him was a ghastly grey. The aura and smell of death were on him immediately. He had evacuated his bowels and bladder. I was pretty sure I had broken his neck.

Thank goodness it was night. I don't think anyone observed Zeke and I hauling the two deceased agents into the trunk of their automobile.

Zeke wrote a note to the landlord telling him he had been called away on army business and left the note with his key on the kitchen table. We left the apartment unlocked.

We drove out toward Charlottenburg and through the Grunwald Wood and parked near Lake Havel. It was a deserted and dark wooded part of the forest. There was no one around; we did not want to take a chance of being seen.

We untied the agents and placed rocks under their clothing close to their bodies so they would sink into the deep part of the lake. We slipped them into the water. Both bodies floated for a brief time before the rocks pulled them under the water.

We drove the government car back to the section of Berlin near the Reichstag. This building was the center of the *Nazi* Party's power base. We left the car in a large parking lot next to the Reichstag. We wore gloves the entire time, so there was no evidence of our involvement with the automobile or the agents. We walked to the Central Berlin Rail Station and purchased tickets for Greifswald in Northern Germany.

I had a little trouble getting Vitali into the base. Once the *SS* guards read over my orders and carefully examined Zeke's Italian passport, one of the Wehrmacht guards drove us to the officer's quarters. I could tell Zeke was paralyzed with apprehension as the SS guards interrogated us. I had told him to say very little and to fake a little bit of an Italian accent with his German.

The next day I introduced Vitali to our chief of operations for the Flight, Guidance, and Telemetering Device Laboratory, Dr. Ernst Steinhoff. The doctor complimented Vitali, "Your command of the German language is excellent."

Vitali's response was, "I do a lot of reading in the scientific literature."

Vitali was amazed at the amount of space and with the testing devices housed within the laboratory.

"These laboratories are enormous," he commented.

Vitali mentioned everything seemed so orderly and smelled very clean for a busy laboratory.

"This is our guidance department," said Dr. Steinhoff. "Our main problem is we don't have exactly pinpoint accuracy with the V-1 flying bomb. Half the time we aren't even positive what part of a country they might attack!"

Vitali had not even heard of this weapon, and his amazement flashed briefly across his face. With tact, he said nothing but nodded seemingly with knowledge of the subject.

"To further clarify," continued Dr. Steinhoff, "The V-1 carries approximately 165 gallons of medium octane gasoline. Whenever the gasoline runs out, the bomb crashes to earth and explodes. Accuracy is a problem, and the weapon is not effective for destroying military targets. However, it does act as a terrifying weapon for the population hearing it overhead. The pulsejet makes a rather remarkable, almost alarming sound. The sound resembles a loud, poorly timed motorcycle engine when heard from a distance."

"The problem is we never know what the target will be. Whenever the pulsejet engine runs out of gas, the target is wherever it happens to fall to earth. It could be in the middle of a deserted field, or on top of a city block."

"Perhaps, Vitali, you would be able to help us improve our accuracy?"

"I would be happy to work on the problem," stammered Vitali. "I would need to look over the design of the guidance and fuel systems. I would need to know the total weight of the weapon with its' warhead when loaded with fuel, and the aerodynamics of the fuselage.

Dr. Steinhoff gave Vitali drawings of the pulsejet flying bomb and some equations and drawings to look through to evaluate the guidance system. The complete specifications for weight and length of the missile were included. Both fueled and unfueled weights were on the drawings.

In the evening I had dinner with Vitali at the officer's dining room at the Research Center. I had something significant to discuss with him.

I selected a table in the far corner of the officer's mess hall. The hall itself contained *Nazi Swastika* flags, mirrors, and photographs of the *Führer*. There were little *Nazi* flags on all the tables next to small vases of flowers. The tables were covered with white tablecloths and had gold-colored linen napkins. The entire dining room reeked of elegance.

Our waiter appeared immediately and offered water and asked for our drink order. He was extraordinarily polite and addressed me by my rank of Lieutenant, and called us gentlemen.

"Vitali," I said, almost at a low whisper after the waiter had departed, "We have to be very sure and careful of what we are doing now. Anyone could overhear us at any time, so we have to be guarded with our speech."

"What do you mean, Jenz."

"As you can see, Zeke," I uttered in a whisper, "Germany is becoming a police state. Our parents, scientists, ordinary citizens, virtually no one is safe to speak their mind in Germany. Our countrymen cannot carry on many forms of business, or even belong to their religious organization or political party."

"Hitler, the *Nazi Party*, and a handful of thugs are leading Germany into a very dark and dangerous place. We are going to have to take a stand and very quietly fight back. We have no money and no political strength. Our only resource is our inner determination and the inner goodness of God-fearing Germans. We can rely on each other, but we cannot trust anyone else in this struggle. The torture tactics of the *Gestapo* have ensured no one can be thoroughly trusted. Once you start losing fingers, one at a time, no one can remain silent."

"But Jenz," Zeke whispered in a shallow voice, "How can we fight the *Gestapo*, the *SS*, and the *Wehrmacht* with determination alone?"

"We have already started, Zeke!" I uttered in an excited whisper. "Remember, we have already eliminated more than a half dozen *Gestapo* agents, perhaps more in the explosion at the Hamburg office. My contacts in the *SS* tell me the *Gestapo* fears there is a traitor in their midst. There is a lot of rivalry between the *SS* and the *Gestapo*. We must keep them guessing about their missing agents, and encourage this rivalry."

"Jenz, how are we going to stop Germany from making war on its neighbors and its citizens, especially Jews?" He tilted his head toward me and cupped his hand to ensure his voice would only travel to my ear.

"Our part is to make sure we can eliminate as many of these police-state *Gestapo* agents as possible. Also, make sure the weapons developed at this research center are never completely effective."

We assumed a normal conversational tone and sat up a little straighter as our waiter arrived with our dinners. Although formal and polite, one never knew which waiters were listening or trying to pick up threads of conversations from the scientists and officers in the dining room.

After the waiter had left, Zeke suggested in a hushed tone, "Perhaps we could make a slight modification in the fuel supply or tank size. The flying bomb would then run out of fuel and crash prematurely."

"Or," Zeke continued, "I could suggest the gyroscopically controlled stabilizing system be pre-set for a specific geographical location and distance. The system I would build would be able to handle all sorts of weather and climatic conditions. I would need to be able to control the system so it could be preprogrammed to explode in flight or over farmland outside of a major city."

"Excellent!" I suggested. "But we have to be careful any modifications we install are completely hidden and undetectable. Remember we are dealing with very bright scientists, not goons from the *Gestapo*. Most of the workers and technicians here are more or less totally on board with the *Nazi* philosophy of racism, pure German blood, and harsh penalties for disloyalty."

"Although I should mention Dr. Von Braun seemed only reluctantly to accept his appointment into the *SS* this past summer. The doctor saw the importance of joining the *SS* when Himmler threatened the continuation of his aerodynamic research and life's work on space exploration.

"Also," I commented, "Some of these flying bombs would have to be successful. If they all failed, the scientists and the military would be able to trace the problem directly to your lab. We have to approach this business with a certain amount of realism and plausibility.

"Tomorrow, I will begin inquiries about your parents. The Reich cannot afford to lose valuable doctors and their families. We have to find them quickly because in short order they will be suffering from malnutrition."

We switched our conversation to the base housing and how delicious the food tasted when the waiter approached to clear our table.

As the waiter left us alone, I emphasized to Zeke, "Remember, you are a well respected Italian mathematics student studying aerodynamic engineering. Make sure you have a ready story about your family and where they live in Italy. Make it a large city where you have dozens of prospective relatives."

"Thanks, Jenz. I will start getting my thoughts organized this week on how I can 'improve' this flying bomb."

"Remember Zeke, after the invasion of Poland this past September, Germany is at war. Our loyalty cannot be in doubt. War rarely generates personal animosities between opposing people. The Poles, British, French, Russians and all of Eastern Europe may get pulled into this war. It is important for you and me not get pulled or swept along with any particular political ideology.

"Our hatred is certainly specific, but not for the people who fight us on the battlefield. Our hate is directed at the forces of evil and criminal forces who have brought Germany to this destructive place in history.

"Our goal must be sincere yet kept very secret: the destruction of the *Gestapo* and the *Nazi* politicians who have hatched this violent pogrom against our people. And the limitation of the capability of these terrible new weapons."

We walked and whispered on our way back to the base housing. It was a cold and damp winter on the Baltic Sea. We were right on the Pomeranian Bay near the Oder River. Snowflakes sprinkled in the headlights of the few cars traversing the base. In contrast, the officer and scientist housing on the army base were surprisingly warm and comfortable.

"Tomorrow, dear friend, all the technicians involved in the rocket research are going to hear from our Technical Director of Research, Dr. Wernher Von Braun. He has been appointed the head and running the *Heeresversuchsanstalt Peenemünde*, (Peenemünde Army Research Center) since 1938."

"It was Von Braun's early work with the *Vereine Fur Raumschiffahrt*, or *VfR*, Society for Space Travel, which first brought him to the attention of the *Wehrmacht* in 1940."

Vitali and I were whispering in his room. Vitali went over some of the basics of the control and guidance system for the developing V-1 or flying bomb. The drawings and formulas looked pretty intense and challenging to interpret for me, but Zeke seemed to understand them reasonably well.

He asked me about Ilsa and her family, and we talked about my father's work at *I.G. Farben.* As I got up to leave and head back to my room, there was a loud knock at the door: **Bang, Bang, Bang.**

I put my finger to my lips to hush up Vitali. I spread my hands to stop motion in front of me. I then pointed at Vitali and motioned him to open the door slowly. I stood behind the door and waited.

As Vitali opened the door, two armed Gestapo agents barged into the room; both brandished their pistols.

Jeez, Louise, I thought; these goons are everywhere. Is there no end to their stupidity? Since there were two of them with their firearms in their hands, I saw no good outcome to surprise them from behind the door.

"What can I do for you, gentlemen?" Vitali asked while introducing himself and me.

The mean goon stated tersely, "I am Agent Hofmann, and this is Agent Krause. We are here from the *Gestapo* to detain a student activist, Vitali Carapezza."

Agent Hofmann looked foreboding. His pockmarked face had a scar across the left cheek, but you could tell he wasn't military. His florid face and bulbous nose complimented his flabby out of shape body.

Agent Krause, on the other hand, looked in better shape. He was lean with steel gray eyes. His eyes seemed to look right through you and bore into your soul. He was the one who had to go down first.

I immediately spoke up, "We are very sorry you agents are misinformed. Both Vitali Carapezza and I worked with the *SS* to root out student activities counter to the *Reich's* philosophy stated by the *Nuremberg Laws*. We are here at the Army Research Center to work on special weapons programs for the *Reich*."

Both agents looked a little questioning at me. I furthered my question and addressed Agent Krause who seemed to be in charge: "Let me see your warrant, perhaps I can clear up the confusion."

Since we weren't combative or resisting, Agent Krause ordered, "Agent Hofmann, please retrieve the paperwork from the car."

As soon as Agent Hofmann left the building, Vitali distracted Agent Krause by asking, "Herr Krause, could I get you something to drink?"

"No!" he replied forcibly. "This is not a social visit. You are being placed under arrest and taken to Gestapo Headquarters for thorough questioning about student activities at the *Technische Hochschule* in Berlin."

I knew then we were in trouble. We would have to eliminate these agents right here and right now.

I casually stepped toward Agent Krause and brought my clenched fist down on his gun arm with all the force I could muster. I heard a crack as the radial bone snapped and the pistol went flying. He let out a horrible sound silenced in mid-scream by my second blow to his neck. His body went violently back against the wall. He clutched his throat with his right hand as his eyes seemed to bulge out of his head and then rolled back.

He slid to the floor, gasping and panting. Blood was collecting and dribbling out of his mouth. He couldn't get any air into his lungs; my blow had crushed his trachea and larynx. However, he could still expel air in a fit of coughing and guttural sounds. I then punched him in the solar plexus to expel any air still left in his lungs. His eyes rolled back in his head, and he gave a horrible death rattle with his expelled air. His neck was a bright red from internal bleeding where my fist had landed. He started gushing blood from his foaming mouth.

Zeke and I dragged him into the bathroom. I told Zeke, "Let's stuff a washcloth in his mouth to make sure he doesn't make any noise at all when the second agent returns."

Agent Hofmann burst into the apartment without knocking. He had holstered his pistol. He probably thought Agent Krause was still holding his.

"Where is Agent Krause? He demanded.

"He is in the bathroom," I shot back.

Agent Hofmann turned to look toward the bathroom. At the same time, I planted my fist firmly in his solar plexus; he went down with a whoosh of air from his lungs. I immediately removed my belt and cinched it tightly around his neck from behind. His arms and legs flailed uselessly as I held on tightly to the belt, jerking him off the floor. I brought him to the center of the room by placing him over my back while holding on tightly to my cinched up belt.

Although I was much taller than him, I didn't want the agent to kick any of the furniture over or create any other noise. He clutched at his throat as he desperately tried to get air into his lungs. I just wasn't about to let him gasp for air.

He kicked his feet and flailed his arms to get me off his back, but I had a firm grip on my belt and wouldn't give an inch. He twisted and turned trying to get me off his back or to kick me, but I held on with all the firmness I could muster.

The agent's face then turned reddish purple, and his eyes bulged and rolled back in his head. He tried to scream, but there was no air left in his lungs. I let him slump to the floor, but kept my belt tightened around his neck. His legs gave one final spasm of activity before he fell silent.

Vitali remarked, "Now where are we going to deposit these two?"

"We'll put their weighted bodies in the Baltic Sea on the outgoing tide. Perhaps their bodies will make it to Stockholm or Danzig in a month or two."

Vitali and I drove their car with the two dead agents in the trunk. We went out to the coast on road L-264 and drove south toward Karlshagen, but only for a few minutes. There was a small dirt track winding into the woods on our right side, away from the beach. We only saw one other automobile on our way along the shore. The road was practically deserted on this desolate and wind-swept land adjacent to the North Sea.

The government car wouldn't drive too well on the dirt tracks. It was an older Mercedes and not quite high enough to avoid the higher ground between the ruts. We purposely turned off the road into some brush after only 100 yards or so into the dirt road. We parked the car well off the dirt track and covered it with brush and branches.

Zeke and I dragged the two agents from the trunk and down to the beach. We placed some small rocks a little larger than my fist inside their shirts and tied their shirts tightly to their bodies. We then carried their almost floating remains out about thirty yards into the surf, and slipped them into the Baltic Sea. The water didn't seem as frigid as I thought it should be for the time of year. It could have been my adrenalin coursing through my body so fast nothing seemed too cold at the time.

It was a cold, night so I'm sure no one observed our actions. It took us about 40 minutes to walk back to the base housing. We were pretty cold by the time we got back to our rooms. My pants had started to freeze; my legs looked a little blue. I asked Zeke, "Do you think God will forgive us?"

CHAPTER 29

Modifying the V-1

Over the next few weeks and into the spring, Vitali and I got to meet most of the scientists working at the research facility. We also tried to find out which camp had detained his parents. I notified our base doctor there was a surgeon in one of the concentration camps who could be of great benefit to the center. The doctor replied, "please be careful about even making inquiries about detainees. You never know where the inquiry could lead."

"Thanks for your kind warning, doctor. I just thought it might be helpful for you to have a well-regarded surgeon on your staff."

Vitali worked on the fusing mechanism of the V-1 and modified the fuse so it wouldn't explode on impact. It was a rather ingenious little mechanism consisting of a small propeller on the front of the warhead. The propeller would have to make at least 100 revolutions before a pin would drop into an electrical circuit and activate it. Once the electrical system was activated, the bomb would explode on impact.

However, by removing the pin, or re-wiring the fusing mechanism, the V-1 would explode prematurely, or never explode, even as it crashed to the earth. Vitali showed me in a diagram of how the doctored device worked. It was quite simple and hard to detect. Our problem was to get the forced labor workers to go along with the deception without them turning Vitali in for a better food ration or better treatment. We had to make it look like a requisite from higher up the engineering chain of command.

The name of the officer in the "Top Secret" file came to mind.

In addition to the contact fuse, there were two additional fuse mechanisms; both were electrical. The first could be set off by a radio signal, in case the V-1 flew erratically off the catapult. The second was a time delayed fuse, to prevent inspection by a foreign power in case the rocket was a dud. A special wrench and removal procedure would deactivate the rocket for approximately two minutes before the missile would explode.

My thoughts went back to the officer in charge of testing the propulsion mechanism for the V-1 guided missile system. I certainly did not want it discovered his father was Jewish. It would, however, make a plausible excuse if our deception was ever revealed. *Generalfeldmarschall* Erhard Milch would make an excellent candidate for blame if any "irregularities" were discovered.

One spring morning in 1940, Vitali and I were invited to a meeting with the department heads and all the personnel from the guidance department. Dr. Steinhoff and Dr. Thiel and the entire Flight, Guidance, and Telemetering Devices laboratory were there at Dr. Von Braun's meeting. Also, several high ranking officers from the Luftwaffe, many of whom I had never seen, were in attendance.

Dr. Von Braun began the meeting. "Gentlemen, thank you for coming to this meeting and thank you for all your hard work on our first vengeance weapon. The V-1 will be a tremendous success in our quest for space travel. Our military advisors have suggested it will be effective for retaliation for our cities being bombed by the British. We have a few imperfections to work out, but it is nearing completion and should go into production over the next few months.

"Our prison laborers are producing thousands of the parts and the outer fuselage for the rocket as we speak. We have excellent German technicians overseeing and 'encouraging' these prisoners to produce the rockets quickly. The *Führer* has given us orders to build up to thirty thousand of these vengeance weapons as soon as possible!

"You will notice I described the V-1 as our first vengeance weapon. I have purposely done this to announce and differentiate it from our second, very secret, vengeance weapon the V-2. This weapon was originally designed as the A-4 Rocket for travel into outer space. Since it has obvious uses as a military weapon, this missile has been modified by order of the Luftwaffe to carry a warhead directly to the heart of our enemies.

"This weapon will arrive at our enemies doorstep undetected. It can be launched from anywhere in Germany and reach our enemies anywhere with some modifications. Right now the accuracy is within five kilometers of our target. Our goal is to get it within 150 meters of our target. Our range with the current configuration is approximately 350 kilometers. This rocket flies at the height of 60-300 kilometers and is capable of traveling above the ionosphere. With modifications and improvements, this rocket would be capable of hitting any target on the planet from anywhere in Germany."

There was a hushed silence in the room as Dr. Von Braun's words sunk in for the scientists and military personnel.[*]

---

[*] *There was a rumor it was Von Braun's mother who at Christmas in1935 suggested to her son Wernher he consider Peenemünde as a site for rocket testing. She told Wernher*

"Are there any questions, Gentlemen?"

"Yes, doctor." One of the military generals from the Luftwaffe had a question. "What is your estimate of when these new 'vengeance' weapons will be available for full service?"

"It is a difficult question to answer exactly, general," Von Braun continued. "Full service for these weapons depends on two factors. First, we are having some trouble convincing our *Führer* of the necessity for funding for our research and development. He has indicated he thinks these weapons are just a costly artillery shell with a longer range, but much more expensive. Also, and also very important, it will take the workforce and training to assemble and build the V-2 rockets in the number we may need."

"Manpower will not be a problem, doctor." The general continued, "I will be speaking with our *Führer* tomorrow. I will bring both of your concerns to his attention. There are plenty of highly trained workers in our labor camps. Most would be anxious to trade their current circumstances for improved food, housing, and medical care available here at the Research Center.

"Your grandfather use to go duck-shooting there."

In 1937 at Peenemünde, on the island of Usedom along the Baltic seacoast, the German Army secretly acquired the secluded site to develop and test rockets for the Wehrmacht.

Von Braun received his doctorate in physics at the age of twenty-two in 1934 from the Charlottenburg Institute. The title of his thesis carried the cryptic title "About Combustion Tests" and was classified secret and went unpublished for many years. His father never joined the Nazi Party, and Wernher didn't for several years. He looked so young to be heading up such a prestigious and secret part of the Wehrmacht.

Most of the scientists at the research facility at Peenemünde were apolitical and much more interested in their work than developing weapons for the Third Reich. Von Braun never wore his swastika lapel pin, a symbol of Nazi Party membership. He wore his SS uniform with the swastika armband only once, during one of Himmler's formal visits.

"Besides, the Reich has confiscated enough gold, jewels, and rare art from the Jewish rabble where I think the funding for your research and development should be able to continue unimpeded."

"Thank you, general. Anything you can do will be appreciated."

"Your work here doctor is very appreciated by the *Reich*. I will inform our *Führer* of your progress. Please let the *Luftwaffe* know of any developments we may be able to coordinate for you."

"Your efforts are sure to be a help in our progress, general."

There were a few additional questions about logistics and timing, but most of the queries were not as crucial as the prior questions of launch dates and production. The cost of the V-1 and V-2 programs were immense. These missile programs were funded from the confiscation of the wealth of others in the *Reich,* mainly hardworking imprisoned innocent Jewish citizens.

At the end of the question and answer session, another one of the Luftwaffe generals asks for our attention since he had an announcement. "Fellow countrymen, the *Führer* this day has announced an essential pact with our friends from Italy. On the 18th of March, the *Führer* met with Benito Mussolini at Brenner Pass in the Alps to ally against France and the United Kingdom. This alliance will be beneficial to the *Reich* and the goals of the *Führer.*"

Vitali and I just glanced at each other during the presentation. I silently cringed over the thoughts of placing German lives against those in Britain and France. The idea of another Great War could hardly be pleasing to any rational person. How could the scientists and officers assembled in this room of this army research center think any of this preparation and production for war was rational?

Vitali mentioned as we strolled out of the meeting,

"Jenz, I have some ideas we should discuss this evening. Let's try to meet at an off-base restaurant."

We made definitive efforts not to be seen together too often, but we had a lot to talk over.

"It would look too suspicious, Vitali, if we check on and off the base together. The Wehrmacht guards are not fools. I am already worried about the two *Gestapo* agents might have checked in, but we know they didn't check out at the gate. I hope they haven't been missed at their headquarters."

Zeke and I met for dinner at a small off-base eatery. The establishment was pretty informal, but the food was decent. Although early evening, it was already crowded with regulars and a few Luftwaffe personnel. The standard fare was knockwurst and sauerkraut, *Kieler Sprotten,* which were smoked Baltic *Sprats*, or fish, and a bowl of delicious potato soup or stew called *Kartoffelsuppe.*

There were several favorite beers on tap, including Pilsner and Einbecker.

"Vitali, excuse me, Zeke, I asked in a lowered voice, what looks good to you?"

"I think I'll try the Knockwurst with Sauerkraut with a Pilsner.

"Sounds excellent, Zeke, I think I'll try the same.

I got serious for a moment and quietly asked, "Zeke, you know what will happen to us if the *Gestapo* catches us."

"Yes. We will probably be tortured and killed. Or, if we are lucky, just killed."

"Jenz, you are the one doing most of the eliminating of these hateful people. I'm sure you have done some serious soul-searching over the past few months. Do you think God will forgive us for all of our actions with the *Gestapo*?"

"I'm not sure, Zeke. Both of us come from a religious upbringing. My prayers include my hope God will look at us as warriors against the evil in Germany as shown itself in the *Gestapo*. So in reality, we are not fighting decent Germans, but the enemy of decent people everywhere. I hope our eliminating these hated agents isn't just an excuse to try to eliminate evil, but a realization for both of us to rid this scourge from our country."

"I agree with you, Jenz. I do hope the Good Lord will forgive us.

Zeke continued, "Let me tell you about the procedure I have developed for minimizing the effectiveness of the first vengeance weapon.

"Just before launching, the weapon is filled with 165 gallons of medium octane gasoline. This fuels the pulse jet engine. As discussed with the engineers in the Guidance Laboratory, many weapons will be launched against the English in London. The range of the weapon is in line with the London destination from the launch sites.

"I have devised a method of changing the fuel consumption so many of these 'super weapons' will harmlessly crash into the English countryside before they arrive at a population center. And, more importantly, I have done it without any evidence of tampering with the weapon."

"And just how do you propose to accomplish this?"

"I have made a slight change in the meter on the fuel trucks which pump fuel into the rockets. The meter will read 165 gallons of fuel, but the exact amount will be 3-5 gallons less. The discrepancy will be impossible to detect unless testing the amount or quantity of fuel is compared against the meter. Testing would be tough to do with small quantities of fuel. Irregularities will only be detected if amounts larger than 200 gallons are metered."

"However, with favorable meteorological conditions, temperature, wind speed and direction, and humidity, some of these rockets will still reach their destination. I estimate twenty to thirty percent of them will fall short or explode before they reach their destination."

"How will you get them to explode prematurely?" I was still not convinced we could throw the V-1 rocket off its mission without being discovered.

"This was fairly simple, Jenz. Most of the papers done by the scientists here at Peenemünde call for using medium 75 octane fuel for the pulse-jet motor. However, the higher octane fuel burns too hot. About twenty percent of these vengeance weapons failed because the fuel burned so hot the weld joints for one or more of the stabilizing fins melted off. Without one or more fins the weapon will fly erratically and crash into the ground or the sea short of the target.

"Now, I have convinced, through a slight deception in the fuel manifests, for the fuel loaders to use only high octane gasoline for these weapons. The newer research findings are sidetracked to ensure higher temperature burning fuel for all V-1 weapons. The scientists believe the higher octane gasoline will increase the range of the missile.

"I will admit, if a fin from the rocket does fall off while over a major city, the weapon will truly act as a weapon of terror. It will fly erratically over its target until it runs out of fuel, then drop to earth detonating the warhead. I have not dared to request adjusting the detonating device to explode prematurely because I'm not sure who to trust in the prisoner population responsible for loading the warheads. All of these procedures are carefully watched and monitored by the *Wehrmacht*."

"You have done a remarkable job, Ezekiel. Someday you may earn the gratitude of a grateful nation. I have heard subtle rumors from the scientists even Dr. Von Braun thinks Hitler is a bit of a horses ass; a 'Napoleon with a Charlie Chapman mustache.' Furthermore, Himmler himself had pressured von Braun when he 'invited' him to join the *SS*. The doctor said if he hadn't joined, Himmler would have made sure he would have to give up his life's work in rocketry and space travel."

CHAPTER 30

Encounter with Wehrmacht Deserters

After several months and weekly letters from Ilsa, I decided to put in for a week's leave to see her and her family in Hannover. Because of the impending war, one week was the maximum leave anyone was allowed. I missed her very much. It was time for me to make clear my intentions to her family and ask her father for permission to marry my dearest friend.

The next Friday evening I took a bus to Griswold and a train to Hamburg with a continuation on to Hannover. I was able to sleep fitfully on the train. Many of the passengers stared at me because of my uniform. I decided not to wear it during my stay with Ilsa's family.

I arrived close to midnight, but Miss Ilsa was waiting for me in the middle of the station at the ticket office window. Her embrace and kisses were like rocket fuel to my body. Suddenly, I wasn't tired, but fully energized for the walk to her home.

On our walk, she admitted her parents would probably be asleep when we got there. She also mentioned her parents had planned an enjoyable hike and picnic on Saturday deep in the woods north of the city. I told her a picnic sounded terrific. Of course, I didn't mention to her anything involving food always looked fantastic to me.

"Mom has been making German delicacies and baking some of your favorite deserts this week, Jenz, I hope you will enjoy them."

I have to admit, whenever anyone mentioned any food, even tangentially with words such as picnic, deserts, dinner, snack, or lunch. It would get my attention. I was perpetually hungry.

We spent the night in Ilsa's bed. She was warm and beautiful and came to me in her very own style of teasing and lovemaking. I always found her gentle teasing thoroughly enjoyable. She took her time with me, and though I was exhausted, I found myself riveted with passion at her touch. We fell very soundly asleep in each other's arms.

Saturday was a lovely spring day in late May. We drove for an hour deep into the woods north-west of Hannover. We decided to hike in toward a small picturesque lake in the forest. Steinhuder Nature Park and Lake was a beautiful scenic area for a picnic even though it seemed a bit isolated and off the beaten track. By the time we had hiked at least 5 kilometers into the lake area, we were miles from any civilization; I was starving. I remember the enchanting smell of the pine woods. It was a beautiful day to be alive.

Mr. and Mrs. Huber was very respectful of Ilsa and me being together. After we had set up the picnic area with a blanket, I rolled a log over for seating for Ilsa and Mrs. Huber. I took Mr. Huber aside and asked if he would like to walk down to the lake for a few minutes.

While we strolled along the lakeside, I asked Mr. Huber if he would permit me to ask his daughter for her hand in marriage.

He said he and Mrs. Huber would be grateful to have me as a son and I had his full permission, blessing, and support without reservation. I was relieved and thankful for his acknowledgment of our being a couple and his words of comfort and acceptance.

When we trudged back up to the picnic area, the women had a beautiful spread of sandwiches and cheese set out on wax paper on the blanket. Mr. Huber was about to give a blessing. I was about to launch into a chicken sandwich when three young men appeared out of the woods.

The three men looked unshaved and scruffy and had old worn and tattered *Wehrmacht* uniforms in a bit of disarray. I couldn't tell their rank or rate, and I feared they might be deserters.

"Can I help you, men?" I was sitting cross-legged on the blanket, and perhaps they couldn't tell how big I was. Each of the men carried clubs made from stout branches in the woods. They were not unusually large men, but they looked menacing with the clubs.

"We thought we might like to help you," said their leader. He spoke in a rather loud and arrogant voice. **"We thought we might be able to help ourselves to your food and then your women!"**

I could see Ilsa, and Mrs. Huber inwardly cringe at the remark. Mr. Huber started to stand and protest. I addressed Mr. Huber directly.

"Mr. Huber, **please**, I said rather forcefully, relax, these boys are just kidding around. Please let me talk to them. I'm sure they meant us no disrespect."

It was becoming evident to us these men were deserters from the *Wehrmacht* and up to no good. But I thought I should at least make an effort. I remembered my dad's words about trying to avoid fighting, if possible.

"Look, men, you haven't caused any trouble, yet. How about we give you each a sandwich, and you can be on your way. You will get something to eat, our hospitality, and you will be able to walk away. This way, no one gets hurt."

The largest one spoke up in a loud and commanding voice. **"Look dumpkopf,** we make the rules here. If you are smart, you will leave immediately; the cute one stays with us. If you play it smart, **you** will not get hurt." He came over to me and brandished the branch like a club above my head.

My reply was not to his liking. "If you brandish your club one more time, your friends will be taking you to the local hospital emergency service."

Then I added, "My apology for appearing somewhat impolite, but I'm always a little bit peckish when I'm hungry."

My remark did it for this deserter, he took a dreadful swing at my head with his club yelling, **"you swine, I warned you!"**

I grabbed the club as it careened toward my head. I jerked it out of his hand on his down-swing and stood up at the same time. I then grabbed his club hand and extended his arm to its full length. I towered over the little bastard. I let the forearm of this unnerved deserter feel the full force as I came down on it with his own club as hard as I could. It was a short swing, but I knew from his stagger and squeal of pain I had broken every bone in his forearm and wrist.

As he fell backward, his two friends started to come to me. "If you boys want to play rough, who will be left to take all of you to the hospital? I would suggest you all leave quietly, while you can still walk."

One of them started to raise his club to take a swing at my face. It was a well-placed swing, but I just ducked out of the way. The blow glanced off my back. Now I was starting to get a little perturbed, in addition to being hungry.

I quickly bent down on one knee and braced myself. I brought the club which had crushed his colleagues' forearm to bear with a sharp crack on the attacker's knee. With the break of the bone and his death-like gasp of pain, I knew I had shattered his leg and kneecap.

Both deserters were down and screaming, so I addressed the only one left standing. "I would suggest you take your friends to the nearest hospital. Unfortunately, you will have to walk, limp or crawl out of the woods." Then I added in a somewhat firmer tone, **"If I ever see any you near my friends or me again, I will bury you where you stand."**

As they limped off whining and whimpering into the woods, Mr. and Mrs. Huber looked visibly shaken. Mrs. Huber was staring at me and remarked in a shaky high-pitched voice,

"Jenz, I had no idea you were such an expert fighter."

"I'm not, Mrs. Huber. But if I'm hungry, sometimes I lose my polite demeanor and perspective. My friendly disposition takes a back seat to my hunger pangs.

"These men were relentless, cruel, and sadistic. They deserved nothing less than a beating. Please put them out of your mind. I don't believe they will bother us again. If the Wehrmacht takes them into custody, they will be shot or hanged.

"Thanks for preparing this delightful lunch, Mrs. Huber; let's give thanks and enjoy our time together. Mr. Huber, I'm so sorry we were interrupted, would you like to give our blessing and thanks to the Lord?"

"Thanks, Jenz. Dear Lord, we thank you for watching over and protecting our family today. We are blessed to have you in our lives every day. Please watch over and protect Germany as it struggles to find its way during this upheaval. Protect us from evil politicians who do not have God in their heart. And finally, please bring some semblance of peace to those who tried to harm us this day. In his holy name, Amen."

The rest of the picnic went undisturbed. We relaxed and enjoyed each other's company; Ilsa and I walked down by the lake. We made plans we hoped would not get torn apart by a war neither of us could control or fully understand.

I did confide in her some of what Zeke and I had planned. I didn't dare speak of the vengeance weapons developed at the Army Research Center in Peenemünde. I only discussed the vengeance Zeke, and I had wreaked and would continue to bring to the *Gestapo*. She begged me to be careful.

It was by the lake northwest of Hannover where I pledged my life to my Ilsa, and she agreed to pledge her life to me.

CHAPTER 31

Joseph Göebbels Comes to Peenemünde

It was a pleasant four-day respite with Ilsa and her family. Zeke did seem genuinely relieved to see me on my return to Peenemünde. He would get nervous with all the *Nazis, SS, Gestapo* Agents and *Wehrmacht* roaming around Berlin. At the research center, he was far less stressed because the scientists weren't so hard-core about their politics.

"I agree with you, Vitali. I think many of these scientists are much more interested in their work than politics. It was rumored doctor Von Braun was pressured into joining the *SS* because Himmler wanted to get his 'finger in the pie' at the Army Research Center."

"Jenz, I fear someone somewhere will get wind of the fact we have begun eliminating *Gestapo* agents and try to arrest us. You know it would not go well for us at a concentration camp or the *Gestapo* Headquarters."

"We cannot allow our capture to happen, Zeke" We were talking in hushed tones in his room at the base housing facility. "Also, there are spies everywhere." I was pointing at the ceiling ventilation fixture. Our conversation resumed at a normal tone, and we talked in general about how relaxing and refreshing a few days of leave had made me want to work harder for the Fatherland. Ezekiel just shook his head and rolled his eyes.

At the end of June 1940, our research facility had a visit from a prominent *Nazi* politician. Joseph Göebbels, the Reich Minister of Public Enlightenment and Propaganda. He arrived on a Friday afternoon and spoke to all the senior employees of the center. There were over two hundred of us gathered in the facility housing the main dining area for the base. It was an "all hands" speech required for the senior officers and the scientists.

Not too many of us were happy to be there. Göebbels discussed the latest German offensive at Dunkirk and the annihilation of the British Army. Most of us found this disturbing and a little difficult to believe. What none of us could doubt, however, was the virulent anti-Semitism spewing from his every sentence. He droned on and on about the declining number of Jews remaining in Poland.

His most ludicrous suggestion, however, got most of us embarrassed, yawning, and looking at our feet. It was the discussion of how noted Nazi politician Franz Rademacher, Head of the Jewish Department of the German Foreign Office, was making plans to remove all Jews from Eastern Europe and ship them to Madagascar! I wasn't sure if Vitali was going to vomit, get up and leave, or fall asleep. As my eyes were rolling to the back of my head, I noticed his head was starting to nod and fall asleep. How much of this crap were ordinary Germans supposed to stomach?

What brought us back to stark reality was Göebbels vivid and enthusiastic description of the supreme *Nazi* accomplishment: the building of a large concentration camp in southern Poland and its' use for the forced labor of the Jews of Eastern Europe. I think everyone in the room knew this was not a good idea for the long-term health of our nation. Auschwitz was supposed to be the

Nazi's answer to most of the 1000 year Third Reich's issues for marching into Poland last September.

Originally Auschwitz was developed to house Polish political prisoners. Its maximum capacity was approximately 50,000 detainees. It wasn't until a year later, after combining with another concentration camp at Birkenau, when it became a death camp destination for Jews, Catholic and Protestant Clergy, Russian prisoners of war, children, disabled people and anyone with views adverse to the Nazi "pure-blood" racial philosophy. Jews and others who could not meet the "urgent" work requirements of the camp were immediately selected for extermination.

Those who survived immediate extermination were subject to many methods of torture used on innocent Jews and other detainees at Auschwitz. Whenever the *Gestapo* or the *SS* wanted to get information from prisoners, often they would use a contraption called the "Boger Swing." This "swing" was a method of beating a prisoner to death while trying to get information on other Jews or members of the community who did not hold to the German ideal of racial purity.

The "Swing" was developed by Wilhelm Boger, a police commissioner and overseer of the Auschwitz Concentration camp. His nickname, "The Tiger of Auschwitz," was given to him because of his ghastly and horrific crimes committed while serving at the camp run by fellow *Nazi* and Gestapo chief Maximilian Grabner.

The Boger Swing was a meter long iron bar suspended from the ceiling by chains. The prisoner would be brought in, stripped naked and bent over the swing. His or her ankles would be shackled to their wrist, and a guard would gently push the victim on a long slow arc on the swing. The guard would often sound very caring and explain to the prisoner if the bar might be cold to the touch, he could put a towel on the bar. Boger would start in a low friendly voice to question the inmate. Boger would then gradually increase the tone of his voice and eventually work himself into a bellowing rage while another guard would smash the victim across the buttocks with an iron crowbar.

The victim would pass out from the cruel torture, but then revived with a bucket of cold water. The "swing" would continue until there was nothing left of the innocent prisoner but a bloody collection of broken bones.

Older men and women, young children, and anyone not capable of prolonged hard labor were immediately shunted off the freight cars of the trains, stripped of all clothing and jewelry and herded into the "showers." The unsuspecting victims were then subjected in this locked and sealed gas chamber to a pesticide gas called Zyklon-B, manufactured by the I G Farben chemical company which, conveniently enough, had a plant just a few miles away.

The gas pellets were dumped in through a roof vent and the vent was then closed off and sealed. Their ghoulish and demonically cruel executioners could observe the cries of anguish and terror from the poor souls locked in these chambers through a thick glass sealed portal.

Perhaps the majority of the German people had little knowledge of the wholesale murder of its' citizens by the *Gestapo, SS*, and the other officers and men of the *Wehrmacht*. But many of the participants of the Holocaust who ran the camps knew. Their families must have known people were being experimented on while alive.

Bayer, then a subsidiary of I G Farben had a practice of purchasing prisoners to test new experimental drugs! Unfortunately, these drugs were not just the Bayer Aspirin many people use today. Inflicting pain on the purchased innocent Jews and experimenting with pain relievers was common practice. This inhumanity was very difficult for many Germans to understand.

I think what bothered Ezekiel and me the most, was the officers of the *SS* and *Wehrmacht* viewed their murderous work as a career opportunity for advancement and a way to curry favor with the officers higher in rank. Our goal was the reduction, alteration, mitigation, or even the complete cessation of this murderous behavior. We certainly knew the risks. Also, we knew without an uprising of the German people, our efforts were doomed for ultimate failure.

Most German civilians were utterly intimidated by the all-powerful politicians and their backing by the *Gestapo, SS* and the *Wehrmacht.* German citizens knew one word of protest against the political policies of the day could land them in the same concentration camp as their Jewish neighbors. Many German citizens knew in spite of the horror engulfing their country, not belonging to the *Nazi Party* marked them as "unreliable patriots." This knowledge only enhanced the terror many God-fearing Germans experienced.

On our way out of the meeting Ezekiel, in a hushed tone of voice commented,

"Jenz, our interference with the work of the development of these vengeance weapons is taking us further and further into danger. Some of the laboratory technicians are asking me questions which are difficult to answer.

"Karl, one of the head lab technicians in the Guidance Laboratory, was asking pointed questions about my family in

Italy. I think I was pretty smooth, but he was a little too persistent; bordering on the impolite."

"Do you think he might suspect you or us, Zeke?"

"He might; let's be extremely cautious."

"Caution is my only method, friend. Let's find a place for dinner; somewhere where we can talk without the fear of being overheard by a hidden microphone."

CHAPTER 32

The Gestapo Interrupts Dinner

We settled on the small restaurant near the base. We had the smoked fish and delicious potato soup. Although it seemed safe enough, we still spoke in low, hushed tones.

"We have to redouble our efforts at work, Jenz. It's important we make ourselves valuable so they will not suspect anything."

"You're right Zeke! Have you thought of any innovative ways to 'improve' the V-1 program?"

"The only improvement I discussed with the scientists and technicians in our lab is the use of a lighter metal for the housing of the rocket. The metal could be lighter, but it also has to be extremely heat-resistant."

"Our assistant chief of lab operations has asked me to research the possibilities for this important part of the rocket."

"What makes the metal so critical?"

"I used calculus to discover for every kilogram we can take off the total weight of the rocket, also means a reduction in the amount and weight of the fuel. The result is another 35-40 kilometers in range of the weapon. The improvement in range was a real victory for our lab. Now the head of our lab wants me to research the metal or alloy to find one which will work best for this weapon."

As we were talking and eating our meal, two men came into the eating establishment, looked around the room, and headed directly for our table. I mentioned to Zeke, "please do not turn around but I think this could be further trouble coming our way. Try not to display any anxiety and act slightly indignant. I will try to do the talking."

They came up to our table rather abruptly and asked our names.

"Are you men associated with the Research Center? What are your names."

I pointed to my name tag on my *SS* uniform while chewing my last mouthful of food and said in a kind, light tone, "I am Lieutenant Jenz Ramsgrund and this Vitali Carapezza. We are both affiliated with the Army Research Center here in Peenemünde."

"Who would like to know who we are? And, how did you get on the base?"

Both men looked a cut above the average *Gestapo* thug. They were both well dressed in suits and their clothing looked to fit well. One of them was reed thin and had a little *"Hitler"* mustache. He was probably the lead spokesman. The other, a powerfully built gentleman, with minimal neck, but lots of bulging muscles, looked like a weight lifter. Although stuffed into his suit, it fit him pretty well.

The reedy one spoke up hurriedly. **"We will be asking the questions here. Agent Baumann and I are from the *Gestapo* special intelligent unit. We are detaining you both on suspicion of anti-Nazi activities involving students at the university in Berlin."**

"Humph." I stifled a laugh but regained my composure immediately. I was sure it was no laughing matter. I just had trouble put those two words together in my mind: *Gestapo* and intelligence. Special was the watchword for these two.

I thought it best to be as agreeable as possible. "Would you gentlemen care to sit down while we finish our dinner? And, could we, please see your credentials?"

The beefy agent stepped right in front of my face and said in an officious tone, **"I'm Agent Baumann, and this is Agent Weber."** They both opened a leather wallet and displayed their badges. **"And, we cannot wait around while you two finish your dinner. You are to come with us immediately to *Gestapo Headquarters* for questioning. We will notify your unit if we detain you for longer than 24 hours."**

I didn't say anything, but adjusted my seat a bit and kept on eating. Agent Baumann or "agent beefy" as I started to think of him then drew his Lugar and shouted, **"Now!"**

The outburst drew the attention of every dinner guest in the restaurant. The cook in the kitchen came out to see what was going on.

Since I was sitting down, evidently both agents Weber and Baumann had no idea how large I was.

I then stood up and said in a commanding voice, **"Agent Baumann, you have just made a career-ending mistake. Pointing a weapon at an *SS* Officer has only proven fatal for your career with the *Gestapo.***

"We shall see," hissed Baumann.

Vitali and I reluctantly left our meals on the table and walked out of the restaurant at gunpoint with the two *Gestapo* agents right behind us.

The dinner guests in the restaurant looked aghast. They were shocked and stunned. I wasn't sure if the patron's discomfort was the sudden appearance of the *Gestapo* or my response to their demands.

I should try to explain myself here a little more clearly. Ever since I was a young boy growing up in Düsseldorf, my mom always, gently, wanted to get me to eat nutritious food and in sensible portions. I was growing fast and usually still always hungry.

Left to my diet desires, Mom was afraid I might get overweight.

For some reason, if anyone other than my mom tried to interrupt or restrict my meal, I would get a little annoyed. Now, if someone interrupted my meal with a loud command, and stuck a Lugar in my face in a public place, well, I would get downright irritable and grumpy.

I kept trying to keep a refined and cajoling note to my voice and asked, "Vitali, did you pay for our meal?"

"No, Jenz," he replied as we got into the back seat of a recent vintage Mercedes Benz. "We left rather abruptly after we were interrupted and I didn't think of paying for our meal."

I mentioned, "We should come back later this evening and apologize to the staff and get a chance to finish our meal."

Agent Baumann then challenged, "You men will not be back to this base for at least 24 hours or possibly much longer."

We started driving, and it looked like we were heading for the main gate.

"Where are you taking us, Agent Weber," Vitali asked.

"Don't worry, gentlemen. The Gestapo has an unusual detention and interrogation facility outside of Greifswald about 30 kilometers from here. It is called Stalag II. It is currently being used to house any prisoners-of-war lucky enough to avoid the concentration camps.

With a smirk, Agent Baumann claimed, "I'm not sure you gentlemen will be quite as comfortable as on the *Wehrmacht* base at the Research Center, but you will get used to it.

It was then I noticed there were no handles on the inside of the rear doors of the Mercedes. We were locked in the rear compartment. I tapped Zeke on the knee and pointed to the doors where the handles should have been. Zeke looked sick.

I held up one finger as the wait sign and gently shook my head. I hoped to alleviate the panic feeling Ezekiel might be experiencing.

I then raised my foot to my knee and unlaced my boot.

Then I switched my position on the seat and brought my other foot up and quietly unlaced my other boot.

I then tied my shoelaces together in a very tight knot ensuring it wouldn't slip. Thank you, Hitler Youth Camp.

I then whispered to Zeke to keep the conversation light until I had a chance to loupe the shoe-lace around Weber's neck. Then he was to push forward as hard as possible on the seat in front of him to make it so Agent Baumann couldn't reach for his pistol. I told him we should wait until we were in an isolated spot at a slow speed to avoid a traffic accident.

"Quiet! No Talking." Agent 'beefy' commanded.

After about ten minutes, we came to a stop sign at a crossroad heading for the Baltic beach region. I lifted my chin to alert Zeke, and we went to work.

I wound both ends of the shoelace around my hands, quickly looped it over agent Weber's head and pulled back tightly on his neck. I put all my strength into a downward and backward pull.

His head snapped back as I pulled him up in the seat so his feet couldn't reach the foot pedals of the automobile. He made some horrible gurgling sounds in his throat, his face turned to beat red, his eyes bulged out, and he tried kicking the dash to get leverage on me. His hands went to his throat to try to remove the garrote, but I was putting my weight into the downward pull.

Zeke had pushed the back of Baumann's chair forward, making it difficult for the agent to get his pistol out of its' holster.

"Watch his gun hand, Zeke!"

I hoped I had crushed Weber's larynx and the esophagus because I had to let go with my right hand to bring my closed fist down on Baumann's temporal bone as hard as I could.

There was limited room in the automobile for a decent swing at Baumann, so my efforts only stunned him. I grabbed the shoelace garrote and looped it around his neck, but he was so muscular, I wasn't sure it would be quite as useful as the garrote used on Agent Weber.

As I was pulling him back over the seat, I shouted at Zeke, "hold on to the laces and pull as hard as you can."

I reached over and opened the driver side door and pushed Weber out on to the street. We were still rolling slightly to the side of the road.

I crawled over the seat and out the door on all fours, which wasn't easy for me with my long legs. I ran around the car, pulled open Baumann's entry, and grabbed his Lugar from his holster.

He looked at me with terror in his eyes while trying to clutch at my shoelaces Zeke was holding and pulling on for dear life around his neck.

I considered putting two bullets in his chest, but I was afraid the sound might carry and alert someone.

Instead, I just watched and tried to explain to him this is what I meant by a career-ending mistake. He tried to kick at me, but the car was too confining. His neck was so thick, and I thought it might take Zeke quite a while to end agent beefy's sad life. I didn't need a passing car to stop and ask questions.

In the end, I looked in the trunk, pulled out an old blanket, placed it over the Lugar and beefy's chest, and pulled the trigger twice putting two Parabellum bullets into his heart. I had to fire at an angle so the bullets wouldn't deflect toward Zeke if they were to get through beefy's massive body and the seat-back.

"Now," Zeke commented, "we could have a real problem. How are we going to make this mess disappear?"

"Ezekiel, our *Gestapo* 'friends' have had a tragic accident."

"How is an accident going to cover up to two bullet holes in the chest of agent beefy?"

"Unfortunately their car burst into flames after it went off the road. Their bodies will be burned to an unrecognizable crisp."

"Let's get Weber in the back seat until we find a likely curve for an automobile accident."

I told Zeke, who was in the back seat, to brace himself, we were coming up to a curve, and I wanted skid marks on the pavement. He folded the blanket in his lap and held on to the seat.

I accelerated, jammed on the brakes, and turned into the biggest ditch I could find.

"Hold on Ezekiel; we are going into a ditch!"

As we went off the side of the road, the car tilted on its side in the shallow road swale. It looked like a pretty authentic roadside accident. We threw a little dirt and sand from the bottom of the road onto the car; which was probably unnecessary considering what I had planned.

We carefully arranged both passengers in the front seat and banged the glass where their heads would have cracked the windshield as they went into the ditch. I used the bar for the jack I found in the trunk to break the windshield.

Zeke unwrapped the Lugar in the blanket, reached under the rear of the car rewrapped the Lugar to muffle the sound, and shot a hole in the gas tank. The diesel fuel didn't burn or explode, but he did get a steady stream of diesel fuel flowing onto the blanket. After soaking the blanket with fuel, we placed it over both of them on the front seat. Zeke set it on fire using matches he found in agent Weber's pocket.

Zeke and I started walking rapidly back to the base on the deserted road we had just traveled. The Mercedes was burning quite brightly as we picked up the pace and jogged out of sight.

The guards challenged us, but we showed our identification, and I had a copy of my orders, which I always kept with me. They always seemed a little respectful to the *SS* emblems on my uniform and hat.

Zeke asked me later, "How do you always stay so calm in these tense situations?"

"Because, I know we are doing the right thing: eliminating these evil agents of doom. "I'm planning my life with the sincere hope and prayer God will forgive us. These people are torturing our fellow citizens and placing them in concentration camps. Who will forgive them?"

CHAPTER 33

Planning for The Failure of the V-1 and V-2

For a year Vitali and I had not been bothered by the *Gestapo* or *SS* at the Army Research Center. Our laboratories were making continual improvements in the V-1 and V-2 rocket motors and guidance systems. The liquid fuel in the V-2 burned very hot and produced a powerfully explosive rocket thrust, but we had continuous and ongoing failures trying to launch the rockets with consistency.

Our experiments with the liquid fuel involved using minimal quantities, usually less than a tablespoon, in a controlled burn in the laboratory. The temperature, and the explosive force, was always carefully measured. The power of the explosive force was still pre-calculated with mathematical formulae, but the heat and energy of the explosion always surprised us.

For every successful launch, we had three unsuccessful launches and sometimes catastrophic explosions with loss of life. Hitler came to one of our launches in 1942 and witnessed a rocket rise to approximately 200 feet before it exploded in a fireball. I asked Zeke if he had anything to do with the failure, and he just winked at me. I never did learn the intimate details of how he did it. We think it might have been part of the reason Hitler didn't back the rocket program as enthusiastically as his scientists and rocket specialists.

Many generals thought the V-1 and V-2 programs just took money away from the production of tanks and artillery and other conventional arms. The Wehrmacht elite looked at the missile program as just another artillery piece, but with a more extended range.

Zeke had mentioned the fuel was highly volatile and had a low threshold of combustion. He said, "I'm working on the problem of lowering the flash point of the liquid oxygen and naphthalene by including some stabilizing pollutants into the naphthalene."

"The most successful mix I have been able to come up with," added Zeke, "was a mixture of 75% alcohol and water mixed with the liquid oxygen. This formula is relatively stable, but I have not introduced it yet to the fuel scientists, because it would just advance the date for use of the missiles."

Also, he cautioned, "The metal skin of the rocket has to be durable, lightweight, and not too temperature conductive. If the overall surface of the missile gets too hot, two things may happen: the fuel in the holding tanks will ignite with catastrophic results, or the oxygen will boil off. The rapid increasing pressure in the liquid oxygen tanks will cause rupture and explosion. We are working on a venting system for the liquid oxygen holding tank to self-vent to the exterior of the weapon or into the combustion chamber for added thrust.

"As you can see," Zeke continued in hushed tones, "The V-2 has many problems. "My biggest concern is the completion of the weapon in the next year or two. Then Hitler's dreams of world conquest could come to fruition. Unfortunately, the V-1 is ready to go into production and London, and all of England will feel the consequences within twelve to eighteen months.

"Last month on the third of October," Vitali remarked, "was the first completely successful flight of a vehicle capable of reaching outer space. The rocket, an A-4, which the politicians want to use as their second vengeance weapon or V-2, was successfully launched from our Test Stand number VII here at Peenemünde. The V-2 could be a dangerous weapon, if the guidance system is perfected. It reached a height of 84.5 kilometers and flew down range for 147 kilometers.

"Hitler's armies may be facing defeat in Stalingrad," Vitali said. "I hear stories in the laboratory. These stories of defeat would be very upsetting if true. Let me explain," Vitali continued, "General Paulus has written to Hitler the German Sixth Army is surrounded. It could mean the end of this ridiculous and tragic war; perhaps the war could be almost over for Germany. If we lose an entire Army to the Soviets, how would we continue the war effort?

"Jenz, if the rumors about the Sixth Army are true, it will mean our work here at the Army Research Center will be even more critical for the politicians. We have to be extremely careful and vigilant. Let's concentrate our brains to see if there is anything additional we can do to slow down these vengeance weapon monsters from becoming fully operational."

Throughout the spring and summer of 1943 Vitali and I thought of all sorts of mechanical and technical engineering changes to advance, and perhaps, at the same time, slow down the development of these weapons.

Late in July, the allies bombed the military targets in Hamburg. The resulting firestorm was rumored to have killed over forty thousand people. The buildings in the center of the city and the areas around the military targets looked like burned out hulks.

"Jenz, this war is now coming to Germany with very dramatic and deadly repercussions. Won't the politicians see the futility of continuing this madness."

"I'm sorry to think, Vitali, Hitler and the rest of the thugs running the country seem to have an all or nothing approach for Germany. Let's face it, the allies can build more bombs and aircraft faster than we can. If you and I can understand this, certainly the politicians must see it."

"One of Hitler's ministers, Albert Speer, Reich Minister of Armaments and War Production for the *Nazis,* has been spending time in our laboratories quizzing us as to when these vengeance weapons will be ready to wreak havoc on the English cities."

"Has he described a time table for you, Vitali?"

"Not specifically, but he says he has prisoners building launch sites on the French coast from Calais to Le Harve. Also, more slave labor is employed digging an underground factory someplace in the middle of our country.

"We will have to think of some additional methods to slow down these terror weapons."

CHAPTER 34

The First Vengeance Weapons Arrive

Our laboratory heard the first V-1s were launched toward London on the 13th of June, 1944. Their launch and deployment were prompted because of the Allied landings on the coast of France on June 6th. Of the ten missiles launched, only four reached London.

When the news of the V-1's forty percent "success" reached our lab, Vitali remarked, "Perhaps the missiles will need a little more tweaking."

Much of the missile construction had moved underground in a laboratory near Nordhausen in the geographic center of Germany. An old gypsum mine had been enlarged with slave labor from the Dora concentration camp and made into production facilities for the vengeance weapons.

Vitali tried to be outwardly ashamed and embarrassed even disconcerted because of the forty percent success rate, while inwardly Vitali and I shared the joy of knowing, perhaps we had something to do with only four of the missiles reaching London.*

---

* *From June 13, 1944, until the end of the war in May 1945 almost ten thousand V-1 vengeance weapon cruise missiles were fired at London. Each steam catapult launching site could fire 10 to 15 rockets per day. Of the 10,000 launched, only 2400 reached London. Many fell short on the Croydon area southeast of London; many were felled*

Vitali asked, "Jenz, are you able to consistently alter the fuel mix for these V-1 weapons?"

"I have to be extremely careful, Vitali."

"The weapon calls for 165 gallons of 75 octane gasoline. One of the prisoners who fuel the weapons launched from the site near Peenemünde will, under my orders, mix 10 gallons of diesel fuel in with the gasoline. Mixing the fuels will cause the weapon to run out of fuel early or to sputter as the fuel mix cannot correctly power the pulse-jet engine. Fuel starvation will cause the missile to crash prematurely and not reach the target.

"Another method I have used is to fill the tank with 165 gallons of 90 octane gasoline. High octane fuel makes the pulse-jet engine burn too hot, and the rocket will explode over water long before it reaches any populated areas. My problem with this technique is the higher octane gasoline is in critical shortage and much harder to get after our politicians have blundered so severely on the Eastern Front."

"What happened in Russia, Jenz?"

"It looks like the Russians have stopped the Wehrmacht advance at Stalingrad."

"The rumors we have heard in the laboratory about the Sixth Army look to be true. Not only was this entire army surrounded, but they surrendered to the Red Army on the 31st of January 1943. Our 'brilliant' politicians lost over 280,000 of our nations precious young *Wehrmacht* troops!"[*]

---

by British and American aircraft and other countermeasures like barrage balloons and anti-aircraft fire.

[*] *Of the troops captured by the Red Army, only 5,000 men made it home to Germany at the end of the war. Most of the rest perished under horrific circumstances with poor nutrition and disease; much like the conditions in the Nazi concentration camps.*

"Why wasn't the country notified?"

"Zeke, think about it for a minute. News of a massive of defeat would demoralize the *Wehrmacht* and bring the entire country back to its senses. Especially since Hitler demanded they resist until the last bullet!"

"Worse, this past January the First Ukrainian Front of the Red Army has entered Poland. Now, in 1944, our armies will be fighting a defensive battle for our homeland. If our current politicians stay in charge, the Russians will be in Peenemünde within a year.

"Most of our research and manufacturing material has now been moved underground to Nordhausen since the RAF bombing last August, but our testing laboratory is currently minimally stocked.

"Well, here is another interesting thought, Jenz. In our Guidance Laboratory, the rumor is last month, in July, there was an attempt on Hitler's life. So far, the *Gestapo* and the *SS* have rounded up almost five thousand people linked to the conspiracy. Those arrested included high ranking officers of the *Wehrmacht*, their families, and even their children.

"Jenz, we should be planning some exit policy to escape from this place. If we could find my parents, I would love to take them with us.

"Have your parents move from Düsseldorf, Jenz?"

"Yes, they had to move. There were too many questioning *Gestapo* agents in his plant. I got a letter last week telling me they have moved in with family members in Stockholm. So I can assume they are safe for now. I wish I could have ordered the *SS* to release your parents to go with them. Sweden is still maintaining its neutrality, so the 'brilliant' politicians in our country probably will not invade them.

"I will make some further discreet inquiries for your family, Vitali, but the news, if there is any, may not be good. These labor camps can be challenging and life-threatening for the detainees."

"Thanks for trying, Jenz. Please be careful not to jeopardize yourself or our 'important' work here at the Army Research Center."

"Has your laboratory made any progress with 'improvements' for the V-2?"

"Jenz, this rocket is a monster! It is three times the size of the V-1, and it travels to the edge of outer space before re-entering the atmosphere at two or three times faster than the speed of sound. The victims cannot hear it coming. All of a sudden, the target is just obliterated. There is no known defense for this weapon."

"How is the guidance system?"

"The gyroscopes are much more sophisticated than in the V-1, but the rocket is still only accurate to within a three-kilometer circle of the target. There are three stabilizing gyroscopes, but radio control is not yet perfected. The missiles are now under construction, and the first one will be fired as a weapon this fall.

"However, Jenz, the V-2 warhead laboratory has not yet developed a proximity fuse, so an airburst is not possible. The only detonation possible is the moment the rocket hits the earth. This 'contact only' fuse, will limit its destructive power."

"What the devil is a proximity fuse Vitali? Are we trying to develop one?"

"It detonates the warhead near the intended target. It could be set to go off at the height of 300 meters. An explosion at a 300 meter height would be quite devastating in a congested area. Or it will go off if the intended target immediately starts to travel further away. A proximity fuse would be quite useful for an antiaircraft missile when attacking enemy airplanes."

"Will they develop one for these rockets, Zeke?"

"Probably, eventually. Unless I can think of a way to build one we can depend on consistently failing, I'm working on a proximity fuse right now, along with what I quietly and humorously call a 'Never Find' guidance system."

"What the devil is a "Never Find" system all about Vitali?"

"It is a pretty simple guidance system which will direct the missile precisely to the target with almost ninety-five percent accuracy. However, it will detonate the warhead at least ten miles before reaching the target!"

"Vitali... Zeke, sometimes you exhibit true genius! I depend on your clear linear thinking to get us through some complicated and challenging situations. I have never told you this, but many of your suggestions helped me through the Hitler Youth Camp when I was a teenager."

Vitali and I would often take walks along the beach in Peenemünde to discuss the safest way to slow down the development of the missiles. The beach was the only place where we could discuss in complete privacy the slowing and completion of the missile development. We were both very much afraid of the possible capabilities of these monsters.

"I should mention one more item of gossip from our lab, Jenz. The *Reich* is building or planning to build over 10,000 of these V-2 vengeance weapons. One of the main problems is our country doesn't have enough explosives for the number of many warheads the *Führer* is planning.

"It's rumored some of the warheads will be filled with cement and will rely on the kinetic energy alone for the devastation of the targets."

"The political thinking doesn't make a lot of sense to me on several levels, Vitali."

"Jenz, does this whole decade since Hitler's rise to power make any sense to you?"

"You make a good point, Zeke. Let's plan an exit strategy before the whole country collapses. I also want to make sure Ilsa and her family are safe. I have urged her and her family to avoid going anywhere near the downtown areas of Hannover. The central city has seen extensive air raids because of the military value of war production materials, including military vehicles and aircraft production. Sometimes, especially with inclement winter weather and strong winds, those bombs could easily drift into the suburbs of Hannover."

"What do you think we should do, Jenz, traveling through Germany to Switzerland or Spain might be very difficult with the Allies coming in from the west and the Russians coming in from the east."

"No Zeke, we will plan our exit for the summer of 1944. I have thought a lot about various escape plans, but none of them are without danger. Our best bet will be to get orders to our base in Denmark. From there we will make our way to Sweden where I have relatives. This winter and spring, let's see how much more we can 'improve' the V-2 rocket."

CHAPTER 35

Delaying the V-2

"**T**his wind is relentless here in Peenemünde, Zeke." We were talking in hushed tones in the early morning on their way to the research laboratory, before the research and construction of the missiles was move to the Mittelwerk factory. It was a penetrating cold which kept most sane people inside.

"It's an Arctic wind, Jenz. It blows across Russia, Finland, and down over the Baltic Sea. It is an unlikely spot for a rocket development laboratory. I think it's why the *Nazi* politicians liked it so much; it's very remote."

"Can you think of any way your lab could further delay the deployment of the V-2? I understand the politicians want it ready for launch this summer."

"Jenz, if everything goes the way I hope this winter and spring, I will be able to delay the beast for a month or two, but probably no longer. Hitler is calling this rocket his 'wonder weapon' and is pinning his hopes for victory on its rapid deployment. Our laboratory is feeling enormous pressure to iron out any problems with this weapon as soon as possible."

"When will be the next big test launch?"

"Probably late spring, unless we can think of a way to delay it. This rocket is truly a monster. Its overall length is just under forty-six feet with a circumference of five feet five inches. Fully loaded with an explosive payload, it weighs almost 27,600 pounds!

"The most dangerous feature of the weapon, Jenz, is there is virtually no defense against it. After it achieves lift off, it will travel up to the edge of space and speed toward its' target at up to 2,500 miles per hour. At impact, it could be traveling at two or three times the speed of sound. Its' victims will never see or hear it approaching!"

"Is there anything you can do Zeke to disable the rocket completely?"

"Not without the extreme danger of being discovered."

"I know your laboratory is working on the warhead and fusing for the weapon, can you think of anything to slow down its development?"

"Nothing yet Zeke. But I have heard rumors our laboratory will be constructing mobile launching vehicles for both the V-1 and the V-2 rockets. There is even talk of building a launch pad on the submarines to launch the V-1missiles into New York City in America so we can kill more Jews.

"Our politicians are truly deranged. It is just so hard to believe our Jew-hating leaders could get so much power."

"Also, as shortages get more intense and even necessities get more scarce, ordinary citizens could get more desperate. Let's try to find my parents, Jenz, and make our exit before the boarders get impossible to cross. Do you have any final plans to get out of this quagmire of a country?"

"We will wait until next summer. Our final plans will have to include a lot of flexibility because the *Gestapo* seems to be everywhere. Our first step will be trying to get or forge orders to our base in northern Denmark. Although the Reich occupies Denmark, the Danes are not happy about being subjugated by bullies and tyrants. My feeling is we would have a better chance of freedom if we could leave from occupied Denmark."

"The fear hangs over our country has been unrelenting, like a continuous fog penetrating every nook and cranny of our lives in the *Reich*. Friends, neighbors, even families, have turned against each other. It is hard to know whom to trust in this atmosphere of implacable, tenacious fear."

"Have you had any luck with the fuel mix for the V-2, Ezekiel?"

"I have been looking at the liquid fuel mix pumped into the combustion chamber during takeoff and flight. It is a mixture of alcohol and liquid oxygen. It has explosive characteristics and burns for only about 60-70 seconds. It develops enough thrust to lift the monster. When fully fueled with a warhead, it weighs almost thirteen tons!

"It is complicated to alter the fuel, Jenz, because it comes from very secure storage areas from other parts of our country. The difficult part about altering the rocket in any way is it can be set up in a matter of 4-6 hours and launched from any flat spot in the country, even from a clearing in the middle of a forest."

"All the fuel is expended after the first 65 seconds of flight, and the control is only in effect from the gyroscopes. The gyroscopes control the fin trimmers in the veins of the exhaust for only the first twenty miles of flight. Afterward, it is almost like any other artillery round, except the range is up to 200 miles. This range is over ten times further than any artillery piece ever developed. It travels up to a height of over 50 miles and then comes roaring back to earth at almost 3000 miles per hour. How is anyone supposed to prepare for any kind of supersonic weapon?"

"Is there any flaw to be built into the guidance system, Zeke?"

"I'm working on the possibilities right now. I'm searching for anything which could cause an error in trajectory or targeting location. It could be minimal, but even a slight change in the trajectory could cause a significant change in the flight path of the missile. Even if I could get one of the electric motors controlling the trimmers on the fin veins to fail, it would make a sizable difference in targeting malfunction."

"Zeke, how are the gyroscopes controlled to keep the missile on its' tract?"

"This is the tricky part, and the missiles are all programmed ahead of their launch. Each missile carries a new small analog computer. Once the rocket is in flight, its gyroscopes will continuously track the position of the rocket in three dimensions. If there are deviations in the course of the missile, the rudders attached to the fins on the monster automatically adjust to keep the rocket on its deadly path to the pre-programmed target. If weather at the launch site isn't stormy and the winds are calm, there is no stopping the missile once it is launched."

"Well, Zeke, I appreciate anything you can come up with to interrupt the accuracy of this deadly monster of a weapon."

"Many before me have tried. The rumor in our laboratory is many hundreds of prison workers have died so far in the fabrication and mass production of these missiles. The new facilities are being placed underground, away from Allied bombing attacks."

"The Nazis have used slave labor from the concentration camps. Any prisoners with electrical, welding or mechanical or engineering skills of any kind are being used. An underground factory, *Mittelwerk* has been dug into the mountain near Nordhausen in Thuringia. It is near the center of the *Reich* away from the threat of Allied and Russian air strikes.[*]

---

[*] *During the summer of 1943, the Royal Air Force instituted bombing raids on the Army Research Center at Peenemünde on the night of August 17th and 18th. The attacks*

"As of the 22nd of August, our *Führer* has authorized the use of slave labor to ramp up the mass production of both the V-1 and the V-2 missiles. The extreme cruelty and desperation of the *Nazi* Regime has come together to complete the nightmare of living in the concentration camps."

The original work for preparing the gypsum mine for the underground factory was given to Himmler and his construction chief *SS* General Hans Kammler. This contractor built most of the concentration camps in the *Third Reich*. Kammler used forced labor to blast and expand the existing mining tunnels at the southern edge of the Harz Mountains into the largest subterranean factory in Germany.

This sizeable underground factory is used for the production of submarines and aircraft as well as the main production line for the V-2 missiles. Over twelve thousand slave laborers are toiling in this factory in the underground gypsum mine.

Ezekiel, (Vitali) and I, wanted to view the production line of the rockets to see if we could institute any "improvements" in the V-1 or V-2 missiles. What we witnessed was not only shocking but genuinely horrifying.

Hundreds of concentration camp prisoners were working on fabricating, assembling, and finishing the V-2 rockets. If a prisoner slowed production, he was whipped or beaten by one of the kapo guards.

The prisoners appeared in deplorable physical condition. All of them looked emaciated with their skin and clothing just hanging on their skeletal frames.

---

destroyed much of the testing and research facilities. The missile production was moved to the center of Germany near Nordhausen away from the bombing raids. Some of the testing and laboratory research for the rockets was kept at Peenemünde.

I was in my SS uniform, and Ezekiel was beside me as a witness when I asked one of the guards, "Where do the prisoners sleep?"

"These sub-humans don't need or deserve to sleep." answered the guard. "When they cannot stand up any longer, we ship them to a side tunnel to sleep on a mat. There are no malingerers here! When they drop from fatigue, we usually send them back to the camp." The guard was disheveled looking. His uniform was unkempt, and he needed a shave. I could smell him from five feet away.

"What happens to them there?" was my question, although I was afraid I already knew the answer.

"Usually they are sent to the showers for 'rejuvenation' therapy," the guard said with a mean sneer on his lips.

"What do they eat?" I asked.

"Oh, they get a thin potato peel soup every night."

"Is potato peel soup all the workers get?" I was incredulous. "Wouldn't they perform better if they were better fed?"

The guard shot back, "If they don't perform or attempt any act of sabotage, we hang them from the crane." He motioned to the high crane and pointed three stories up toward the ceiling with his unshaven chin.

There at the end of a rope, a worn out prisoner was hanging from a noose around his neck. He looked more like a collection of rags than a human being.

I thought Vitali might lose his temper, his face reddened and contorted. I immediately wanted to tell the guard this might reinforce negative feedback from the workers.

The Kapo, however, ended our discussion with a facial sneer, "Herr Himmler feels this will remind the sub-humans of their fate."

I whispered to Vitali, "let's get out of this living hell."

As we walked outside to catch a bus for the officer and scientist housing, Vitali asked me, "Do you have any idea if we are going to be able to escape this sewer?"

It was an early spring day with a chill accompanied by a low hanging fog to help exacerbate a depression we both felt as we exited the tunnels. The deplorable exploitation of our fellow Jews and German citizens gave us both a deep heartache.

"We have two objectives, Ezekiel, first, we will try to do everything in our power to delay or sidetrack the work on these 'wonder weapons,' and second, we will try to find a way for us and our loved ones to escape this tyranny we once proudly called Germany."

"Jenz, the *Reich* is building hundreds, perhaps thousands of these monsters. If we are to be effective, we must avoid being caught up and imprisoned in this madness."

"I know Zeke; even Von Braun doesn't like the idea of his spacecraft rockets used as weapons. The *Reich* Minister of Armaments, Albert Speer, is probably under a lot of pressure from Hitler to produce these missiles in quantity to overturn what looks to be the inevitable outcome of this crazy war."

"Remember Zeke; these weapons represent Hitler's last-ditch effort by the Nazis to reverse the course of the war."

"The 'Vengeance Weapons' could kill or injure thousands of innocent civilians because of their inaccurate guidance systems. They are being fired rather indiscriminately at major population centers as retaliation for the bombing of our major cities."*

---

* *During the final stages of the war, an estimated nine thousand civilian deaths resulted from the use of the V-2 rockets. However, at least twelve thousand wrongly imprisoned laborers and concentration camp prisoners died as a result of forced participation in the production of these weapons.*

"We should form some plan, Jenz, for getting the hell out of *Nazi* Germany before it's too late. I can't help but feel a trap of our own making is slowly closing in on us."

"Vitali, I am trying to think ahead. Right now I am working with the chief of our laboratory and suggesting a launching site in a German-controlled air force base in northern Denmark called Aalborg Air Base. The German *Luftwaffe* has controlled this air base since the 9th of April 1940."

"How do you even know about such things, Jenz?"

"I read about the reports of an air raid on the base in August 1940 by the Royal Air Force. They attacked with Bristol Blenheim Bombers. All eleven British aircraft were brought down by anti-aircraft fire or our Messerschmitt BF 109 fighter aircraft.

"The base has been substantially expanded and would make a wonderfully convenient and remote launch site for the V-2 rockets. Both Moscow and London could be easily targeted. It is remote enough and easily defended to make it unlikely to be targeted by Allied aircraft again.

"We need to convince my boss, Dr. von Braun, or General Dornberger to get us orders to conduct a survey and write up a report on the suitability of the air base as a launch site. I would much rather discuss my idea with Dr. Walter Thiel before talking with them. However, the August 17 raid killed our highly respected chief of rocket engine design and development.

CHAPTER 36

Labor Camp Prisoners Building Rockets

"**B**efore we request orders, I would like to make an approach to one of the prisoners from the factory inside the gypsum mine. Talking with one of the prisoners who is working on the production line could prove enlightening."

"Wouldn't talking to a prisoner be taking an unnecessary risk, Jenz? The Kapos or guards are always watching the prisoners very closely, and they always seem to be belligerent and humorless. Why would you want to talk to a prisoner?"

"Well, I have two main reasons. First I would be interested to know if any of the prisoners have heard of your parents, and second, I would think it important for these victims of *Nazi* oppression to know they are not alone in their resistance to the *Reich.* Perhaps they could even help us slow down the V-2 rocket production."

"Jenz, it sounds hazardous, you know what could happen with the betrayal of the *Gestapo.* How were you thinking of accomplishing this without winding up in the camp ourselves."

"Zeke, we are going to have to pick a fight! You and I will have to rehearse it this evening. Our actions will have to be carefully staged; you can be sure the Kapos will scrutinize whatever we do near those rocket production lines."

"The Kapo, *(Funktion shaftling)* or prisoner functionary is also a victim of the *Nazi* concentration camp system. The *SS* is saving money by turning a victim against the victims. Keep in mind, these guards or Kapos are often criminals recruited because of their brutality."

"What the devil are you talking about?"

"Tomorrow, on our inspection tour, I will approach one of the men working on the production line and yell at him for some minor infraction. As the guard comes over to intervene and discipline the prisoner, I will need you to step in front of the guard and tell him the *SS* officer has the situation under control and not to interfere."

"It sounds dangerous."

"It is. We both have to speak with authority and be firm. We will both need nerves of steel. But I know you can do it, Ezekiel, look what you, look what we have accomplished the last few years. We have both developed a little 'command authority' in our voice."

"Jenz, I think you are a different person after you attended Hitler Youth Camp."

"Hitler Camp was beneficial. I learned how to recognize evil, and I learned how to be strong. And when necessary, how to confront evil."

"Did you have any regrets from Hitler Camp?"

"**No!** I also learned about love. Ilsa and I have pledged our lives to each other."

"Did you get married?"

"How would I get married without you there as my witness?"

"Let's get some sleep, Zeke. I want to pull off our charade just before noon tomorrow."

Late morning, after a short bus ride, we approached the underground factory facility. Zeke's nerves were on fire. I looked great in my *SS* uniform. My boots added another inch or two to my height. It was odd, I didn't feel even slightly nervous. Zeke mentioned he thought I should pursue an acting career if this war would ever end.

We looked for a guard who would at least smile or not seem so severe while we were walking around the production line. All the V-2 rockets were in various stages of production. We walked toward the end of the line where the slave laborers were assembling the missiles.

Jenz approached one of the guards and asked, "Excuse me, Kapo, I would like to take a closer look."

Jenz walked to the assembly area for a look at what one of the prisoners/technicians was doing.

After about 30 seconds, Jenz accosted the prisoner in a loud voice, **"How dare you eye-ball me, keep on with your work!"**

The words rang out like a pistol shot up and down the assembly line.

The prisoner glanced at Jenz in his *SS* uniform. I thought the poor soul was about to have a heart attack. He got down on his knees and started praying for Jenz not to hurt him. Jenz recognized Jewish prayer.

"Please God watch over my family and keep them in a better place. I worship you alone, God of my ancestors. Please deliver me from this evil."

Jenz bent down and whispered in the prisoner's ear, "don't move, I have a question for you. Have you ever heard of Dr. or Mrs. Leven in the camp?"

"Sir, how long ago did they go to the camps?" asked the surprised prisoner in a quivering voice.

"It's been almost three years now," returned Jenz.

"They are gone, lieutenant. No one lasts more than three or four months in any of the camps. Lasting over six months would be a miracle."

Jenz then whispered to the prisoner, "get back on your feet, I am going to yell at you again and hit you across your back. Don't worry. You won't feel anything but my hand brushing your garment. If you and your fellow prisoners can find a way to slow down the production line of these monsters, please do so. And remember, we did not have this conversation; it would mean the death of both of us."

As the prisoner got back on his feet, Jenz yelled, **"back to work, you idiot, can't you see the *Reich* needs these weapons?** Jenz took a vicious swing at the prisoner, but just grazed his shirt.

Vitali was busy with the guard, "Sir, we need to know how the production of these weapons is staying on track. How many will you be able to assemble each week?"

The guard was very proud to answer, "we are now producing ten to twenty each week. But with more workforce, we will get finished up to one hundred each week."

"Wonderful!" I interjected.

I also stated firmly, "do not discipline the prisoner further. I will check on him later to make sure he is doing his job well."

As we were exiting the tunnel, Zeke whispered, "I thought I was going to pass out when I heard you yell at the prisoner. You really should look into an acting career at some point in your life."

"Why don't we go into Nordhausen for the lunch hour?" suggested Zeke, The lunchroom is often too crowded at the officer's mess hall."

"Good idea. It will be much easier to have a conversation."

CHAPTER 37

Downtown Nordhausen

We took a bus into the center of Nordhausen and walked a bit down Taschenberg Street looking for a small and quiet eatery. The town itself was picturesque. There were narrow streets off the main town road. Many of the businesses or homes had flower boxes with spring bulbs just beginning to bud. The homes and businesses were well-kept. Everything looked neat and orderly.

It was a chilly early spring day with a light breeze waving the green shoots of 1944's first tulips. It seemed a very stark contrast to what we had witnessed just a few miles away earlier in the morning. Leaving the underground factory was much like exiting a nightmare and finding yourself in familiar surroundings. You don't want to remember your horrifying dream, but you know you can never forget it.

The streets had almost no traffic, and only a few people were out and about. We stopped in a clock shop and asked the proprietor where he would suggest for a quiet meal.

"Sir," I asked in a very gentle tone, "could you direct us to a quiet spot to eat?"

The owner seemed almost miffed we would enter his establishment and said in a rather gruff voice, "Oh, you must be from the missile factory, you are the only ones who can afford a meal out."

"I thought the facility was supposed to be secret," was Vitali's quiet observation.

"Oh, no!" The shopkeeper shot back, "The whole town knows what's going on in the hidden factory buried in the Kohnstein. We know all about the abandoned gypsum mine and the tunnels in the hill. And we know where you are getting the labor to run it! You are taking hard working decent German citizens and turning them into slave laborers. **Oh, Yes**. The entire town is aware of what you people are doing in the mine.

Then he couldn't keep his mouth shut and continued, "It's going to act like a magnet for the Russians or the Americans, whoever can overrun our beautiful country with its stupid leaders first."

Vitali put his arm on my shoulder and repeated, "Sir, we are just looking to get a small bite to eat, do you have any suggestions?"

"Yes!" he announced in a harsh voice, "you can both go to hell, it's where our country will be in short order. If it's closed, try the Gashouse Restaurant further on down Taschenberg Street toward the city center."

Vitali nudged me toward the door. My anger was not with his words, but with his tone. I guess the local folks had about enough of this fiasco of a war. They seemed terrified of the Red Army advances into the Eastern Territories. The fact that I was a tall, imposing SS officer didn't seem to faze or worry him in the slightest.

Once out on the street, Zeke's comment was, "I would say the local population doesn't feel too secure with the military presence in this area."

My observation was, "When the shortages get severe enough, no one is going to have enough to eat. The *Führer* and the rest of the politicians have ensured hell will come to our beloved Germany."

We continued down the street toward the center of Nordhausen and came across a small cafe with a tiny "Gashouse Restaurant" sign in the window. It was a small but well-kept establishment. I removed my uniform hat as we entered; I had to duck my head to get through the doorway.

It was evident the proprietor and the two guests at one other table were not expecting the *SS* to visit their small restaurant this afternoon. I wasn't sure if the look from the patrons and the owner was hostility or chagrin. My six foot almost five-inch height probably didn't help.

Vitali gave a cheerful "hello," and a "good afternoon" to the owner, and we made our way to a table.

The owner came right over with two menus and asked what we wanted in his restaurant. "What is the SS doing in my restaurant?"

I spoke up, "Sir, we would just like a lunch meal. What do you suggest?"

"We have very little of what is on the menu. There is some soup with some beans and a little broccoli, and some cheese for a cracker or sandwich. My daughter will bring it to you in a few minutes." He grabbed the menus before we even looked at them and retreated.

The owner's lovely daughter, she couldn't have been more than sixteen, came over in about five minutes with two bowls of steaming soup and a plate of two different kinds of cheese with two slices of hard dark bread.

I had to tell Vitali the word from the work camps was not encouraging. I told him the prisoner at the missile production factory said the detainees rarely last even six months. Vitali's face showed resignation and anger.

"What has our country come to, Jenz?"

"This news means it is even more important for us to make sure we can get out safely."

While Vitali and I were munching on our food, the daughter came over and asked if she could sit with us.

Of course, both of us registered our surprise. The owner's daughter had the first kind word for us we had heard in the entire town.

She introduced herself, "I am Greta," and said, "I'm sorry I overheard you, but you were saying you wanted to get out safely."

"Could you please take me with you?"

Vitali and I were utterly astonished.

I tried to respond, "Miss, this is a bad time for Germany. You must be very careful when confiding your confidence with anyone. Vitali and I work at the factory just out of town, and the factory is no place for a young woman."

"Sir," she responded in a rather loud and sad yet plaintive voice, **"When the Russians arrive, there will be no place in Germany safe for a young woman!"**

Vitali and I just looked at each other. He finally asked, "When do you think the Russians will be in this part of Germany?"

"Within one year!" she shouted with authority, she looked terrified.[*]

With Greta's two outbursts, the other couple in the restaurant fled in a huff.

The owner came from the kitchen and looked forlorn, almost defeated.

------

[*] *The Russian Army entered Nordhausen fourteen months later on the 26th of May 1945.*

I put my hand over the young woman's hand and told her in a lowered voice, "Journey toward the American lines and be very cautious about any of the men you might meet along the way." I spoke loud enough for the father to hear what I was saying. I didn't want him to have any confusion about our intentions.

He nodded and walked back into the kitchen.

"You would fare much better taken in by the Americans than the Russians. The Russians have been treated very poorly by the *Wehrmacht* in the Eastern Territories.

There are many Germans in America, especially in the western part of the state of Pennsylvania. These German-Americans would be very kind and understanding of your family's situation. I have also heard there are many German-speaking men in the American Army. I believe you and your family would do much better to be captured by the Americans."

"How will you get out safely," she responded.

"I cannot honestly say at this point. But, let me tell you again, please trust no one but your family. Most men wearing this uniform may not treat you as well as you might like."

"You and your friend have shown me precious kindness, Lieutenant, God Bless you."

She looked so vulnerable; my heart went out to her.

Vitali and I paid, edged out of the restaurant, and headed back to the bus for Mittelwerk. The meeting with the young girl and her spoken fears were a little unsettling for Vitali. He asked, "How did you know the Russians might treat those people poorly?"

"The word is 'vengeance.' But you could also say 'revenge' or 'retribution' for very sinful or cruel behavior. I read reports of death squads roaming throughout the Eastern Territories and on the Russian Front. These death squads are encouraged, condoned, or instigated by the *Gestapo* and the *SS*. I think they are called *Einsatzgruppen*. This group of thugs was formed after the Anschluss or the annexation of Austria. The *Einsatzgruppen* are under the direct authority of *SS Obergruppenführer* Reinhard Heydrich, a true Nazi political monster."

"What are the death squads purpose in these conquered territories?" asked Vitali.

"I have read from reports their chief function is to deport people to death camps. These death camps are numerous in the conquered areas."

"Are they just killing innocent civilians?" asked Vitali.

"According to the reports, yes! First, they make them dig their graves and then shoot them so they will fall into their freshly dug graves."

"Are you sure those reports are true, Jenz? It sounds completely barbaric!"

"Vitali, the cruelty of these monsters is completely unabashed and blatant. And to my knowledge, unknown in a civilized society. We must be cautious, careful, and well-timed with our escape from this regime."

CHAPTER 38

A Chance Meeting with Gestapo Agents

"**L**et's walk back to the factory. We must be almost halfway there by now. I don't want to run into any Wehrmacht or Gestapo patrols."

It was a cool spring day with a hint of warmer weather on the way. The leaves were coming out on some of the early spring flowering trees. The walking felt good in the spring air.

The words were hardly out of my mouth when an older black Mercedes sedan came around the corner up ahead and stopped abruptly right next to us. I leaned toward Vitali and whispered, "These bastards are everywhere. Let me do the talking."

Both men in the car seemed a little eager to quiz us about our business near the town of Nordhausen this afternoon.

"Why are you two out here today?" The driver addressed us in a harsh tone. He was anything but friendly. His face clearly displayed the hate in his heart.

I turned so the driver couldn't see my hand and motioned with my finger then pointing to my mouth for Zeke to circle the back of the car and engage the man on the passenger side in conversation.

I then turned back to the driver and explained, "We had been in Nordhausen on business and decided to walk back to the factory at *Mittelwerk*. **And who exactly are you,**" I asked in a firm but pleasant tone.

"We are the Gestapo," as the driver pulled out a leather wallet with a badge attached.

"We will give you a ride back to the base at *Mittelwerk.*"

I declined as politely as possible saying, "Oh, no, thank you, we are enjoying walking in the fresh clean air outside of the tunnels.

The driver then changed his position in his seat, unholstered his weapon and pointed it out the window at my chest saying in a firm and demeaning tone, **"You will come with us, get in the car."**

Unfortunately for the two agents, our lunch at the restaurant didn't even come close to satisfying my hunger pangs. And although I was still quite hungry and a little irritable, I certainly didn't want to chance the Lugar going off in my face.

Vitali knew me well enough so he was at the passenger window, engaging the other agent in some conversation.

I opened the back door on the driver's side as fully as it would go, which is pretty wide in a Mercedes. Next, I stepped as close to the door hinges as I could with the door opened. I pretended to enter the automobile. My feet were still standing outside of the automobile. I then reached in from the back seat with my right hand and slammed the drivers head onto the window sill of the open window as hard as I could. I grabbed the pistol from the driver's side at the same time with my left hand.

I then opened the driver's door, and he spilled out with a bloody head onto the road.

I leveled the pistol at the other agent's head, Vitali opened the passenger door and with one smooth motion, relieved the agent of his firearm.

I opened the trunk and encouraged the agent from the passenger seat to get in. He wouldn't get in until I pulled back the firing mechanism and chambered a round in the Lugar.

I slammed the trunk and pulled the injured agent back into the back seat of the car. His face was very bloody, and he was moaning and swearing. Blood seemed to be flowing freely from his nose and mouth. He was clearly dazed.

We couldn't afford to have anyone else come by on the road and see what was happening. I next removed my uniform belt and looped it around the agent's neck in the back seat. I then tightened the belt as hard as I could on his neck and held it in the stretched position. He thrashed around and kicked so hard he broke the front seat, but after a while, he just stopped breathing and turned blue. He did make some awful gurgling noises through his nose, but in the end, he watched me while the light dimmed in his eyes.

"Zeke, hop in. We have to get the car off the road.

"What are we going to do with the automobile?

"We will hide it. We cannot let anyone recognize the car and talk about it later.

"But Jenz, we still have a live agent in the trunk!"

"He isn't going anywhere just now. Let's get this car hidden and off the road."

The broken front seat kept wobbling on its tract. We drove south-east of Nordhausen and came to a little town of Bielen and turned right and went through the main street on to *Market Strasse.* We followed this street out of town until we came to a small lake or canal. We drove off the main road onto a dirt road running along the edge of the lake. The car was parked out of sight in a grove of trees and bushes. The sun was almost down.

We were out of sight of the road. The agent in the trunk was kicking the boot and trying to get out. Mercedes have pretty strong trunks, but probably not watertight.

I spoke to Vitali, "Zeke, I might have to get a little wet with this one."

"Why, Jenz. Will we need to go swimming?"

"Perhaps. I'm not sure I can get the car submerged any other way. Let's open the front windows so the car will fill with water. I'll check the depth of the lake near the shore."

We eased the car near the shore and waited for the approaching evening.

After dark, I stripped down to my undershorts and drove the car into the water. It floated for about four or five minutes, giving me enough time to force the door open, climb out of the vehicle, and swim the short distance to shore. The water was surprisingly cold. I was shivering and cold when I climbed up to the dirt road.

Vitali asked, "What about the agent in the trunk?"

"We will give him the same chance as he was about to give us when they stopped us on our way back to the research facility. I'm sure it is about the same chance he has given to all the folks he has sent to the labor camps."

I stripped off my underwear and buried it near the shore and redressed in my *SS* uniform. It was pretty cold, so I hurried to get warm. We walked back to the small town of Bielen and found the bus stop for the ride back to the Army Research Facility. We wound up walking at least three or four kilometers from where the bus left us off on the outskirts of Nordhausen.

The next morning Vitali and I were discussing the close call with the *Gestapo* we had experienced yesterday.

"Jenz, we have to be very cautious now there are missing agents from this area. Let's get back to work in the laboratories and see exactly when the brass are planning on launching these beasts."

We worked through the spring of 1944, trying everything we could think of doing to delay the imminent launch of the V-2 rockets. We certainly did not want to be discovered, so all of our efforts were quite subtle.

It was April when we heard about the arrest of our lead scientist and head of missile development at Peenemünde by the *Gestapo*. Dr. von Braun and two prominent members of his missile team, Klaus Riedel and Helmut Gröttrup were arrested in their quarters in the dark of night and taken to a nearby prison in Stettin.

These arrests were of grave concern to both of us. If the *Gestapo* could arrest three of the most prominent scientists working on Hitler's critical weapons program, what would their arrest mean for the rest of us.?

Himmler was angry with von Braun for not stepping up the pace of missile development and getting the A-2 into production. Himmler had lured General Dornberger away from the Research Center on pretense, and had complained "von Braun was more interested in space travel than winning the war."

To Himmler, this amounted to high treason. However, von Braun looked at his imprisonment "as a wonderful way to catch up on my sleep."

Within two weeks General Dornberger had convinced Hitler the V-2 program would falter without von Braun and he and Albert Speer, Berlin's war production chief personally intervened on von Braun's behalf and had him and the other scientists released.

The V-1 pulsejet flying bombs were already in use against London since the second week of June. The Reich had ordered thousands of these missiles. The trick was getting them off the launch catapult and on their way to the targets.

Vitali exhausted all efforts with the V-1. Still, about 25% of them were getting through to their target London and its suburbs. Many of these missiles were being fired from several sites on the north coast of Europe, so it was much harder to alter the gasoline mix or the rudimentary navigation systems before launching.

During the first attack against London, only one of the missiles caused any loss of life. Of the four landing successfully in Britain, one caused six fatalities in the city of London. Five of the first ten missiles crashed very near their launch site. I'm not sure any of the failures resulted from the work we designed into the rockets. But, I remember Vitali said it would be a mistake to ensure they all failed.

As we approached fall in 1944, I got a letter stating all *Waffen SS* officers were ordered to the Eastern Front within 30 days. The Wehrmacht was withdrawing from the Eastern Front. I immediately went to see Vitali in his makeshift laboratory.

I sat next to him at his desk and showed him the letter I had received. It looked like the Red Army was breaking through the German lines. Zeke whispered, "It might be a good idea to talk with our station head about the launch site in Denmark."

"I couldn't agree more," was my quiet response. "Is there anything you can think of to 'improve' the mechanical engineering of the V-2s?"

"I have a couple of last minute 'improvements' I can share with you later. Let's meet for dinner, and we can discuss these ideas. Zeke pointed to the electric motors. The motors moved the fins in the rocket's exhaust.

Some of the other scientists and technicians were giving us sideways glances so I folded up my letter, thanked him for his tireless devotion to work and our *Führer,* and left through the main laboratory entrance.

I went directly to my desk and got out the schematics of the V-2.

CHAPTER 39

An Exit Plan to Get Out of the Reich

Vitali and I dined at the main mess dining room for the officers and scientists. The officer's dining at Mittelwerk wasn't as elaborate or as tastefully decorated as the one in Peenemünde, but the food was pretty decent. There were plenty of *Nazi* flags and posters of our *Führer* everywhere. I got to thinking about the thin potato peel soup they were feeding the prisoners in the tunnels.

The room was quite large, so Vitali, and I chose a table away from the other diners. The meals were served buffet style from long high benches up against the kitchen wall. The tables for seating were wood with wooden chairs. The chairs were not entirely comfortable. There were paper placemats to place our plates on; the eating utensils and napkins were on the buffet table. The entire atmosphere was one of a cafeteria setting, not the comfortable dining room we had in Peenemünde.

The food selection left something to be desired, but I kept thinking about the prisoners in the tunnels. There was some meat, boiled potatoes, onions, and sliced cabbage. The type and quantity of food throughout the *Reich* were becoming restricted, so we felt fortunate to eat as well as we did.

"Vitali," I began, "Tomorrow I will submit a report for our chief of operations, Herr Frits Gosslau. I plan to have him and

Dr. Ernst Steinhoff from the Flight, Guidance, and Telemetering Devices Laboratory discuss the report about the rocket launching site in northern Denmark at the air base at Aalborg. If they agree the station would make an ideal launch site for the V-1 and V-2 rockets, I will suggest they make the presentation to General Walter Dornberger.

"If General Dornberger gets behind the idea," I mentioned to Zeke, " Von Braun will be on board. I will need them to get me orders to travel to the Aalborg base with you to plan a launch site and bunkers for the controls and missile storage.

"My report includes the population of the base, surrounding towns and distances to significant community and military targets. The report also includes on the ground and atmospheric weather conditions along with the number of favorable launch dates per month. My report, in addition, includes the availability of technical help to store, set up, and launch the rockets.

"If we cannot get orders for the Aalborg Air Base, you realize our exit from the Reich will be much more complicated, difficult, or impossible."

"Unfortunately," replied Zeke, "I understand completely."

He looked miserable.

I showed up at Herr Gosslau's office just before lunch the next day. It was a beautiful late spring day. If it were not for all the disastrous war news, it would have indeed been glorious. "Good morning, sergeant," I introduced myself.

"Morning Lieutenant, what can I do for you."

"I would like to speak with Herr Gosslau or Dr. Steinhoff, if either of them is available?"

"So sorry, Lieutenant, they are both tied up at meetings with all the difficult war news."

"Have the Allies landed at Calais?"

"No, Lieutenant, they are gaining a foothold on our Atlantic coast, they have breached our anti-tank armaments and have begun to land supplies on our coast. The Allies have temporarily breached our defenses in the Low Countries.

"But the *Führer* has some surprises for them tomorrow."*

"Can you tell me when either of these gentlemen would be available, I have an important report for them to look over?"

"Yes. Of course, Lieutenant, leave the report with me, and I will see it is delivered first thing this evening when they return from their important meetings."

"I'm sorry sergeant, this report contains 'eyes only' information for the *Führer*, I cannot let it pass out of my hands undocumented."

"Understood, Lieutenant. Herr Gosslau and Dr. Steinhoff will be back in this office by eighteen hundred this evening."

"Thank you, sergeant. I will return this evening. Please contact me at the Warhead Laboratory if they get in sooner."

The sergeant contacted me in our laboratory at 1730 to let me know both men had returned from their meeting.

---

* *The "surprises" turned out to be the initial launching of the V-1 guided pulse-jet missiles against the city of London on the 13th of June, 1944.*

Of the almost eight thousand launched between June of 1944 and the end of the war in May of 1945, only twenty-three hundred reached London and its surrounding suburbs. Anti-aircraft balloons accounted for two hundred and seventy-nine interceptions of the V-1 missiles. The anti-aircraft fire brought down another fifteen hundred, and fighter planes brought down another two thousand.

The remaining four thousand which were unsuccessful in reaching London, some were fired at other targets, and a certain percentage just never made it very far from their catapult launch pads, and never to their intended destination targets.

Vitali and I hoped some of the launched failures were due to our intervention of "improving" the missile technology.

Although a little nervous I might have "oversold" my report, I went directly over to their office.

"Thanks for the contact sergeant."

"Wait here for a moment, and Herr Gosslau will see you."

The offices seemed small and cramped compared with the spacious offices in Peenemünde. But the Allies had discovered our secret Army Research Facility last summer, and we lost a lot of our laboratory testing equipment, power plant, launch testing site, and of course, our inventory of V-1 rockets, as well as some key engineers. We were fortunate to be able to move here to Mittelwerk after the Allied bombing attack in August.

The only decorations were large photos of our *Führer* and *Luftwaffe* posters. The walls had been quickly painted a light "Army Green." The whole complex of offices seemed rather hastily arranged, but understandable after getting bombed and forced out of the research center. The sergeant seemed to be in charge of several of the small offices.

The sergeant signaled with his hand, "Lieutenant, this way, you may go in now."

I picked up my brief with the report and followed him down the hall.

Herr Gosslau's office was quite small; his desk was overflowing with paperwork. The proliferation of paper and folders made the office seem even smaller and more insignificant. He sat behind a mound of books and papers with a balding head peaking over the top. What hair he did have was wispy, graying, and combed over his ears.

"Good Evening, Herr Gosslau, thank you for seeing me on short notice."

"Yes, Lieutenant, what is it? Is your breakthrough so important you think our *Führer* would want to see it?"

"I have a report right here, Sir, I think is worthy of looking at by at least our group here at Mittelwerk." I started to explain it to him as I handed him the report.

"Do you want me to read it or are you going to tell me about it!"

I sat back quietly in my chair while he read over the report.

After a few minutes, Gosslau commented, "This is a somewhat interesting report, Lieutenant, what made you think of Aalborg?"

"I was trying to find a safe and secure location for our new missiles; yet a location not too remote from military targets. I was fearful the Russians, as well as the British and their American Allies, might need convincing not to invade our country."

"I will pass this on to Dr. Steinhoff first thing tomorrow morning. If he agrees, we might be able to discuss this report with General Dornberger. The General has plans for a production and launching schedule which includes launching three hundred to three hundred fifty V-2 missiles per week. His goal of one hundred per day is possible, if we can build the rockets in sufficient quantities."

"Excellent, and very heartening news Herr Gosslau. We will do everything here at Mittelwerk to meet those production goals for the *Führer*. Do we have sufficient men to work the assembly lines?"

"We are working on production personnel, Lieutenant, but do not concern yourself with the problem. The *Reich* has sourced from several labor camps and can supply a constant stream of very skilled labor."

"Also, this is a busy time for the *Führer*. He is effectively directing the war the Allies and Russians have instituted against the Fatherland. Herr Hitler has had episodes of nervousness with the way some of his generals are conducting the war. The Aalborg project might come as refreshing news for him."

"As you probably know, many of the Führer's closest generals have been sacked and replaced since the 20 July plot by Von Stauffenberg. Over four thousand eight hundred conspirators have been arrested and executed. Many of their families are also imprisoned. This fall he is now relying on many trusted members of the *SS* to prosecute the war."

"Thank you for your time, Herr Gosslau. I wish you well."

I met with Ezekiel in the evening at the officer's dining commons. He was alarmed and astonished when he heard over 300 V-2 missiles per week could be launched against the British and Russian forces closing in on Germany. Our country was in the grips of a vice.

Earlier this month, on the 8th of September, 1944, the first V-2 was fired against London. Since no one heard or saw it coming, people at first thought it was a natural gas explosion. There was no defense against a missile traveling at over 2500 miles per hour at impact, more than three times the speed of sound.

Even if the incoming missile could be detected on radar, there was still no known defense against such a weapon.

Zeke's astonished comment in hushed tones after hearing about the conspiracy to assassinate the *Führer*:

"At least we know we aren't the only ones who want this madman taken out."

He then exclaimed, "How the devil is Germany going ever to build so many missiles?"

"I'm not at all sure our country could build even a fraction of the amount," was my quiet comment. "Besides, each V-2 rocket consumes eight and a half tons of fuel. Where is the *Reich* going to procure or make so much liquid oxygen and alcohol?"

"These sound like pipe dreams from the Führer's deranged mind," was my quiet comment.

Vitali spoke up a little above a whisper, "Jenz, we are going to need those orders soon, or we will be trapped here in Germany when the Red Army or the Allies come into Nordhausen."

"We need to wait until Dr. Steinhoff and General Dornberger can discuss my report. I know it is dangerous staying in the *Reich,* especially in light of our recent efforts with the *Gestapo.*"

"The *SS* and *Gestapo* Agents seem to be everywhere on this base," said Vitali. "They make me nervous because now I understand how to spot them."

There was a little zip to the wind as we walked on the gravel path to the laboratories after dinner. You could feel the cold starting to ride the wind down the Harz Mountains into our forested base in the middle of the *Reich.* There was a rustle to the leaves in the wind. Much of the foliage and bushes had died down for the fast approaching winter season.

Ezekiel and I wanted to brainstorm a little on methods to slow the production and launch of the V-2 liquid-fueled rockets. Several rockets had been launched. The potential of the missile could change the course of the war. A continuation of the war would mean extending and prolonging of the torment and suffering of the Jewish population in Germany and the Eastern Territories. The citizens in the *Reich* suffered from lost loved ones, and the deprivation of the freedoms they once enjoyed.

"Jenz if we received orders to the airbase in Denmark perhaps we could drain off substantial numbers of V-1s or better, V-2 rockets and prevent them from being launched at all."

"It's possible Zeke, let's give it a little more time for the Aalborg idea to ferment. My report only included the movement of the V-2 missiles to the Danish air base."

One week later, I received a note from Dr. Steinhoff's office to come in for a conference. I immediately dropped any work I was calculating for warhead production and went over to his office.

"Good afternoon, sergeant," I greeted as I entered the group of offices.

"Afternoon, Lieutenant. Dr. Steinhoff will see you now; he is expecting you. His office is the 4th door on the right in the same corridor as Herr Gosslau. If he is not in his office, he will be in the lab at the end of the hall."

I knocked on the fourth door. **"Come In!"** Herr Steinhoff announced through the door.

I stepped into another small office and said, "Hello, Dr. Steinhoff, I am Lieutenant Ramsgrund."

His office was crowded with a desk overflowing with paperwork. The adjacent file cabinet was piled high with folders and reports. There was no other seating except the desk chair.

"Yes, Lieutenant, I have your report here. Please come in and close the door."

Dr. Steinhoff dispensed with any pleasantries by stating, "I discussed your report with General Dornberger, and he had some additional comments and suggestions he brought to our *Führer's* attention."

I stated, "I was glad the General thought my report worthy of comments to our *Führer*."

"Would it be possible, Lieutenant, for you to journey to the army base at Aalborg to get some hard data for a missile site? The *Führer* does not want to trust this information to the men operating the base for fear of the Danish underground getting wind of the secret missiles."

"I would certainly be able to leave whenever the General orders me to, doctor. My only concern is with the travel arrangements with all the Allied and Red Army bombing of our cities. Is the airfield at Tempelhof still in good working order?"

"Of course, Lieutenant. You might have to travel by rail for part of the way, but your orders will stipulate you are to take the quickest mode of travel available."

"The most direct mode of transportation would be helpful, Doctor. Thank you."

I had one other item on my agenda, but I wanted the doctor to think it came up as an afterthought as I was leaving.

"Oh, by the way, doctor, it would be helpful if my colleague Vitali Carapezza could also accompany me. He is very good with the physics and calculus needed to help judge the suitability of a launching site and the storage needed for the missiles.

"I would also suggest we launch only the V-2 rocket-powered missiles from the Aalborg base so our adversaries will have no idea where the launch site is located.

"We would need a secure rail line to transport the missiles directly to the base. I don't think the Red Army or the Allies will be bombing rail lines in Denmark. As long as a launch team, with the proper technicians accompanied the first shipment of missiles, they could be ready for launch within a few hours after the arrival.

"Thank you, doctor. I appreciate your time. Let me know what the General would like to do with our base in northern Denmark."

"You're welcome, Lieutenant, the *Führer* appreciates your suggestions."

CHAPTER 40

The Gestapo Provides Our Transportation

I went back to my laboratory and tried to contact Vitali in the Guidance Laboratory. His colleague said, "He had just met two men who had come into the laboratory looking for him."

"Where were they headed," I asked.

"One of them said something about questioning him at headquarters. You came in from the hall, and they had just left out the front of the building."

I hurried through the laboratory and out the side entrance to try to catch them before they left. They were getting into a car across the street. They sure looked like the *Gestapo* type.

I walked across the street and approached the driver's side of the car. The driver was about to close his door. Vitali was already sitting in the back seat. I noticed there were no door handles on the inside of the rear doors of the automobile.

I put myself between the driver's door and the driver while I asked, "Excuse me, gentlemen, where are you taking my colleague, Dr. Carapezza?" "We are to be at an important meeting with the general in an hour."

"I'm afraid the general might have to wait, we have been informed this man is a 'dirty Jew' and a traitor to the *Reich*, masquerading as a scientist." quipped the agent.

Now the last time someone called my friend Ezekiel a "dirty Jew," I think it was in grade school in Düsseldorf. If I remember correctly, it didn't go too well for the bullies in the schoolyard. And I had just finished lunch.

This parade of slurs against my friend happened to occur too near suppertime for me to be polite. But I tried.

My first words were a signal to Zeke: All I said was "Zeke, the shoelace maneuver."

Then I politely asked, "Would it be all right with you gentlemen if I rode along with you to headquarters?"

"Impossible," the driver spit out in a slightly firm and sarcastic tone between yellowing tobacco-stained teeth.

"Perfectly okay," I said and started to back away so the driver could close the door. I then reached in to tap the driver on the back of the neck gently, to signal his denial of my request was not going to be a problem.

I took the opportunity to then grab the back of the agent's neck and pulled him toward me. My hands were always a little oversized, and I was able to grab the side of his neck, almost encircling it. At the same time, I gave his chin a violent shove with my other hand in the opposite direction. The loud **crack** of his vertebrae indicated to me this agent wasn't going to be a further problem.

In the meantime, Zeke had removed his boot laces, tied them together, and had wound them firmly around his hands. As the audible crack of the driver's vertebrae, Zeke looped the noose over the other agent's neck. He was pulling up and back with all his strength.

I reached past the driver and rabbit chopped the passenger on his trachea with the backswing of my hand. Since there wasn't too much room for a full backswing, he might have still had a way to breathe. Both agents were down for the count, the passenger was possibly still alive, so I told Zeke to keep the pressure on the noose.

I then slid the driver over to the middle of the seat; his head was lolling back and forth. I got into the driver's seat and drove away slowly. The whole take-down lasted less than two minutes, and I don't think anyone noticed. It was late in the day, and the shadows were long.

We drove over toward the gypsum mine and pulled off on a deserted unpaved road running off to the right into the woods. The path was overgrown with weeds barely broad enough for the car to pass. The car bumped along until we were sure we couldn't be seen from the road. We parked off the dirt path in a tangle of bushes.

Ezekiel's comment, "I'm afraid the *Gestapo* is on to both of us now. I thought it was all over when these two goons showed up."

"Don't let this get to you, Zeke. We will get rid of these two evil agents, but we need to hide the car because we may need transportation for our exit plan. I am still hopeful we can both get travel orders to Aalborg Air Base in northern Denmark. But it won't hurt to have a backup plan."

We stripped both agents of their identity and most of their clothing and buried them in a shallow pit we had dug by using sticks and the jack handle from the trunk. We covered the bodies with rocks, and filled the shallow grave with dirt, leaves, then brush. Their identification, handguns, and clothing went into another shallow hole we had uncovered from rocks we had placed over the dead agents. We put additional stones and leaves over their belongings.

We put their car in the lot by the gypsum mine with about 20 other automobiles. The lot would hold over 100 vehicles, but the restrictions on gas and oil at this time in Germany were so severe only politicians, physicians, the *Gestapo,* and very few others were allowed to drive cars. Most of the petrol went for the war effort.

Zeke and I walked back to the laboratories. "If they ask you anything about your meeting with the *Gestapo*, tell them you answered their questions. We may have to make a retreat from this area before we had planned. I will check on our orders in a couple of days. We may not have too much time left. Please don't get too nervous with the waiting. I know that time is not on our side right now, but orders from our *Führer* would facilitate our exit plans."

"How much time do you think we have before the *Gestapo* is on to us and comes for us again, Jenz?"

"A lot of the turmoil caused by the war going badly for the *Reich* has helped us. More and more of the reserves are heading east to try to stop the Red Army. There was a *rumor* in the warhead laboratory the First Ukrainian Front, the most powerful of the Red Army, is rolling on to the Vistula River. The Russians will be on German soil in the conquered territories in less than a month."*

---

* *Germany was being squeezed in a vice. On July first, 1944, the Supreme Commander of the German Army, Field Marshal Keitel telephoned Field Marshal von Rundstedt, who was the German commander-in-chief of the West Army. He asked a simple question. "What shall we do?" The Red Army was advancing on the Reich from the east and north. The Allies were advancing from the west and south.*

Von Rundstedt's reply was short and pointed: "Make peace, you idiots. What else can you do?"

"Is there anything we can do now to delay the massive launching of the *Führer's new* 'wonder' weapons?"

"Zeke, it is our best interest to keep our heads down and keep working toward the development and production of the vengeance weapons."

"We will somehow get a decent map of the best route to northern Germany and the Danish coast. We could take the *Gestapo* agent's automobile; it was almost full of petrol. Our biggest problem will be traveling without orders. We will need to procure orders somewhere."

"Why will lack of orders be our biggest problem?" Asked Zeke.

"Two military-aged males traveling without orders would be suicide in the *Reich* at this time. We will need some authorization to travel, and it could still be hazardous. There are the possibilities of running into deserters, military fanatics who would like to shoot first and ask questions afterward, and hoards of civilians fleeing for safer areas. All in addition to the *Gestapo* looking for trouble at every corner of the *Reich*."

"Is there anything we can do, Jenz?"

"Yes. We will wait 12 hours and see which happens first: a visit from the Gestapo, or orders to Aalborg Air Base. I know this is very difficult for you Zeke. Quiet prayer might be in order. Think of our prayers as many of our Jewish friends think about chicken soup when we are ill - it couldn't hurt. I thought a bit of levity might make us both feel better.

We didn't have to wait long. Orders authorizing travel were on my desk when I returned to my office. I busied myself with sorting the paperwork for a hasty exit. Vitali's name was not included on the orders so I typed his Italian name on the line where his name could have been. I thought it looked pretty authentic.

I heard a disturbance in the adjacent laboratory. It was the *Gestapo* looking for their agents and their automobile. They were questioning Vitali, so I put on my uniform tunic and went into the Guidance Laboratory.

"Gentlemen, can I help you?"

The lead agent was quite large, at least 6 feet and broad-shouldered but his head looked far too small for such a large frame. His hair looked bristly and graying at the temples above his clean-shaven face. His face had a mean sneer across his lips.

I thought to myself, don't these morons ever smile?

The second agent was almost five foot ten inches with a sour disposition; he smelled like stale tobacco.

The foul smelling agent started complaining, "Our agents came here earlier today to bring Vitali Carapezza in for questioning. Now I find him back here at work, and our agents and their car are missing."

"Agents," I replied, "I don't think our scientist, Mr. Carapezza has lost your agents. Mr. Carapezza explained to me two agents showed up here earlier today with some questions for him, which he answered in their automobile. He said they then headed away from the base."

I had to put a little implied threat into my retort. "Furthermore, agents, we are doing very secret work on special weapons for our *Führer*. If you delay us in our progress, you will hear **directly** from the *Führer*. Besides, I have secret orders here from the *Führer* stating our scientist, Mr. Carapezza, and I are to travel in conjunction with our work here."

The larger more substantial agent shot back, **"I will need to see those orders."**

"Come into my office, gentlemen, and I will allow you to read them as long as you will swear not to make them public."

"**Let me see them**," was the agent's rather loud response.

"In my office, please. Right, this way."

We went through the Guidance Laboratory to the hall and into my office. As I closed the door to my office, I thought about a convincing way to get these agents on their way.

I picked up the orders just arrived from the General's office and placed them in the more substantial agent's hands.

"Both of you please read them. Because the orders are top secret, I cannot offer you carbons to take with you."

Since it was late in the day, and our arguments seemed to hold up for them, the more substantial agent said in a slightly less threatening voice, "Thank you for your cooperation, but both of you would need to come to our headquarters tomorrow for further questioning."

"What time would you like us there, agent?"

"We would need to see you, and your orders at 8 am in our office in Nordhausen."

"We will be in your office in the morning, agents. Good afternoon."

CHAPTER 41

Our Hasty Retreat to the Land of the Danes

Vitali and I spent the evening with an early dinner and packing whatever essentials we needed for the trip to Denmark. We had no intention of showing up at *Gestapo* Headquarters in Nordhausen or anywhere else for this group of thugs.

"My friend, pack lightly. We can use the last agent's car, as long as it is still at the mine. It is probably a bit large for our purposes, but it's the best we have. I will leave a note with a carbon of our orders with my chief at the warhead laboratory with a note to inform your department head. We do not want to be hunted by the *Wehrmacht* and the *Gestapo*."

At 9:30 in the evening, we walked to the gypsum mine car park. It was completely dark with no lights on. It was a little disconcerting to be wandering around the automobiles. We almost had to feel our way around the cars.

We got in the black Mercedes we had left in the lot by the mine. The Gestapo agent's automobile had not been touched. Thanks to God, no one had siphoned the diesel fuel from the tank. The engine turned over, coughed once, and started. We drove off without headlights. The visibility was marginal, the road barely visible.

It was late fall, and there was a chill in the air. "Zeke, we are going to need some warmer clothes for northern Denmark."

"Can we make a slight detour to whatever is left of Peenemünde Army Research Center and see if we can pick up something warm?"

"Good suggestion, Zeke, but it could be dangerous. We may have to be on the lookout on our trip for messages these clowns might send from the local *Gestapo* headquarters. Unfortunately, because of our orders, they can find out where we are headed.

"Hannover might be closer. Let's see if Ilsa can get us some warm coats. We are going to have to travel pretty slowly at night. The blinds on the headlights will make it slow going, especially on the back roads. Did you pack any food in your bag?"

"No." Replied Zeke. "You said to pack light. We need to depend on the kindness of strangers in the small villages and towns on our way."

We traveled very carefully through the first small town north of Nordhausen. There was a complete black-out in effect throughout the *Reich*.

Our travel was prolonged, usually under 20 miles per hour. But we were headed toward Denmark or at least north-west on a very lonely road. We followed a small secondary road parallel to the Zorge River. The first village we came to was Cleysingen.

We didn't even realize we were in a town until the sidewalks and small buildings appeared beside the automobile. I could tell Zeke was getting very nervous about our nighttime escape. His voice was getting a nervous twinge to it, and he kept asking and repeating his questions.

"I don't blame you for being somewhat nervous about our slow progress Ezekiel. I don't dare to go much faster with our minimal visibility." The blackout was complete in Germany at this stage of the war.

We crawled through the small town without seeing anyone at all. It was strange to be in a complete and total blackout; it was unnerving for both of us. Almost like the whole town had been abandoned. There was no bomb destruction. The Allies and the Red Army wouldn't waste ordnance on small pieces of civilian real-estate. It was so dark, we could barely see the buildings, even in the town center. We slowly felt our way through the town.

The next major town was Ellrich. It was quite large, and we suspected it might have some war damage. Dawn was rising out of the east as we entered the town. I wore my tunic and cover as we were skirting around the center in the city. We drove as quietly and as conservatively as possible. We tried not to be too obvious, but an *SS* officer and another adult military-age male in a large black Mercedes Benz just couldn't be easily overlooked.

A police officer stopped us as we were traversing around the town on Muhlendamm Street just next to the Zorge River.

"What can we do for you, officer?"

"I need to see your papers and orders Lieutenant."

"Of course, officer. What is your name and badge number?"

"Why would you need badge information, Lieutenant?"

"As you can see from our orders, we are on a mission directed by the *Führer.*"

"Everything looks in order here, Lieutenant. Please do not let me slow or hinder your journey. Drive safely. There are some bands of deserters from the Eastern Front just north of here toward Hannover. Use extreme caution with these people; they have been under intense duress and shell fire from their battles with the Red Army."

"Thank you, officer. Which would be the safest route to Hannover?"

"Stay south-west of the Hertz Mountain Range and try to get to Herzberg. If possible, stay off the main roads, and by all means, avoid roving bands of deserters. These folks do not take kindly to *Wehrmacht* or *SS* officers because they know they will be hung or shot if caught. If they outnumber you, be extremely wary of them and do not trust them. It would be best to shoot first and then ask your questions."

"I should also mention, Hannover has sustained major damage. The city has suffered many raids by the British and American Bombers. The B-17s and the B-24s have dumped tons of bombs on the rail yards, factories, and armaments of the city. It has been almost as bad as Hamburg."

"I would strongly advise staying away from any major cities."

"Thank you, officer. Thanks for the advice."

We crept along at 25-30miles per hour and came to the outskirts of a small town called Walkenried. We very carefully took the scenic route around the town center. It was mid-morning, yet there were few people about and no young men. There was very little traffic of any kind.

We stopped at a farm just north of the town and asked to purchase food or a place to have a meal. The older woman told us to get out and not come back. She said the soldiers had confiscated all her food and she had none left. She said she had not heard from her husband or two sons since they had left for the Eastern Front five months ago.

I told her we were very sorry to hear about her family. She mentioned all the families she knew had lost their men in the war. She felt very few would come home.

In the end, she gave us two apples and warned us about roving gangs of hungry and dangerous men between Bad Sachsa and Königshütte.

We thanked her and were on our way, slowly. We drove between 20 and 30 miles/hour through some very scenic countryside and arrived on the edge of Bad Sachsa in the early afternoon. The country was green with crops, although it looked like many of the farms were overgrown and untended. There was hardly any traffic on the roadways.

We decided to go a little further north to a tiny town called Warteberg, where we found a farm with two women working in a garden out front of a low home with a moss covered roof.

We stopped and asked one of the women for directions. It was a mother and her daughter using hoes and picking weeds out of a few rambling tomato plants near the side of the road.

The mother gave us some suggestions to get to Hartz with again the admonishment to watch out for gangs of deserters. She suggested we stay in a town for the evening and not get caught alone out in the country at night.

She added, "Many of the deserters from this area feel they have nothing left to lose. They have lost their families, most of their friends, and they are starving. Be careful!"

Our goal was to reach Herzberg am Hartz by nighttime. It started getting dark between 6 and 6:30 so we were confident we could get a little north of the town before we had to stop and find lodgings for the night.

As we were traveling very slowly through a wooded section just north of the small town at the foot of the Hartz mountain range, we came across a young soldier lying on the side of the road. I stopped the car to see if he needed help.

"Jenz, be careful. It might be a trap with military deserters from the Eastern Front."

"The front is too far away, Zeke. This soldier looks injured. He has bandages on his head and leg. If he is dead, we can see if there is any identification."

As Zeke and I stepped out of the car, the injured soldier seemed to come back to life. He jumped up and pointed a pistol directly at my face.

He then yelled, "**Okay, comrades, out of the woods. I have their car.**"

Four more "injured" soldiers came trooping out of the woods from behind the trees and rocks and a ditch beside the road.

It looked like a total of five deserters. One of the soldiers had an older Lugar pistol. The firearm was probably either inoperable or without ammunition. The other four had clubs fashioned from short pieces of hardwood.

"Lieutenant, we just want your car. Give me the keys and your money; then no one gets hurt," intoned the bandaged soldier with the pistol.

Ezekiel just looked at me and shrugged his shoulders.

I raised my hands and stepped toward the gunman.

He reacted by flourishing the pistol and warned me not to get any closer.

Of course, waving the pistol was a mistake. Now I was just one stride away from disarming the bastard. I needed a distraction, so I pointed skyward and said, "It looks like the British, are bombing during the daylight hours in this part of Germany."

As the bandaged soldier looked up, I took a step forward and slammed my closed fist down on his pistol hand hard enough to break the deserter's wrist.

As he yelped in pain, his four friends moved closer around the car to confront Zeke and me with their clubs. I picked up the pistol, ejected the empty clip and threw the gun into the woods.

Now the bandaged soldier was indeed injured.

I announced to his four comrades, **"If you would like to leave here uninjured, then slink quietly back into the woods. If you persist in challenging us, you will not be able to leave except on a stretcher."**

The most massive idiot with a stout stick immediately made a rush to club me into submission.

I ducked out of the way of his downswing, grabbed his club as it hit the road, and shoved the hand end of it hard into his solar plexus with such force he went down with a whoosh of air escaping from his lungs and immediately began vomiting significant quantities of blood. He lay still on the road with blood trickling out of his nose and mouth.

I suggested to the remaining three soldiers, **"You could all three try to rush us to be successful, but I guarantee your results will be similar. Please walk away while you still can."**

I probably should have confided in the attackers I hadn't eaten much all day and I was a little testy.

They must not have had a lot to lose because the three remaining deserters rushed toward me anyway. Zeke started to come to my aid, but I yelled, **"I got this one, Zeke!"**

I held up one hand and begged them to reconsider, as the first assailant tried to hit me with his heavy stick.

I bent down low as his club bounced harmlessly off my back. As I stood up, I grabbed his ankle then his wrist in one swift motion. I then swung him like a battering ram at his fellow deserters. I could feel his shoulder dislocate during this maneuver, and I then hurled him at the side of our Mercedes.

The other two were down. I stepped on the leg of the first one and heard the lower leg bone snap. I kicked the last deserter in the head with the heal of my boot. He didn't move again.

I suggested to Zeke, "Well, I guess we've accomplished enough good deeds for the day. Let's get to the next town before it gets too dark."

We left the injured deserters, who were now truly injured, on the side of the road.

By evening, we made it to Lüderholz, a small town a few miles north of Hartz. We hoped to make it to Hannover the next evening.

Unfortunately, there wasn't much going on in the town, and we saw no lights and no one moving around after dark; we wound up sleeping in the Mercedes automobile. Not fun. Although not yet winter, cold air seemed to flow down from the Hartz Mountains and cool down the whole area as soon as the sun went down. We would have kept driving, but it was just too dangerous with such limited headlamp visibility.

We woke up with the birds the next morning. We were both pretty hungry. We had parked off the road, so no one saw us at first light. Hannover was only about 50 miles away, but it was slow going on the back roads. We didn't want to get involved with any military police or *Wehrmacht* movements in and around any major cities.

Our immediate goal was food and an attempt to make Hildesheim, a city just south of Hannover, by early evening. We went around the main parts of Osterode am Hartz and found a tiny restaurant in a home on Schulweg Street in the country town of Landwehr, just north of Osterode am Hartz.

The two old folks who owned the home were the cook and waiter. The Becker's were kindly but had an unfortunate story to tell. Since our army connection was evident, they told us about how their son went right from Hitler Camp into the *Wehrmacht*, and their daughter went from Hitler Youth directly into a hospital in Hamburg to help with injured veterans. Her hospital suffered Allied bombing damage, and she had been killed in 1943. They hadn't heard from their son in almost a year.

I didn't quiz them on politics or the war, but they let me know their feelings about Hitler in a roundabout way: "Perhaps his initial intentions were helpful for the German people, but now he has just gone crazy. Why can't we end this war?"

Ezekiel and I had plenty to eat and wanted to pay for the food, but the old folks wouldn't take anything. I left a hundred mark note under my plate.

We took country roads around Holle and stopped in Wendhausen just south of Hildesheim to switch drivers and to figure which routes to take to get around Hildesheim without difficulty. We talked with the local authorities, and they told us to avoid Hannover.

"There is too much bomb damage and too many homeless and desperate people. The fires have destroyed whatever the bombs missed."

I desperately wanted news from Ilsa and her family in the northern suburbs, but the only way I was going to find any accurate information was to go there. Zeke and I had to be careful in our travels anywhere near Hannover.

From Hildesheim, we went west-northwest to a suburb of Hannover called Barsinghausen. The back roads were a little rough, but we could see signs of smoke on the horizon toward Hannover. It was getting dark, so we found a small boarding house in Barrigsen to spend the night. The proprietors offered what they could for breakfast. Their warning: avoid Hannover at all costs. There were roving bands of very desperate and starving people.

The next day we passed through Garbsen and on toward Langenhagen. It took us most of the day to get to Ilsa's parents home because we were continually on back country roads. At one point we had to get around an airport which had taken some bomb damage. Also, roving groups of men looked very out of place. We did everything possible to avoid them.

We came eventually to what we thought looked like a narrow part of the country road. There was a fallen tree blocking almost three-quarters of the roadway. Vitali and I stopped by the side of the road a few hundred feet before we got to the partially blocked area. We debated whether or not it might be a trap for unsuspecting motorists, although we saw very few cars or trucks on the roads.

We got out of the car and stretched. It felt good not to be driving. If it hadn't been so cold, I would have removed my uniform coat. I wasn't sure if it might anger the local population to see a healthy *SS* Lieutenant this far from the front. Ezekiel and I had no illusions about the direction of the war and the German population's attitude toward the *Nazi* leadership.

Just then Zeke cried out in a hushed tone, "Jenz, I see movement of some men the other side of the tree across the road!"

It was late afternoon, and I hadn't eaten much all day. I certainly didn't want to hurt any innocent civilians. As these men came toward us, it was evident they were quite young. The oldest looked to be about sixteen; the rest were probably younger. There were six of them; they were all carrying clubs fashioned from tree limbs.

Zeke and I debated, "They don't look exactly friendly," said Zeke.

"You might be right," I returned. "Should we make a run for it in the car, or see what they want?"

"We can't afford to lose the car," said Zeke. "I'm not exactly sure where we are or how we would get up to Denmark without it. They are getting too close now to avoid some dialogue. Let's hope they won't be confrontational."

"We must plan to take them down if necessary Zeke. Come over to my side of the car. I have the keys in my pocket."

"Hey," One of them shouted, **"We like your automobile!"**

"He is the largest one, Zeke, and probably their leader. Perhaps if I take him down first, the others will disappear. He is so young, and I don't want to hurt any of them."

"It may be true, Jenz, but they don't look exactly friendly. Six against two isn't terrific odds either."

Their leader then shouted, **"We're taking your car and any money you might be carrying."**

He then broke into a run and came at me with his club ready to take a swing at me.

I shouted, **"Please stop. I don't want to hurt you!"** I held up both hands in the stop position. Had he stopped, I could have explained to him I hadn't eaten much since breakfast, and I was a little testy when I was hungry.

But he didn't stop. He took a swing at me with his club anyway and yelled, **"How are you going to hurt me, old man!"**

I thought his comment was completely uncalled for; so I had to show him what this "old man" could do.

Rather than duck, I just grabbed his club as it headed for my face. I jerked the club away and caught his jaw with my elbow as I stepped out of the way and he kept going by me. I tripped his ankle with my foot as he went by and sent him sprawling onto the pavement. I was pretty sure I had broken his jaw, and he was going to lose a few teeth.

The rest of the crew looked threatening, but now I had a club.

I ran at them and yelled, **"Who's next!"** as I brandished the club over my head.

They did the right thing and scattered. Zeke helped the injured fellow to the side of the road. He was bleeding profusely from his mouth where his teeth used to be. I hoped his jaw was going to be okay.

We drove around the tree on the road and headed for Langenhagen. We found the streets in deplorable shape as we went around the outskirts of Hannover. The city had a smoky red glow hovering over it on the horizon.

We arrived at Ilsa's family home in the early evening. The house was dark; no one answered the door. There was a dim light at the neighbor's home across the street, so I knocked and waited.

After knocking several minutes, a young woman came to the door. When she saw my uniform, she at first thought it must be bad news regarding her son or husband. Both men had left for the Eastern Front over a year ago.

I assured her I had no news about how the battles were going on the Eastern Front, but I was inquiring about her neighbors, the Huber's across the street. I thought it best not to add my comments or feelings about the crazy war except to say I hoped and prayed it would be over soon.

"I am a friend of their daughter Ilsa; she is my promised mate."

"Oh!" Exclaimed the neighbor," Mrs. Huber has mentioned you. Are you Jenz?"

"Yes. Do you have any idea where the family has gone, they don't answer the door."

"Mr. Huber said if you came around he has left a letter for you on the kitchen table. The key to the kitchen door is under the mat by the back door."

"Thank you so much, Frau. I appreciate the message."

Zeke and I crossed back over the street and went around to the back door. We got inside okay, but the home was cold and dark. I saw the note and read it by moonlight:

> *Dear Jenz,*
>
> *I hope this finds you well. My family has moved up north until the war ends. We are staying at my grandmother's summer home in a small town in the forest called Höbek. It is up north of Hamburg near Kiel. We are directly west of Rendsburg. We are far away from the bombing, so Dad feels we will be safer here. Please come and find me. I will leave my grandmother's address and directions for you in an envelope at the Rendsburg police station. I miss you, and love you.*
>
> *Ilsa*

"Zeke, her family has moved north. It shouldn't be too far from Denmark. Let's check the house here for warm clothing and any food they might have left. Let's spend the night here. I don't think Ilsa or her parents would mind."

"Is there any way we could warm it up a bit?" asked Zeke.

"There is kindling wood and coal in the box beside the stove. Let's get it going," was my quick reply.

We also looked around for some warmer clothing. We washed out our clothes and let them dry in the warmed-up kitchen over the stove.

CHAPTER 42

On the run to Northern Germany

The morning started with an early morning knock on the door before the sun was up. A local police officer wanted to know about the car in the driveway. He said it was registered to the German State Police. I hadn't even finished dressing or shaving.

"Sir," I started, "Can I get you some tea while I tell you about the car in the drive."

"No!" replied the officer in a quite firm voice. **"Tell me about the automobile registered to the *Gestapo.*"**

"Please officer, here is a copy of my orders and a note from the daughter of the homeowner. Read them over while I finish dressing.

He looked very suspiciously at me, but I reassured him I needed to finish getting dressed.

I then went upstairs and finished putting on my uniform, including my boots. The boots made me another inch and a half taller! I grabbed my dry officers tunic from the kitchen and returned to the living room in full *SS* uniform with Lieutenant's bars.

The officer seemed satisfied but said he had to report the car and my excuse for it to the *Gestapo.* He also told us to stay in the home until the *Gestapo* returned to interview us.

Ezekiel and I knew our waiting wasn't going to happen, but Zeke asked, "What time should we look for the agent to get here?"

"It might be later this morning or early this afternoon," replied the officer. "We have to contact the Gestapo office where the car was registered. But a local agent should be here within the hour."

Zeke rolled his eyes a little, and we both answered, "Yes, Sir."

As soon as the police officer had left, we started going over the map to find the safest way to Ilsa's grandmother's home and the Danish border. We also packed any supplies or clothing we could borrow. None of the coats would fit me, but Zeke found a jacket to borrow. I did find a worn sweater I stretched to put on, but the arms barely covered my elbows.

I told Zeke, "I'm just going to walk around the neighborhood to see if there are any suspiciously parked cars. We do not want anyone following us when we leave."

I found a few cars around the neighborhood, but no one was about watching Ilsa's parents home. No one looked suspicious or out of place. The sun was coming up, yet there was still a glow of fire and smoke from recent bombings in the direction of Hannover. The smoke in the atmosphere gave the sunrise an eerie red-orange glow. I couldn't imagine what the population of Hannover and all the people of the bombed-out cities were going through. They had an immediate need for shelter and food with the coming colder weather and winter in Germany.

Our automobile was parked as far back as it would go into the driveway. We hoped we didn't look too overt as we packed a couple of winter garments to keep us warm and some stale crackers we found in one of the kitchen cupboards and a jug for water.

Today's goal was to pick our way carefully around Hamburg and get to one of the small northern towns like Pinneberg or

Norderstedt. We had been warned by several people to not go into Hamburg, Hannover, or any major city because of the bombing, looting, fires, and gangs of deserters or Hitler Youth squads.

As we got within a few miles of Hamburg, we could see lots of smoke and a few scattered fires burning on the horizon. We could only imagine the devastation responsible for killing upwards of 40,000 residents. It was apparent to Zeke and me, if Germany were to continue the war, our country would be ruined. The bombing raids were ongoing day and night.

The nighttime raids were particularly terrorizing. You could hear the droning of the aircraft and hear the whistling of the bombs as they flew toward their targets, then the jarring explosions as the explosions seem to walk their way into your cellar, or wherever you could find a bit of shelter.

We were on the outskirts of Hamburg when our disguise started to slip. It started in such a benign and minor way I almost missed the significance. Ezekiel was driving, and we had to stop at a checkpoint on the way around the city. I thought Zeke handled the officer's questions with directness and sincerity.

Then the officer asked, "Sir, where did you get the automobile? And where are you going?"

"It was loaned to us for our mission, officer," was Zeke's retort. We are on our way to the German base in Aalborg, Denmark."

I could tell by his tone Zeke was getting a little stressed and possibly intimidated by the police officer's questioning.

"Officer," I chimed in we are on a mission from our *Führer*. Please do not delay us further."

"Oh, I'm sure you are gentlemen, please park over there in the lot behind the truck."

"Sir, If you delay us, I will have to make a report to the local *Gestapo,*" I tried to make my voice sound pleasant, yet slightly commanding.

"This will be easy for you to do Lieutenant." scolded the police officer. "Their office is in the building the other side of the parking lot. Present your paperwork to them. You will need a pass to continue north on this road."

I suggested to Zeke in a low whisper, "Let's pull over into the lot, but park so as not to be hindered or blocked by any trucks or other vehicles, in case we have to leave abruptly."

We parked at a distance from the checkpoint. Only a small gravel parking driveway would prevent our quick exit to the road north if necessary. We then decided to go into the *Gestapo* office and present our orders and get a pass to try to get through the checkpoint.

The *Gestapo* office looked old and had been converted from a municipal building. If a stray bomb from an Allied raid had mistakenly hit the building, it would never have been missed. The floor looked like it hadn't been swept in weeks.

The older woman at the reception counter had steel grey very thin hair, a too strong lower jaw, and paunchy pale skin which hadn't been out in the sun for decades. The atmosphere reeked of old sweat masked by stale perfume and cigarette smoke.

The receptionist seemed a bit startled by a Lieutenant in an *SS* uniform standing in front of her, but she was mildly pleasant. "Can I help you, gentlemen?"

"Yes," Ezekiel replied, we have orders to our airbase in Denmark and require a pass for the checkpoint."

"Let me see your papers," shot back the steel-haired functionary.

I pulled out our orders from a large envelope and carefully laid them out in front of the woman. She took her time reading through the papers and then said the officer at the checkpoint had called and said something about your automobile.

Ezekiel asked, "Is there something wrong with the automobile?"

The lantern-jawed lady replied, "Yes. It was reported missing from the Gestapo Headquarters in Nordhausen two days ago. We have informed the office we have the car and are holding the two occupants here in Hamburg."

"What do you mean, 'holding' us," demanded Ezekiel.

"We have been asked to detain you both until the local Gestapo agent can clear the problem with headquarters," replied the woman. He will be in right after the lunch hour this afternoon.

Since it was only 9:30 in the morning, Zeke and I were not about to hang around for an interrogation meeting with some goon from the local *Gestapo* office. We also were not anxious to waste the morning waiting for incompetence to show up.

Zeke looked troubled and looked like he might start to be confrontational, but I immediately answered, "Of course, Frau. Where would you like us to wait? And, if I may, where would our pass for the checkpoint be held?"

The passes are here in my desk drawer, and you will get one as soon as the local headquarters clear you. Please go with Gus. He will take you downstairs to a cell.

Gus was the only other person in the reception area. I truthfully hadn't even noticed him. There might have been more people downstairs. Zeke had a panicked look on his face when he heard the word "cell." I held up my hand and said, "Gus, lead the way."

We went down a wide rather steep stairway to a dank and filthy cellar rife with odors from something I couldn't place. The smell of mold was quite strong. The handrail was a blessing since the stairway was so dark. There were three empty cells, and I could see no one else in the area.

Gus opened a cell with a set of keys from his belt and motioned us to enter the cell explaining he was sorry to lock us up, but, "It probably won't be for too long."

"You're correct about it not being too long, Gus."

As I entered the cell and passed in front of Gus, I turned suddenly and caught Gus on the side of his face with a sharp blow from my elbow. It wasn't a "killing blow," but it was lights out for him for a while. I had no reason to harm the older gentleman, but I knew being locked in a cell would not be suitable for Zeke or me.

It was just more comfortable for me to strike someone, if I had to, with my elbow. I would bring my fist up to my chin and then cuff the opponent with the flat side of my elbow. Most of my opponents were shorter than me and my elbow, padded with muscle and my uniform coat, seemed to be at the same level as their chin. My padded elbow also saved my hands from getting injured.

"Zeke, find something to tie him up and gag him. I will go up and collect the nice lady upstairs. Let's get some extra rope or cloths to tie her up also.

I hustled up the stairs.

"Time is not on our side at this moment," I called back to Zeke.

I yelled across the room, **"Ms., I think Gus might be having a seizure or fit, could you come down and let me know how I might help him!"**

When she reached the bottom of the stairs, she saw Gus trundled up like a Christmas turkey, bleeding from the side of his face. I informed her the *SS* was detaining her, and if she were cooperative, no harm would come to her.

She started to resist and turned to run back up the stairs. I grabbed her arm, turned her around, and gave her a mild slap on the face. I didn't mean to bruise her, but my slap left definite red markings, and it certainly surprised her. **"Ms, you will not be harmed if you cooperate!"**

Zeke and I tied her up and gagged her then tied them together in the same cell, locked the cell door, and quickly went upstairs to grab a pass from the reception desk for the checkpoint. It was signed and stamped.

Zeke said he was grateful we didn't have to injure them further. I agreed and said, "Let's walk slowly and calmly to the car.

The officer at the checkpoint gave me a hard look but gave us no further trouble. We proceeded north and crossed the Elbe River. This river flowed into and through Hamburg. Further north we passed what must have been the airport for the city of Hamburg. It was a mass of bomb craters and smoldering wrecks of military aircraft.

We kept off the main roads and headed north to Norderstedt. We inched our way around the city and headed due north to the outside suburbs of Neumünster. There looked like some damage to the central part of town. We kept to the small roads leading around the city.

It was late afternoon as we took back roads through the town of Nortorf and Thienbüttel on our way to Rendsburg. We needed to get Ilsa's grandmother's address at the local police station on Moltkestraße in Rendsburg. We were not entirely sure if going to the police station was going to be a smooth or seamless proposition.

The more Zeke and I talked about going to the police station in Rendsburg, the less we liked the whole idea.

Meanwhile at the station in Rendsburg, the chief of police had received a message from the Hamburg *Gestapo* office: **Alert! Immediate detention of two adult males, early twenties. One quiet tall in *SS* uniform, one medium height. Both claim to be on a mission for the** Führer. **Orders may be forged and counterfeit. Traveling in stolen *Gestapo* automobile from the Nordhausen Office. Detain/Detain/Detain.**

The chief of police immediately put out a call to the local *Gestapo* office to get some back-up involvement from the German State Police. Four agents responded to apprehend the two adult males quickly. The Gestapo felt their extensive questioning methods would get a quick resolution and answer to their questions.[*]

"Zeke, let us approach the police station on Moltkestraße very cautiously to see if there is any unusual activity."

We were coming down Hollorstraße and getting close to the station. As we approached the station, Zeke noticed, "Jenz, does there seem to be quite a few cars around the station?"

---

[*] *During World War II, The German State Police (the Gestapo) did not follow the norms or niceties of democratic societies or international conventions. They were unrestrained by and had no fear of internal or international laws; acquiring information was their only goal and requirement. The Gestapo had almost no intention of ever releasing a prisoner unless it was to terrorize other members of a family or group.*

The Gestapo methods of brutal torture varied according to the immediate circumstances, and included, but were not limited, to the following, in addition to removing one finger at a time: electric shock, hanging by the feet, beating with a baton, use of a blowtorch or red-hot pokers, whipping, and rape for women. Also, there had been reports of hungry, ravenous dogs, attacking naked prisoners who would not talk and chewing their privates and tearing the flesh off their bodies while the subject was still alive.

"It's hard to tell. Two of the black automobiles could be *Gestapo* cars. Let's park up the street and see what develops."

"Jenz, do you remember Ilsa's grandmother's last name?"

"I think it was Müller or Möller.

"Do you remember the name of the small town east of here on the way to the city of Kiel?

"Don't test me Ezekiel, but I think it was Höbek. I can check Ilsa's letter."

"Let's drive over to Höbek it can't be too far from here. We could try to find her address from the post office or local police station. It might be a lot safer," claimed Ezekiel.

"You're probably right, Zeke. But remember, the authorities at Rendsburg have Ilsa's grandmother's address and possibly her last name. They could be there ahead of us. We should approach her home with caution."

We left Rendsburg and drove over to Höbek on Hauptstraße. It took us less than an hour, and we stopped at the first municipal building we saw, the local fire station. There was only one fireman on duty, but he was accommodating and directed us to Mrs. Möller's summer home a few blocks away.

As we approached the home, we noticed one strange black sedan parked out front. It might have been my desire to see and hold Ilsa and feel her next to me, but I remarked to Zeke, "How many of them could there be there, with only one car out front?"

"Let's take in our orders, Jenz, in case we need a distraction."

The neighborhood was a collection of scattered homes and farms set in a beautiful pastoral rural setting. It was near sunset, and we parked on a hill overlooking what we hoped was the grandmother's summer home. The neighborhood was tranquil; almost too quiet.

"Zeke, if we wait for it to get dark, perhaps the black sedan and its occupants will leave."

"Or, Jenz, perhaps more of the cavalry will join them. Time is not on our side."

"I could knock on the door and see who is in there. If I don't come out in five minutes, you could think about coming in after me."

As we assessed the situation, I realized Zeke was right. Time was not on our side. It looked like the *Gestapo* was out to arrest us and take us in for questioning. Perhaps Ilsa and her family also. We had to convince whoever was in the home with Ilsa's family we were on a legitimate mission for our *Führer*, or eliminate any obstacle and escape to a safer place.

Immediately after we approached and knocked on the door, the decision was made for us. We were met by an agent from the Gestapo who pushed a pistol into Zeke's face. There on the couch in the living room were Ilsa, her parents, and her grandmother. All were bound hand and foot, gagged, and tied to the furniture. They all looked frightened, unnerved, and cowed.

It was a pathetic and sad group on the couch, but the two Gestapo agents looked even worse.

The taller agent was almost six feet tall, balding with a bit of a pointy head, but muscular enough not to be underestimated. He was probably in his early forties.

The second agent was almost as tall with bushy unruly hair rapidly going to grey around the temples. He wasn't quite as muscular, but he was the one waving the pistol.

The one with the pistol spoke first. "Come in gentlemen; we've all been waiting patiently for you."

The balding agent with the pointy head spoke up. "You are both to sit over there." He pointed to back to back chairs set in a hall. "We have been ordered to detain you until our chief gets here."

"And when is your chief due to arrive?" I inquired.

"Soon enough in the morning!" Pointy head shouted. **"Now, both of you sit over there!"**

"Yes, agent, we will sit down, but here are our orders from our *Führer*. As I passed them to the pistol-waving agent, I purposely let them flutter to the floor at his feet.

As the agent bent down to pick up the paperwork, my knee caught the pistol and his chin almost simultaneously. I thumped him so hard my knee was quite painful. The pain might have been a combination of the barrel of the gun and his lower jaw on my knee.

There was a loud **crack.** The agent's unruly hair became even more unruly as his head snapped back. The sound was the agent's jaw breaking. He pulled the trigger of his pistol at the same time, but he hadn't chambered a round. I guessed I had snapped off both condylar heads of his lower jaw and perhaps driven them into his skull. He moaned once like a deflated balloon but never moved.

As he was going down for the count, I grabbed his pistol, chambered a round by cocking the gun and leveled it at the balding agent declaring in a firm voice, **"Now, you pointy-headed bastard, please be so kind to sit and do not move. I would hate to mess up this nice lady's living room with your pointy-headed brains scattered all about."**

In a calmer voice, I continued, "You *Gestapo* 'gentlemen' are now to be detained by the *SS* for interfering in a mission of great importance for Germany and our *Führer*. You will be held and dealt without judicial review or trial."

Zeke could tell I hadn't eaten in a while. I wasn't quite as polite as I probably should have been. But under the circumstances of seeing my intended and her family all bundled up on the couch like so much luggage, I thought I did pretty well.

Zeke untied Ilsa's grandmother first and used the ropes to tie up the agent to the chair snugly. The bushy haired agent was still out cold, but Zeke securely tied him up and gagged them both.

I apologized to Mrs. Möller and Ilsa's parents for the rough language with the excuse I hadn't eaten since breakfast.

Mrs. Möller's comment, "Wow, Jenz, what a fine piece work subduing both Gestapo agents!" It is a pleasure to meet you.

Ilsa threw her arms around me and said, "I knew you both would find us, thank you so much. These agents were hinting at all sorts of ways they would be able to get information from us. They even told us they would rape me in front of my parents and grandmother."

"Ezekiel and I will make sure, Ilsa, these animals will never assault another God-fearing German again. And they will pay for their impropriety and indecency."

The family was grateful to be free of their bonds but also terrified. Mr. Huber asked in a quiet voice, "Jenz what shall we do with the *Gestapo* agents?"

"Mr. Huber," I started, "Laws passed in Germany in 1936 gave the *Gestapo* the freedom to operate without judicial review. In other words, the German State Police could act above or outside the law. They could arrest, detain, imprison, or execute our fellow citizens without court involvement or review."

"We are going to give these two putrid examples of human trash the same opportunity they were planning to give us. Also, they will pay for the way they treated you kind folks and the way they intimidated my lovely fiancé Ilsa."

"Mrs. Möller, What is the largest and closest body of water on our way north?" I asked.

"Well, if you are going north, I guess it would be the *Kaiser Wilhelm Kanal*. It is a few miles north of here up near Sehestedt."

"How deep is the canal, Mrs. Möller?"

"Oh, it's very deep. Large battleships have traversed the canal."

"Then our Gestapo friends will be able to see just how deep it is."

The conscious agent gave me a quick head snap and a look of abject terror on his face as I announced their fate. He would have screamed if the gag had let him. All he could do was look woefully afraid, and gurgle swears at me. They were both wretched examples of humanity.

I had to lay down a few rules for the family. "Let's, please gather any food for travel; even crackers, cheese, bread, and water. We have to leave this location very early in the morning because these nice agents could have alerted their fellow thugs we would be coming here."

"Mrs. Huber spoke up, "But Jenz, where will we go?"

"We can discuss our plans after we visit the canal, Mrs. Huber. However, we have to leave this place just before the first light in the morning. Let's pack up this evening and be ready to go before sunrise. Please include warm clothing.

"Mr. Huber, can you help Zeke and me load these two thugs into the trunk of their automobile? It's dark enough so we should be able to load them unobserved."

CHAPTER 43

Fleeing the Reich

Ilsa and her grandmother traveled with me. We were a two-car caravan and left early in the morning before the sun was up. There was a faint glow of sunrise on the horizon. Mrs. Möller read the map to me for the quickest back road shortcuts to the canal. We took a right out of the driveway to Hauptstraße, and then after a few minutes, she suggested a right on Bahnhofsweg which eventually turned into Brückenweg. Ezekiel was following in our car we had liberated from the *Gestapo* in Nordhausen.

After a few minutes, the sun was coming up on a smoky horizon. The bombing and destruction of cities throughout northern Germany's industrial heartland gave an eerie glow to the sunrise. There was a yellowish haze on the horizon. The nighttime dew hadn't burned off yet, and the roads were a little slick. I drove as cautiously as I dared, but I wanted to put some distance between us and Ilsa's grandmother's home.

We went through a couple of small towns including Ostenfeld and Ehlesdorf on our way to Sehestedt Süd. As we approached the canal, I asked Mrs. Möller if she knew of a secluded spot we could get rid of the agent's car. She suggested we turn off and drive into the Kiebitzmoor woods to the left of the road we were traveling.

Both cars turned onto the dirt road leading into the woods. Since the local agent's car looked a little newer and had an almost full tank of diesel, we put all the "trash" in the Nordhausen automobile's trunk. The conscious agent fought us and kept mumbling swears through his gag. Zeke gave him a good slap with his gloved hand, and he went quiet. We pushed him into the trunk with his diabolical fellow agent.

Zeke and I said we would be right back and continued driving down the dirt road into the woods with the local agents in the back trunk of our older automobile.

Zeke asked, "What are we suppose to do with the automobile and the two agents in the trunk, dump them into the canal?"

"Exactly, Zeke. They are going for a ride into the canal. We will need to open the windows so the car will sink quickly. It's a little cold for a swim, so a little slope to the canal would be helpful. It might be good to get rid of the car; it has been traced since we left Nordhausen."

The dirt road paralleled the canal and came out of the woods for a brief period. The path running along the canal was higher than the water level, so there was a slight slope down to the canal. We positioned the car, checked for water traffic, and placed a flat stone on the gas pedal. I put the car in first gear with the clutch depressed.

I opened the door, and Zeke held my arm as I popped the clutch. Zeke pulled me out of the automobile. The car moved slowly and deliberately into the canal. It floated for almost a minute before the windows and opened front door filled the car with water, and it sank below the surface. The engine quit as soon as the air filter submerged and water soaked into the engine.

"I'm not sure what the depth of the canal is here Zeke, but I can't see the roof of the car anymore. A few bubbles are coming up, but they should die out pretty quickly. Let's get back to Ilsa's family."

We jogged back to the newer car with the full tank of diesel fuel.

"What did you do with the car, Jenz?" asked Mrs. Möller.

"The automobile and the trash sank in a deep portion of the canal. Those *Gestapo* thugs will not be bothering decent Germans any longer.

"But wouldn't drowning them be murder?" asked Ilsa's grandmother.

"Mrs. Möller," I began. "It is not my place in God's heavenly realm to act as judge, jury, and executioner for these *Gestapo* agents. *I paused for a moment because I wasn't sure how far I should go trying to explain myself. Also, I had my doubts about how the Good Lord would look at the actions Zeke and I had taken against the agents we had killed.*

Ilsa's grandmother had brought me to an ah-ha moment. But I continued, "Mrs. Möller, I sincerely pray God will forgive Zeke and me for our actions. Also, instead of trying to deal with the facts of our actions, we are trying as best we can to protect our families our loved ones, and indeed all God-fearing German citizens."

Zeke interrupted, "My parents have already been lost in the concentration camps, Mrs. Möller. Jenz and I have seen what is happening to the honest, hardworking Jews, and other members of the German community. These honest folks are treated as slave laborers under terrible conditions of food and sleep deprivation. Most honest Germans wouldn't think of treating a dog the way the *Gestapo* and the *SS* treat our neighbors and fellow citizens."

"In addition, Mrs. Möller, we have never eliminated any *Gestapo* agents using any of the torture methods the agents frequently use on our fellow countrymen, women, and children. The elimination techniques Jenz learned at Hitler Youth Camp dispenses with the agents in the most humane and rapid method possible.

"Jenz has been in some of the concentration camps, Mrs. Möller. You would not be able to comprehend or even imagine the types of torture inflicted on our German citizens or the citizens of the Eastern Territories. Thousands of countrymen, women, even children, have been lost to the gas chambers and the heinous, incredibly cruel torture of depraved members of the *Wehrmacht, SS,* and *Gestapo.*"

Mrs. Möller then mentioned she had an elderly Jewish friend living with her. This friend had gone with a Gestapo agent for questioning and never returned to my home. "When I asked at the local police station what had happened to my friend, no one could tell me."

Mrs. Huber interrupted, probably to halt Zeke's description of the torture being inflicted on her fellow Germans, "Jenz, we have nowhere to go; where can we go without the *Gestapo* following us and arresting us ?"

"Everyone, please listen. Ezekiel and I have orders from our *Führer* to travel to an airbase in Denmark called Aalborg. We will be sizing up the now German airbase as a possible site for the *Führer's* 'Wonder Weapons.' We intend to get all of you into Denmark, then on to Sweden. I have family and friends in the Stockholm area. My family will help us and put us up until the German generals decide to end this war. Since Sweden is a neutral country, we should be safe there. Or at least safer than near a major German city."

I continued with the hope of ensuring their cooperation and alleviating some of their distress.

"Our initial goal today is to take the back roads to Flensburg, which is near the Danish border.

"What happens if we get stopped again by the *Gestapo?*" asked Mr. Huber.

"Don't forget, sir; we now have hats and coats, and better still, identification for Ezekiel to be an agent of the feared *Gestapo.* He will be wearing a holster and a loaded Lugar if anyone wants to challenge us. We certainly hope we never have to use the pistol, but it can be intimidating if anyone starts to ask too many questions. We will rid ourselves of all the *Gestapo* material as soon as we can in Denmark."

"Including the weapon?" asked Mr. Huber.

"Especially the Lugar," answered Zeke. "These weapons may be able to be traced to a specific German State Police headquarters and possibly the agents who had them. We have kept most of the cash carried by the several agents we have eliminated. The money will aid us in procuring safe travel. We had to leave Nordhausen rather abruptly and were not able to secure our normal pay."

We traveled without incident to Flensburg, although it was a little challenging to get much food along the way. We had some success at a well-kept farm in the small town of Südensee outside of Sörup. Ezekiel and I approached the farmhouse with a little trepidation and not a lot of hope. The fields looked well tended, and the outside of the home was clean and well maintained.

The farm owner was an older gentleman who at first offered us nothing but heated criticism of the war and its generals. I decided to try a little different conversation with the old farmer.

As he could see from his front door, we had a full complement of people crammed in our automobile. His disdain and loathing for the war were obvious.

"I've already lost one son and a nephew to Hitler's war. I have little hope of seeing my youngest son since he left a year ago for the Eastern Front," intoned the elderly geezer.

"Sir, even though I'm wearing an *SS* uniform and am traveling under orders from the *Führer,* let me assure you, our efforts are in no way linked to supporting or furthering the goals of a murderous regime. My lifelong friend who stands before you, Ezekiel, is Jewish. He has already lost his family in the concentration labor camps. I am half Jewish and half Swedish. Our intention for the past five years has been to end the power and authority of the German State Police. We are on our way to Denmark and then will attempt to travel to Sweden and live with relatives until this diabolical war is over. Also..."

"Enough! The old farmer held up his hand and interrupted. My name is Svensson. My family is also from Sweden. What do you need for food to get you to your destination?"

Not only did the farmer invite us into his home for a very decent lunch of cheese sandwiches with crackers and cider, but gave us a bag of apples for our journey to Denmark.

I asked him, "How difficult is it to transit the border into Denmark in this area? Are there any border crossings more difficult than others?"

"Your best bet is to cross at Niehuus just north of Flensburg," replied the old gentleman. "None of the crossing points have been reinforced since the *Führer* in his wisdom decided the Danes would all rather be Germans!"

We thanked Mr. Svensson and headed for the checkpoint just north of Flensburg at the town of Niehuus. The farmer said to follow the Schloßberg road to the border.

As we neared the border crossing, we could see two army vehicles and a patrol of Wehrmacht guards reinforcing the border patrol. None of the guards seemed to have a strict military bearing and were waving the two cars ahead of us through without searching them.

"This might be tricky, I warned our passengers. Please let Zeke, and I do most of the talking."

CHAPTER 44

....

The Danish Border

There was some nervous chatter from the back seat as we pulled up to the guard shack at the Danish border. I rolled down my driver's side window.

"Good afternoon, Sergeant."

"Welcome to the German-occupied country of Denmark, now part of the *Reich*." Heil Hitler was his stiff arm greeting.

The *SS* uniform persuaded the guard not to question us further.

I waved through the window and drove on through the checkpoint and into the town of Padborg, Denmark. The relief in the car was palpable. We were all very chatty, almost euphoric. It was quite a relief to get out of Germany so easily. The only problem, we were now in a German-occupied country.

Ezekiel's comment was telling, "I hope it is as easy to get out of Denmark as it was to get in. It might be a bit more challenging to get out of Denmark and into Sweden if the Wehrmacht guards the border."

The countryside was pastoral and beautiful. There were many small farms with cows and sheep in the pastures. The air in this agrarian setting even smelled fresher. Perhaps because we were getting farther away from the bombed-out larger cities in the *Reich*.

We had driven about 20 kilometers north on smooth roads to the town of Kliplev and pulled over and stopped. I wanted to give everyone in the automobile a chance to take a little break, perhaps get some food at a local Inn and make a decision on going directly to the coast at Fynshav to continue by ferry to Copenhagen.

I knew we needed to get to the easternmost city in Denmark, either Copenhagen or Elsinore, to get a ferry to Sweden. I was considering taking the automobile with us whenever Zeke and I were able to take the ferry.

I explained I was going to follow my orders to Aalborg to try to persuade the Wehrmacht to send a trainload of missiles to this particular base. If the rockets arrive at the army base in Aalborg, I will make every effort to delay or dismantle or change them to make them ineffective and not capable of being launched.

"Oh Jenz," Ilsa proclaimed, **"Wouldn't dismantling the missiles be very dangerous!"**

"I appreciate your concern, Ilsa, but Ezekiel and I have been doing this for the past five or six years. We always take certain precautions, but these missiles are very dangerous. There have been rumors the missile developers have thought about even more dangerous warheads for these weapons."

Ilsa's dad asked, "What sort of warhead could be more dangerous than the ones they are now using?"

"The stories I have heard at the Army Research Center, Mr. Huber, is the German research scientists are trying to develop an atomic warhead since 1939."

"What is an atomic warhead, Jenz?" inquired Mrs. Huber.

"It's a bomb capable of flattening an entire city. It gets the explosive force and energy by splitting the atom. However, it needs a substance called 'heavy water' which is produced during the process of making fertilizer. The heavy water contains deuterium oxide, which can be used in making atomic bombs. The explosive force and radiation is the danger of an atomic warhead."

"Where could the Wehrmacht possibly get heavy water?" asked Ilsa's dad.

"The first production plant is, unfortunately, in Norway and under *Nazi* control," added Zeke.

He continued, "Norwegian saboteurs had attacked the Norsk Hydro plant named Vemork, at the Rjukan Waterfall in Tinn, Norway on the 27th of February 1943. This Norwegian plant was the first plant capable of producing 'heavy water' in any quantity. They could produce about twelve tons each year."

"The brave Norwegian saboteurs, with the aid of the British SOE or Special Operations Executive, blew up the electrolysis units as they were producing the heavy water. Their aim was to prevent the *Nazi* regime of Adolf Hitler from developing an atomic capability."

"It was two German chemists, Otto Hahn and Fritz Strassmann who correctly determined nuclear fission could be a source of great power if it could be controlled. Heavy water was needed to control the power of nuclear fission."

"Where do you get all this information, Ezekiel?" Asked Ilsa.

"Oh, it's all scientific stuff and published for the world to read in the German scientific journal, *Naturwissenshaften*. You understand, the *Führer* and the rest of the *Nazi* thugs in their 'brilliance' have swept many of the most valuable physicists into the *Wehrmacht* to be used as cannon fodder on the Eastern Front. Many scientists with Jewish names or heritage who have worked on nuclear fission have either fled the country or have wound up in the labor camps, never to be seen again."

I mentioned I would be happy to drive everyone to Fynshav where they could board a ferry to make their way to Copenhagen by bus, or they could stay with me for another fifty miles north and make a decision when we reached the small town of Frederica, Denmark.

Everyone decided to stay with me, at least for another few hours while we traveled north. We ate at a small inn at the quaint little town of Aabenraa overlooking the harbor. It was going to get dark early, so we decided to try to make it to the city of Aarhus about seventy kilometers north.

I convinced everyone except Zeke to leave us at Aarhus and take the ferry and bus to Copenhagen. From there they could take a bus to Stockholm, Sweden. Ilsa protested, but I told her it would be much too hazardous to both of us to bring her into the Wehrmacht base at Aalborg.

I wrote down my family's address, where they would be staying and contact information for my dad's relatives. I promised we would try to get there by the first day of Spring, 21 March 1945. I also gave them all but a few Marks we had confiscated from our *Gestapo* "friends."

CHAPTER 45

The Wehrmacht Air Base at Aalborg

The next morning Zeke and I took our time and got to the air base at Aalborg by lunchtime. I was hoping to catch up on our food rations. For some reason, I was continuously hungry. We showed our orders at the gate and got directions to base housing, the officer's club, and the commandant's office. The base seemed well laid out with several newer looking buildings.

There was snow everywhere, but the roads were well-plowed, and all the buildings were numbered and well-marked. There was a brisk cold wind-driven light snow blowing all around the base, but the sky was a bright blue, so the snow was blowing off the frozen ground.

After finding rooms across the hall from each other in the officer's quarters, we decided to walk over to the rudimentary officer's club across the street. They served hot food, but hot was the only similarity to the club at the Army Research Center. It was certainly not as well-kept or luxurious as the one at the Research Center. There were no linens or candles on the tables or decorative art on the walls.

We had some sort of meat and gravy, and some hard little cabbage-like vegetables. The vegetables were palatable as long as they were soaked in the gravy. They also served the meal with a rather hard dark bread. But again, it was tasty only with a good soaking of gravy.

After lunch, we went over to the commandant's office to present our orders and ask permission to tour the base. The CO's office was in the air terminal for the station.

We knocked, and we could hear the door being unlocked. A sergeant opened the door and asked, "Sir, what can I do for you gentlemen?"

"We have orders from our *Führer* sergeant." I kept the envelope in my hand and indicated to the sergeant these orders were for the Commanding Officer's eyes only.

The sergeant responded, "Come in, gentlemen." As we entered the office, he locked the door behind us. At the time, I thought it odd the CO's door remained locked during office hours, but I said nothing; Zeke had the same question on his face.

The sergeant knocked on the door behind him and told the commanding officer we were in the office. To our surprise, a rather portly officer in a rumpled major's uniform waddled out to meet us.

"Good afternoon gentlemen, we had a message from our Nordhausen office you would be coming."

"Excellent," I advised. "Would it be possible to have a tour of the air base?"

The major replied, "Your orders were explicit in stating you would come here, but what is the purpose of your visit?"

"Could we go to your office to discuss them," I mentioned. The major seemed helpful but guarded in any response. The officer turned and led us into a small office.

After he closed the door, I explained, "Major, we are looking at the base here at Aalborg as a possible launching site for an advanced missile system."

The Major shot back, "Wouldn't our airbase receive unwanted notoriety with a missile site here? Do you understand, Lieutenant, how important this base is for our operations in Norway?"

Probably notoriety was the last item this overweight functionary wanted. Any unwanted notice might mean lard-ass might actually have to produce results or get noticed by his superiors.

"Of course, Major. The airbase here would be primarily providing storage space and launching facilities." I inadvertently rubbed my knee where it had come in contact with the *Gestapo* agent's jaw and pistol yesterday.

"How long does it take to launch one of the missiles, Lieutenant?"

"This particular missile can be set up, programmed, and launched in under an hour. The beauty of the rocket is it is impossible to detect where the missile originated. It travels at almost three times the speed of sound. It is impossible for the target of these missiles to learn their origin. Moreover, the targeted cities cannot see or hear it coming. Defense against this missile is impossible."

"They sound dangerous, Lieutenant. What sort of warhead does it carry, and are they reliable? Is there any chance they could shorten this war?"

"Much of this information is classified, Major. I can tell you the *Führer* has indicated this is our best chance to win many battles. If we can attack the Russians on the Eastern Front and ruin some of their cities, it may affect the outcome of the war dramatically."

"Here is a map of the airbase, Lieutenant. You and your colleague are permitted access to all the secured areas. My sergeant will drive you around. It's cold up here this time of year, and it can be dangerous to be caught out in the open after dark. The wind can be unrelenting in the winter."

After our tour, I asked the sergeant if he would send the following message to our office at Nordhausen:

Aalborg air base cleared for the first shipment of V-2 missiles. They can accept up to 20 weapons transported by rail or ship. Launch sites and storage facilities favorable. After launching the first twenty, the base could service, store, and launch up to 50 missiles per week. Radiation protective storage is available for warheads. Lt. J. Ramsgrund.

Zeke and I got word in the evening the Russians were closing in on Germany, and could be in Berlin by the Spring. Suddenly it seemed like an excellent time to get out of Germany. We had accomplished most of our goals of minimizing Gestapo Agents, slowing missile development and deployment, and trying to divert missiles to northern Denmark. We thought it might be a good time to head to Sweden. We had no idea how much longer the war could go on.

CHAPTER 46

The Gestapo Comes Calling at Aalborg

My room was direct across the hall from Ezekiel's room. We had turned in for the evening. I was about to drop off to sleep when I heard a sharp knock on Zeke's door across the hall. I cracked my door and peeked out. There were two large men at his door. The meanest looking one had drawn his Lugar. Both men were quite large with close haircuts under black fedoras.

I eased my door closed and dressed rapidly in my *SS* uniform. These folks looked pretty serious and could well have come over to my room next. I wasn't about to let them take Zeke out of the building.

After a few minutes of listening, I heard Zeke's door open. Since they didn't come directly to my door, I opened it a crack and saw them starting down the hall. Zeke was handcuffed with his hands behind his back. I called out to the three of them, "Vitali, where are you going this time of night?"

The mean looking agent with the pistol waved it in my direction and answered in a threatening voice, **"The Gestapo has questions for this man, do not interfere. This is police business."**

"I'm sorry gentlemen, but Vitali is my valued colleague from the Army Research Center. Where are you taking him at this time of night?"

"He will be at *Gestapo* Headquarters, you may see him in the morning. **This is a police matter, stay in your room.**

I had a pretty good idea what the Gestapo does to people once they get them to their headquarters. Torture for information was their primary goal. Their techniques were inhuman.

I took a step toward the pistol-waving agent, and he took a step toward me and leveled the Lugar at my head. As the agent took a step toward me, Zeke put his foot out and made the agent stumble slightly while I took another step forward and grabbed the Lugar out of the distracted agent's hand.

"All of you, come into my room so we can sort this out." I was pointing the weapon at the larger agent and had chambered a round in the barrel.

Once I had closed the door to my room, I fished the key to the handcuffs out of the agent's pocket and gave it to the other agent. I instructed him in a firm but polite manner while holding the pistol with both hands and leveling it directly at the goon's head. **"Please unlock my colleague's hands, so I don't have to mess up my room with your brains.**

Zeke had both agents sit on the bed and placed the handcuffs on the first agent through the iron bed frame.

Zeke started to tie the other agent up with the first agent's shoelaces, but the agent swore and struggled to get free and took a swing at Zeke. I jabbed the agent with my elbow into his solar plexus and then gave him a crushing blow to his right temple with the side of my closed fist.

Blood spurted out from his temple around the spot where the side of my fist had impacted and probably fractured his temporal bone just above his ear. Blood was running out of the agent's ear. He was going to have a massive headache if he ever woke up.

He went down on the bed and either passed out or decided not to move for health reasons. We both went to work, making sure the agents were securely tied and gagged.

"What should we do with them?" queried Zeke.

"We will take them back to Germany to face a court for their crimes," I winked at Zeke. "We will take them in the car."

We left the first agent cuffed to the bed with his feet bound together and gagged while we carried his pistol-wielding friend to the trunk of our automobile.

We went back for the first agent and wrapped him in a blanket and tossed him on top of the other agent in our trunk. The agent was wide awake. Zeke told him the blanket coverage would help keep him warm. Now we had two live agents in our back trunk and another pistol with our belongings. Neither agent would last long in the freezing weather. We were pretty sure they wouldn't have further use for the cash in their wallets.

"Zeke, we are going to have to leave this evening to be safe. I don't know how the *Gestapo* found us, but we cannot take a chance of them catching up with us again. I will leave a note for the commanding officer telling him we were recalled back to Germany. All members of the *SS* and the *Wehrmacht* not involved in critical defense have been called to the Eastern Front."

"Won't the Gestapo intercept us on our way out of Denmark?"

"Probably Zeke, especially if we were to travel south. We will start south, but after going a few kilometers, we will pick up a secondary highway listed as number 180 North on the map. This winding but paved road will eventually take us to Frederikshavn.

"Where the devil is Frederikshavn?"

"It's about forty miles north of here. The map shows secondary roads to our destination, but they have a morning ferry going over to Gothenburg, Sweden. From there we could take the car or bus to Stockholm. The agents in the trunk will be frozen by then, and we can either abandon them in a remote location or leave the car within walking distance of the ferry parking lot."

"Will it be difficult to get out of Denmark and onto the ferry to Gothenburg," asked Zeke.

"It might be more difficult with the automobile. We could leave it in Denmark. It's possible the *Gestapo* has been tracking us through our use of the automobile. It is a rather large black distinctive automobile. There are so few cars on the road, this one stands out. Let's get on our way and see what the ferry schedule looks like."

It took us the rest of the night to get to Frederikshavn over snowy, icy-cold conditions. We stopped in Saeby to change drivers. Nothing was open at such an early hour; it was 2 am. It was only another ten or fifteen kilometers or so to the ferry, so we kept going.

Before we went into the terminal for the ferry, I changed out of my uniform tunic and put on one of the overcoats we had "borrowed" from the *Gestapo* agents we met at Ilsa's grandmother's summer home. We left the *Gestapo* credentials, pistols and hats locked in the car and parked on a small dirt road off a side street two blocks from the ferry terminal. We covered most of the car with some pine branches and snow.

There was an icy wind blowing as we made our way down to the terminal and across the parking lot. It was early, and dark and cold. Money from the last four *Gestapo* agents we had eased out of the system bought us more than enough cash for breakfast and tickets for the ferry. The one ship each day wasn't until 9 am. so Zeke and I lingered over coffee until we could get our story straight for the encounter with the ticket agents at the terminal.

Zeke's story was uncomplicated. He was Vitali Carapezza, a Jew fleeing the Nazis. My account was also straightforward. I was Swedish and a resident of Jakobsberg, about seven miles north of Stockholm. I showed the ticket agent the address where my folks were staying with relatives. Thanks to God the agents weren't sticklers on visa requirements. I guessed we were not the first folks getting out of the *Third Reich* while we could. The two *100 Reichsmark* bills I folded into the address paper probably didn't hurt either.

Zeke mentioned in a low tone as the ferry was getting underway, "I think we can breathe a little easier to at least be out of the *Reich*. It feels almost like awakening from a bad dream, a nightmare might have come true."

"Don't relax too much yet, my friend. Do not turn around, but two large thuggish men are looking our way. Let's walk down to the other end of the ferry to see if they follow us."

We knew the ferry ride from Frederikshavn, Denmark to Gothenburg, Sweden was about a fifty-mile trip. The one way trip would take six to seven hours. We preferred not to be harassed or detained by the *Gestapo* on the way over to Sweden. The trip carried us across a portion of the North Sea which can be very rough at this time of year. This particular route was semi-protected by the countries of Denmark, Norway, and Sweden.

Zeke whispered, "Jenz, what do we do if they try to arrest or detain us?"

"We may have to deal with them, but let's not be too concerned unless these two or someone else approaches us."

Zeke turned sidewise to look over my shoulder, "I just have an uneasy feeling about those two. They look like *Gestapo* only meaner, if it's possible. Do you think it we could avoid them until we dock in Sweden?"

"We can certainly try, but it would be important not to get separated on board the ferry. If the *Gestapo* is up to mischief, they will deal with the Swedish authorities in addition to us. Let's always stay in visual contact with each other. I'm thinking of finding a chair and sleeping for at least the first portion of our trip."

Zeke and I found some large well-cushioned chairs in the corner of the passenger deck and sacked out for probably over an hour. They were very comfortable chairs with well-padded cloth seats. The chair was turned to face the wall so I could stretch out my legs without bothering anyone trying to get by. Sleep came on me almost immediately with pleasant thoughts of my pledged mate.

I was rudely awakened when I heard someone asking Zeke questions about his travel plans. Both suspicious looking thugs were right next to his chair, talking about how they had been following him for the past few hours.

"What are you talking about," exclaimed Zeke in a somewhat surprised tone. He spoke loud enough to wake me up.

"We are the *Gestapo* from the Frederikshavn office," said the first thug as he flashed his badge. I am agent Rasmussen, and this is agent Poulsen. We need to question you about two missing agents from the Aalborg Air Base."

Hearing this made me think. How the heck had these two agents found out about our altercation back at the officer's quarters at the Aalborg base? Had they witnessed our loading their bodies into the trunk of their car? And, if they had seen something, why didn't they arrest us on the spot and prevent the agents in the trunk from turning into blocks of ice?

"What would I know about *Gestapo* agents?" Zeke shot back in a sleepy but direct retort.

Agent Rasmussen, the one closest to Zeke, replied, "Two agents from the Aalborg office were sent to the barracks to pick you up for questioning. This morning their automobile was spotted by the local police in Frederikshavn."

Our ferry was starting to react to the wave swells and the continuous howl of the wind out of the north. The two standing agents kept bracing themselves.

Zeke quickly answered without hesitation, "You should ask the agent's what their car is doing here."

We have two specific problems, gentlemen. The agents and their automobile are not able to be found. How did you get to the ferry in Frederikshavn?"

Zeke pointed at me, and I answered, "I drove him up here agents." I stayed seated. Both agents were not very tall, perhaps five feet seven or eight but broad shouldered and stocky. I didn't want to intimidate them by towering over them.

Agent Rasmussen came over to me and asked, "What did you do with your automobile?"

"It is in the car park agent Rasmussen until my cousin comes to pick it up this evening."

Agent Poulsen then interjected, "You should both come with us down to the office we have below decks. We need to question both of you further. We might have to detain you until the return trip on the ferry to check out your automobile at the ferry pier. We will have the local police hold your cousin for questioning. What is the year and make of your automobile?" The disappearance of two agents last night is a serious problem."

Zeke answered for both of us. "Lead the way agent Rasmussen, my friend and I will be happy to answer your questions."

Agent Poulsen followed our little procession as we descended two flights of stairs to what looked like an oversized walk-in closet. I didn't want to get locked in any small space in case the agents tried to keep us onboard and take the ferry back on the return trip.

I stepped aside as agent Rasmussen opened the door. I followed Zeke and both agents inside and closed the door behind me. I didn't lock it because I was afraid the agents might get spooked if they heard the latch click. The room had wooden benches on the side with symbols indicating the area was for the storage of extra life jackets.

Agent Rasmussen was the first to speak. "Gentlemen, I'm afraid we will have to take you into custody today until we get the problem of our two missing agents solved. We have many questions for you regarding what might have happened to them."

Zeke protested first. "Agents, we are surprised you have missing agents. However, how do you link us to their disappearance?"

Agent Poulsen spoke up. "Vitali Carapezza, you were the last person on our agent's list to apprehend last evening. When we heard his automobile had traveled to Frederikshavn, we immediately looked for the agents. Imagine our surprise when your name came up on the manifest for the ferry to Göteborg, Sweden."

Agent Poulsen pulled out a set of shiny handcuffs and slapped them on Zeke. I held up a finger to Zeke, indicating we should wait before we protested.

Agent Rasmussen declared, "And you, sir, are being held as a material witness in this case since you are involved by bringing Mr. Carapezza to the ferry."

I pretended to go along with the agent's absurd request by holding out my left wrist. Since I was a foot taller than the agent, he had to reach to place the handcuff on my wrist. As he was about to put the other cuff on my right wrist, I nodded to Zeke, spun around on my right heal, and smashed my elbow into agent Rasmussen's throat.

As agent Poulsen turned to see Rasmussen writhing on the deck with his fingers clutching at his collapsed pharynx, Zeke immediately placed his cuffed wrists over agent Poulsen's head and pulled hard on the chain across the agent's throat. The handcuff chain crushed the agents' thyroid cartilage and closed off his ability to breathe.

I took a swing at agent Poulsen's solar plexus and diaphragm to quickly expel any air in his lungs. I buried my fist in his gut. His eyes were bulging out of his head, his face was turning purple, and he was making hideous sounds from his nose and throat. He and Zeke collapsed in a heap on top of agent Rasmussen. I informed Zeke he could probably let go of the choke hold he had with his handcuffs. The entire take-down took less than a minute.

I waited a few minutes and checked for a pulse on both agents and found none. I then fished a key out of agent Rasmussen's pocket and took off Zeke's shiny handcuffs.

Now we had two dead *Gestapo* agents and nowhere to put them.

Zeke suggested, "Should we deep six the both of them."

"I'm afraid someone would see them going overboard. Let's lock the door while we figure this out," I suggested.

"How about putting them under all the lifejackets in the wooden cases?" suggested Zeke. "We only need them concealed for another four hours."

"Good idea Zeke, let's remove most of the lifejackets and put them over the agents. We should remove their identification, badges, and wallets to hinder any investigations into their disappearance.

We emptied the cases and put the agents in the bottom; then piled the lifejackets on top of them. My comment, "As long as we don't have a lifejacket drill over the next couple of hours we should be fine. Let's lock the door on our way out."

The rest of our trip to Göteborg was smooth and without interruption. The wind died down a bit when we approached the lee of the Swedish land mass. Food on the ferry was rather rudimentary, but the cheese along with dark bread seemed to fill us up.

Göteborg was a large and beautiful city compared to Frederikshavn. There were many tall buildings; the streets were busy with traffic and bustling shoppers and businesspeople. The air was clear, with no smoke or threat of Allied bombing. As we disembarked the ferry, Zeke asked directions for the bus to Jönköping. The bus trip seemed almost as long as the ferry ride. All the stops and waiting times in the small towns added up as we traveled through the hills and valleys of western Sweden.

I had a strong feeling of guilt for leaving my homeland in time of war. Zeke and I had, however, slowed down the development of two terrible weapons systems. This knowledge alleviated some of the guilt. The V-1 and the V-2, if fully developed in time, could have easily changed the course of the war against the Allies and the Russians. Had Zeke and I been fully aware of the possible nuclear capabilities of the Reich, we would have taken even more risks to ground the entire missile system.

I couldn't get the poor souls in the Mittelwerk tunnels out of my mind. They were suffering and dying at a rapid rate.

The bus stopped at our destination in Jönköping. We switched coaches and continued to Stockholm. The bus traveled in a slow and almost leisurely pace as we wound around the hills of eastern Sweden. . We got into the city very early the next morning.

The bus ride had to be hard for Zeke. His parents were lost in the camps, and we were in the process of finding my relatives and Ilsa's family. Of course, always being hungry, I thought it might be best if we could find a decent breakfast in a local hotel.

It was wonderful to eat fresh eggs, ham, and bread. These common breakfast items were no longer available in my homeland. We had a very hearty breakfast including the most exquisite fresh coffee. Real coffee had not been available in Germany for years.

Another strange phenomenon happened at the hotel restaurant: people seemed happy to be there and were smiling. It almost seemed we were on a different planet.

Zeke remarked, "These folks are happy. I'm not sure if anyone in Germany will be smiling for a long time after this war."

We found the bus station for the short ride to Edsviken just outside of Sollentuna. My relatives home was within walking distance of the bus stop.

As we approached the house, Ilsa came running out to meet us.

"You made it!" She shouted and gave Zeke and me a big hug. "We have been waiting anxiously for word from you both. Was it difficult getting out of *Nazi*-held Denmark?"

"Well," I started, "Let's just say the ferry ride wasn't completely uneventful."

"What happened?" queried Ilsa.

"Two *Gestapo* thugs from the Frederikshavn office followed us out on the ferry," said Zeke. They wanted to detain and question us about two missing agents from the Aalborg office. Jenz and I felt we did not want to be arrested and brought back from Sweden for prolonged questioning so we 'discouraged' them."

"Jenz, I missed you so much and was worried about you both being caught up in the *Gestapo* or *SS* sweep in Germany or Denmark."

"Peenemünde was the most dangerous spot for us because of the security. We were almost trapped a couple of times on the base for the Army Research Center. The British bombing of August 1943 saved us because some ongoing investigations were starting to close in on us."

"Jenz, I want to make our stay here at your uncle's home enjoyable for us, but are we going back to Germany after the war?"

"Germany might not be safe for us for a long time, Ilsa. Your parents could go back, but it might be too dangerous for us. I feel an obligation to my fellow Jews to return, at least for a short time. I want to try to help those prisoners in the gypsum mine."

I continued, "You and I might consider emigrating to America. I have some relatives and an old classmate in Massachusetts. I could contact them to see if they might help us get settled."

Germany could be a very dangerous place for us, even after the war is over. We cannot take a chance of compromising our children's freedom with a Nazi or Communist regime.

It was wonderful to be reunited with my uncle, parents, and the rest of Ilsa's family. Ilsa's parents were quite receptive to my staying with their daughter and even about the possibility of our emigrating to America.

The next evening at dinner, I told my family I was considering returning to Germany to help more of our countrymen escape the *Reich.*

"Oh Jenz," Ilsa stammered, "I am not at all comfortable with you returning to Germany."

Both of my parents protested, "Jenz, no! It could be immensely perilous for you."

"I know dad. Believe me, it's not the most appealing idea for me either. The love of my life is here at the table and safe from the clutches of the *Gestapo.* It could be a death sentence for Zeke to return to Germany before the end of the war.

"Going to America, living with my sweetheart, and starting a family would be pure heaven for me. It is my fondest dream. But, I have seen how the Kapos at the camps treat our fellow citizens. I would never forgive myself, if I didn't at least try to get some of them out or improve their conditions. None of us know how long this damn war will last or when the Russians or Allies will overrun the country."

"I feel a strong pull on my heart for my fellow Jews. I need to go to some of the camps and attempt to restore a semblance of sanity, if even for myself."

My speech became halting as I thought about the prisoners working in the gypsum mine at Mittelwerk near Nordhausen. Water came to my eyes, and I hung my head at the table. I felt like a fool and was embarrassed. Why should such a big guy like me break down after achieving the gift of freedom for his family and loved ones?

Because I knew what was going on back in the concentration camps at Dora and Dachau, I had witnessed first-hand the horrors of Auschwitz and Treblinka; Jews were being used for slave labor for furthering the *Reich's* reign of terror. The fate of these prisoners was always assured. They faced certain death in the gas chambers of these hellish camps. Treblinka was set up with thirty gas chambers. The goal was to kill twenty-five thousand Jews each and every day.

I had heard or visited some of the death camps in Poland including Sobibor, Belzec, Auschwitz-Birkenau, Majdanek, Chelmno, and Treblinka as well as countless others used to kill many thousands of my countrymen and others from the conquered territories.

CHAPTER 47

A Very Hard Goodbye

The next day I took Ilsa with me into Stockholm for a little shopping. She was so happy to see shops which weren't smashed, and people who were smiling. I wanted to purchase a suit and a new shirt and tie to wear to Germany. I was formulating a plan to circumvent the *Gestapo* by getting another *SS* uniform at their Berlin headquarters or wherever I could get one inside Germany. I knew I had left another uniform in my locker in Mittelwerk. I just wasn't sure how difficult it would be to get into the research center.

I also needed a suit for the most significant reason. Ilsa and I wanted to get married in a church, with as many relatives as possible for witnesses. Also, I wanted Zeke at my side. We chose Engelbrekt Church, a member of The Lutheran Church of Sweden in the Lärkstaden section of Stockholm. The pastor gave us counseling for an hour before the 30-minute service. After the ceremony, we went back to my uncle's home for a celebratory dinner.

Our wedding was magical. Since we were now married, I feel embarrassed to discuss our lovemaking. It was humbling for me, and I was transported to a heavenly realm for the evening, and really, for the rest of my life.

In the morning, Ilsa wanted to know what our plans were for returning to Germany. She also wanted to do a little long-term planning. Ilsa hadn't mentioned children in any of our discussions since Hitler Camp.

I was almost twenty-six and replied as carefully as possible. "Ilsa, I very much look forward to having children of our own to bring up and educate in this world, but I think our future would be better and certainly safer in America."

"However," I continued, "I must keep you safe. None of us know how long this infernal war will continue, but the Allies have a firm foothold in Europe. And the Russians are advancing from the East. Hitler will be forced to sue for peace at some point, hopefully very soon. In the meantime, I will take the train tomorrow for Malmo and make my way to Copenhagen and the Danish border with the *Reich*.

Her protests diminished when I implored her, "Please make sure your parents and grandmother are safe. They should not return to their homes until Germany is safe."

"Thank you so much, Ilsa, for trusting me and being my wife. I would appreciate it if you could stay with my uncle here in Stockholm until I am in a safe place. Once I get a uniform, I will go directly to the gypsum mine to inspect the missiles. I still have my orders, and I will be on a legitimate mission to ensure delivery of the V-2's to the Aalborg *Wehrmacht* Base."

"Jenz, I will miss you so much."

"Stay and help your parents and grandmother get resettled in the Reich when you feel comfortable returning to your home. Many things will have changed for Germans and Germany after the war."

Although the love of my life was my responsibility, Ilsa was very much involved with my decision to return to Germany despite the dangers and chance for arrest. She knew how important it was for me to help the Jews from our Düsseldorf synagogue and our country. I decided to head for Mittelwerk and the gypsum mines. I knew I had another uniform in my locker in the newly placed research center outside of Nordhausen; getting to it might be a little bit tricky, however.

I left the next morning for southern Sweden and then on to Denmark. Traveling into Germany wasn't at all problematic with my orders and passport. The *Reich* needed every non-disabled service-age male to oppose the Allies and the Russians.

I had been to Denmark and Sweden for the better part of two weeks. Getting into the research center near Nordhausen was routine: I had on a suit and tie, and I had my orders. I looked very respectable; no one questioned me.

I went to my locker first and put on my Lieutenants uniform; I informed the technician in the warhead laboratory I would be over at the gypsum mine.

"Mr. Ramsgrund," was the technician's retort, "Be careful, we have orders to destroy the mine and these buildings if the Russians or Americans get within 50 kilometers."

"How close are they now?" was my initial question.

"Approximately 1500 kilometers! The Allies are a little closer, the Russians are a little further. The buildings and mine are all wired with explosives!"*

"I'll be careful. Is the bus still scheduled for transportation to the gypsum mine?"

---

* *Hitler had made an order titled "Demolitions on Reich Territory Decree" which ordered the destruction of any infrastructure of some use by the Allies. Albert Speer, Minister of Armaments and War Production, deliberately ignored the order and the Nordhausen facility was evacuated without damage. It would be approximately one year before the Allies marched into Nordhausen on the 11th of April, 1945.*

"Yes, but watch out for the prisoners. Some of them have become a little unpredictable and have had to be shot."

Good Heavens, I thought. Now the "master race" is killing off the very workers who could help ensure victory.

I approached the first guard I came across in the underground tunnel and yelled, **"You idiot! what are you doing?"** He was whipping one of the assemblers of the V-2 housing. The prisoner was on the floor and looked like he couldn't get up.

"Give me the whip!" I shouted.

"Sir, he wasn't working fast enough," was the guard's retort.

"No, I shouted. You have no idea what a valuable resource to the *Reich* this man represents. You are fired! Get out now. If you linger one more minute, you will find yourself on a train for the Eastern Front."

The guard ran for the tunnel entrance.

I helped the prisoner to his feet and apologized for the guard's behavior. "Sir, what is your name?"

"I...I...I don't remember.

"How old are you?"

"I have just turned 35 years."

"What did you do before you landed here?" I asked.

"I think I was a shopkeeper in Berlin. I use to repair watches and jewelry in my shop on Friedenstrasse. The Nazis brought me here for my repair skills. The head guard at Dachau thought my hands could help assemble these monster rockets. I remember now; my name is Benjamin Frankel."

Benjamin resembled an emaciated, skeletal form wrapped in draping rags which were having difficulty clinging to his frail frame. His eyes seemed to have sunk into his skull. He was all bent over. My guess would have been he might be in his mid-seventies, not his mid-thirties. His skin looked bleach-white and hung on his bones.

I asked, "Benjamin, how long has it been since you have had food or water?"

"I can't remember," was his weak reply.

"Please stay here at your work station. I am going to see about procuring some food rations for all the workers in this stinking hellhole."

"Thank you, Lieutenant. Why are you doing this?"

"Because you folks working in this mine are precious to the *Reich*. We need you very badly," I told him. "You may not realize it, Benjamin, but without you and others like you, Germany doesn't have much hope in this conflict."

CHAPTER 48

Into the Lion's Den

It took me almost an hour before I found my way to the general manager's office of the entire *Mittelwerk* complex. Since I was quite tall, and I still had the guard's whip in my hands, I might have looked a little imposing. The first obstacle I came across my was the head kapo. He was a prisoner functionary or guard and wore the green triangle designating him as a previous criminal. I engaged him in conversation.

"Kapo, where did you come from before being stationed here at *Mittelwerk?*

He braced himself and stood at attention. "Sir, I was a loyal *Lageraltster* at *Buchenwald* Labor Camp before being promoted to this position."[*]

"Where do I find the manager's office?" I asked.

"Oh, he would...ah... not be available, ...sir."

---

[*] *His position at Buchenwald labeled him as a prisoner who was doing the bidding of the SS in guarding the other prisoners. To reach the status of Lageraltster one had to be a man or woman who was fierce, cruel, inhumane, and helped the SS torture, kill, and dispose of any prisoner in the concentration camp who was out of line in any way. Violent career criminals had a leg up on achieving this status. These despicable prisoner/guards usually did the bidding of the SS for additional food rations, alcohol, or the ability to wear civilian clothing and sometimes to get their own room. The male Kapos would often rape the female prisoners in the camps without fear of retribution or punishment of any kind.*

"Kapo," I stated in a firm voice, **"What did I asked?"** Smack! I shouldered the whip I had in my hand and hit my other open hand with the handle.

"Where do I find the manager?"

"Yes, Sir. Go to the end of this tunnel and take a right onto the 'B' tunnel. At the end of the 'B' tunnel, there will be a set of stairs. The manager's office is on the third deck across from the stairs."

I had no idea how extensive and how many tunnels were under this large hill in Thuringia. It's proximity to the Mittelbau-Dora slave labor camp gave the underground factory plenty of workers for assembling the V-1 and V-2 rockets. There was also a tunnel for manufacturing aircraft engines and even a liquid oxygen production plant.

Life was cheap at Mittelwerk. It was not unusual for the kapo guards to have to remove two to three hundred dead prisoners each day because of the appalling conditions in the factory. The prisoners were worked to death under conditions of poor nutrition, poor sanitation, and little sleep. There was a constant fear of retribution if they were not fast enough in assembling the rockets. I noticed one prisoner shackled to a bench on the assembly line who had only one leg. Why was the Kapo afraid of the prisoner. He certainly wasn't about to run away. The stench of the place was dreadful.

The mine was initially used to obtain gypsum for the manufacturing of cement, some fertilizers, cement blocks, and other building materials. When the gypsum is first mined, it is in the dry crystalline state. When gypsum mixes with water, a chemical reaction occurs and turns the powdery crystals of gypsum into cement. The moisture in the tunnels was often from urine because of the ghastly sanitation conditions. The smell made me almost pass out.

The long lines of prisoners working at benches bending and lifting rocket parts in assembly lines was a sight I will never forget. There must have been hundreds, if not thousands of slave laborers working on manufacturing the V-1 flying bombs and the V-2 rockets. I kept looking for just one worker who appeared healthy or in decent physical condition.

Only the Kapos seemed well-fed and healthy. The Kapos reminded me of barking dogs screaming at the occasional collapsed prisoner who didn't have the strength to finish his twelve-hour shift. While on my way to the manager's office, I saw five or six prisoners fall off their bench. The Kapos just dragged them away. Although I never said anything, I wept inside.

As I climbed the stairs at the end of tunnel "B" the rank, nauseating odor seemed to follow me to the third floor. As I stepped through a doorway and closed the door, the fresher air was a welcomed relief.

There was a door across the hall with the name: Georg Rickhey, General Manager. I took a moment to calm down because my emotions were raging inside of me. I knocked and walked in. I wanted to present myself as a very confident *SS* Lieutenant, but my insides were still rumbling.

A woman greeted me as I came in. "Good afternoon, Lieutenant, what brings you up here?"

I was in full *SS* uniform with my boots adding another inch or two to my height. I removed my cover as I stepped into her office.

She was a mid-thirtyish woman with very pale, almost ashen skin and short mousy-brown hair. She appeared very thin, but reasonably well-dressed. I wasn't sure if she was one of the prisoners or just a very skinny *Nazi*. She was either hired help or one of the luckier prisoners. I figured on the latter after she said a few words. With a little sun and a little meat on her bones, she would have been quite pretty. I recognized her as most likely Jewish.

"Hello Miss, I'm Lieutenant Ramsgrund here to see Georg Rickhey. What is your name?"

"I'm called Batya, Sir."

"Ah, Yes," I replied. "Daughter of God."

The poor woman looked aghast, frightened and shocked. Perhaps even a little frightened.

"I am amazed you would know what my name means," she looked astonished. "How would you know what my name meant?"

"I had a Jewish friend growing up. Occasionally I would go with him to schule at his synagogue.

"Oh," she replied with apparent surprise. "Well, the manager is with someone in his office right now. If you don't mind waiting a short while, I'm sure he will finish soon. Please sit just over there." She motioned to some chairs against the wall.

After about fifteen minutes, the manager's door opened, and the Kapo I had admonished when I first entered the tunnels walked out. He took one look at me and developed a stunned and concerned look on his face.

I asked him in a firm voice, **"Why are you still here? I am going to make a recommendation to the manager. You are immediately to be on the next train to the Eastern Front. Now get out the hell out of this facility and pack your gear!"**

The receptionist spoke up and announce to the manager, "Sir, the Lieutenant would like a word with you."

Herr Rickhey looked perplexed but stammered, "C, Come in Lieutenant, what can I do for you?"

I pulled out my orders to the Aalborg *Wehrmacht* Air Base and let him read them. I gave him a couple of minutes to let Hitler's orders sink in.

"As you can see, sir, our *Führer* wants missiles sent to the base in northern Denmark for defensive purposes. I need at least twenty V-2 missiles immediately for transport by rail without delay. Our plan is to transport up to fifty missiles to the air base in northern Denmark each week.

"But Lieutenant, we are producing these weapons as fast as possible. What can I do to speed up production? I am already loosing over 200 Jews each day from overwork!"

I was steamed, so my reply was a little more heated than was probably necessary. **"I don't give a damn about dead Jews,"** I shouted, **"I care about live Jews! You are killing them faster than the gas houses! Now listen to me very carefully."**

It was pretty evident I had his attention. Although he was tall, probably around six feet, I still towered over him. The firmness and directness of my voice caught his attention. Also, I was pretty sure he was familiar with the workings of the camps and their gas chambers.

I pointed up in the air but in his direction. **"Two things are going to happen immediately. First, you are going to feed these workers with decent meals. They are precious workers for the *Reich*. I don't care if they eat the same meals as our troops on the front lines, but they are of equal or more value and need to eat if they are going to produce the missiles we need for the Fatherland.**

I took a breath to let my words sink in for Herr Rickhey.

"And second, there will be no more corporal punishment for prison workers who are sick and cannot produce their

quotas. You have plenty of Jews and other prisoners in the camps, get them out here producing for Germany."

"Also, I want your last visitor to have orders to the Eastern Front tonight! He is a criminal and needs to use his hateful conduct on the Russians, not loyal hard-working Germans."

Rickhey responded, "Sir, I will see what can be done."*

"You realize," I continued, "The Russians or the Americans or both will be in Nordhausen within a year if we cannot defend ourselves with these missiles. Would you like it if they discover what you and our labor camp leaders have done to our countrymen and women who are hard working prisoners for the *Reich*?"

"Careful, Lieutenant, you could be talking treason."

I then exploded and talked much too loud. The problem was, firmness was all Rickhey seemed to understand.

"You damn imbecile!" I bellowed. "I'm talking common sense! Do I have to go to our *Führer* himself to help you understand? You do realize Germany is in a desperate situation!

"I want these loyal working prisoners better fed today! Meaning now, right now! Right away!"

I walked out of his office. I winked at the receptionist who was holding her arms over her chest with her hands on her throat. It was pretty clear she could not believe what she had just heard. The look of shock and surprise on her face wouldn't have been quite so evident if she had been able to close her mouth, but her jaw had dropped too far.

I waved at her and said, "Peace Batya, may God be with you!" And as a little added confusion for her, I mentioned in Yiddish,

---

* *Georg Rickhey was indicted at the Dachau War Trials in 1947 because he had worked closely with the Gestapo and the SS and had witnessed executions. He was acquitted because the evidence was not strong enough specifically against him.*

"This war is meshuggeneh (insane or crazy). As I walked out of her office, I caught a glimpse of a confused and questioning smile. I found my way out of the underground factory the same way I had come in.

I briefly thought about what Batya might look like without her clothes but felt an immediate pang of guilt. I missed my Ilsa.

It felt good to exercise a little command in my voice. Although it was not my plan to bring myself to the attention of the *Gestapo,* it was indeed now a possibility.

CHAPTER 49

My Appointment with the Gestapo

I took the bus back to the relocated Army Research Center and checked in at the Warhead Department. All the information we had gathered from the Aalborg Air Base in Denmark had to be written up and given to Dr. Steinhoff and General Dornberger. High on the list of "things to be done" was better food and sanitation for those prisoners building these critical weapons for the *Reich*.

Listed in my report under "Necessary to Achieve Victory" were the critical contributions of our prison workers. The workers needed better working conditions to get optimal effort from them. If Hitler needed more of these "wonder weapons" built, it didn't make sense to kill off the folks who were building them. Then again, it didn't make any sense to many Germans to have their friends, neighbors, and countrymen arrested and forced into concentration camps in the first place.

Another section of the report discussed the value of the Aalborg Air Base as a storage and launching site for the V-2 rockets. The distances and time to targets and launch sequences were carefully calculated. The defenses of the airbase were fully disclosed and reinforced.

As I was wrapping up the report, I could see two quite large men coming across the laboratory floor out of the corner of my eye. I was putting the finishing touches on the report for General Dornberger and did not want to be interrupted. They came right to my desk and ordered, **"Lieutenant, you need to come with us."**

My first thought was the *Gestapo* hadn't gotten a lot smarter over the past half dozen years. My additional opinion was I didn't "need" to go anywhere with these two buffoons. But I answered in what hopefully was a friendly tone, "How may I help you, gentlemen?"

"This is agent Burk, and I am agent Rikker from the Nordhausen office of the *Gestapo.* We have questions for you about two missing agents from our Nordhausen office and their automobile. Come with us **now!**

When I got up from my chair, I asked my closest colleague at the next desk, "Please make sure this report gets to General Dornberger. Our *Führer* is expecting it today."

I then turned to the agents and said, "Let's go. Where would our illustrious *Gestapo* agents like to go?"

"You need to come to our headquarters in Nordhausen Lieutenant. We need to question you further about our missing agents."

"Well, I can assure you I have not seen any missing agents."

We left by way of the front entrance, and I rode in the back of an older Mercedes with no handles on the inside of the rear doors. I noticed it was a few years older than the one we had "borrowed" a couple of weeks ago. I wasn't too worried about the two agents, but it would be difficult to take them both on without Zeke. I didn't want a stray bullet intersecting anywhere with my body. I was tempted to discuss dinner plans with the agents since I was getting a little hungry.

There was nothing too worrisome about the ride to the agent's headquarters until we pulled up to the Nordhausen city jail. I guessed the *Gestapo* had appropriated it for their use early in the war.

Agent Rikker opened the rear door and tried to place handcuffs on me. I suggested it was unnecessary, "You should be very careful about placing restraints of any kind on a member of the *SS*."

"It is the procedure, Lieutenant. I need to put these handcuffs on your wrists; place your hands behind your back. **Now!**"

"You will suspend procedure this afternoon, agent Rikker. I am coming to your headquarters without complaint," I suggested. "And after I show you my orders, you would be very careful not address me in a condescending tone of voice."

We walked into the Nordhausen police station, now serving as *Gestapo* headquarters. The woman behind the counter seemed surprised to see an *SS* Lieutenant in full uniform towering over her. We were immediately ushered into a separate room for initial questioning.

The room looked a lot like a jail cell. There were bars on the one high window, a unique locking mechanism on the door, with only a key access to exit the room. A sturdy wooden table and three sturdy wooden chairs were in the center. The ten by twelve foot room had light army-green walls.

There was one overhead bulb hanging from a wire giving the room an eerie glow, but not quite enough light for comfortable reading. The tile floor was recently polished, but no amount of buffing could bring the original grey-green colored tile back to life. Agent Burk motioned me to sit in the wooden chair on the far side of the table.

Agent Burk started right away. "What have you done with our agents, Lieutenant?"

"I do not have your people, agent Burk. Were your agents armed when I was supposed to have met them?"

"Yes, of course. We are always armed whenever we need to pick someone up. The agents had you and a Vitali Carapezza on their list to bring in."

"No one ever came to me for questioning. If the agents had come, I would have no reason to argue with an armed agent of the German State Police. What has my colleague Herr Carapezza discussed with you about your agents?"

"We are unable to locate Vitali Carapezza at this time," answered agent Rikker. "But, we will find him, Lieutenant. The long reach of the *Gestapo* touches every corner of the *Reich*. He will be located and brought in for questioning at our headquarters. We have very efficient methods to reach the truth in every situation."

"I'm sure your methods are very effective agent Rikker. You would do well to **never** threaten a member of the *SS* with any of your inept or blundering questions or procedures. I have heard about some of your common practices for eliciting the truth from our fellow German citizens. Your methods are barbaric and outside of German law.

"What about the agent's automobile," Was agent Burk's accusatory statement? "We had a report this car was stopped outside of Hamburg at a checkpoint and it was later noted transiting into the *Reich* protectorate of Denmark."

"You are correct agent Burk. Here, take a look at my orders." I unfolded them from my pocket. "You will see it says to transit to the Wehrmacht Air Base in Aalborg, Denmark, by the most expedient method possible. We were not sure we could get a flight from Tempelhof, or if the airport would be opened with all the Allied bombing.

"Since time was of the essence with the Russians and the Allies invading the Reich, we went to the car park at the gypsum mine and found an automobile. It looked like it hadn't been used in several days or weeks. We used it to get to Aalborg as soon as we could."

"Was there anything to report at Aalborg you found unusual?" Queried agent Rikker.

"Nothing I would be able to share with you. I gave my report to a colleague for General Dornberger just as you were requesting my presence here. The report is 'Eyes Only' for the General and our *Führer.*"

"For what purpose did you need to get to Aalborg in Denmark so quickly?" Asked agent Burk.

"Since you are both well aware of the purpose of the Mittelwerk factory operation I can at least tell you this much: our mission to northern Denmark involved the transportation, storage, and launch sites for the vengeance weapons manufactured at our Nordhausen plant. Further information would involve the disclosure of state secrets. You may be able to obtain additional technical information from General Dornberger, Dr. Von Braun, or our *Führer.*"

I continued, "Since I have missed dinner, gentlemen, I would be happy to discuss anything you would like at a later visit. Unfortunately, now, I have to get back to the research facility.

Agent Rikker put a hand up and jumped to his feet as he stated, "Not so fast, Lieutenant! From this room, we need to place you in a holding cell overnight." He surprised me and grabbed my left wrist and slapped a handcuff on it. He tried to grab the other wrist and pull it forcibly behind my back.

Unfortunately for him, grabbing my wrist was a big mistake. I had already mentioned I hadn't eaten dinner.

"Perhaps, agents, Rikker, and Burk, you do not understand my need for keeping my hands unrestrained or not letting my stomach get too empty."

"Agent, Rikker," I began, "I had asked you very politely not to restrain any member of the *SS*. Now, because I am a little hungry, it is more difficult for me to observe all the formal niceties of a professional *SS* officer. In addition, I would strongly advise that you unshackle my wrist and unlock the door to this room. I am telling you this, not to be impolite, but for your own health and safety.

As agent Rikker grabbed for my right wrist again, I quickly pivoted on my boot heel on the tile floor and brought my right elbow into substantial and abrupt contact with his lower jaw.

Crack! It wasn't a killing blow, but I was reasonably sure I had snapped the condylar head on the left side of his lower jaw. The killing blow was the flat of my palm as it was aimed firmly, quickly, and forcefully on the point of his chin. The immediate blow to the agent's chin drove the fractured end of his broken jaw bone directly into his brain. He gave a shocking scream immediately cut short as he grabbed his head where his brain suffered an instant of very sharp pain. Blood sprayed from his left ear, and he bounced when he hit the floor. His death rattle was immediate and chilling as blood was flowing freely and spurting from his ear.

His partner, agent Burk, sat stunned in his chair. He looked as if he were in a state of shock and disbelief. The whole takedown lasted less than five seconds. Burk didn't even have the chance to draw his weapon. I went over and stood directly in front of him and pointed my finger into his face.

"Agent Burk, if you or any other members of the Gestapo comes anywhere near the Wehrmacht Research Center or the underground factory and bothers me, any of our staff, or any of the prison workers in any way, I can assure you your death will be much more prolonged and painful.

"If you reach for your shiny Lugar Agent Burk, I assure you, hospitalization will be required for you with multiple broken bones, including a broken wrist. I tried to very politely warn agent Rikker not to attempt to restrain any member of the *SS*, but he didn't listen. I sincerely hope **you** are listening now."

I grabbed the key ring off his belt, removed the dangling handcuff from my wrist, and opened the door.

"Agent Burk, get out here and explain to the receptionist how your colleague has had an accident and may need medical attention or an undertaker.

"You can send someone to pick up your car tomorrow in the research center parking lot. However, the person better not be **you!**" I said with a bit of emphasis.

"Good evening, mum," as I gave the receptionist a toothy smile and walked out the door and headed toward the agent's automobile.

When I got back to the office, I got word Dr. Steinhoff would like to see me as soon as I returned to the warhead laboratory.

I thanked my colleague at the next desk, "Appreciate your getting the Aalborg Report over to Dr. Steinhoff and General Dornberger. Did either of them seem interested in it?"

"Oh, definitely yes!" he replied. "I think the doctor wants you to discuss it with the General and possibly our *Führer.*"

"Thanks, I will have to refine it a bit later this evening or tomorrow before I review the report in person with Dr. Steinhoff."

CHAPTER 50

A Return Visit to the V-2 Factory

The next morning, I was in the reception area for Dr. Steinhoff right after breakfast.

"Good morning, sergeant. I am here to see Dr. Steinhoff."

"Yes, Lieutenant, he is expecting you. Right, this way."

The sergeant led me down the hall to Dr. Steinhoff's office. He knocked twice and opened the door for me.

"Good morning, doctor."

"Yes, Lieutenant, come in," summoned Dr. Steinhoff.

"Was the report acceptable, and useful for our purposes, doctor?"

"Very adequate Lieutenant. The *Führer* was pleased. He asked me if I thought you would be the officer who could accompany the first shipment of twenty missiles to Aalborg."

"I would be delighted to accompany the missiles to the Wehrmacht base in Denmark as long as the proper launching technicians could come with me and the missiles, doctor."

"There is a bit of urgency in the air, Lieutenant. The Russians are on the border of East Prussia and will be to the Vistula possibly by the end of August. The Americans have a tanker general named Patton, who has many of the same characteristics as our Rommel.

The Americans are at the Seine and France has been lost to the Allies."

A V-2 missile attack delivered to a major city in Russia and England would make them think twice about invading the Fatherland. It is essential to develop the proper destructive warhead for these missiles.

"It seems imperative then doctor we get the missiles we need as soon as possible. Am I correct?"

"Yes, Lieutenant, as soon as humanly possible. I could also add our *Führer* is planning an offensive operation later this year in the Ardennes Forest, but most of the general officers are not in favor of it. I'm sorry I cannot enlighten you further. But just let me say we need many missiles as soon as they can be manufactured."

"Doctor Steinhoff, would you be able to take an hour or two out of your busy schedule today to come with me on an inspection of tunnel B at the Wifo Gypsum Mine? I would like you to see for yourself how I think the speed of missile manufacturing could be greatly improved."

"I could go over this morning if you think there might be a way to increase our production of the missiles. How do we get over to the mine, Lieutenant? Is there a bus?"

"I will drive us, doctor. Our friends from the *Gestapo* have loaned me an automobile."

We entered the main tunnel A, which was the main assembly line for the V-2 rocket. Dr. Steinhoff was amazed when I went over to one of the prison workers and called him by name.

"Ben," I asked. Have you seen any improvement in your diet since I was here yesterday?"

"Yes, Lieutenant. It might be just a fluke, but last evening we got a full portion of the same meals our front line troops were getting. Did you have anything to do with the improvement in our diet?"

"It's possible," I returned. "I just want to make sure all the food for our very precious workers is adequate for the valuable work you people are doing."

"Lieutenant, I'm not sure if this is appropriate to say, but this is the first time since I have been working here anyone has addressed any of us as a human person."

I decided to use the same Yiddish phrase on leaving the assembly line I used for Batya the day before. In a low voice only the prisoner could hear: "Ben, this war is meshuggeneh! God be with you."

The prisoner said nothing, but he stopped what he was assembling, looked up sharply, and his eyes got huge. His lower jaw almost hit the floor. His eyes filled with tears; he blinked several times to hold back the flow of his tears. I nodded, and he got back to work.

We crossed over to tunnel B and went right to the work station for the German engineer in charge of the assembly lines. His name was Guenther Haukohl, and his associate was Hans Fridrich. Our visit was a total surprise; we had not announced our intentions for an inspection of the V-2 line.

Guenther Haukohl was in his work station, while Fridrich was out in the factory somewhere. We introduced ourselves, and Dr. Steinhoff asked, "What is your rate of production for the V-2 missiles here at Mittelwerk?"

Haukohl took one look at his name tag and responded. "Doctor, we have approximately twelve thousand prisoners working on four projects in this factory. We produce the V-1, the V-2 missiles in addition to jet aircraft engines for high-performance planes, and we have just started construction of a new liquid oxygen plant."

"We produce and finish approximately eighteen to twenty V-2 missiles each week. If we had better-trained workers, we could easily double our production. Unfortunately, we lose approximately two hundred and fifty Jews each day due to accidents and exhaustion."

"Herr Haukohl," I began; how is it there are so many accidents and exhausted workers at this plant?"

"Most of our workers have some sickness when they begin work in this factory, Lieutenant. They come from the Buchenwald or Dora Camps and although somewhat skilled, are often too sick to be effective workers."

"How are they fed, Haukohl?"

"Generally all the workers get potato soup for their evening meal. However, for some reason, last evening the prisoners received full field rations at the dinner meal.

It was nearing the lunch hour, and I was starting to get a little testy. This engineer was trying to gloss over the fact most of his workers were starving.

"Isn't it true, Haukohl, most of these prison workers for the *Reich* are starving? Are not they living in inhumane lice-ridden crammed accommodations in the cross tunnels without proper sanitation or ventilation?"

"Isn't it also true, Herr Haukohl, all the production and efficiency of this plant is ruthlessly executed with utter disregard for anything resembling humanitarian considerations?"

"Well...I..."

I cut him off before he could say more. "Furthermore, Herr Haukohl, do you know the value of these prisoners to the timeliness of missile production? Do you have any idea of their value to the *Reich?*"

"Well, we lose so many Jews each day; it's hard to produce more missiles."

His answer did it for me. Even though Dr. Steinhoff was with me, I started to smolder inside. Perhaps my blood sugar had dipped, but this *Nazi* engineer was beginning to give me a deep and throbbing headache.

I started quietly and politely, but I couldn't contain myself.

"You, Herr Haukohl, seem to be quite concerned about the number of Jews you lose each day and each week." Then I ramped it up a notch.

"Dr. Steinhoff and I, however, are very concerned you are losing more workers each day than are killed by gas in the Dora camp. Don't you understand the value of each worker for the production of these missiles; and their value for protecting the *Reich?*"

Then I lost it completely.

"We are at war, you idiot! You are killing off the very workers who could save the *Reich* from total annihilation. If you fed them properly and made sure they were living under better conditions, perhaps you would lose fewer Jews each day and missile production could be greatly improved!

Let it be known throughout the *Reich,* and I will see to it you receive an official memo from Dr. Dornberger: No further gassing of our precious German citizens, whether they be adults or children. We need these missiles for the protection of the Fatherland."

Dr. Steinhoff then spoke up. "Let's try increasing the worker's daily food ration and get a better hold on the sanitation and sleeping conditions for these workers.

"Yes!" I chimed in, "Double their food allotment amount each day for a start. We will return within a week to check on production. We cannot stress the value of these prison workers for the protection of the *Reich*.

Dr. Steinhoff and I left and discussed the situation in the automobile on the way back to the research center.

"You saw how the workers lived in those cross-tunnels, Herr Doctor?"

"Yes, Jenz. It was pathetic. The workers I saw on the assembly line didn't look at all healthy. I have no idea how they could even lift the parts they were installing in the rockets. We should probably make a report to General Dornberger and the manager of Mittelwerk."

"I have already spoken with the factory manager, but I'm not sure he was listening to me. If the General talks with him, it would probably be much more effective."

Over the next few days, the reports to General Dornberger seemed to have some effect on the living conditions and improvement in food rations for the prison workers. Perhaps I could have done more for these poor folks, but the *Gestapo* kept bothering me about their car and missing agents.

Interestingly enough, the *Gestapo* never mentioned anything specific about the agent who tried to detain me with the handcuffs. However, I was sure it was the reason they were keeping a close eye on me.

CHAPTER 51

V-2 Missiles to Aalborg Air Base

Just three weeks before the 1944 Christmas Holiday I received orders to take twenty V-2 missiles to the Wehrmacht Air Base at Aalborg, Denmark. I was ordered to stay with the rockets along with a team of technicians. The lead technician and launch control officer was an enlisted sergeant named Albert. I was never sure if Albert was his first or last name. He had been a civilian technician under contract with the Wehrmacht. He now wore the Wehrmacht uniform.

Most of the trains were still running in Germany except through the major cities. All the rail lines in Hamburg were unfortunately bombed and smashed and completely unusable, so we had to take a slower local train route around the city. It occurred to me our train full of twenty missiles would be an excellent target for the Allies or the Russian air force.

The Danish gauge or parallel distance between the tracks was, fortunately, the same as in Germany. The Russian guage measure was somewhat different, and none of the German trains could travel into Russia without special alterations of the wheel axles.

We arrived at the Danish border two days before Christmas. The train was comfortable but very slow. We had so many detours I got to know Sergeant Albert and the other technicians quite well.

One day I asked Albert where he thought the target areas for the missiles would be programmed.

"Oh, he replied, They are already set to attack Moscow and London."

"Wouldn't it be better," I asked, "if they were used to protect the Reich?"

Albert was very frank in his quick answer. "Lieutenant, you make too much sense," he muttered almost quietly to himself. "These are vengeance weapons meant for revenge. They are meant to kill without warning, not to defend the Fatherland."

I got Sergeant Albert aside and asked him a simple question: "Is there anything we could do to make these deadly missiles more useful in protecting the Reich?"

He then asked me a question: "Would it be treasonous to answer -- never launch them?"

I told him, "I will take your suggestion under advisement Albert. I appreciate your candor and truthfulness."

The entire northern part of Germany and southern Denmark had been under a heavy cloud cover for weeks. The inclement weather could do nothing but help our brave Panzer divisions in the Ardennes Forest. However, as we crossed the border into Denmark, on a very slow train, the skies cleared and the weather became colder and quite beautiful.

Unfortunately, good weather for us in Denmark was terrible for our brave troops in the Bastogne area. Now the RAF and the American Army Air Force could have a field day picking off our Panzers and severing our supply lines. Hitler's gamble was not going to pay off for the young men fighting and supporting the German Wehrmacht. The Allies would slaughter them with the return of clear weather.

Hitler's gamble with this entire sad excuse for war had brought nothing but death and destruction to our beloved Germany. Millions of my countrymen, women, and children would never grow up to see their dreams realized.

After a slow and tortuous train ride, we arrived at the Aalborg base the day after Christmas. The missiles were unloaded and trucked to a secure warehouse near the building used for the base power plant.

I took a room at the officers quarters although I wasn't sure how long I would be there. I missed my new bride, Ilsa. My best comfort was knowing Ilsa and her family were safe and we had her complete support in our subterfuge of slowing down the V-1 and V-2 programs. She was completely on board with Zeke and I helping our German countrymen and women in the camps while I was appearing as a loyal *SS* officer supporting the *Reich.*

In the evening, I changed into civilian clothes and went into town for dinner at a local restaurant called, from the Danish translation, "The Excellent Pub." I heard there were many Germans in our area of Denmark who frequented the particular eatery. At this stage in the conflict, any German who wanted to exit the *Reich* was more than likely to be a deserter or a Jew.

As I entered the pub, the dim light made it a little hard to focus, so I made my way to the bar and ordered a beer.

"How is the food here?" I asked the bartender innocuously.

I stood at the bar and mentioned I had come up from Hamburg. We discussed the bombing, and the war for a bit and I asked him if any of my countrymen were in the pub so I could sit and have a meal. He pointed me to a table of three men in the corner.

I took my time wandering over because I wasn't sure how friendly or anxious they might be to have an outsider join them.

They didn't look like Wehrmacht deserters, so my hunch and hope was they might be Jews.

I asked them in Yiddish, "May I sit at your table for a while?"

All three men looked stunned and a little skeptical. The older gentleman asked in German, "You speak fluent Yiddish, are you ...."

He probably felt reluctant to ask if I were Jewish. I was pretty tall with sandy hair and steel-blue eyes, so I volunteered. "I'm half Jewish and half Swedish. The Swedish half is probably the boring half. My name is Jenz, pronounced Yenz."

This comment brought a bit of a smile from the older gentleman, and he said with some emotion, "Yes, please join us."

We chatted amiably for almost half an hour before I made the statement, "You men probably know the *SS,* the *Gestapo,* and the *Einsatzgruppen* are killing our people by the thousands.

One of the men started to weep. His name was Barto, perhaps short for Bartholomew. The older gentleman prodded Barto, "Tell our new friend your story, Barto."

Barto explained how he had escaped from an *Einsatzkommando* unit near the town of Rivne in western Ukraine. "After the *Wehrmacht* swept through our town, a special commando unit came in and told all the Jews and prominent townspeople to gather in the town square for transportation for resettlement to another location."

"One of my friends had been a kapo at a labor camp, so I knew exactly what resettlement meant--certain death. I tried to get my wife and ten-year-old daughter to leave with me immediately. I pleaded with them, these men are here to kill us. But my wife argued hysterically she and my daughter Myra would go to the resettlement camp with their friends and neighbors and meet me there later. Then, I did a very foolish thing I will regret the rest of my life."

"What could you do?" I asked.

"I left my family. And after scavenging some food, I walked into the forest. I walked through the woods and circled to the area where the 'resettlement camp' was supposed to be set up. There was some earth moving equipment there in a large clearing. Many of the town's residents were released out of the transport trucks parked near the large mound of the earth."

"Please continue Barto." I implored him to finish his story, but I could see it was excruciatingly painfu for him. I added, "no one here is judging you, Barto, only God can judge you."

After a minute or two, he continued in a halting voice. "There was a man there with a large whip. He ordered everyone to disrobe completely leaving all the shoes in one pile, all the outer garments in another pile and all the underclothing in a third pile. If anyone hesitated, they got whipped.

"Then the townspeople, including all the children, were ordered and whipped to the edge of the pit. A member of the Death's Head *SS* with a machine gun shot each group of townspeople as they went to the side of the hole. Their young and beautiful bodies tumbled into the pit.

"I saw my wife and ten-year-old daughter murdered by this group of German fiends. Blood was splattering everywhere!"

I bowed my head and said a prayer for Barto's family:

> *Dear God, please watch over Barto and Barto's family*
> *in your heavenly realm. Please bring peace to Barto*
> *and justice to those who murdered his family. We ask*
> *you this God, and please keep us all close to you.*

It was a very sobering dinner experience with these three Jews. Barto continued his story and told how he had walked, much of the time at night, almost fifteen hundred miles back into western Poland. He then hid on a cargo vessel in Danzig, Poland and sailed into Denmark.

As I was thinking about saying good-bye to this hospitable group, the older gentleman, his name was Horace, asked me what my story was all about. Since they had accepted me, I thought it would not be too dangerous to give them a little background.

"Horace, if I told you my entire story, you might find it difficult to believe. It will be sufficient to let you know my friend Ezekiel and I have done everything in our power over the last half dozen years to bring down the *Führer* and everything he represents in Germany. I left as a profound sadness was overtaking me. My heart was heavy as I tried for a cordial good-bye to my new friends and headed back to the officer quarters on the base. There was a note on my officer quarters door stating the *Gestapo* wanted to "interview" me as soon as I returned.

CHAPTER 52

Facing the Gestapo without Ezekiel

In addition to having no idea where the local *Gestapo* headquarters was located, I wasn't too keen on running around close to midnight trying to chase them down. Besides, I wasn't about to present myself anywhere near their headquarters.

I had planned to sleep in my clothes in case they came late at night. I changed back into my uniform from my evening civilian clothing, left my uniform tunic on a hook on the back of the door, and lay on the bed. I wanted to think about, perhaps even dream about, my life with Ilsa.

My sleep was interrupted in the first hour by a loud knock on the door. **Bang-Bang, Bang!**

I got out of my very comfortable bed, interrupting my warm thoughts about Ilsa, put on my uniform tunic, and gave what I hoped was a rather cheery call, **"Come in!"**

There were two of them. One larger than the other. Both agents were over six feet, but one looked pretty muscular. Both were armed, but neither had yet unholstered their weapon. The fact their guns were still in their holsters was somewhat encouraging. Zeke and I could have taken care of them, but I was a little curious about how I was going to do the take-down alone.

"What can I do for you, gentlemen. I was attempting to get some sleep."

"Your sleep will have to wait, Lieutenant. You have to come with us! We are from the Aalborg *Gestapo* office."

They sounded pretty serious, so I thought I might try to lighten the conversation.

"Agent, where could we possibly go at this time of night for me to even have the slightest interest?"

"Lieutenant, we need to question you at headquarters about two agents and their automobile. They have been missing for a little over three weeks."

"I'm very sorry gentlemen. You have come out here on a very blustery evening. However, I know nothing about your missing agents or their automobile. I am here on orders from our *Führer*."

I brought out my orders from my inside pocket and spread them out on the bureau for them to read.

"These orders are classified as 'Top Secret' so you may not be familiar with our work here at Aalborg."

After reading over my paperwork, the largest agent said he was sorry, but his orders were to bring me in tonight.

I told him, "I'm sorry you feel you need to bring me in this evening. You could be making a career-ending mistake."

"No, Lieutenant! It is you making the error by resisting arrest. I need to place handcuffs on you for your security."

"Oh, I said, you have an arrest warrant? Let me get my gloves and coat."

I knew the *Gestapo* didn't bother with arrest warrants or any of the other legal niceties. So I just put my leather gloves on. I didn't want to get into a brawl with these two gorillas, especially without Zeke with me. But at the very least, I wanted gloves to protect my hands.

I decided I had to make the takedown go quickly. I reached back to some of the tactics I learned as a teenager at Hitler Camp. I had been practicing these tactics off and on over the years.

My first objective was to get the more substantial and muscled agent to look up to the ceiling to expose his pharynx. He had a rather short neck, so I needed him to look directly up for the best chance of crushing his trachea.

"As I'm sure you gentlemen are aware, these rooms all have listening devices in the ceiling light sockets."

Both agents looked up. I was pointing with my left forefinger as I brought the side of my right gloved fist into abrupt and crushing contact with the larger agent's pharynx. I put some real weight behind my blow and could feel his hyoid bone snap as the side of my fist crushed his trachea. I could well have broken his neck vertebrae.

He staggered for a step or two then collapsed on the floor of my room. Blood gushed from his mouth; probably where his lower teeth went through his lip.

The other agent looked shocked but made the mistake of going for his Lugar.

I stepped over the larger agent and brought the side of my leather gloved fist down on the other agent's Lugar hand with plenty of force. I'm sure I broke his wrist as well as his trigger finger.

I pleaded with him not to also make a career-ending mistake, but he bent over to retrieve his handgun. My legs are pretty long so as he bent down my knee caught him on the chin so hard, his neck snapped back. My fist found the anterior soft tissue of his neck with a lightning-quick blow and crushed his windpipe.

When this agent hit the deck, I turned him over and put my knee with all my weight on it directly on his solar plexus. This pressure on his diaphragm had the effect of shortening his death rattle by expelling any air left in his lungs. He turned purple almost immediately.

Now I had the problem of how do I dispose of two dead *Gestapo* goons and their automobile. I decided their automobile might come in handy to get me to southern Denmark and over to Copenhagen. From there I was pretty-well assured I could get a ferry to Malmö in southern Sweden. I would have to dispose of the two agents on my way into southern Denmark, perhaps in the sea near Aarhus.

When I thought about a timeline for leaving, Zeke's famous quip, "time may not be on our side," came into focus.

I felt the head technician who had accompanied me with the missiles was not in favor of launching the twenty monster missiles we had brought with us to Aalborg. I wrote a note not open to interpretation:

> *Albert, I was called back to the Reich on urgent business. Please use your discretion when launching these weapons. Wait on word from me to confirm targeting and launch timing. We may need these weapons to protect the Fatherland. Lt. Ramsgrund.*

It took me almost an hour to get our "illustrious" agents trussed up in my blankets and tied into convenient carrying bundles. I had to use my sheets as ropes to tie them tightly. They were pretty heavy, especially the muscular one. I had to drag him much of the way to the trunk of their automobile. I was thankful their

Mercedes had a spacious trunk. By the time I had finished loading them and packing up my duffel bag it was well after midnight.

Admittedly, Ilsa was foremost in my thoughts as I contemplated my drive south in my overtired condition. I also realized how much of a true partner and friend Zeke had been these past nineteen years. I could never have carried out many of the "interruptions" in the Gestapo organization without him.

Zeke and I met in our first year of school. For the past six or seven years, we had worked together to thwart the heinous, atrocious, and unspeakable crimes committed by the National German State Police, otherwise known as the *Gestapo*.

My best consolation was each hour spent driving south in Denmark would bring me a little closer to my beloved Ilsa. If I closed my eyes, I could almost feel her in my arms. It was so tempting to lie down for a short nap and dream of being in the arms of my cherished new wife. Her hair smelled so sweet to me, her breath on my face gave me a new life. Her arms holding me tight thrilled me beyond description. I adored my Ilsa.

I sat on the edge of my bed, I was very tempted to lie down, just for a few minutes. Zeke's words came rushing back to me *"time might not be on our side!"*

Zeke's words prompted me to get up, splash some cold water on my face, and use the facilities. I glanced at the note to Albert and walked out into the cold, crisp midnight air.

The government automobile was an older Mercedes, but the tank was nearly full of diesel fuel, and it had a decent heater. The heater blew warm air on my legs. I took the main road south-east out of Aalborg. It was probably ninety to a hundred kilometers to Aarhus where I could feel comfortable disposing of the trash occupying my trunk. I wanted to dump it before first light.

CHAPTER 53

Sweden Bound

The night was clear and cold. The visibility was excellent with no snow. Some windblown snow and dust were blowing across the highway, but the stars were bright. Somehow I felt invigorated knowing I was getting closer to Ilsa.

I pulled into the Aarhus area just past four in the morning. Since the sun was still a few hours from coming up, I drove slowly south of the city to the Tangkrogen section. I past an old automobile racing track and followed Strandvejen Boulevard south. I passed the Helnan Marselis Hotel and slipped the bodies of the *Gestapo* agents into the sea by the Marselisborg Kajak Club. I weighted the bodies with some small rounded rocks I found just off the beach. I unbuttoned their shirts and placed the stones next to their underwear and buttoned up the shirts and retied their coats.

I was only in knee deep water, but my legs were turning blue, so I shoved the bodies out to sea one at a time on a falling tide. Thank goodness the Mercedes had a pretty decent heater; my legs felt like they had turned to ice.

Luckily no one was around to observe my disposal. It was still dark without a hint of glow on the eastern horizon. I continued driving south to Skanderborg and Horsens and eventually to the town of Vejle, Denmark, where I found a small breakfast restaurant in a hotel. The breakfast of eggs and thick fresh bread tasted abnormally great. Perhaps I was overly hungry. I picked at but then avoided the cold fish.

By the time I arrived in Copenhagen, the sun was almost down, and I was dog tired. The days were pretty short this time of year. I found an inexpensive hotel just north of the city in the small town of Lyngby on a side street off Buddingevej Boulevard. A few Deutschmarks got me a room and a decent meal before I fell into a very sound sleep. Ilsa kept my dreams very sweet.

The next day I got up early and drove up north about twenty miles and took the ferry to Helsingborg, Sweden. My German passport wasn't questioned, although I was ready for some negative feedback. I left the automobile in the ferry parking lot. It had a Danish Government plate on it so I figured it might be at least a couple of weeks before it was checked and identified.

The bus trip to Stockholm took most of the day. We did stop in Jönköping and Norköpping for meals and rest stops and arrived in Stockholm at about seven in the evening. I was pretty tired when we arrived in Stockholm.

I did have an interesting conversation on the bus with a retired Swedish engineer, who called himself Lars. He had done some work for the German Air Force the Luftwaffe in the past couple of years. He claimed at their peak, the German factories were able to produce over five hundred aircraft per month, and in the second half of 1943, the production of single-engine fighters peaked at 851 planes per month.

He also mentioned by the second half of 1944 the Luftwaffe's effectiveness was almost destroyed. The Germans had lost nearly twenty thousand two hundred aircraft in the air and on the ground through the bombing of airports, and the almost total destruction of factory production facilities.

Also, the RAF and American Eighth Army Air Force were able to have fighter escorts to Berlin and back to their bases in southern Britain. These fighter aircraft not only protected the bombing fleet but also took a significant toll on the German interceptors. By the end of 1944 most German cities had to rely on their ground 88-millimeter antiaircraft weapons and antiaircraft flack weapons for protection from the Allied bombers. The engineer mentioned by the Christmas Holidays in 1944 the major German cities were a real turkey-shoot for the attackers from Britain.

Lars had been working in Hamburg during the devastating and catastrophic bombing of the war armaments factories in the summer of 1943. He claimed on the night of 25 July the RAF bombers dropped so many tons of high explosive and incendiary bombs on the city an immense firestorm of unprecedented proportions broke out. The result was the incineration of the city with many thousands of civilian deaths.

Lars verbalized in a shaky voice, "I was on the edge of the bombers north-south run. As soon as I heard the air-raid sirens, I immediately got my fellow engineers up from our apartment building and fled east away from the city. My German and Danish colleagues who went into the air-raid shelter in the cellar were burned to death or suffocated by the intense heat."

He also added, "The heat and smoke were so thick many of those who tried to flee were caught in the melting tar on the road surface and suddenly just vaporized. I saw people running from burning buildings with their hair and clothing ablaze!"

Lars then, in a low almost conspiracy-tinged voice added, "You know Jenz, many Germans blame the Jews for the massive destruction of their cities."

"Placing blame on the population one is terrorizing is pretty interesting, Lars, how did they come to a conclusion?"

"Oh, easily enough. There are two points of view, both with an anti-Semitic tinge. First, world Jewry has teamed up with the Allies and the Russians to wipe out the German technological advances because of competition and jealousy. And second, and probably more accurately, the attacks count as retaliation for the German treatment of the Jews."

Lars was a veritable font of information on how the major cities in my homeland were coping with the bombing destruction from the air. As I removed my duffel bag from the overhead rack, I thought about how the bombing might have affected my home in Düsseldorf. If the destruction was truly payback for the way my countrymen treated the Jews, it wasn't nearly enough. I wondered about the future of those who turned their backs on their Jewish neighbors in their time of need. Would there be some form of retribution for those folks?

The taxi ride to Jakobsberg took less than a half hour. It was such a joy and almost spiritual pleasure to be back with my family. Zeke was now part of my family, and we all had a celebratory meal the next day.

The best way I can describe the joy I felt being back in Ilsa's arms was it felt like I had, indeed come home. It was pure exhilaration! She was tender, warm, and loving toward me. She was always the greatest joy I had ever experienced in my life. I will be forever grateful to God for bringing her into my life on a summer afternoon down by the lake at Hitler Camp.

Ilsa truly embodied everything right in the world for me. I depended on her wisdom and reveled in her beauty. I was continually learning from her.

My uncle and my father questioned me about my motivation for going back into the *Reich* after Ilsa, her parents, and Zeke were safe in Sweden. When I told them about the gypsum mine and the deplorable conditions our countrymen had to endure, they understood.

They also seemed to understand why I couldn't return to Germany. Many in the *Gestapo* and the *SS* would someday learn of what Zeke and I had done. It was easier for Zeke to return because he could return as Ezekiel Leven and not as the "terrorist" Vitali Carapezza. The long arm of the *Third Reich* would probably not be able to locate him or bother going after him. After consulting with my bride, I asked Zeke if he would consider emigrating to America with us. He said he would give it some thought.

CHAPTER 54

America Bound

When I wrote my grandfather's brother and my uncle in Massachusetts, they both were encouraging and promised me a job and one for Zeke as well as help in getting settled whenever we came. They encouraged us to come as soon as possible. Their delight in our considering moving to their area was tempered by their comments about the many young American men who would not be coming home after the war.

The German provisional government signed a surrender agreement in May. We stayed with relatives in Sweden until the end of June of 1945. Since we had a sponsor and employment waiting for us in America, our transit to Massachusetts went smoothly in the summer of 1945.

I will admit I never made too much of my involvement with the *SS* or the *Gestapo*. The explanation might be too difficult. Besides, I didn't want either organization knowing where my family was living.

Ezekiel returned to his home in Düsseldorf, Germany. When he went to the door of his family's home, another family was living there. The man at the door told Ezekiel to "get lost" and slammed the door in his face. He eventually worked for a civil engineering firm while he finished his degree at the Technical University in Berlin.

Zeke often visited our family in a small town near Boston where we had settled. Sudbury, Massachusetts, was a town next to historic Concord where the early settlers in the late 1700s had begun their fight against the British for independence.

Zeke visited us in the 1950s as my children were growing up. While he was here, we attended services at a local Temple as well as the Methodist Church in Sudbury Center. It was always an exceptional time whenever Uncle Zeke would come to Sudbury for a visit.

I have been very grateful to everyone who helped our relocation to our new country. My first girlfriend, Marlene from the first grade in Düsseldorf, emigrated before the war. Her parents owned gas stations in America. When I contacted her, she was more than gracious in helping with all the paperwork and practical issues of emigration.

Marlene teamed up with my uncle and helped us find our first house on Concord Road in Sudbury; it overlooked my uncle's farm. The farm land, approximately sixty acres, was later taken for the public high school by some local law called "eminent domain." I found employment at a local high-tech firm called Raytheon.

I was eventually blessed with two grandchildren. Konrad became a research engineer after studying at Rochester Institute of Technology and Georgia Tech. He works for Georgia Tech Research as a Research Engineer and does something for the military in robotics. He can't talk about his work because of security considerations. Verity studied history at Mt. Holyoke College and did graduate work at Simmons College in Boston. She is brilliant and hard-working. She will make essential contributions to her field. I know I shouldn't be prideful, but I can hardly contain my enthusiasm for both smart, loving, and thoughtful grandchildren.

CHAPTER 55

Freedom

I have learned to appreciate the many institutions, values and political freedoms in America. It hurts when I see even slight parallels to what happened in Germany in the 1930s.

I feel most people in America are protective of their freedoms. Americans are wary of changes in firearm laws, especially laws taking away or eliminating firearms. In addition, Americans are wary of changes in a political balance, especially if the balance veers away from the protection of their freedoms and leans toward socialistic societies.

In Germany, we saw a rapid erosion of all of our most cherished societal ideals. Freedom of assembly for protesting was not allowed. The right of judicial review was severely limited, employment was restricted for many individuals, and strict racial "pure blood" policies were put in place. God help you if you were Jewish, Catholic, Protestant, or an ardent religious follower of any particular denomination. If you were disabled, Gypsy, homosexual, or didn't believe in what the Nazi political party was embracing, Germany could be a terrifying place in the 1930s and into the 1940s.

The earliest Nazi programs included registration and then confiscation of all guns, handguns, rifles, and ammunition from law-abiding citizens. Next, additional freedoms started to be curtailed. Summer camps were banned except for the Hitler Youth

Camps. There were no more Lutheran, or any church or Boy Scout camps; they were all consolidated into the Hitler Youth. Then all Jewish people were prohibited from working for the government or attending public schools or universities. Eventually, anyone who disagreed with the "pure blood" theory of Nazi doctrine was subject to arrest and imprisonment or even death without the possibility of judicial review.

If longevity permits, I will write about a very brief period of my life in East Prussia and Poland at the Auschwitz and Treblinka Concentration Death Camps. It is tough to write about my time in Poland. Every time I even think about the winter of 1942, my blood turns cold, and I get nightmares. Zeke knows precisely what I went through because we went through the horror of those concentration death camps together.

In the summer of 1941, The Wehrmacht Commanding General at Peenemünde ordered Zeke and I to investigate why the prisoners from certain labor camps were so ill. When they arrived at our rocket testing facility, they rarely lasted more than a month or two. Poor nutrition and diseases had ruined their physical bodies. The General wanted to know if improvements could be made in the series of labor camps. These labor camps were proliferating like mushrooms throughout the *Reich*. In our efforts to help our fellow countrymen, we had no real idea of how dangerous entering those camps could be. Unfortunately, we found out!

At my advanced age, I probably shouldn't complain, but I lost my Ilsa 15 years ago. I still miss her very much every day. We had a beautiful life together with over 50 years of marriage. Our two terrific and talented children were such a bonus to a wonderful friendship. Our grandchildren are thriving and surprise me every day.

I am looking forward to seeing my dear Ilsa in heaven.

THE AUTHOR'S FAMILY HISTORY

In the 1870s my Swedish ancestors traveled to America and settled in Massachusetts. The reasons they chose to live in New England were two-fold. The coast mimicked much of the country they had left: rock strewn coastlines with occasional beautiful beaches. Also, they were assured of employment at a Norwegian's factory near Worcester, Massachusetts. This factory employed many men from Scandinavia. The Iver Johnson Arms and Cycle Works was expanding and had moved to Fitchburg, Massachusetts. The company needed more extensive facilities to meet the demand for reliable, safe, and inexpensive handguns, and classic well-engineered bicycles.

The three Swedish men who came over together, were Misters Rehnquist, Ramsgrund, and Ahlin. There was a reason they came across as a family group. These three men had married three sisters in Sweden. Mr. Ramsgrund had a son who was the grandfather of the main fictional character in this novel. A branch of the Ahlin family became interested in dry-goods marketing in 1899. Today, under different ownership, the Ahlen's Department stores are plentiful in Sweden.

The author has served in the United States Navy as a dentist on the USS Kitty Hawk from 1969 to 1971 in Vietnam. "Traitors" is his second novel. His first novel, "Overrun, The Battle for Firebase 14," included some of the author's experiences in the Gulf of Tonkin and the country of South Vietnam. His first two books were dental textbooks on Maxillofacial Orthopedic Technique published while he was teaching at Harvard University, School of Dental Medicine. His son Konrad is a research engineer at Georgia Tech Research, his daughter Verity is in graduate school in Boston. He currently lives and practices dentistry in Gloucester, Massachusetts.

AUTHOR'S NOTE

It would be the author's fondest wish none of the horrible crimes committed against the men women and children of the Jewish communities in Europe were true. However, history cannot be glossed over or excused.

The era of Hitler, Himmler, Göebbels, Heydrich, Göring, Bormann, Eichmann, Hess, Rohm, and hundreds of other criminal officers of the Reich is over.

I want to thank S. Falthzik, and Doctor Anne Marie Lasoski for their incite editorial skill and their contributions to what happened to innocent citizens of Germany in the 1930s and 1940s.

Dr. Lasoski has become a dear friend and confidant, and I appreciated her input on the treatment of the citizens of Eastern Europe and the treatment of Russian prisoners of war during the Nazi era.